### ■ ■ ■ THE EAVESDROPPER

"Sorry I couldn't call earlier," he heard the man say. "I haven't had a free moment all day. So much is going on and I can't seem to shake loose from the secret service."

"Damn, I bought a new dress today," said the woman. "It was especially for you. I had planned to wear it when we went dancing."

"Save it," the man said. "I'll get to see you in it."

"You should see me when I'm not wearing it." She giggled.

"I think about that often enough. If there was a way I could see you before—" he started.

"Find a way." The woman insisted. "I love you and I have to see you, that's all there is to it."

The listener broke out in a cold sweat.

The voices were definitely recognizable. These tapes would shake up the whole damn country....

# ■ ■ ■ GOSSIP

a novel by

## Marc Olden

FAWCETT GOLD MEDAL • NEW YORK

For my brother and friend, David Kramer

■ ■ ■

My deepest gratitude to my editor for indispensable editorial direction and creative contribution to this story. Unsung no Mo'.

*GOSSIP*

© 1979 Marc Olden
All rights reserved

Published by Fawcett Gold Medal Books, a unit of
CBS Publications, the Consumer Publishing Division of
CBS Inc.

ISBN: 0-449-14260-4

First Fawcett printing: November 1979

Printed in the United States of America

10  9  8  7  6  5  4  3  2  1

# ■ ■ ■ One

To celebrate his last night in Los Angeles, Burt Anthony checked into the Ambassador Hotel on Wilshire Boulevard carrying just a brown paper bag containing an Oscar. He'd purchased the chipped and tarnished statue the month before in a downtown L.A. pawnshop for fifteen dollars. Since then, he'd come to look upon the Oscar as his lucky charm. On the day he bought it, Burt was down to his last twenty dollars and that afternoon an Englishman named Harold Monmouth telephoned asking if Burt, an investigative reporter, would come to Manhattan and write a gossip column at one thousand dollars a week.

Since Monmouth, at the other end of the phone, couldn't see a stunned Burt nodding *yes,* the Englishman repeated the offer. Somehow Burt found his voice. *Yes.*

Oscar the lucky charm. Its appearance had meant going from hard times to a smoother, sweeter ride down life's highway. That's how Burt saw it. Oscar was a job offer from Harold Monmouth, a man who owned newspapers in seven countries and who had just taken over the *New York Examiner-World*, the paper in which Burt's gossip column was to appear. Oscar was two weeks' salary in advance from Monmouth, plus moving expenses, which meant not being overdrawn at the bank or behind in the rent.

Oscar was not having to park the car in a different spot every day to keep it from being grabbed by collection agency goons. It meant good-bye to the low paying, frustrating field of freelance investigative reporting and hello to a fat and regular paycheck.

Oscar meant good-bye to California where earlier this year newspaper editors and politicians had combined to kill a story Burt had worked on for almost three months, a story that might have freed an innocent woman from prison or at least gotten her a new trial. Stopping Burt had been ridiculously easy for them because he was a freelancer, a reporter working out of telephone booths and the front seat of his car. He had no powerful newspapers behind him, no one paying his expenses, no battery of well-connected lawyers to get him out of jail, which was where he had landed because of this particular story.

But thanks to Oscar, Burt now had someone behind him. Harold Monmouth was bringing Burt Anthony to New York to make him a star, to promote him into a nationally known writer. Burt had a six-month contract with expenses, secretary, paid assistant, and, if at the end of this time Monmouth was satisfied, Burt would get a two-year contract with guaranteed raises each year. All he had to do was give Monmouth a provocative and controversial column that sold newspapers, attracted readers and most important, attracted advertising.

In his luxurious room at the Ambassador, Burt walked barefoot across gray shag carpeting to place Oscar on top of the television set. Four-thirty on a hot, dry Los Angeles afternoon. Time for a shower and maybe a nap before Leslie got here. Leslie was a twenty-three-year-old secretary at Paramount Pictures and she and Burt were going

6

to stay at the hotel tonight, order room service and watch television. Plenty of time for fond farewells, too. Let Oscar watch a real love scene for a change. Lights, camera, action.

On Burt's last night in the City of Angels, *The Maltese Falcon* and *Mask of Demetrios* were scheduled on the tube. Four hours of Sydney Greenstreet, Burt's favorite actor, and if he and Leslie hadn't fucked their brains out, there was *Key Largo*, with Bogie and Claire Trevor, and you couldn't beat that. All this and Leslie, too, who got more out of sex than any girl Burt had ever known. Once he had told her that he would like to be her for a night just to feel what she felt. Leslie's response was typical California spacey: she offered to tape her sex life for a few weeks and give the tapes to Burt as a birthday present. He declined.

Burt loved the Ambassador Hotel. It was where, as a seven-year-old, he had met Gary Cooper, who seemed like the tallest man God had ever made. Burt's father, an attorney for a major film studio, had introduced them and the warm, friendly Cooper had bent from the waist to shake hands with Burt as if they were two men meeting after a long cattle drive. To Burt, the Ambassador was old Hollywood, a time he had heard his father speak of, a time he had read of and wished he could have lived in. D. W. Griffith had stayed here and so had Clara Bow. The Academy Awards were held here in 1943, when Greer Garson had won Best Actress for *Mrs. Miniver* and set a record for longest speech. It had run over forty minutes and Burt's father had fallen asleep during it.

The Ambassador sat in the middle of almost thirty acres of beautiful grounds, with palm trees burned brown by California drought and its famed Coconut Grove nightclub now just a huge room rented by conventions. The hotel had a swimming pool and boutiques in the lobby; there was luxury living on its premises but no more stars driving up to the Coconut Grove in Dusenbergs and Pierce Arrows. Renting a room here tonight was as close as Burt was ever going to get to those distant glory days.

Nikita Khrushchev had stayed here and so had Neil Armstrong, John F. Kennedy and Harry Truman. Robert Kennedy had been assassinated here, an event that had burned its way into Burt's life in more ways than one. At the time of the killing, Burt had been a junior at UCLA and the killing had torn him apart, creating a sorrow that had driven him to write two stories for the campus newspaper, stories pulled from his guts, stories on fire with indignation, pain, fear. A Los Angeles newspaper had reprinted them, as had several newspapers around the country. Ten days later, Burt got married, quit school and became an investigative reporter working only for himself, refusing to work for a newspaper or any organization.

The marriage had taken two years to fail; to walk away from investigative reporting had taken ten years.

The Ambassador. It was locked tight in his mind and heart and he couldn't think of a better way to say goodbye to his old life and hello to the new than by spending his last few hours in this town in one hell of a hotel.

He headed for the bathroom, carrying with him the tiny plastic razor, shaving cream, toothpaste and deodorant he had bought downstairs in the hotel drugstore. All of his belongings had been shipped east. Tomorrow morning he would walk out of this room with nothing but Oscar and a first-class airplane ticket to the Big Apple, courtesy of Harold Monmouth, who was waiting for him with open arms.

A naked Burt looked into the bathroom mirror and grinned. After ten years of trying, it had finally happened for him. Money, a chance to make a name for himself. Finally. He was thirty, just under six feet and lean, with two small scars near his left eyebrow and a nose that had been improved by a club in the hands of a cop during a sixties' campus riot. His brown hair was parted in the middle and worn down to his collar; long hair was something you never worried about when you were your own boss. He was good at what he did. One of the best, with journalist awards, plaques and scrolls to prove it. His stories had appeared in national magazines and in publications across the country. He was a man with a reputation, but he was gladly leaving it all behind. As Samuel Johnson said, "No one but a blockhead ever wrote except for money" and Burt was at that point in life where he was tired of being a blockhead.

In the shower he let the hot water beat down on him until the bathroom was filled with steam. Even the soap in the Ambassador was special; it smelled like a beautiful Hawaiian girl Burt had once spent three memorable days with in Honolulu. Honolulu reminded him of green trees and running water, which also reminded him of the Polo Lounge, where Burt had met Harold Monmouth the day after the Englishman had offered him the job.

Monmouth was fifty-two, small and well dressed, with a receding chin and alert brown eyes that rarely blinked. His dark hair was combed sideways, neatly trimmed and parted on the left. He appeared at the Polo Lounge in an expensive, conservatively cut three-piece suit of gray wool with an antique watch chain across his chest. Always polite, never raising his voice, Monmouth always gave the impression that he was in total control of himself and his world. Later Burt had learned that Monmouth was a little killer with good manners and an excellent tailor. The Englishman never perspired, cursed or spilled food on his tie, but he could cut your throat and you wouldn't know it until you nodded and your head fell off.

"I've checked on you," said Monmouth. "You're an excellent reporter, a fine writer and I think you're the man who can do the job for us. You don't belong to any organization, therefore I feel you would fit perfectly into mine. No bad habits to undo, that sort of thing."

Burt, his mind on six months at a thousand dollars a week, nodded.

Monmouth poured tea for himself. "You'll be working with English and Australians, in addition to Americans. Is that all right with you?"

"Fine. Whatever you say."

"The paper needs new blood, people experienced in

giving the public what it wants. There may be a problem in just how well my people get along with the Americans, but that shouldn't concern you."

Burt smiled. "You're hiring me to be a gossip columnist, not a social worker."

"Yes. Quite." Monmouth eyed him carefully, as though trying to read his thoughts. Taking a sip of tea, he said, "It all comes down to advertising, you know. A newspaper absolutely must have it to survive. But advertisers follow the readers. What I demand from you is that you get me those readers."

"I'll try."

"That won't be good enough. I'm not hiring you to try. I'm hiring you to go out and win."

Burt put his hands under the table to hide the shaking. "I'll win."

"Good." Monmouth sipped more tea and stared at Burt over the cup. "Your sources," he said. "They are good, I assume."

Burt learned fast. Monmouth was a man in a hurry, a man with no time to spare. "My sources are very good, Mr. Monmouth." He almost added, if they weren't, you wouldn't be sitting here sipping tea and eyeballing me as though I were in the crosshairs of an elephant gun.

"Yes," said Monmouth. "I assume they would be. You appear well acquainted with those people who have their knives out. People on the way up in sports, politics, the arts. People with an ax to grind. They always make the best gossips, those. People who want to get even."

Burt reached for his Scotch and water. "Same thing holds true in all reporting. Look for somebody out to even the score; he's the key to your story." He wished Monmouth would stop staring at him.

"You keep notes, records on your sources?"

Burt nodded, eyes going over Monmouth's shoulder to the open-air patio behind the Englishman. "Little black books with names and telephone numbers. Ten years' worth. They don't mind talking, just as long as they don't see their names in the papers."

10

"Back stabbing is such a delicate art. And so necessary at times. Would you like another drink?" Monmouth gave him the first smile of their meeting. It was to be the only one.

Burt stepped out of the shower and began drying himself with one of the Ambassador's huge towels. For a second he debated whether or not he should steal a towel, then decided no. Somehow it would spoil his last night if he did something like that to the Ambassador.

In the bedroom, Burt, towel around his waist, stood deep in thought. By agreeing to work for the Englishman, Burt was going to war. Harold Monmouth owned publications that had made him a multimillionaire, a status he had achieved because he didn't like to lose. Buying a New York newspaper had put Monmouth in conflict with Robin Ian D'Arcy, an old and bitter enemy. D'Arcy had recently come over from London to write a gossip column for the *New York Journal-Herald* and from the moment he had set foot in the city, D'Arcy was a runaway hit. His column quickly boosted the paper's readership and advertising—a fact not lost on Monmouth, who despised him.

To have his first New York acquisition fail was unthinkable to Monmouth. To have it fail because of Robin Ian D'Arcy was *beyond* unthinkable and that was why it had been made very clear to Burt Anthony that he was being brought to New York from California to *win*. Robin Ian D'Arcy had to be defeated. Burt had six months to do it, to pull down the hottest gossip columnist in town and lay him at Monmouth's feet. Otherwise Monmouth was going to find someone else to do the pulling down. He wouldn't keep Burt around any longer than it took to write one final paycheck. Burt was on thin ice and the only way to travel across that was to move fast.

Forty-five minutes until Leslie. Burt turned on the television set, patted Oscar on his bald head and returned to the bed. Lying on his back, he watched the picture emerge on the tube. Another used-car commercial. In Los Angeles a car was more important than a regular heartbeat and you couldn't turn on your television set without used-car commercials jamming the channels. Used-car lots stood on almost every corner. Auto exhaust filling your lungs; but you did have the advantage of being able to make a right turn on a red light, providing your car wasn't repossessed, which had happened to Burt more than once.

After the used-car commercial came a commercial for a drive-in bank. Los Angeles. A city built around the automobile. Good-bye L.A. Shove it up your exhaust. Burt brightened. Back to the movie, *Mark of Zorro,* with Tyrone Power, Linda Darnell and Basil Rathbone. Burt's father had known all three. All three actors were dead now. His father had told him that Linda Darnell was one of the most beautiful women ever to appear on screen, a sweet woman. Twentieth Century Fox had placed her under contract when she was fifteen. She *was* beautiful, thought Burt. Reminded him a little of Leslie around the nose and mouth.

Burt's father. They hadn't gotten along until very recently. Whose fault was that? Did it matter? Except for four years spent in the army's Judge Advocate Corps in World War II, Burt's father had worked almost thirty years for the same film studio. That was how Burt happened to know more about films than most people, meet so many stars, to go on the lot. And that was where he had first learned that the world lies, deceives and covers up as much as it can. His father made a living doing those things.

Gary Anthony was a big, tanned man with silver hair, a lawyer with the looks to become a movie star if he had wanted to. He hadn't. And yet he had become as valuable to the studio as any star. Burt's father was the man who covered up a star's off-screen indiscretions by paying off anyone who needed to be paid off. Police, newspapermen, Hollywood gossip columnists, pregnant waitresses, male and female victims of beatings, rapes and other moral lapses, and Mafia hoods who tried to muscle in on the film industry. Gary Anthony paid them all off in cash from a black bag he kept around the house, sometimes with as much as $200,000 in it.

Cover up. The charming, silver-haired Gary Anthony did it well. He had plenty to cover up in his own life, too. Though he loved his wife he cheated on her with studio starlets all the time. When Burt was old enough to know what was going on, he had accused his father of being a phony—a man who had his name on the letterhead of a half-dozen Hollywood charities and his hand up the skirt of as many women as he found time for—and they quarreled violently.

Burt had started writing for high school newspapers because he wanted to be a writer and he found he wrote better when he was angry about something. From the time he was fifteen, Burt was angry about his father. And Burt used that anger in his writing, something he wasn't aware of until he was older. The traits that brought Burt into conflict with his father, also made him an excellent reporter. Obstinacy, never taking no for an answer, saying what was on his mind, detesting cover-ups, enjoying finding out what others had done wrong.

His father, attractive and successful, the close associate of stars and others in *the industry*, as movie-making was always called, started out as someone to admire. Despite the cheating, Burt's mother adored him. So did Burt's two younger sisters. He was daddy, he was good looking and he worked in movies. Loving him was easy. But there didn't seem to be much love left in their hearts for Burt, who felt inadequate, and had to prove he wasn't. Which was why he wanted his father to make a mistake, to do something wrong, to somehow show that he didn't really deserve the love of the Anthony women after all.

Burt had watched his father use an easy charm and wit to claim center stage at will. So there was a malicious, hidden satisfaction at finding out that his father used his legal talent and charm to handle all the dirty work for the studio. He was fifteen when he first accused his father of being a phony, provoking him into slapping Burt in front of the Anthony women. At nineteen and in college, Burt

13

held nothing back in telling his father where he had gone wrong, in how he had wasted his life. It was the 1960s and time to tell your parents that you were living in a world you never made, a world *they* made, a world of war, assassination, corruption, chaos.

But as the sixties passed and Burt's generation proved to be as human as the parents they were fighting, the relationship between father and son improved. Any revolution is just a new hand on the whip, said Gary Anthony. Make the slave a master and all you've done is create a new master and perpetuated slavery. All solutions become problems, which is why the world never runs out of problems. Burt smiled and agreed. What finally made Gary Anthony easier to talk to was that he had lost center stage. The studios were fading fast, selling their costumes to museums and private collections, their backlog of films to television, their real estate to developers of shopping centers and apartment complexes.

Stars were no longer under contract and studios no longer were allowed to own theaters, so film production was cut by almost two-thirds. Without pictures, without stars, there was less need for a Gary Anthony and his black bag of money. Now stars had their own lawyers and personal managers to handle difficulties involving sex, drugs and assorted misdeeds. A prudish Hedda and Louella no longer reigned over mores and stars no longer jumped when a studio said to jump. It was a new time and a Gary Anthony didn't belong anymore. He looked older, sadder; his face was lined, still permanently tanned, but the smile was tentative, weak, lacking confidence. Burt pitied him and no longer felt in competition with him.

He would call his parents later tonight from the Ambassador, Burt decided. They were in Phoenix, Arizona, on their way north to the Grand Canyon, something Gary Anthony never had time to do while working for the studio. Burt's mother had always wanted to go, but his father was too busy. Burt's sisters were in college; neither one had any idea of what she wanted to do. All three kept in touch with each other and were closer now that they

14

were older and no longer in competition for their father's love and attention.

Thirty minutes to Leslie. No sense getting dressed. The two of them weren't going anywhere and anyway Leslie enjoyed walking around nude. More used-car commercials on the tube, followed by supermarket ads and guys shouting the joys of fast foods. There were commercials in Spanish now, a concession to the growing illegal Mexican population in Los Angeles. Even illegals had money to spend. The movie was almost over and Burt wished he had something to read. He hadn't bought the local papers because they were a waste of time. Heavy on classified ads, because Los Angeles real estate was a booming industry, with houses selling for small fortunes. But as far as news or good reporting was concerned, don't bother.

All of his books were on their way east, along with his records, his Dodgers warm-up jacket and San Pedro Eagles batting helmet. The Eagles were such a rotten ball club that Burt couldn't resist wearing something belonging to them. It was a contrast to the Dodgers, who were his team. He was going to miss the Dodgers.

As for San Pedro, not only was its ball club lousy, but so was its district attorney and two of its leading newspapers. The D.A. and the newspapers were keeping a woman in prison who shouldn't be and Burt, who had tried to get her out, was lucky he wasn't there with her. A tip that the district attorney, about to announce his candidacy for lieuenant governor, had obtained a murder conviction of an Armenian woman on some very questionable evidence, sent Burt digging. Burt's source was a man who had been fired by the D.A. and wanted revenge.

Burt spent weeks on the story, checking into the district attorney's record of convictions, appeals, overturned decisions, relationship with local police and informants. He talked to the imprisoned woman, her family and friends and he learned that two people testifying against her were up for criminal prosecution themselves. But deals were made and the two people never went to trial. Witnesses friendly to the Armenian woman were never called and

**15**

perhaps most damaging of all, the people who testified against her at the murder trial were now running her very prosperous vineyard. If Burt's story were printed, it could have finished the D.A.'s political career.

But the story was never printed. *Far West,* the magazine that had commissioned the story, refused to buy it, as did four California papers. A big reason for their refusal lay in the fact that the D.A. was the son-in-law of a wealthy family which was the second largest advertiser in California's magazines and newspapers. No one wanted to risk losing that money. Also, it seemed that the governor wanted the D.A. as his running mate, since he would be bringing a few million dollars with him as campaign funds. With the governor almost certain to be re-elected, no newspaper wanted him or the new lieutenant governor as an enemy.

Not only was Burt's story not published, but on his last day in San Pedro he was arrested and his notes and files on the case confiscated. His telephone had been tapped and he was threatened with prosecution for having secretly looked at the D.A.'s files. Burt had wound up spending a very nervous night in a San Pedro jail cell. In the morning, he was released and his notes returned. Burt Anthony was nobody to worry about, but just the same he was warned that it would be a good idea if he got out of San Pedro in a hurry. Burt covered the hundred and twenty miles back to Los Angeles in record time.

If he couldn't get his story published, he couldn't help the Armenian woman. He had been threatened before, jailed, had his notes stolen and his stories thrown back in his face. He had run into timid editors and publishers in the past, but this one really bothered him because the people responsible for the cover-up, such as the D.A., were going on to bigger and better things. They were climbing higher and higher on the bodies of other people and that hurt. It was time to quit, to leave reporting and go into a trade where the heartache came in smaller doses.

Go east, young man, and reach for the brass ring. Do

a gossip column that will make the country sit up and take notice. Get your share and get it now.

A knock on the door made him sit up.

"Yeah?"

"Leslie."

"Just a minute."

He opened the door.

Leslie, carrying a small overnight bag, laughed and pointed at the towel. "You really did send everything you own to New York, didn't you."

Burt pulled her into the room, drew her close to him and stuck his tongue in her ear. She smelled of lemon. "Not everything. Wait 'til you see what I've got under the towel."

They kissed. Her tongue sped into every corner of his mouth. She was a small, tanned redhead with clear blue eyes and the only girl Burt knew who rouged her nipples. She wore a short-sleeved lavender blouse, pale green skirt and white anklet socks, a fashion fad that Burt found a sexual turn-on.

She took her mouth from his. One of her hands was under the towel, squeezing his penis as if she was trying to knead it into a different shape. "What time you leaving for the airport?"

"Nine."

"Gives us a little over twelve hours." She continued to knead.

"That it does, that it does."

"Tell you what." She spun away from him with a smile, her skirt swirling up and away from her thighs. She wore no panties. "Why don't we order dinner and see if we can do our thing faster than room service can do theirs?"

Burt grinned. "You want to order, then hop in the sack?"

Leslie nodded, the tip of her tongue running across a row of the most perfect teeth Burt had ever seen, teeth that had left marks all over his body.

She noticed his Oscar. "Hey, that's neat. Far out. Really far out."

Burt leered. "Want to see what I won it for?" He dropped the towel and Leslie fell back on the bed howling. Burt ran, flopped on top of her, a hand under her skirt.

Her legs came up around him and he entered her easily and she closed her eyes and shuddered under him as she quickly disappeared into a world where Burt couldn't follow. He could only stay behind and envy. There goes room service, he thought, and then the pleasure of lovemaking reached from his toes to the tops of his eyes and he really didn't give a damn about room service or anything else. Later, as they were lying in bed, he told her he would call from New York, which made her smile up at him and touch his nose with the tip of a finger. He didn't add that he would be calling her because he was now a gossip columnist and interested in anything she could tell him to help him keep his job. All reporters used people. All reporters said one thing and meant another. Then it hit him. It was the kind of thing his father had always done, too.

The telephone rang. Burt frowned. He hadn't told anyone except Leslie where he was going to be. Tonight was special, something for himself, a going-away present. No friends, no relatives. Who the hell was crashing his party?

He snatched the receiver. "Yeah?" Leslie pressed close to him, her bare breasts flat against his back.

"New York calling. One moment please." Then— "Burt? Harold Monmouth here. Just wanted to say we're looking forward to having you with us tomorrow. Did the champagne arrive?"

"Champagne?"

"Sent you some. Thought you might want a little libation. Helps one sleep soundly, I'm told. Never touch the stuff myself."

*How did Monmouth know where he was?* "Uh, no. Haven't gotten it yet. How did—"

"It will be there, I'm sure. Well, don't want to keep you. Just wanted you to know we're pleased to have you aboard and we're looking forward to working with you. Call me from the airport when you arrive. By the time you get in the city, I will have my schedule cleared. We're having dinner at my apartment. Seven-thirty." He didn't ask Burt. He *told* him. In a pleasant English accent and ever so politely, but he *told* him.

"Yeah, sure." Burt was too surprised to say more. Monmouth had a way of making telephone calls one-sided.

"Well, cheerio. See you tomorrow. Enjoy the champagne." And he was gone.

Someone knocked on the door. A naked Leslie raised her eyebrows. "Can't be room service." She scampered under the covers.

"Champagne."

"Hey, far out. I'm into champagne, really, really into it."

"Yeah, sure." Burt stood up slowly, his mind on the telephone call. Monmouth knew a lot about him. Too much. Too goddam much. Reaching down he picked up the towel and wrapped it around his waist. The champagne was free and so was the room, but Burt had a sinking feeling that they weren't really free at all. Monmouth was going to give him a bill for them starting tomorrow.

## Washington, D.C.

Alone at the hotel's front desk, Gypsy signed the register as "Mr. and Mrs. Lucchese," giving an address on Manhattan's West Side which, had it existed, would have been located at least a mile out into the Hudson River. He looked over his shoulder casually, as though expecting his wife to arrive momentarily, out of breath and apologetic for being late.

Smiling, he turned to the desk clerk and said Mrs. Lucchese would be arriving soon. Would the clerk please send flowers up to the suite for Mrs. Lucchese as soon as possible?

A bellboy picked up Gypsy's bags and reached for the attaché case. Gypsy, a large white-haired man in his fifties, had placed the case on the front desk as he was check-

**19**

ing in. Smoothly, firmly, Gypsy laid a thick hand on the black leather case, keeping it in place and the bellboy nodded his acceptance of Gypsy's decision to carry it himself. The attaché case was the reason he had taken a bus from New York rather than a plane. A plane would have meant going through airport security, where its contents would have set off a metal detector and caused Gypsy's arrest. He had come to Washington, D.C., to tap a telephone in this hotel. In addition to a .22 pistol with a silencer he had made himself, the case contained all of the bugging equipment he needed, as well as three thousand dollars in cash to cover expenses and emergencies.

Gypsy, an expert wiretapper, had been approached a week ago in New York by a precise and arrogant young man calling himself Simon, who had offered him this job for big bucks without once mentioning who was to be bugged or why. Gypsy was to be at a certain Washington hotel before 4:00 P.M. on the last Friday of the month, prepared to record telephone calls made from a particular suite. Other than time and place, there would be no further details nor was it necessary to make copies of the tape. Just bug the phone and then give the tape to Simon, who spoke as though the world were filled with bad smells and Gypsy was one of them. Simon gave him the code name Gypsy and then asked some shrewd questions about wiretapping, about the equipment to be used and, at the same time, revealed that he knew quite a bit about illegal taps done by Gypsy in the past. For a few seconds it disturbed Gypsy that people he had never met and would be working for knew so much about him, but the disturbance faded when he thought about the money he would be getting.

After the bellboy placed his bags on the bed, Gypsy tipped him, and called room service to order three Cokes with plenty of ice. Then he pressed the gold-plated stud on the side of his digital watch. Almost five-thirty. He was an hour and a half late for his meeting with Simon, a man who didn't like to be kept waiting. But it was February and the entire East Coast from Maine to Florida had been hit by a snowstorm that had made travel almost impossible.

After hanging his suit in the closet, he patted the pockets, touching the extra wires hidden there. Though he had been fired from the telephone company seventeen years before, he hadn't forgotten something important he had learned there: never come up short. Always carry enough cable, enough wire, enough line. On the day he had left the company, Gypsy had stolen enough company wire to last him his first two years as a wiretapper.

Gypsy walked with a limp, the result of a badly broken leg suffered ten years ago when he had jumped from a third-story window in the Bronx onto a gigantic pile of trash to avoid three shotgun-carrying Puerto Ricans, who had learned he was hiding in the next room and listening to bugs planted in a whore's bedroom. Gypsy had been hired by a politician anxious to learn how much anti-poverty money a rival politician had stolen. The information wasn't to be used to expose anyone. Both politicians were partners in the theft but one suspected he wasn't getting his fair share of the ripoff. To save his own life that night, Gypsy had quickly burrowed a hole in the incredible stink of the trash and garbage around him, cutting his hands on broken glass and the jagged edge of tin cans, hearing rats squeak and brush across his body as they panicked. After that, he had started bringing the gun along on jobs, fitting it with a silencer. It was a .22, a light piece easy to handle and not likely to go off and hurt him. In ten years of carrying it, Gypsy hadn't fired the gun once. But he never went on a job without it. His reason for carrying it was the same as carrying extra wire. Never come up short.

Gypsy was sitting on the bed, reaching into his shirt pocket for the key to the attaché case when the telephone rang.

"Mr. Lucchese?"

"Yeah."

"Simon here. I'm downstairs in the lobby." He sounded as though he were forcing himself not to get angry.

21

Gypsy looked around for his cigarettes. "Come on up."

"I'd rather not. You come down. To the left of the front desk you'll see some telephone booths. Take the last one on your right and wait."

"Guess that means you'll be calling me again," said Gypsy.

"You're late," said Simon coldly.

"You been outside lately? Nothing's moving on the roads. You could have checked the bus terminal and found that out."

"I did. And I still don't like being kept waiting. I'll see you downstairs as soon as possible." He hung up.

In the lobby, the elevator doors slid open and a group of tourists, cameras dangling from their necks, hands filled with guidebooks, filed out first and Gypsy wondered what they were going to see or photograph in this weather and the early darkness of a winter's evening. Gypsy was dying for a cigarette and an ice cold Coke, but he didn't see a bar where he could sneak one. He did see the row of telephone booths, and went directly to the last one as instructed.

A second after he closed the door, the phone rang.

"Mr. Lucchese?"

"Christ, why the hell can't we meet face to face where I got room to stretch my legs? We already know what the other one looks like so what's the big secret?"

"The big secret," said Simon, "is we're both in Washington and it wouldn't do for us to be seen together here. Someone might make a connection I'd rather not have made. That's why we picked you instead of using local talent. There isn't a wiretapper here who isn't known to somebody else in this town. You aren't that strong here, which is an advantage to us."

Gypsy opened the door a crack to give himself some air. "You going to tell me who I'm after?"

"No. I'm only going to tell you where and when. When is tonight, starting at 9:00 P.M. Where is the suite next to yours."

As Gypsy grinned, Simon continued. "A special request was made for you to have that suite because tomorrow's your 'wedding anniversary' and your wife has a sentimental attachment to the suite. I think you'll find the bathroom the best place from which to work. Have you checked the vent there yet?"

"No," said Gypsy scratching his throat. "Haven't even had time to unpack."

"Check the air vent. It's connected to the vent in the bathroom of the suite you're going to bug."

"So much for listening," said Gypsy. "What about the telephone tap?"

"When you hang up, go to the front desk. You'll find an envelope with your name on it. There'll be a passkey inside. We didn't want to leave it until we were sure you'd arrived. You'll have to work fast because I don't know how soon someone will be using that suite. Get in, do what you have to do and get out in hurry. After that, stay in your suite until you hear from me and I mean don't leave the hotel, don't go down to the lobby, don't even set foot in the hall. You'll have to listen through that toilet vent and work your tap and when we give you the word that the suite next to you is empty again, then and only then do you leave your room. At that point you hustle your ass and use that passkey again. Take out whatever bugs you planted and don't forget to leave your own suite clean as well."

Gypsy wiped perspiration from his forehead with the palm of his hand. "That brings up another problem," he said to Simon. "How do I get the tapes to you if I don't know where to reach you?"

Simon made no attempt to keep the smirk out of his voice. "At the proper time you'll receive instructions regarding the tapes. It all seems perfectly clear to me."

Gypsy opened the door, swung his legs out in to the lobby and stretched them. Simon didn't like long telephone conversations or long good-byes either, and even though he talked tough, Gypsy had him pegged as a little man trying to stand taller than he was. Something about Simon said he wasn't calling the shots on this deal. Somebody else was and Simon was only a puppet, another clown on a string to be jerked around by the string-pullers of this world. Who were Simon's string-pullers and who were they out to get? Gypsy wondered. Right now he had to get that envelope with the passkey and get upstairs into the suite next to his.

In the elevator Gypsy put a few pieces of the puzzle together. Simon's backers had money. They were organized enough to have checked on Gypsy, learned his background and even smart enough to know about the use of toilet vents. They had had no trouble booking Gypsy into the suite next to the target or in obtaining a passkey. In the lobby Gypsy had toyed with the idea of asking the desk clerk the name of the party in the suite next to his but then decided against it because there was always the chance that the desk clerk was in with Simon's people.

Back in his own suite Gypsy took off his jacket and went to work fast. He sat down on the bed and opened the attaché case. Laying aside a pair of thin rubber gloves, he removed a small can of Johnson's baby powder and carefully holding his arms away from his body so as not to spill any on himself or the case, he sprinkled powder in the palms of both hands. After rubbing his hands together he pulled on the rubber gloves, again looking around to see if he had spilled powder. Satisfied that he hadn't he closed the case without locking it, stood up and pressed the stud on his digital watch. Ten minutes to six. If the hall was clear and the suite next door was empty, Gypsy could plant his bugs and be back in ten minutes. *If.*

Cracking the door to his suite, he stared out into the hall. Two men in overcoats, their backs to him, were walking toward the elevator around the corner. At the opposite end of the hall, a white-jacketed waiter with a tray of drinks in one hand gently knocked on a room door. Seconds later the hall was empty and Gypsy eased through his own door, the passkey in his right fist. In front of the suite he was to bug, he slowly inserted the key in the lock while looking left and right. Then he was inside, back against the now closed door, holding his breath and listening. Hearing nothing, he stepped forward. The suite was like his, only bigger. There was a large living room, two bedrooms, a bathroom and wall-to-wall carpeting everywhere. Laying the case on the living room coffee table, he opened it, removed the .22, tucked it in the small of his back, then took out a four-inch screwdriver and two bugs, each no larger than a dime. In minutes he had unscrewed the mouthpiece on the receivers of both telephones in the living room, inserted the bugs inside and replaced each mouthpiece.

Leaving the attaché case in the living room, he hurried to the bedroom where he inserted a third bug inside the mouthpiece of a telephone on a small night table. While his orders had been to bug the telephones and not the room, Gypsy would be listening and recording whatever went on in here, via the air vent in his toilet. His curiosity was growing, and one way or another he was going to find out who he was working for and who he was bugging.

He was back in his own suite one minute after six. The flowers for his nonexistent wife had arrived, along with three Cokes. He went into the bathroom to take off the rubber gloves and wash the powder from his hands. Then he walked back into the living room where he removed an unopened box of brown sugar and a teaspoon from the attaché case. Heaping three spoons of sugar into one Coke, he stirred it until the sugar dissolved, then drank the entire glass almost without stopping. He did the same to a second Coke. Gypsy loved his sweets.

With almost three hours to go until he was to begin listening, he had time to kill. So he wandered over to the television set and turned it on to watch the news. The picture was clear, no need for focusing, though there was a light green tinge to all of the faces. Then the station cut to film footage on some kind of congressional hearing and Gypsy turned his back to the screen to get his third Coke. He was sitting on the bed stirring sugar into the Coke, his mind half on the news and half on the bugging job when he stood up quickly, squinting and frowning at the television set.

On screen several congressmen sat at a table in a room

crowded with press and spectators, each congressman with a microphone in front of him and behind them stood Simon. Simon leaning forward with his arms around the shoulders of two senators. Same bony face, pointed chin, cowlick hanging down on his forehead and looking like he belonged. He wouldn't be standing so close to men like that unless he was somehow involved with them. One senator covered his microphone with a hand, leaning back in his chair to say something to Simon who nodded, reached forward to take a briefcase the senator handed him, then turned and walked off camera. A second later, a blond female reporter was on camera in the rear of the crowded room, saying something about this particular congressional committee making trouble for the President of the United States, but Gypsy hardly heard her. He stood looking blankly at the set, his brain whirling around in his skull. Now he knew who was pulling Simon's strings and that meant tonight Gypsy was involved in something special, something very, very important. He also knew he wouldn't stop until he had uncovered all there was to know about tonight's bug job, until he had found a way to get as much out of it for himself as possible, because a few seconds ago he had seen Simon standing next to power and power meant money.

■ ■ ■ **Two**

"Gossip," said Robin Ian D'Arcy, "should hurt. It must have a knife edge. Gossip should draw blood."

"Come now, Mr. D'Arcy, aren't you being rather severe? You're saying that as a gossip columnist you deliberately set out to be destructive, to hurt people?"

"Dear girl, if to oppose hypocrisy is to be destructive, then I'm destructive. Those with money and power in this world go to great lengths to hide their true selves from the rest of us. As a gossip columnist I'm concerned with telling the truth, with seeing that the public swallows a minimum of the elite's dirty little deceits. Dare I say that wealth and position are used more often to deceive than to enlighten." He lifted an eyebrow at the TV camera.

"If I hadn't read your column, I'd say you were a puritan. But I *have* read your column, Mr. D'Arcy, and I find it a collection of nasty revelations rather than a call for uplift. I wonder if the hypocrisy you speak of isn't in *you* more than in the people you write about."

"I *do* have moral standards, Miss Warren. Without them, I could not write an effective gossip column. Believe it or not, I'm shocked at the sordid behavior I see in the world today and under no circumstances would I ever condone it. If I did, then my journalistic credibility would vanish in a second."

Daniela Warren crossed her legs, tossing her head back to clear ash-blond hair from her face. She jumped on the opening D'Arcy had given her. "Does *any* gossip columnist have journalistic credibility?"

"Indeed yes. It usually comes after respectable print journalists or even television journalists like yourself read his column, then steal his stories and pass them off as their own."

She blinked once, began a smile then stopped. It would take more than that to knock her off her chair. Daniela Warren had a reputation as one of the toughest interviewers in television—"Dirty Dan" one critic had called her—and she'd sent better men than Robin Ian D'Arcy crawling out of the studio. At forty, she was at the peak of her career, with a three-million-dollar contract that said so.

D'Arcy smiled down at the well-defined creases in his dark gray flannel trousers. Seven-thirty in the morning and the silly bitch sitting across from him on this asinine television program was under the delusion that her questions were difficult, that she was actually capable of causing him uneasy moments. Hardly, dear heart.

Robin Ian D'Arcy. British, thirty-five, lean, with blond hair, long nose and small mouth. Currently the most controversial and talked about gossip columnist in America. Two months ago he had arrived in Manhattan from London to begin writing gossip for the *New York Journal-Herald* and in those two months he had become hated, admired, feared, widely read, loathed, praised, widely read. And talked about. Above all talked about, with his provocative brand of British journalism straight from London's cutthroat Fleet Street.

As a gossip columnist, Robin Ian D'Arcy was ruthless,

outrageous, highly entertaining and never dull. If some found him deliciously arrogant, Daniela Warren wasn't among them. D'Arcy's reputation as a hard-ass made him nothing more than a target, just another dart board for "Dirty Dan." She read from the clipboard, her voice frost and ice, thinking that D'Arcy was a man who carried his own precipice around with him.

"Mr. D'Arcy, I have descriptions of you which I'd like to read if you don't mind. I warn you they're not exactly flattering."

"I wondered what that little clipboard contained. Does it weigh heavily on your knees?"

"Let's see if these descriptions weigh heavily on you. I'm quoting now—'a repulsive snoop'—'an unctuous journalistic pervert'—'the wizard of ooze'—"

"Rather like that one."

" 'An odious, treacherous toad.' "

"And the animal kingdom is heard from."

" 'A back-biting cobra with a typewriter instead of fangs.' "

D'Arcy linked long fingers in his lap. "Now that conjures us a picture of me slithering across someone's front lawn with impure designs on a sparrow."

Daniela Warren pressed her lips together to kill a smile. "Harsh words. Do they bother you?"

"Should they? I've traveled and moved among the famous and the well-connected and I found myself repulsed by their actions. I said so in print. Whereupon I was cursed, insulted, threatened. Miss Warren, I have chosen to write about sex, money, power, all commodities usually abused and misused by those who possess them in any abundance. Now who can I possibly offend, save that tiny minority which controls most of the world's power and privilege? History says of this little band that it never willingly takes its foot from our throats. I say to them that they are all fair game, especially since they usually seek the public eye. And, dear girl, anyone in the public eye invited attention and as such, to my way of thinking, has no right to a private life whatsoever."

He leaned toward her, a forefinger tilting up at her hair which he felt had been lacquered to the consistency of polished wood. "In England, Miss Warren, I had seven million daily readers. Seven million, mind you. More than any other gossip columnist in the world."

"With so many readers, Mr. D'Arcy, why did you leave England, where you were so obviously at the top of your profession, to come here to New York, to America? Were you forced to leave because of something you wrote?"

D'Arcy snorted. "Dear girl, I came here for the money, for the same reason that you are now at your third network in less than three years."

Daniela Warren went rigid in her chair, her nostrils flaring.

D'Arcy, appearing to be bored, looked down at the backs of his manicured hands. "There were no worlds left to conquer in England and *no* I did not leave my native land out of fear or any other such rubbish. I came to New York because I was told the streets were paved with gold and the trains ran on time. I am in the land of hamburgers and women who talk through their noses because the *New York Journal-Herald* made me an offer I could not refuse, as they say in certain circles. I am the highest-paid gossip columnist in the history of what passes for journalism in America."

Daniela Warren's voice now had a harder edge to it. "In your column, you seem to gleefully pounce on the failure of what one might call your betters. You seem overjoyed when the high and mighty are unhappy or fall from grace."

"I'm ecstatic, if you must know."

"Really?" Daniela Warren almost purred.

"Oh come now. We both know that there are few things in life more satisfying than hearing the worst about public figures. Makes one's own existence seem bearable. A man living on cold oatmeal and hard bread cahn't be expected to relish that sort of diet. But if he hears that King so-and-so or Sarah Smartarse choked to death on beluga caviar, well the man smiles and eats his oatmeal and feels that perhaps there is some divine justice in the world after all."

"Ah, I see. You're saying bad news is good news."

"Quite. Give me a lurid tale of anyone's decline and fall, rather than some prattle about a great man romping on his well-tended grass with his favorite cocker spaniel. Gossip is the only way the ordinary man can feel superior."

D'Arcy closed one eye and looked at Daniela Warren. Too hard looking to be pretty. Dyed blond hair, too much orange makeup and a horrid green dress and black boots on a fashionably undernourished frame. She looked like an asparagus stalk half-dipped in ink and dressed by a blacksmith. She was part of the famed American process of promotion, hype and merchandising that was going to make D'Arcy famous and solvent. Beyond doing that for him, she had no place in his life. D'Arcy, ambitious and determined to succeed in New York, was appearing on radio and television as though running for public office; it was necessary to sell the column.

The column. It was a collection of harsh truths, for D'Arcy made no attempt to ingratiate himself with anyone, nor did the *Journal-Herald* expect him to either. It expected him to boost circulation by delivering five columns a week, avoiding libel suits wherever possible. With that in mind, D'Arcy pursued information with a vengeance and in the words of Cocteau, he knew how far to go in going too far. At the moment he had readers and he had an exorbitant American salary. God was in his heaven and all was right with the world.

Daniela Warren lifted a page on her clipboard and read from the one beneath it. "Explain, please, the difference between gossip writing in England and gossip writing in America."

D'Arcy shifted in his chair, which was as far as he could go in escaping the hellishly hot lights drilling down into his skull. "American gossip is boring, if you must know. It's infantile, heavily censored, with no more bite than a guppy. As to why this sad condition prevails, blame it on the American tendency to seek love from every corner of the universe. Your gossip writers don't wish to offend anyone. They seem to have this fear that if they say nasty things about people in power, they won't be invited to any more dinner parties or the people in power will stop talking to them. Your gossip columnists play it safe, which is why they are so puerile. They lack the stomach for complete truth, which, quite frankly, can be said of you Americans as a whole."

"Mr. D'Arcy, there *is* such a thing as taste. I think it's important not to harm someone's reputation or career."

"Really? You've made a career of asking impertinent questions, many of which have been quite embarrassing and even harmful to those you've interviewed. For reasons which escape me, you've had a rather disgusting attack of piety this morning, brought on no doubt by the thought that talking to a gossip columnist is akin to talking to a child molester."

She chewed a corner of her lip and kept her eyes on the clipboard. Bastard. Supercilious bastard. Well, the program wasn't over yet. "I take it, Mr. D'Arcy, that you suffer from what the civilized world calls a lack of restraint."

"I admit that any appeal to my better nature is a waste of time, since I have none. To answer your earlier question regarding gossip in England, nothing is sacred and I do mean nothing. Whether you are a member of the royal family or some cheap tart waiting on the dock for the navy to arrive, you are a target for any gossip writer. In England, I'm happy to say, you cannot bribe the press nor can some highly paid flunky prevent you from being flayed alive in print if you deserve to be."

Daniela Warren, still seething from D'Arcy's insult, kept her eyes on the clipboard. Interviewing this son of a bitch was like riding a tiger. You couldn't get off and you couldn't control him. Just stay put and hope he doesn't eat you alive. Her eyes quickly took in the studio. For a change the camera crew and technicians weren't yawning or scratching their collective crotches. They were watching D'Arcy, hanging on his every word and in the control booth, the director and the knob-turners had both eyes open and aimed at D'Arcy. Damn it, this English bastard was right. Everybody loves gossip.

"Is it true that you are fighting with Philip Trainer, the New York film critic?"

"He would prefer to think so, yes. I pay as little attention to him as possible, which is the best position from which to view Mr. Trainer."

"What brought this on?"

"I wrote that he often sends someone to a screening in his place, or has someone interview an actor. The review or interview then appears under Mr. Trainer's byline."

Daniela Warren's eyes gleamed. "And he didn't like your printing that?"

"Nor did his newspaper. Nor did a book publisher who had been prepared to offer him $75,000 to write a book. With Mr. Trainer's reputation now somewhat tarnished, the publisher felt reluctant to give critics a reason for panning the book unseen."

"I'm told your newspaper is pleased with you."

"They jolly well should be. Circulation up fifteen percent in two months and that's a fair increase in readers and advertisers. What's more, my syndication is increasing quite handsomely as well. I'm in over two hundred newspapers across America, with more to come."

Daniela Warren caught her producer's signal from the control booth. A minute left. She leaned forward. A parting shot.

"Harold Monmouth."

She couldn't be sure but she thought she saw a flicker of alarm or uneasiness cross D'Arcy's eyes before he leaned his head back and smiled into the bright, hot lights above him. His fists were clenched.

"Ah, yes," he said. "Mr. Harold Monmouth."

Daniela Warren, sensing that Monmouth's name had caused some sort of disturbance in D'Arcy, pursued that

**33**

disturbance. "Monmouth's hired a new gossip columnist with the express purpose of challenging you."

"Burt Anthony. Bright-eyed, young, eager. A former investigative reporter. We've met, he and I. Both of us are being enthusiastically publicized by our respective employers, so our paths cross on various talk shows and at public executions."

"What was that?"

"Nothing. You were saying?"

"Harold Monmouth."

"He hates my guts. I loathe his."

"Can you expound on that in less than thirty seconds?"

D'Arcy unclenched his fists. "Not in thirty years." In England, Harold Monmouth had hired thugs who had beaten D'Arcy so badly that he had been hospitalized for almost two weeks. A ruthless man, little Mr. Monmouth. No, D'Arcy would not care to expound on that this early in the morning, thank you veddy much.

She said, "Why do you think Harold Monmouth is buying newspapers in America? He has a newspaper and two magazines here, plus newspapers in Florida, California and Oregon."

D'Arcy's nostrils flared. "Let us not forget England, Canada, France, Italy and Australia. He's such an eager beaver."

"Yes, but why America?"

"Money. That's always at the top of the list. He feels he can make a profit. Your American press had been run in a most unimaginative fashion. It lacks a certain energy that I must say the English and Australian press possess in great abundance. Monmouth intends to supply it, while turning a dollar or two for himself, of course."

"Care to comment further on Burt Anthony, your young rival?"

"Not especially."

"Are you as confident as you sound? You seem to be dismissing him as though he were nothing to worry about."

D'Arcy lifted one pale blond eyebrow. "At this point in my career, I feel rather kindly toward him, but wasn't it Oscar Wilde who said one can always be kind to people about whom one cares nothing."

Daniela Warren lifted a page on her clipboard. "Somehow, Mr. D'Arcy, I don't get the feeling that you are kind at all. You seem the type to pour water on a drowning man."

"I've been known to cup my hands and do it that way, whenever I lacked a bucket or a pail."

Mmmm, yes." She looked up. "Final question. Why are you so harsh on Renata Zachery in your column?"

"She's news. She's the wife of the vice-president of the United States, a man who quite possibly is your next President if things go his way at the next nominating convention. Therefore everything she does is news."

"You zero in on her personal life quite a bit."

"I'd be a poor gossip columnist if I didn't. She's twenty years younger than her husband and spends more time away from him than she does at his side. She seems to be addicted to New York nightlife, the theaters, discotheques and art galleries in this fair city and she borrows other women's husbands to take her out and about. Yes, I write about her a great deal and plan to continue doing so."

"Some people think you shouldn't."

"I assure you I don't give a fig what some people think. Renata Zachery is beautiful and, I feel, rather thoughtless when it comes to her position. If she wants to lead a less conspicuous existence, let her stay closer to hearth and home."

She laid the clipboard on the small table in front of her. "I get the impression it's hard to keep a secret from you."

Thank God this little meeting is about to be terminated, he thought. It's too early in the morning to be put upon by an American career woman who has all the subtlety of an alligator in one's bath tub.

"Dear Miss Warren, I leave you with the words of Samuel Johnson who said, 'three can keep a secret if two are dead.' It has been my good fortune to be in touch with that one survivor. Anyway, if I were you I'd worry about

**35**

that young man the network is bringing in to co-host this show with you beginning next month."

Daniela Warren's mouth dropped open.

D'Arcy's grin was malicious. "You mean you didn't know? Dear me. We learn something new every day, don't we."

Two seconds later, the program broke for a commercial and a stunned Daniela Warren stood up and looked towards her producer in the control booth. She was too shocked to speak. *This was the first she'd heard of any co-host!*

"Jack—" She called out to her producer. "Jack?"

He turned his back to her.

And when she turned to look at Robin Ian D'Arcy, he was gone.

"Jack?" Daniela Warren's eyes were blinded by tears and she fought against rage, pain, and a sudden horrible hurt. "Jack!"

From far in the distance, she heard a cue from the floor. "Five seconds, Miss Warren."

As he turned off the television set which he had carried into the kitchen, Burt Anthony slowly bit into a piece of whole wheat toast covered with raw honey and thought about what he had just seen D'Arcy do to Daniela Warren. A wipe out. D'Arcy had just knocked the lady off her surfboard and she was now drowning. That last little piece of news about the show getting a co-host was as easy for Daniela Warren to swallow as cement. From her expression, she really hadn't known it was coming. Burt sipped his tea and looked at the clock. Almost eight in the morning. Maybe he ought to go back to bed and curl up beside Monica, who had told him not to wake her unless the room was on fire. She wasn't about to get out of bed in the morning to watch D'Arcy or anybody else.

In his five weeks in New York, Burt had run into D'Arcy several times. On two occasions they had had short conversations while promoting their gossip columns on radio and television talk shows. D'Arcy had been polite in a snotty way, waiting until he got on the air to zing Burt. He had done a lot more to Daniela Warren this morning. God, the look on her face when D'Arcy said *co-host*. D'Arcy was a fierce opponent, no two ways about it; his column was strong, with the wildest stories, all of which had held up so far. D'Arcy's reputation as a heavy in the field was well deserved.

Burt's column was good, but it wasn't as good as D'Arcy's—as Harold Monmouth had pointed out, often. Be more sensational, be dirtier, said Monmouth. D'Arcy was ever on his mind and he never let Burt forget it.

Sunlight through the kitchen window bounced a glare off the television screen into Burt's eyes. Pushing the set farther back on the kitchen table, he closed his eyes then opened them wide again. He dropped another piece of whole wheat bread in the toaster and reached for the teapot. His California breakfast, Monica called it.

Monica Hollander was a publicist employed by Monmouth to promote Burt's column and show him around New York. She was twenty-eight, almost as tall as Burt when she wore heels, and her black hair hung down below her shoulders. She had the round face, wide mouth and dimples of Burt's favorite Italian actress, along with gray eyes and long lashes.

Monica was intelligent, sexy and very good at promoting Burt and his new gossip column. Burt liked her more than any woman he had met in a long time. A week after they met, the two had started sleeping together. Burt smiled. That was something else Monica did very well.

She made the rounds with him at night as he gathered items for the column. Manhattan discotheques, restaurants, parties, Broadway and film openings, clubs with new talent and no talent. Burt and Monica side by side. If he had another Oscar, he would give it to her for making life in the big city a lot easier for him. New York was no place for the weak. It was a tough town and only the strong survived. The few times he had been here in the past, he had enjoyed the energy, the feeling that something was always happening twenty-four hours a day. It was. Everybody was in a hurry here. Everybody was running a great race and if you happened to stumble and fall, most people would run right up your back and down your face and never look behind them.

Burt was determined to be one of those runners who didn't stumble. He was here to become successful and not sit around in his kitchen brooding over what Robin Ian D'Arcy did to women broadcasters with multimillion-dollar contracts. No sense brooding over Monmouth either. Save that for later in the day.

There was a sound at the front door. The doorman coming on duty at eight in the morning had orders to bring up the early edition of the *Journal-Herald* so that Burt could read D'Arcy's column. The doorman was to leave the paper in the hall without ringing the bell. Working as a pub-crawling gossip columnist often meant that Burt didn't get home until three in the morning. He usually wrote his column as soon as he got in. A messenger picked it up at promptly at 5:00 A.M. and took it to the *Examiner-World* on 34th Street and Eighth Avenue; it appeared in print a few hours later.

This morning Burt opened his front door, scooped up the paper and ducked back inside. Quickly finding D'Arcy's column, he stood in the living room and read it. Strong. Fucking strong. Outrageous and off the wall. A slightly nervous Burt closed the paper and softly breathed the words *holy shit*.

Almost every day since Burt arrived from California, Monmouth had either telephoned or met with him and always it was *did you read D'Arcy? Did you see what he did today?* Today's D'Arcy column definitely meant a call from Monmouth and no sleep for Burt. All he could do was crawl into bed beside Monica and worry. Worry and wait to hear from a man who was paying him a thousand dollars a week and wanted his money's worth as soon as possible.

# ■ ■ ■ Three

**Burt drove through the cool March night toward** Kennedy Airport, listening to the frightened woman in the front seat beside him.

She was Renne Blake, a beautiful Manhattan call girl who chain-smoked through a black ivory cigarette holder studded with rhinestones and nervously spoke into a tape recorder on the seat near Burt's right thigh. He wanted her to do as much talking as possible before she took the "red-eye special" to Los Angeles. Renne Blake was leaving New York permanently. If she stuck around after her story appeared in Burt's column, she could wind up dead.

Monica sat alone in the back seat of the rented dark blue Mercury, saying nothing as Renne Blake told her story. "They only went after the best." There was a sad pride in Renne's voice. "You had to be young and beautiful. Had to have a little style, some class. They didn't want anything from Eighth Avenue, know what I mean?"

"How young?" asked Burt.

"No teen-agers. Only girls in their early to mid-twenties. Teen-agers are a hassle. Most of them work the street and usually have a pimp somewhere in the background. You got the cops and parents out looking for them all the time. Only independents like me got hit. Girls workin' alone out of their own apartments."

"And you were forced to have sex with these visiting bigshots?"

"Better believe it." She snorted in anger, twin jets of cigarette smoke speeding from her small nose. "New York cops and those government guys, CIA, they said do it or else and I was too scared to ask *or else* what. Politicians, generals, colonels, princes, whatever. All foreigners. It was hop in the sack with those grease-balls or your ass is in a sling, honey."

"Jail, you mean?"

Renne Blake rolled down the car window, threw out a cigarette butt and then blew through the holder to clear it before reaching in her purse for another cigarette. She was twenty-four, a small, pretty blonde who had worked out of an apartment on Manhattan's East 81st Street and right now, her hands shook as she thumbed a slim gold lighter into flame.

"Jail," she said. "They made sure we knew we'd wind up there, with roaches in our food and bull-dykes following us into the shower. Man, that's scarey, let me tell you. First the cops put pressure on the girls they want. You get arrested two, three times in one week. They tell us it's for sure that the johns are gonna testify we ripped them off, stole their wallets or some shit like that. Honey, let me tell you something: When you make the kind of money I do, you don't have to steal from nobody."

Burt slowed down for a toll booth coming up on his left. Whores and politicians, he thought, they both screwed you and liked to brag about it. "What kind of money you talking about?"

"Eighty thousand a year average. Tax free. And I get presents besides."

At the toll booth Burt handed a dollar to the attendant

and turned around to look at Monica. She winked at him, pointed to herself and mouthed the words *no presents*.

"Eighty thousand, huh?" Had to get Renne Blake started again. This was their third meeting and he had found her to be an honest working girl who only wanted revenge.

"Eighty big ones, honey. Beats workin' at Woolworth's."

"Beats working," said Monica Hollander. She and Renne Blake grinned at each other.

Though Renne Blake was a call girl, she was sick of being forced to have sex with men she didn't like. "After I got sent down to Washington a couple times, I get hit on up here by that important cop I mentioned. Starts out he wants one freebie. Just a casual fuck on the house. Next thing you know he's dropping by the apartment once a week. Don't even call up first, just comes 'round and honey, what that asshole did to me, I am tellin' you. Couple times I throw up after he leaves. It was worse than gettin' raped, which has also happened to me but that's another story. Me and a couple other girls who are caught up in this shit figure we just can't go on livin' this way."

Burt glanced at her, then turned back to the road. "You won't have to."

"Yeah, I know. That's why I'm splittin'."

"I don't mean that. I mean when this story is printed, somebody's going to be unhappy and it won't be you."

"I will be if they ever catch me. You don't know cops."

Burt snorted. "I sure as hell do know cops. Every reporter knows cops, especially when they try to frame you and send you to jail for writing something they don't particularly like."

Renne Blake looked at him. "You too?"

"Yep."

"When was this?"

"Last year. In California. Working on a story about Mexican illegals, people who sneak over the border to pick California fruit for two bucks a day. There was a small town in Baja California and some people were making a few bucks sneaking in Mexicans. I found out that a couple of local cops were in on it, too."

Burt braked gently, allowing a speeding station wagon to cut in front of him. Driving in New York was dangerous, but not as dangerous as working on the Mexican alien story.

"Go on," Renne said, touching his thigh.

Burt's eyes went down to her hand then back to the road. He was going to like this job.

"Cops were in on the frame-up all the way," he said. "They'd learned I was around asking hard questions so they decided to set me up. There was a girl down there that I'd been using as a contact and one night I got a quick telephone call from her telling me to hurry over. Says she can't talk to me over the phone. Just get there. So I run out, but when I get to her building I stop. Something tells me don't go in. *Do not go in.* Now I'm thirty years old and I've been a reporter for ten years and believe me, I've learned to listen to those tiny voices in the back of my brain. I back off and return to my motel. A minute after I get back somebody else telephones and says get out of town right away, that the cops are planning to 'flake me.' Plant drugs on me. The gal I was going to meet had a half kilo of cocaine in her apartment and the cops had planned to bust me for selling drugs. The gal was helping the cops frame me. I would have ended up doing time for sure."

Renne Blake frowned. "They can do that to a reporter?"

"Oh, yes they can. And they do. Most people don't like reporters, especially investigative reporters. So people lie to you, threaten, pressure, see that nobody helps you in any way. So now instead of being a starving, hardworking, freelance truth seeker who can't pay his bills, I'm a gossip columnist and so far, nobody's tried to put me in jail."

He wasn't just trying to put Renne Blake at ease by telling her that cops could give anybody a hard time. They had come down on Burt more than once. Threats, arrests, twelve-hour interrogations, vindictive judges, unending promises of lawsuits and never, never anybody backing him up. Newspapers and magazines were far from courageous; most didn't want to stir up a fuss, so they refused to print stories offending important people or advertisers. Burt's ideals were enough to get a story written, but not always enough to get the story published.

The only reporters who ever had it easy were Robert Redford and Dustin Hoffman and their winning streak had occurred on the silver screen. Burt had learned the hard way that the opposition played rough, making up the rules as it went along. He had survived ten years in a tough business but it wasn't something he wanted to keep on doing until his teeth and hair fell out.

He wanted a comfortable life while he was young enough to enjoy it. The idealism of the 1960s, a big part of Burt's life, was dead, as dead as Janis Joplin, Jimi Hendrix, John and Bobby Kennedy and Martin Luther King, Jr. One way or another, they had all died of high hopes. Stone dead from ideals. Long ago and far away, Burt Anthony had embraced those same high hopes and ideals, because you couldn't change the world while sitting in a classroom. And the world *had* to be changed. *Had to be.*

Burt had given a lot of talent and energy to changing it and he had worked up a sweat, nothing more. Moral indignation had kept him going for a time, as did the very little money he had earned. He had chosen to freelance, to avoid organizations and regimentation, to be his own man. He had a suitcase full of awards, commendations, glowing letters but he wasn't rich and the older he got the more important it had become to have money. Money, he had learned, afforded the ultimate freedom.

Turning to Renne Blake again, Burt asked who had told her to go to Washington this weekend. And she told him it was the cop, Clauson.

"The vice lieutenant who's been visiting you?"

"Class A prick. You gonna use the pictures I gave you?"

"Sure will."

Lieutenant Clauson had done more than team with U.S. Intelligence to force Renne and other Manhattan call girls to entertain visiting foreign dignitaries. In addition to those little visits he had been paying Renne every so often, he had also pressured her into spending a weekend with him in upstate New York. He was too drunk and too hot in the pants to notice that he and Renne were being photographed in the hotel nightclub, but Renne noticed. She paid for the photograph and hid it, waiting until the time was right.

The time was right now.

When Clauson told Renne she would have to go to Washington this weekend to entertain Arabs who were there buying arms, she had called Burt. Two other call girls Burt had met through Renne had given him more names, which he had had checked out with his Washington sources. Those names turned out to be involved in intelligence, arms contracting and lobbying. As a reporter, Burt had developed excellent contacts in Washington, a fact appreciated by Harold Monmouth.

Burt turned to Renne Blake. "Does your pal Reynaldo know where you're going?"

"No, you told me not to tell anybody."

"That's right." Reynaldo was a professional basketball player who had gone to college with Burt and who had sent Renne to him in the first place. Renne and Reynaldo had met at an East Side orgy club and maintained a casual sexual relationship since then.

Not even Burt knew exactly where Renne was going, nor did he want to know. After she landed in Los Angeles, she was taking a flight to another western state and what Burt didn't know, he couldn't tell anybody. If there was any kickback from this story, Burt was covered. True he had driven Renne to the airport, but that was at her request since she was too frightened to trust a cab driver. Besides, the trip was yielding another hour of tape. Monica had said that Monmouth might even run the story on the front page.

Burt and Renne sat in the airport terminal and continued to talk while Monica made several telephone calls, one of which was to cancel Burt's appearance on a radio talk show he was to have taped in a half hour. There was no way they would make it back to the city in time. In any case, Burt was set to do two more radio shows and one television show later in the week. Monica was doing her job well.

After Renne's plane took off, Burt and Monica relaxed over drinks in an empty airport bar. One of Monica's telephone calls had been to Burt's answering service. She had taken down several messages for him and he held them unread in his hand while grinning across the table at her.

"You won't believe this," he said, "but you know how much money Renne Blake's carrying in her suitcase?"

"How much?"

"Over sixty thousand dollars."

"You're kidding."

"She tells me she plans to pay ten thousand for a new trick book. It's a list of johns she's buying from a gal who's leaving the business to get married."

Using a toothpick Monica speared a tiny onion in the bottom of her empty glass. "I would have sold her one of my old address books for half that. How about reading those messages."

"Right. You talk with Dave?"

"Yes. Two messages are from him. Says he'll check with you at the apartment in an hour."

Dave Tiegs was experienced in gossip, not as a writer but as a collector. He had been around New York for a few years and was middle-aged, overweight, hypertense, with a mania about gathering personal and private information on famous people. Monmouth had hired him, pending Burt's approval. In a matter of days Dave had proven how valuable he could be as a compulsive collector and leg man and Burt had been glad to keep him on.

Burt looked at the first scrap of paper. "From Dave. Says 'go with the dynamite story for tomorrow's column.'"

"What's that?"

"I had a tip that a top Broadway star, male, was having trouble with stagehands during the performance. They kept talking while the star was onstage and it bugged him, so he complained to the producer about it. The producer spoke to the stagehands. Now one thing you don't do in the theater is take on the stagehands. They don't care who you are, their union is a lot tougher than you'll ever be. So they fixed the star good."

"Who is he and what did they do to him?"

Burt mentioned the star's name and Monica nodded in appreciation of his importance.

Burt leaned back in his chair, smiling. "They found out that the star's birthday was coming up and they planned a surprise party for him onstage after the show. This was the day before yesterday. They gave him the present and told him not to open it until he got on the plane. Our superstar was going to the Bahamas for a day or two. But he was so happy about the crew giving him a present—a fine bit of ego stroking—that he opened it right there."

Monica leaned across the table in anticipation.

"The present was four sticks of dynamite taped to a timer. Phony dynamite, of course, but can you imagine what would have happened if he'd opened that on the plane?"

"Oh, Burt," Monica laughed, "you'll have to run that one blind or his lawyer will be on your back. You don't need that."

"Better believe it." He looked at the rest of his messages. "Jesus. That won't be the only blind item I'll have tomorrow."

Blind items were gossip with the names left out. *What-star - was - caught - naked - in - a - phone - booth - with - a-dwarf-and-two-Tasmanian-hedgehogs* kind of thing. The names were dropped either because you couldn't prove the item was true or it was so libelous that you would be sued whether it was true or not.

Burt frowned. He read the last message again.

Monica touched his hand. "What is it?"

"Call from L.A. telling me to go ahead with something

I've been sitting on a few days. It says my information is correct, but if I run it somebody's going to get hurt."

"What is it?"

Burt looked out at the night-blackened runways, at blinking lights and jets climbing high into a dark blue sky, leaving long gray trails behind them.

He looked back at Monica Hollander. "It's about Rachel Auden, the actress who's been nominated for an Oscar two years in a row. She had a son by Curtis Graham—"

"Short marriage. He's only one of the most glamorous movie stars ever. They're getting divorced. But that's been in all the papers."

"I'll tell you something that hasn't been in the papers. When they started going together, Graham never slept with her. No sex. He's, what, more than thirty years older than she and he just didn't have a strong sex drive. But she works at it and finally one afternoon, she gets him to screw her, which is what she wanted for God knows how long. Then she climbs into her car and drives through Beverly Hills until she sees a guy standing on a corner waiting for a bus or something. She says to him, 'get in.' He's a stranger. She's never seen him before."

Burt shrugged and continued. "Well, who wouldn't get in the car if Rachel Auden says get in. She drives to a motel and she and the guy screw like crazy. She wants to make sure she's pregnant because she desperately wants Curtis Graham to marry her, and since he is over sixty and has no children, she is certain this will do it. She's right. Because Graham is crazy about children. When the motel scene is over, she and the stranger say good-bye and never see each other again. She and Curtis Graham marry and he thinks the child is his. He thinks he's got a son, his first child at over sixty. But it's not his and Rachel Auden told somebody the entire story."

Monica raised an eyebrow. "Who did she tell?"

"Her hairdresser. In Beverly Hills it seems you tell your hairdresser everything. That's where my source heard it. I also have confirmation from a personal manager she fired and cheated out of his commissions. Now if I run this story it's going to have an effect on the divorce. All one of Graham's lawyers has to do is read it, then go into court and put the pressure on Rachel Auden."

Monica nodded. "So far, your West Coast stuff has been strong and it's held up. What's bothering you about this?"

Burt chewed his bottom lip. "What bothers me is if I run it, the kid'll find out someday and Rachel will have to explain. The kid's three years old now but—"

"Burt, you can't live other peoples' lives for them. You do your job. Do what you're getting paid to do and don't worry. As far as Rachel Auden is concerned, that's life in the big city. She called the tune and now she has to dance to it."

Burt looked out into the night, at the red, white and green lights twinkling on the runways. "If I print it, she's got a problem."

"Keep thinking like that, and *you've* got a problem."

He nodded. "You're right and lady, when you're right, you're right."

Monica looked at Burt. He was exactly her height with a long, sad, clean-shaven face and a nose he'd told her had been broken three times though it still looked cute to her. He was thin, which came from being too intense, from trying too hard to remake the world. But he could be a dynamite gossip writer if he'd let it happen, if he'd stop worrying about who got hurt.

Burt smiled at her. "Got to go back and make a few rounds. Hit the discos, which is where it's all happening these days and check out one of Renne's girl friends. Then it's to the typewriter and have the column ready before morning when the messenger knocks at my door. Jesus, what a way to live. Working at night and sleeping in the day."

Monica blew cigarette smoke in the air. "You and Dracula."

"Drop you off at your place."

Her grin was sly. "If you insist."

"Got to do some work on tomorrow's column and on this Renne Blake thing, if it's going to be front page. I produce five columns a week, tall lady, while you sit around enjoying three-martini lunches."

"You know you're doing the Barry Gray radio show this week with D'Arcy."

"I know." Burt was uncomfortable around D'Arcy. D'Arcy wanted to own New York, that much was clear, and it was also clear that he didn't care how he did it.

He was writing some gamey items about Renata Zachery, wife of the vice-president of the United States and when Burt had criticized him for doing so, D'Arcy's reply had been a snide grin and an "everything is grist for the mill, old boy."

"Are you going to print that item on Rachel Auden?"

"Yes." And keep my job, Burt thought. "Yes, I'm running with it."

Monica leaned across the table, took his face between her hands and gently kissed both of his eyes.

Burt said softly. "On the other hand, I don't have to drop you off at your place."

"Didn't you say something about having a column to write?"

"I'm a fast writer, remember?" He kissed the palm of her hand.

"It'll cost you the going rate."

"Which is?"

"Eighty thousand. Forget the presents. I'm not greedy."

"Will you take a check?"

They went back to his apartment. After a delicious, if brief, tumble in bed, Burt sat at his typewriter, while Monica slept and he wrote fast.

■ ■ ■ **Four**

The door opened and Denis Radd, the Examiner-
*World's* editor-in-chief, entered Harold Monmouth's office
with two folded newspapers under his arm. He walked
with his toes turned out, hitting the thick, green carpet with
his heels and bouncing up and down. He was English,
forty-five, a burly man with thinning red hair and rimless
glasses. His appearance was that of a former athlete now
running to fat. Flopping into a chair, he sat and wheezed
for a few seconds and when his asthma stopped bothering
him, he tossed the two newspapers on the table in front
of Monmouth.

Monmouth reached for black horn-rimmed glasses inside his handkerchief pocket. His other hand pulled the
paper containing Robin Ian D'Arcy's gossip column
toward him.

Monmouth read the column. He snorted, shaking his
head. "The bastard. He says the heavyweight champion
got two women pregnant and neither woman plans to sue

him. And here, this one. He claims that ten million dollars which an arms company was sending as a payoff to a Middle Eastern country never got there. One of the company's lawyers stole it and hasn't been seen since."

A strong column, as usual. And as usual D'Arcy's success only angered Monmouth. But he continued to read. There was an item about a television talk show host who was divorcing his wife after catching her in bed with the handyman. Apparently the handyman was also wearing a pair of the husband's finest silk pajamas at the time. D'Arcy named the young comedian arrested for almost beating to death the girl he lived with when he'd learned that she had been turning tricks in their apartment while the comedian was appearing at colleges and rock concerts.

Another item dealt with a lesbian love affair between an Oscar-winning English actress and a top model. While no names were mentioned D'Arcy simplified the guessing game by working in almost the entire title of the film for which the actress had won her Academy Award. As for the model, he mentioned the type of product she was promoting while avoiding the brand name. Cheeky bastard, thought Monmouth, and he's going to get away with it.

Nor did D'Arcy neglect Renata Zachery. She was the current media darling, lauded, picked on and over-publicized and still very much the one woman the public seemed to want to read about. She was beautiful, outspoken, married to a man who could end up in the most powerful job in the world, and she was living her own life with a freedom never indulged in by a woman in her position.

D'Arcy reported that she had spent two days in New York having lunch and dinner with the same "borrowed" husband whose wife bitterly resented the arrangement and had told him so. On one of those two nights, Renata Zachery and her party of ten had gone to a top discotheque and D'Arcy listed their entire drink order, with the result that it appeared as if all had been drinking to excess.

There was a final note at the bottom of the column. Denis Radd watched Harold Monmouth and waited, knowing what the reaction would be. D'Arcy had the item in boldface type, so it couldn't be missed. In it he wondered how much longer Harold Monmouth could continue to prop up his new toy at a cost of $100,000 a week. Perhaps, wrote D'Arcy, it was time for Mr. Monmouth to examine his world more closely.

Monmouth said, "Bloody bugger!" and threw the paper to the floor. He jerked off his glasses. The item referred to the fact that the *Examiner-World* was losing money and Monmouth was keeping it going by dipping into his own funds to the tune of $100,000 a week. It didn't matter how or where D'Arcy had learned this. He had, damn him. The paper *was* losing money and Monmouth *had* to stop the red ink soon or admit defeat, leaving a successful D'Arcy to revile him. *Examine his world more closely.* Damn D'Arcy's eyes!

Denis Radd looked up at the ceiling and waited. Give the guv'nor time to cool down. Harold's hatred for our Robin was hotter than the desert sands. Why not? D'Arcy had gone after Monmouth in England, peeling the skin off the man with fiendish glee. He'd exposed everything about Harold, from his real name to his rapacious business practices to his attempts at buying a knighthood. Denis Radd declined to pronounce judgment on Harold, whom he had known and worked for these past fifteen years. Every man had a right to climb up the greasy pole of success any way he could, and Harold was a climber.

Harold and Robin. They had hated each other in England, and the egos of both men contained no room for forgiveness. The fact that both men had crossed the Atlantic with the intention of conquering New York had not made them hate each other any less. D'Arcy, at the very least, saw Monmouth as crass, a pretender, a man of no taste. Monmouth saw D'Arcy as a gadfly, a tormentor, someone who made him uneasy about his success, someone who would always remind him that he was only a hustler who had clawed his way out of the mud, with the mud still under his fingernails.

Monmouth put his glasses back on and reached for the *Examiner-World*, which was folded open to Burt Anthony's column.

"Well now, dear Denis, let's see how our little shoe-maker is doing."

Denis Radd's eyes never left Monmouth's face. "Some of it's good, some of it's a bit light. Our Burt's got possibilities he does, and in time I think he'll do all right."

"Time is one thing I do not have." Monmouth began reading. Shoemaker was a nickname he and Denis Radd had for Burt Anthony, never to be used to Burt's face. The name came from a story about a princess with very big feet. She wanted a shoe made that was small on the outside and large on the inside. An impossible task, which is how some had described Monmouth's intention of beating Robin Ian D'Arcy at the game of gossip.

"Mmmmm, yes." Monmouth nodded his head in approval. Burt's first story was on a congressional leader who was an alchoholic and often conducted important committee hearings while drunk. Fellow congressmen and lobbyists with vested interests were covering for him. Monmouth looked across the table at Denis Radd.

"What's his source on this congressman thing?"

Radd finished wheezing before he answered. "Thought you'd like to know. I asked Anthony and he says he's got a friend who's an assistant to the senator hoping to replace our drunken congressman on a rather important committee."

"Ah, yes. A leak in high places. Where would we gossipmongers be without 'em."

Monmouth continued reading. There were several juicy items but the one that interested him most mentioned a married eastern superlawyer who had just paid personally for two women to have abortions, both within a six-month period.

Monmouth said, "Who's the lawyer that's continually challenging the Vatican's edict on birth control?"

53

"Don't know. Will check for you if you'd like."

"Do. Perhaps we can use it elsewhere."

Denis Radd smiled. Among the American publications Harold Monmouth owned was *P.I.*, a weekly tabloid that Radd found sordid as hell but it was starting to sell and that's what counted in the long run. It ran stories on farmers who had been taken onboard flying saucers, flown to Venus where they were wined and dined, then dropped back off in Iowa. There were stories on grisly murders and mishapened freaks, with photographs to match and if there was a crazy diet of some kind, *P.I.*, which stood for Privileged Information, would surely run it.

Some of *P.I.*'s stories, Radd knew, were "window stories." A writer sat staring out of the window of his office and let his imagination run wild. After it had run wild long enough, he swiveled around in his chair and began to type and the result would run in *P.I.* the next week. Movie and television stars, professional athletes, politicians, known authors, all received the *P.I.* treatment and, occasionally, some of those stories were true. The true ones cost money, for Monmouth paid handsomely if he wanted the story badly enough. Once in a while he would buy serialization rights to a popular, lightweight book, but most of what appeared in *P.I.* were freak stories, tales of the bizarre and the bloody, with more than a few window stories thrown in.

*P.I.* was lurid and lucrative and Denis Radd knew that no respectable author wanted his name connected with the tabloid. Editors and staff used their true names but no one else did. Respectable writers had to be down on their luck before agreeing to write for *P.I.* under false names. Though *P.I.* paid well, its stench was too strong for it ever to become respectable. Monmouth didn't care, nor did Radd, since he didn't work on or read the publication.

Monmouth placed Burt Anthony's column to his left. "Passable. Just passable. But not a word about Renata Zachery. The presidential convention is coming up in a few months and her husband has every chance of winning the nomination."

"*If* he continues to please the prudish President," Denis Radd wheezed, his round face turning red.

"Indeed. I'll have a talk with shoemaker. I do think Mrs. Zachery should be more prominently featured than she has been of late."

"How do you think he'll take it? These Americans, 'specially the young ones, seem so bloody independent."

"You've heard the expression 'whose bread I eat, his song I sing'?"

"Harold, you're not talking about singers. You're talkin' about a bloody Yank who started out to save the bleedin' world and somewhere along the line he stubbed 'is toe."

"Yes, well I shall be discreet but I would appreciate more attention paid to Mrs. Zachery. I've given orders that she be featured in *P.I.* every other week until further notice."

"Jesus God, Harold." Denis Radd grinned, folding his hands on top of his bulging stomach. "The country will be seein' more of the bloody woman than her husband does."

"Well, dear Denis, at least he'll know where to find her. In the pages of *P.I.* And as soon as I have a talk with Anthony, in the pages of the *Examiner-World.*"

Denis Radd wheezed again, as he polished the lenses on his rimless glasses and stood up.

"I'm for that, as long as it sells papers. Well now, do you feel like takin' a walk with me downstairs and tellin' our American cousins why we intend to bring in machines to replace some of them?"

"Oh, indeed I do, Denis. Indeed I do. After all, haven't I been told to examine my world more closely?"

## New York City

As he sat in his parked car, Gypsy bit into his third Milky Way bar of the night, eyes on the one lighted window on the second floor of an East 72nd Street duplex. Yesterday he had used keys given him by Simon to get inside and bug two telephones, a television set and an air conditioner in the bedroom. By tuning his car radio to an FM frequency Gypsy was able to use it as a receiver, allowing him to overhear and record telephone calls as well as conversations in the luxury apartment itself. This was his third bug job for Simon, who as usual refused to name a target, giving Gypsy only time and place, plus his money in small, used bills.

On the first tap in Washington, Gypsy had heard men talk about government and the weather, all of it boring, though someone had mentioned a congressman caught propositioning a Marine. Because of the blizzard, the men in the hotel room had left early before the storm got worse and only the fact that Gypsy had spotted Simon on television in the company of some heavies had made the trip worthwhile. The second tap had also been in Washington, on a telephone in a Georgetown apartment. The phone had rung and rung while Gypsy waited and listened, but no one had answered because no one had gone in or out of the apartment. The caller apparently had been checking to see if his party was there and receiving no answer, had stayed clear. For some reason this tape seemed to excite Simon more than the first, but as always he remained close-mouthed. Gypsy decided that Simon was the guy in charge of dirty tricks for certain politicians.

Gypsy looked at his watch. Twelve minutes after eleven; he had been sitting cramped in the Chevy for almost four hours. Whoever was left in the apartment was alone because there hadn't been a sound from the place since eleven o'clock, when a group of men and women had left, some of them in chauffeured limousines with diplomatic license plates.

At 7:30 tonight Gypsy had begun watching and listening to an empty apartment; whoever Simon wanted bugged had been in the crowd of two dozen people who had shown up twenty minutes later. Over his car radio Gypsy had listened to and recorded a few phone calls, most of them local, a couple to Washington and one to Germany. The television and air conditioner bugs were useless; too many people talking loudly and at once. If Simon had known about this party he should have mentioned it, and Gypsy would have told him that bugging a crowd was a waste of time. All you'd pick up was noise, because everybody was drowning out everybody else. Gypsy's guess about it being a spur-of-the-moment party was confirmed when he heard a couple of telephone calls from the duplex to a neighborhood gourmet shop and a liquor store.

There wasn't much Gypsy could learn from that. Gypsy had learned Simon's name, however, and who he worked for in Washington—a feat accomplished merely by describing Simon to a New York reporter Gypsy knew. Simon worked for one of the most powerful senators in Washington, a tough, shrewd man who bitterly opposed the current President of the United States and who was rumored to be seeking the office himself in this fall's national election. That was when Gypsy knew there was real money to be made if he were smart and made all the right moves. The first move was to become indispensable to Simon. Once they saw how good Gypsy was and how much they needed him, they wouldn't be able to drop him. That was the time to make a move for bigger money, not before.

Gypsy shivered. The car heater was on and he was wearing thermal underwear and two sweaters under his overcoat, but he was still cold. It was March in New York, the first day of spring and the temperature hadn't risen above freezing all week. Simon had said stay with the tap until one in the morning then leave and have the tapes ready by noon.

Suddenly Gypsy heard the sound of classical music over the car radio, a violin and a piano, probably coming from a radio or a recorder player in the apartment. There was also the sound of papers rustling, as though someone was either working at a desk or reading a newspaper. Still no conversation from the apartment and no telephone calls in or out. Gypsy thought of the food probably left over upstairs and he was hungry. He would love to have some deli just about now. He would also like to stretch his legs and get rid of the milk carton that was stinking up the car. Because he hadn't wanted to leave the car he had used the carton to piss in and the smell was getting to him.

He looked up at the duplex. The light was still on in most of the rooms and the classical music, which he found boring, was coming in nice and clear so whoever was there was in place for the night. Gypsy was hungry; if he hurried he could get to the gourmet shop around the corner and be back inside the car in minutes. The bugs were working perfectly and so were both the receiver and the recorder; they would keep on working while he was gone.

Walking back to the car with the bag of food clutched to his chest was a sensual pleasure, sort of like hugging a woman. The thought of it filled his mind with a joy that was going to be his and his alone. That was the beautiful thing about food. You didn't have to share it with anybody; it was your individual ecstasy and you could have it any time you wanted. He didn't look up at the duplex until he was inside the car and had slammed the door. It was dark. Not a single light in any of its windows. The occupant had probably gone to bed but to make sure he hadn't missed anything, Gypsy checked his recorder and received a surprise that temporarily made him forget about his food. He backed the tape up to the point where he'd left the car, listened to himself locking the car door, followed by a period of silence broken only by classical music from the apartment. Suddenly a telephone rang, was picked up in the duplex and a voice at the other end simply said, "Now." Just the one word and it brought no response from the person in the duplex. But it was obviously what the person inside had wanted to hear because he or she hung up the phone immediately without replying and the only sounds on the recorder were the classical music being turned off, followed by footsteps racing across the carpet and a front door slamming shut and being locked.

58

An angry Gypsy pounded the steering wheel with his fist. Christ. If he'd stayed in one place he could at least have seen the occupant of the duplex come out, maybe even followed that person and learned more about Simon's game. Shit. Nothing to do but sit tight until something else happened or somebody returned to the apartment. Simon would call Gypsy tomorrow and either tell him to remove the bugs or continue listening. Meanwhile, Gypsy rewound the tape and played it once more, listening carefully to the one-word conversation, listening to a hoarse voice that could have belonged to either a man or a woman. The voice could have had laryngitis or a bad cold but Gypsy sensed the hoarseness was actually an attempt at disguise.

Reaching into his bag of food, he removed a hot pastrami sandwich and a quart of chocolate milk. As he ate he thought of what he had come up with tonight. Diplomatic license plates, a late-night meeting now about to take place somewhere in New York, and a voice that didn't believe in talking too much over the phone. Gypsy decided that when he got back to his apartment tonight he would work on that one-word conversation. He was going to run it at different speeds, test it for various voice levels, timbre and several other things. With only one word to go on, Gypsy could still learn a few things about that voice, a voice so special it had only to say one word to make somebody come running out into a damp, cold night. Gypsy's equipment was the finest in the world and in his hands it could do wonders. Before he went to sleep tonight he'd know a few things about the mystery voice. . . .

■ ■ ■ **Five**

**She slept on her left side, back to D'Arcy** who inhaled on a long, thin, black cigarette and lay awake pondering that turn of fate, which found him, at thirty-five, ridiculously infatuated with this sleeping American childwoman, age twenty. She was beautiful and bizarre, sensual and treacherous and since their meeting ten days ago, D'Arcy hadn't been able to stay away from her. She was Johnnie Gelb, daughter of a wealthy New York corporation president; a woman with flawless good looks, too much money and an indifference to any known standard of morality. D'Arcy craved her.

They had met in an illegal gambling casino, a luxurious duplex on Sutton Place South. D'Arcy, who enjoyed gambling, had inquired around until he had found a casino that offered more than the chance for a fool to be parted from his money. If offered a view of Manhattan's polluted East River and two decaying bridges as well as the dreary perusal of the slow passage of numerous garbage barges. Patrons also received free drinks in Styrofoam cups and lukewarm Chinese food piled on paper plates. The casino lacked the ambience of London's elegant Victoria Sporting Club; however, as a confirmed gambler, D'Arcy had no choice but to submit to the rather base environment and lay his chips down on a nearby table. When in Rome, dear heart . . .

Johnnie Gelb. D'Arcy felt the name belonged on a pimply faced schoolboy, not to the most delicious creature he had seen since his arrival in New York. Johnnie had followed D'Arcy around the casino one night, from roulette to blackjack, from one floor to another, to the bar and back, smiling at him until intrigued, he had crooked a finger and beckoned her closer.

"You have a name, I presume."

"Johnnie. Johnnie Gelb."

"You cahn't be serious. *Johnnie?* Really? Did your parents fail to detect your gender at birth or is it traditional in America to present girls with boys' names."

She giggled, covering her mouth with a slim hand. The nails were painted a cinnamon color and there were delicate rings on all fingers. "I like the way you talk. You have a nice accent. I've seen you on television, you know."

"Have you now. And how was I?"

"You talked then the way you talk now."

"How very clever of me. And what brings you to this emporium of chance?"

God in heaven, the child was lovely!

Delicate and sensual and D'Arcy lusted after her. She was slim, with gleaming platinum blond hair that fell straight to her shoulders. The clearest of blue eyes and a mouth with the pout of a French actress. She wore a long flowing lavender dress split to her thighs, and gold sandals laced at her ankles. D'Arcy found himself actually licking his lips.

"Meeting somebody here," she said, tilting her head to the side and studying him. He was tall and she liked that and he spoke with an English accent, like some of the rock stars she had met. Super. Really super.

Her perfume smelled of wild flowers. D'Arcy took a step closer, amazed that such a young girl would choose so subtle a scent.

"Johnnie, if you don't mind my asking, whom are you meeting?"

"A friend—Richie. How did you get in here? You have to know somebody or they don't let you in. Or are you so famous they have to let you in?"

"Young woman, I admit to a modicum of fame but what others *have* to do for me is debatable. I am here because I enjoy gambling, which one can do in London but not in New York, unless one knows a person connected with an establishment such as this. Shall I tell you something?"

"What?"

D'Arcy listened to the tape playing softly in the background. Roberta Flack was singing of a love that had been doomed from the start.

He said, "You must go home and break every mirror you own."

She giggled. "Far out. You want to tell me why?"

"Because you are beautiful and can remain so forever, if you never again look into a mirror."

She touched his arm and D'Arcy shivered as he hadn't since he was an adolescent. "I like you," she said. "You're funny. Buy me a drink." She put her arm through his and D'Arcy took a deep breath.

At the bar she sipped Scotch and water, eyeing him over the glass through long lashes which she assured him were real. He believed her.

"Robin," she said. "That's a girl name, isn't it?"

"Not necessarily. Aren't you rather young to be in a place like this all by yourself?"

"Told you I'm not by myself. I'm meeting Richie. Besides, I was twenty last week."

D'Arcy looked around the duplex at the well-dressed men and women gambling at roulette, craps, blackjack, or who sat and drank and talked. Roberta Flack had been replaced by Stevie Wonder, who also sang about the inevitable pain of love and D'Arcy wondered if Stevie and Roberta weren't warning him against what he had begun to feel for Johnnie Gelb.

He said, "What does your friend Richie do?"

She sucked on an ice cube. Both elbows were on the small bar and she stared out of the window at a bridge far away in the night.

"Richie's a hood."

"A what?"

"Hood. Gangster. Mob guy. Mafia."

She looked at him and moved her sensual pout of a mouth in a small smile. She waited.

D'Arcy frowned. "I do believe you're serious."

"I am."

"And he's on his way to meet you?"

She nodded, continuing to chew ice. "He doesn't like me talkin' to other guys, but what he doesn't know won't hurt him, right?"

D'Arcy nodded. "What would he do if he caught you talking to me?"

"Nothin'. He hit me once when I told him I made it with this black guy who was college football player of the year. But then I told Richie if he ever laid a hand on me he'd never see me again. So now he doesn't hit me. He just yells a lot."

D'Arcy drank more of his gin and tonic. In America people confided in one on terribly short notice. Definitely not the case in England. But this topped anything he had encountered since his arrival in New York. Beautiful Johnnie Gelb was an American primitive and, if she were to be believed, she was leading quite a life. D'Arcy was captivated by her depravity.

"So your friend Richie is a hood. How do you know?"

"He told me. Men like to brag, especially in bed. That's a nice suit. You buy it here or in England?'

"England. Isn't there a rule about that sort of thing? I'd always heard you're not supposed to tell anyone you were a member of that illustrious crew?" Humor the dear darling and see where it leads. To bed, he hoped.

"Robin. I like that name. Robin, Robin, Robin. Robin, there's a lot you don't know. I mean, mob guys, they're just like anybody else. They always want to impress you with what a big man they are. I'd like another drink, please. The same."

D'Arcy ordered. And listened to her with fascination. Johnnie Gelb was rich and her parents, who'd long ago lost control over her, gave her money to stay away and not embarrass them. She was bored with school, private tutors, psychiatrists who were unable to deal with her and she had lost her virginity early to an uncle who had cried afterward. A week later, the uncle died in a car crash, which Johnnie guessed had been caused by his remorse over molesting her.

She was aware of her beauty, but unwilling and unable to be faithful to any one man. She was promiscuous, which she didn't find a problem, and she found life boring most of the time, unless something was happening and what was happening depended on her mood or who she was with. D'Arcy was new, different and he was *somebody,* which was why Johnnie had followed him around the casino.

D'Arcy was enthralled, enchanted. Dear God, *he was in heat!* Johnnie Gelb was as much a child of nature as the Sioux Indian or a gray wolf slinking silently through a moonlit forest. So American, and as sexual a creature as God had ever made. D'Arcy had to have her. The heart knows not why, it only knows when. D'Arcy didn't care to know why. He had to have Johnnie Gelb and there was nothing more to know.

She fingered a gold-plated razor blade hanging on a thin gold chain around her neck. "Do you make a lot of money? I mean you write about famous people and all. I just wondered if it's a kind of thing you make a living at."

"You think I'm gambling to supplement my salary?" He laughed. "I do quite well, thank you." He made $125,000 a year, but he wasn't ready to confide in strangers as quickly as she did.

"How much you make?"

"None of your business, Johnnie Gelb." He gave her his biggest and he hoped, most charming smile.

"How come you're here alone? I mean you're famous."

"If you must know, people bore me. Also, I prefer to concentrate on my gambling, since I am, after all, losing my own money. What is the significance of that razor blade you're wearing, if you don't mind my asking?"

"Hey, come on. Every body knows that. You use it when you do coke. Sets up the lines. Did you win or lose tonight?"

"Depends on you, Johnnie Gelb." He waited, heart in his throat.

She stopped crunching ice and stared at him for several seconds. Stevie Wonder continued singing of betrayal. Johnnie turned away from D'Arcy and looked straight ahead. "When Richie comes I've got to go with him. But I can come to your place later tonight if that's cool."

D'Arcy's hand shook as he took his notebook from inside his jacket. He printed his address and telephone number, then watched as she folded the piece of paper twice before placing it inside a tiny, yellow beaded bag that hung from her left wrist. Leaning toward her, D'Arcy fingered the razor blade. Being so near to her, smelling her perfume, feeling the warmth of her body was almost unbearable. He felt himself get hard and he had to laugh at himself. He now had hot balls over a girl fifteen years younger than he, a girl who had warned him that she would not be faithful.

He said, "Coke? Cocaine seems to be all the rage at the present moment." Americans were starting to treat their own decadence as naturally as they did the wearing of jeans. A casual attitude toward life's sordid side, thought D'Arcy, was the sign of a civilized nation, for one had to work long and hard before learning to sin in an offhanded manner.

"Yeah, cocaine," she said, looking down at the gold-plated razor. "You use this to set up the lines. Put the coke on a mirror, then divide it into lines, tiny little rows and you inhale it from the mirror. I use a silver straw to snort mine."

"Why the mirror?"

"Coke's expensive. This way you don't waste a grain. Mirror's hard. It doesn't absorb any of the coke, see?"

"I see."

"Oh shit, here's Richie—"

She slid off the bar stool and D'Arcy turned to see a tall, handsome, young man striding toward them. He had expensively cut black hair, and wore several thin gold chains dangling from his neck, which were visible in his chest hairs. A dark blue velvet jacket, an open-necked pale blue shirt, black pants and black snakeskin boots completed the contemporary hood look. D'Arcy noticed that men stared at Richie and quickly looked away. Women merely stared.

When he reached D'Arcy and Johnnie, the young man stopped, his hard eyes flicking from one to the other. Then he stepped between them, turning his back to D'Arcy. His voice was low and came from deep within his throat and it belonged to a man used to being obeyed. "Let's go." He jerked Johnnie off the bar stool.

With an animal's instinct, Richie sensed that D'Arcy was about to stand up and, still with his back to the Englishman, Richie said, "Back off, creep."

D'Arcy stood up anyway. His eyes glittered as though pleased with Richie's remark. "*Au revoir*, Johnnie. I enjoyed our conversation."

Then the Englishman, who'd courted danger all his life, added, "How's the family, Richie?"

Richie turned to face D'Arcy. "You talkin' to me?"

"I'm attempting some sort of communication, yes. You did address me earlier and I merely wish to reply. I inquired about the *family*. I believe that is the proper word."

The black bartender, towel and glass in his hands, turned his back to the two men. Better not to see what you shouldn't see.

Richie released Johnnie's wrist and took a step toward D'Arcy.

"Mister, I don't know what your problem is, but you come to the right guy to get it taken care of." There was Brooklyn in his voice and he loosened his shoulders, ready to take care of business. "Maybe you'd be doin' yourself a favor to go back where you come from. Like now."

"When I'm ready, Richie. And *like now,* as you put it, is not the time."

D'Arcy wanted conflict. He was jealous and he didn't like the idea of a third-rate American hood grabbing Johnnie and dragging her away from him. *Incredible.* He hadn't been jealous of anyone in years. What's more, he feared no one, for in the end the gossip writer had the last word, the last thrust, the last attack. Bring on the exhilaration of combat, the emotion D'Arcy lived for; hadn't someone in England written of him as being politely suicidal?

Richie narrowed his eyes, nodding his head several times. A creep with airs, this one. Talking like some fucking butler out of some fucking movie and talking with Johnnie, which was a mistake. Time to put the hurt on this dude.

Richie hooked his left fist into D'Arcy's stomach, folding him in half. As the Englishman slumped toward the floor, Richie drove a short, chopping right into the left side of D'Arcy's face. The Englishman flopped backward, arms wide for balance. He fell into a bar stool, knocking it over, and then he crashed into the bar, slumping to the carpet, his mouth open, his blond hair flopping down on his forehead. He winced, working his jaw left, then right, using the back of his hand to wipe a trickle of blood from the corner of his mouth. There was a dull ache in D'Arcy's stomach and he inhaled loudly through his mouth.

Richie grinned down at him. "Cocksucker don't stand so tall now, do ya?"

He turned and grabbed Johnnie's wrist, dragging her away while down on the floor, D'Arcy narrowed his eyes and watched them leave. *Thank you, Richie. Thank you, indeed. I shall now pursue you with a vengeance that will make the hounds of hell seem crippled.*

Later that same night, an anxious D'Arcy waited in his spacious living room, listening to Beethoven and holding ice to his aching jaw. He sat in darkness and when the doorman buzzed from downstairs, D'Arcy bumped his ankle on a piano bench as he ran toward the intercom.

Seconds later when he opened the door, Johnnie entered and in the darkness, a trembling D'Arcy took her into his arms.

That was ten days ago and once again in darkness, D'Arcy held Johnnie Gelb close to him. Somewhere during those ten days, she had found the time to sleep with a man who had picked her up in Bloomingdale's. She had told D'Arcy about it, even though she had no wish to see the man again. D'Arcy knew she was telling the truth and it was merely a reminder of the only rule that would ever exist between them: Johnnie did as she pleased. Her every action seemed to taunt him, to place her just out of reach. She lived for one sensation after another and still D'Arcy could not give her up.

She was not to be used and dismissed, for in essence D'Arcy never truly possessed all of her; Johnnie was never completely his or any man's. Now he could see the truth to Kierkegaard's "the perfect love means to love the one through whom one becomes unhappy." D'Arcy welcomed that unhappiness, for it meant Johnnie was in his life. Happy, unhappy. Johnnie could make him both; one without the other was as impossible as a stick with only one end.

The pain from her confessed infidelity was something to thank her for, oddly enough, because through Johnnie, D'Arcy had been made to feel concern for another human being. He treated this rare emotion as an experience on the order of a new drug. What *did* he feel for Johnnie? Love, perhaps. Lust, definitely. But he *felt* and that was enough.

She always told him of Richie, of what they did in bed, and, D'Arcy, sexually aroused by hearing these things, pulled her to him and ordered her to do them with *him*. Johnnie was a sexual demon, a succubus, pushing D'Arcy beyond any carnal limits he had known, and sharing her with Richie was a galling and harsh truth that was hard to live with.

Richie. The morning after the incident at the Sutton Place casino, D'Arcy began his campaign of vengeance against him. In a meeting with a federal narcotics agent, the columnist learned quite a lot about Richie. Full name Richard Aldo Suitori, age twenty-seven, American citizen of Sicilian descent and a *made man,* said the narcotics agent. *Richie's got his button. He's made his bones. He's in the Mafia.*

"Not easy to get your bones," said the agent. "Back in '63, Joe Valachi testified before a congressional committee, first made man to open up, and right after that the mob stopped taking in new people. They were afraid of informants. Around 1975, they started making new guys. All five New York families opened up their books and you could get your bones. Richie Sweet's definitely a made man and nobody to mess with. We think he's killed at least twelve people."

"Richie Sweet?"

"Street name. Nickname. All mob guys have 'em. It's a thing, a custom. Richie's comes from his last name, Suitori, plus the fact that he works in a bakery. That's his cover, his legitimate job, so he can show some source of income to internal revenue. He's a baker like you're a camel with two humps."

"What's his actual job?"

"*Soldato.* Soldier. That's actually his rank. He's a hitter. He kills people. When he's not doing that, he's chauffeur and bodyguard to Carmine DiNaldi. Carmine's *consigliere* or advisor to Augie Bonnetti's family, which operates throughout the borough of Manhattan. Sure I can't get you some coffee?"

"No, thanks. It's dreadful and I don't see how you people drink it. Tell me more about Richie and his *consigliere*."

"It's an important position, and being bodyguard and chauffeur to a *consigliere* usually means you're on the way up. That's our boy Richie Sweet. He's headed for bigger and better things, though he's known to have a temper. *Soldato* is the bottom rung. And technically Richie's a soldier, though he's a special case because of working for the *consigliere*."

D'Arcy stopped taking notes. "What do soldiers do?"

"Steal and kill and everthing in between."

"I see. So Richie Sweet is in an excellent position to see and learn a lot from this Carmine DiNaldi."

"I would say so, yes. You might say it's a graduate course in crime. Augie Bonnetti specializes in ripping off Wall Street. Stealing securities, bonds, looting brokerage houses. This doesn't mean he's ignoring the traditional money-makers like gambling, loan sharking, stolen credit cards, illegal cigarettes, massage parlors. Narcotics is where we come in. We know who's in the family and we know who they're selling dope to among the blacks, Cubans and Latins. But knowing and proving are two different things. Getting somebody to testify against these people is impossible."

D'Arcy looked at a series of black-and-white photographs the agent had laid out on the desk for him. All ugly men, except for Richie Sweet. The photographs ranged in quality from fair to poor, most having been taken by agents who had been following or watching the suspects. One group of photographs were of members in the Augie Bonnetti family. A few shots had been taken during an arraignment and they were clearer. Beasts in shirts and dark glasses, D'Arcy thought. There were also photographs of black and Hispanic traffickers involved with the Bonnetti family.

D'Arcy said, "May I have a few of these?"

"No. They're still part of an ongoing investigation, which is also why I can't show you current files on these people. We're still trying to nail them and that's not easy. Anybody they catch playing 'Judas' or informant, gets iced. Richie Sweet's got a neat little trick, I hear."

"Which is?"

"Strips a guy naked, hangs him on a meat hook, then jams a cattle prod in his balls. Throws water on the guy to give the prod more charge. One tap from that prod and you jump around on that meathook like crazy. Of course each time you move, the hook digs in deeper."

"Can I talk to your informant?"

"Mr. D'Arcy, you have friends in high places and one of 'em reached the Justice Department, which told us to cooperate. But there's no way you are ever gonna talk to an informant. Informing is a risky business. We've got to protect these people and we don't do that by sittin' a gossip columnist on their laps. You can go back to your people in Washington, but you'll never get permission to speak to an informant."

D'Arcy smiled. "I stand corrected. I would like to learn more about some of the legitimate business this Bonnetti uses as a front."

"Now that I can help you with." The agent reached for a folder lying on his desk. "He's got two catering companies, a vending machine company, a realty company and some singles bars and restaurants around town. He's also got points in one of the big new discotheques in town. His sticky big fingers are everywhere. The night you and Richie had your run-in, he was probably there collecting Bonnetti's piece of the action. Here, you can copy down the names of his legit places. But you still gotta be careful."

"Why? I'm not afraid."

"I don't mean that way. You're a newspaperman and they know it's not cool to go near you. Fact is, I bet Richie's getting chewed out right now for decking you. The mob does not want publicity. When I say be careful, I mean if you write something about how these legit places are mob-controlled, you better be right, 'cause they got lawyers like you wouldn't believe. You'll be spending the rest of your life in court, which is no fun, believe me. I'm in court enough."

D'Arcy closed his notebook. "I am always careful. Richie Sweet is the one who should have been careful. Thank you most kindly."

"Just remember, you didn't get this stuff from me. The department knows I'm talking to you, otherwise you wouldn't be sittin' here. We just don't like agents' names mentioned, physical descriptions of agents, stuff like that. It could mean trouble for us on the street, understand?"

"You have my word that neither your name nor description will ever appear in my column."

The agent narrowed his eyes. "But you gonna do a number on Richie Sweet?"

D'Arcy touched his sore jaw and nodded.

The agent said, "Remember one thing: Richie's mob. He's a *wise guy* and they've got their pride. He's also what we call 'new Mafia,' young guys, up-and-coming talent and they don't have much self-control. Not like the old 'Moustache Petes.' The new guys fly off the handle quickly. They don't think or look ahead. Richie's like that, though Carmine DiNaldi cools him out a lot. But don't count on Richie always holding back 'cause you're a newspaperman."

D'Arcy slipped into his top coat. "All I ever count on are my fingers. And, of course, my nimble brain. Thank you veddy much for your help. You've been so kind."

During the following ten days, three of D'Arcy's gossip columns contained references to Richie Sweet or the Augie Bonnetti family, and the federal narcotics agent was right. Neither Bonnetti nor Richie Sweet were pleased about being in the newspaper. Tonight, as Johnnie Gelb lay sleeping beside him, D'Arcy suddenly smiled. He'd just decided what to write next in his column about Richie and his publicity-shy employer. Slipping out of bed, D'Arcy took a dressing gown from the bed and walked into the room he used as an office.

It was a little after two in the morning when he began to type. On the desk beside him he had placed a glass of chilled champagne and several wedges of Danish cheese on a saucer. Pausing only to sip champagne and nibble cheese, D'Arcy typed steadily for the next hour.

■ ■ ■ **Six**

"Burt, my friend, here in Washington, power is the name of the game. Actually the game has a *second* name: It's who you know. Hear me well, my young columnist. Now because of this little game, everybody in Washington makes a point of knowing everybody else. Result: one dead town, a dull town and why? Because, buddy boy, there are *no* surprises. Not a fucking one. We know each other and we know exactly, I mean exactly, what's on the other guy's mind. So there are no surprises in D.C. And now that I've told you why your nation's capital is the dullest city in North America, suppose you tell me what brings you here."

"Trying to become rich and famous before the week is out." Burt Anthony took two glasses of champagne from a tray held by a white-jacketed Oriental waiter, and handed one glass to Monica. He looked around, impressed by the variety of people the Saudi Arabian Embassy had managed to gather for their cocktail party.

Monica said, "We're in town promoting Burt's column. Radio, television, and as much print as we can get."

"Hype, hype, more hype," said an almost drunk Max Reid. "Get out the hot air machine, folks. Burt the gossip is running amok in our midst, or is it amidst in our mok." Someone accidentally nudged Reid from behind and he tilted forward. Burt caught his elbow, then watched Reid take two glasses of champagne from the Oriental waiter's tray, drain one in a gulp, place it back on the tray and remove a third.

Reid burped long and loud, then grinned. " 'Scuse. Never trust a man without a single redeeming vice. Churchill said that."

"Did Winston say anything about not stepping on peoples' feet?" Monica turned her face sideways to avoid Max Reid's breath, spearing his chest with a forefinger and gently pushing him away from her.

"Sorry 'bout that, Veronica."

"Monica."

"Monica. Christ, no wonder all my wives divorce me. Always did have trouble with names. Old Burt here, he's got a memory like a Sicilian. Never forgets a thing. When you become rich and famous, old Burt, remember your friends and sources."

Burt wiped the bottom of his champagne glass with a damp napkin and grinned at Max Reid. "Your name's engraved on the wall in the chapel of the cathedral of my heart."

Max Reid burped again. "No shit!"

Both men laughed. Monica closed her eyes and shook her head.

One of the first people in Washington Burt had telephoned was Max Reid, an old friend and a reporter with the Washington bureau of a Chicago newspaper. Max had invited him to this party at the embassy, promising belly dancers, caviar and rumors. It was too good a menu to pass up. Washington had become the gossip capital of the world and Burt was here to collect his share.

He had been in and out of Washington over the years

and had always found it as dull as Max Reid said it was, a town addicted to power and only little bit of news that could increase power. Every breakfast, lunch, dinner, cocktail party, buffet and conversation in a congressional hallway centered around a political purpose or someone's personal ambition. Running the nation and the world made it easy to take yourself seriously. The city lacked warmth; ambitious people were too suspicious and distrustful of each other to be warm.

Max Reid was a short, square-shaped man with a pitted face, a huge, bright red walrus moustache and a bow tie the same color. He was irreverent and drank too much. He had curiosity, moral outrage, and he took pride in his cynicism and in being a loner, qualities that made him an excellent reporter and also caused his three marriages to fail.

Max Reid leaned his head on Monica Hollander's shoulder and leered at her. "Love them tall ladies. Give me a woman I can go *up* on."

Monica, half annoyed, half amused, pushed him away. "Burt, your friend is gross."

Burt gently patted Max's cheek. "Yeah, but did you ever see such a beautiful moustache. Believe me, he's harmless. Talks a good game, that's all."

"Just a silver-tongued devil, I am, I am. As for you, old buddy, how come you don't share your goodies with an old friend?"

"If you mean Monica, forget it."

"Not talking about luscious Monica. Talking about these stories you're breaking in that little gossip column of yours up there in New York. 'National intelligence agency forces call girls to whore for the good of the country. Congressman drunk while officiating at important committee hearing.' Heavy, heavy. You know of course that some of the reporters in this town are taking your stuff and running with it."

Burt raised his eyebrows.

Max Reid snorted. "Not me, scoop. You know better. I never stole from another reporter in my life. Except once

76

or twice maybe. I'm one of your better sources, remember? I'm the guy who telephones you collect, of course, and passes on juicy little tidbits I can't use or prove. No, cute little Max ain't ripping you off, but others are."

"Let 'em. It's flattering. Means I'm doing my job. When *I* write something, it's gossip. You clowns write the same thing and call it journalism."

He felt Max jerk gently on his tie. "You get paid more than we do, so take your lumps, buddy boy. How much longer are you and Veronica staying in town?"

Monica's voice had a hard edge to it, as she deliberately stepped on Max Reid's foot. "It's Monica and we're leaving for the airport directly from here. Burt's doing a TV show in New York tonight. I know you're his friend but I'm not sure if I like you."

A grinning Max Reid withdrew his foot. "Well, Monica Veronica, come to bed and we'll talk it over. Did you know my friend Burt here when he was an ace reporter?"

"No. We met when he came to work for Harold Monmouth."

Max slipped between Monica and Burt, taking each by the elbow. "Let's mingle. Wanna get some caviar and check out the belly dancers. Old Burt here was one of the best investigative reporters ever in this heartbreaking business. We met a few years back when I was in Chicago and I'd come up with a story 'bout a race track murder. Only nobody would print it 'cause the track owner was a pal of the governor and of the people who owned the paper I was working on at the time. So I gave the story to Burt and he dug some more and he got it into *Time* magazine, which isn't bad. Let's move, people. That caviar is disappearing fast."

They pushed through the crowd. Burt recognized several politicians, a few reporters, debutantes, Washington hostesses, cabinet members, White House staffers. Max Reid knew them all. He made a few introductions and Burt mentally filed away names and faces. Some of the people he was introduced to shied away from him as though he had come to arrest them. He sensed their apprehension, their suspicion. *New York gossip columnist comes to town to fuck us over.* That was what they were thinking and that was why the limp, damp handshakes were no more than a quick mutual feel of fingertips, why smiles were forced and eyes quickly swept across Burt's face, then over his shoulder and to other faces in the crowd.

At the buffet, Burt, Monica and Max spread black caviar on salty crackers and listened to the finger cymbals, drums and Eastern string instruments that were accompanying the belly dancers. They could only listen, because a crowd had gathered around both dancers and they couldn't get near them. Max had just finished a funny dirty story about an ambassador's affair with a blond Virginian horsewoman, when Burt looked up to see a woman on the other side of the table staring at him with incredible hatred. She wore an expensive floor-length white dress that appeared to be half toga and half evening gown and the diamonds around her neck and on both wrists had to be real. Her hair was auburn and her face was strong, the face of a woman who could be beautiful merely by believing she was.

She stared calmly, making no attempt to hide what she was doing. When a tall, thin man in a tuxedo came up to her, she leaned back to whisper to him, keeping her eyes on Burt who wondered if the woman was crazy or somebody who just didn't like what he'd written in a column. Then, without a word, the woman took the tall man's arm and walked away.

Monica exhaled. "What was all *that* about?"

Max Reid watched the woman disappear into a crowd, then turned to Burt. "My friend, you seem to be on that lady's shit list. In which case keep your back to the wall and your balls in a safe place."

Burt frowned. "Never saw her before. Who is she?"

"Clare Noel Chandler, one of the top hostesses, in our little town. I'm sure you've seen her name in society and gossip columns."

Burt had. Clare Noel Chandler. Well preserved, filthy

rich, well connected, super hostess. Her parties were *the* parties in this town, where there were usually one hundred and fifty parties a week in a *slow* week. She ran Washington society and a nod or frown from her could make or break your social life.

Burt said, "She's supposed to be worth over a hundred million which is somewhat more than I make in a week. Three ex-husbands, all rich, all of them generous with her in life and in death. And she's got more political clout than half of congress. Why is she down on me? I've never written a line about her."

Max Reid was on tiptoe, trying to peer through the crowd watching the two belly dancers. He gave up and turned to Burt. "The lady is in love, sir."

Burt looked toward the belly dancers. The crowd was applauding and whistling. He turned back to Mac. "So?"

"So she's in love with Robin Ian D'Arcy."

"Ahhhh."

"Ah is right! She's smitten with your rival, only smitten isn't the word. She'd crawl naked on her hands and knees through a blizzard for Robin baby and Clare Noel Chandler doesn't crawl for any man. She's so wired politically in this town, it's not funny. Senators, cabinet members, State department, FBI, CIA, you name it. She knows them all and they know her. She's rich and she's got super clout and she doesn't have to be nice to God if she doesn't feel like it. The lady's a heavy and knows it. Story is she had a brief fling with Vice-President Zachery while he was still a widower and before he married the beautiful Renata . . ." Max's attention strayed.

Burt put an arm around Max's shoulders, cupped his jaw and gently turned Max's face away from a passing voluptuous black woman with a black dress cut down within inches of the crack in her behind. "Max?"

"What? Oh, sorry. You were saying?"

"Clare Noel Chandler and Renata Zachery?"

"They hate each other. Clare thinks Renata took Zachery away from her. Clare thinks *she* should be married to the vice-president, who, as we all know, has a better chance of being President than any of several others I could name. Zach's twenty years older than Renata, which puts him close to Clare Chandler's age."

Burt released Max and reached for his champagne. "Would you say Clare Chandler's giving D'Arcy information for his column?"

"You bet she's helping D'Arcy. Everybody knows that. She feeds him super stuff on what's happening in this town and she's the gal who can do it. We should be so lucky. She got D'Arcy the job in the first place. Bet you didn't know she's a big stockholder in the publishing company that owns D'Arcy's paper."

"No, I didn't."

"Well, she is. She cut through the immigration red tape in record time and D'Arcy got his green card, plus cards for two British assistants. All of them now have permanent resident alien status and they got it quicker than you can say *America the beautiful*. They say Clare Chandler's had four face lifts. A little nip and tuck down in Brazil and she's back here looking like Dorian Gray. But she's still maybe twenty years older than D'Arcy who loves himself a lot more than he loves her or anybody else. That's why she stood there a few minutes ago waiting for you to die."

Monica took Burt's hand. "Don't let it bother you."

He shrugged. "It doesn't. I've had rocks thrown at me before. Let D'Arcy work his side of the street and I'll work mine. Max, is Renata Zachery going to show up?"

"Who knows? I think they're running out of caviar here. If Mrs. Zachery does grace this party with her presence and Clare Chandler's still around, beware the frost. There'll be a chill that could freeze a polar's bear's fuzzy buns. Those two women hate each other. Clare wants no competition as the number-one hostess in town. I mean the President's wife is about as exciting as watching paint dry, which leaves the vice president's wife. Except that Renata thinks this town is something to be avoided. She digs New York and I don't blame her."

Suddenly a belly dancer pushed her way through the crowd and ran past Burt. Her arms were over her bare breasts and behind her, some of the crowd pointed and laughed. Max moved up to see what had happened and listened quietly as a man whispered in his ear.

Joining Burt and Monica again, Max grinned. "Here's something for you, Miss Rona. What White House staffer pulled the brassiere off a belly dancer at today's Saudi Arabian Embassy party, then bit her on the left boob?"

"You're kidding?"

"The number-three man."

Burt got out his notebook. "Everybody else will have it, but I might use it."

"Here's something they won't have." Max looked around, then placed his lips close to Burt's ear. "Said White House staffer's wife filed for divorce this morning and he doesn't even know about it yet."

Burt lifted his eyebrows.

"But," said Max Reid, "he'll soon find out. Might as well name names. Everybody there saw him yank off her bra."

Burt watched the second belly dancer push her way through the crowd; she was angry and didn't want to continue performing. Someone whispered in Max's ear and the square-shaped man nodded his head several times, then whispered back. Max beckoned Burt toward him.

"Renata Zachery's arrived."

"Where?"

"Downstairs. Secret service men are keeping her down there until they check security and finish fooling around with the frequencies on their hand radios. She's with Gil van Lier."

Burt stopped writing and looked up from his notebook. Van Lier was black, an under-secretary of state who was ambitious, a political comer and one of the most talked-about men in Washington. He was good-looking, cocky, brilliant, married and rumored to be a womanizer. At forty-two, van Lier's future was golden. He was good at his job and currently handling behind-the-scenes negotiations to bring a peaceful turnover of power by whites to blacks in the African nation of Chindé.

Downstairs in the embassy lobby, Burt and Monica stood trapped in the crowd surrounding Renata Zachery and Gil van Lier. Some of those in the shouting, shoving mob had been diverted from the cocktail party, but most were reporters with microphones, tape recorders, notebooks and cameras. Harsh, blinding lights told Burt at least two television cameras were on hand and that's when his experience as a reporter said the press wasn't there to photograph Mrs. Zachery and Mr. van Lier at play. Because he wanted to know the reason for tonight's strong media interest in the attractive couple, Burt let the tide of bodies sweep him along.

He squeezed Monica's hand, pulling her with him as the crowd shoved them across the lobby floor, through two large doors and into a large room with high ceilings, black marble columns in each corner and a gigantic portrait of King Kahlid above a black marble mantelpiece. Chilly and smelling of incense, the room was huge enough to have several colorful Persian rugs scattered across its floor. Inside the room the crowd fanned out and tried to again encircle Renata Zachery and Gil van Lier, now ringed by secret service men and embassy guards in black suits, white shirts and thin black ties.

Nose to nose with the bodyguards, Burt winced as a huge, swarthy Saudi stiff-armed him in the chest. Son of a bitch, that hurt. He almost kicked the guard until he remembered that the embassy was considered Arabian soil and the guard, probably carrying a gun under his jacket, was also seventy pounds heavier than he was.

Both the American secret service men and Saudi security guards were tense and edgy, the Americans with the bland, blond looks of professional golfers, the Saudis with dark, oily skins, moustaches and hooked noses. Burt, who'd been in crowd scenes before, hoped the guards would stay calm. The guards had to control both themselves and the crowd, which had now driven them across the room and to the wall under the king's portrait. In back of the mob, someone yelled, "Close the doors! Close the doors!" Burt turned to see Saudi security guards pushing the twin doors shut in the faces of people still trying to force their way in.

"Shouldn't have let them in!" shouted an American secret service agent to no one in particular. "Shouldn't have let these bastards inside! What's with you people, you crazy or something?" He's talking about the press, thought Burt. Why *are* they here? What's the story with the gorgeous Mrs. Zachery and the almost as gorgeous Mr. van Lier? Did somebody catch the two of them checking into a motel? But in that instant, Burt's instincts told him the reason for the excitement was van Lier himself. Had to be.

The doors slammed shut behind Burt and he turned to see three Saudis now with their backs to the door, arms folded across their chest. Ignoring the pounding behind them, the guards stared at the crowd with narrowed eyes. Give those guards some rope, thought Burt, and a few of us won't make it home for dinner. He pulled Monica to him, placing an arm around her waist. A strap on her gown had slipped down her shoulder and she was pale, still angry at having the back of her head grazed by the lens of a portable television camera carried on the shoulder of an aggressive cameraman. Looking at Burt, Monica forced a weak smile.

"Fun, it ain't."

He hugged her from behind, his eyes on Renata Zachery and Gil van Lier. "Glitter and glamour. And you, my love, are a part of it. Van Lier's sitting on something. I want to know what."

"I don't understand."

"Gut feeling tells me these people want to talk with him. Not *her*, but *him*." Burt kissed Monica's ear. "Mrs. Zachery gets a lot of ink, but she doesn't draw hard-news guys, the people who write front page for the *Washington Post* and *New York Times* and that's who we've got around us. These people don't deal in light stuff and the only hard news Mrs. Zachery can make is by shooting or divorcing her husband."

Monica turned and raised an eyebrow. "Maybe van

Lier's getting the divorce. I hear he's not your typical homebody." She looked at the handsome black diplomat. "Mmmmm. Nice. I can see why his wife spends a lot of her evenings alone with cold dinners and Johnny Carson. He's the best-looking thing in basic black since the A-line dress and you can quote me. God, he's not even that black. More like a creamy caramel or yummy peanut brittle."

Burt put his lips to her ear. "Don't get your hormones in an uproar. I hear there's a long line ahead of you."

Gil van Lier *was* cocky and brilliant and, if gossip was to be believed, the married father of four was also a notorious womanizer. Burt watched him reach down and take Mrs. Zachery's hand. The two of them stood with their backs against the wall and van Lier smiled with half his mouth, as though he were Errol Flynn and he had read the script in advance, the script that said Errol Flynn always won.

Van Lier had been a winner all his life, a man with a history of more peaks than valleys and because he was a political comer, a man with an unlimited future in Washington, Burt had read all the clips on him. At the moment van Lier's advice carried more weight with Secretary of State Jerome Rolland than any other diplomat in the entire State Department. Van Lier's thinking was realistic, detailed and not limited to African affairs. He'd also had a hand in shaping administration foreign policy toward Europe, as well as South America and if he had enemies in the State Department, they only served as proof of van Lier's success.

The black diplomat's talent lay in getting people to compromise. He was a charmer, a shrewd master of tactics who could bring both sides to the bargaining table for talks, then send each away with the feeling that it was going away with the edge.

One press clip Burt had read described van Lier as having been born with a silver ham hock in his mouth. It was true. Gil van Lier hadn't crawled out of a ghetto nor had he fought rats and roaches for possession of his crib.

He had been born to a wealthy family, the son of the richest black man in Albany, New York. From birth he had had the best of everything. Fine homes, tutors, private schools and he had wasted no time in showing himself superior to all kids his age, black or white. In addition to brains, he had been an outstanding amateur boxer, which along with his father's money, had protected Gil van Lier from having to endure too many racial indignities. He had won a basketball scholarship to Colgate University in New York, where he had made the starting line-up as a freshman, was voted team co-captain in his junior year and averaged twenty-eight points per game in his senior year.

Van Lier had majored in political science, graduating third in a class of over a hundred and fifty students, while also running track and batting over .400 for the college baseball team. He had turned down the chance to play professional basketball with the Detroit Pistons, nor was he interested in a fifty-thousand-dollar bonus to play baseball for the Philadelphia Phillies. Gil van Lier took the long view; he wasn't going to wind up a burned-out athlete finished at thirty-two, left with nothing but a broken body and broken dreams. Boxing and collegiate sports had given him all the satisfaction he needed from physical competition. What he now wanted was power and so he went to law school.

In law school he made the contacts that got him to Washington where he immediately showed his talent for making correct decisions. He selected the correct political party and social circle while turning down several invitations to join local law firms, an offer made to every incoming congressman or people about to be influential in that town. Law firms that placed a congressman or Washingtonian with clout on the letterhead could better shape legislation than a law firm lacking such foresight. Gil van Lier, however, refused to be anybody's house nigger. He was his own man; he would achieve power while owing as little as possible to as few as possible.

Along with his intelligence went an uncanny sense of

knowing when to make his move. Gil van Lier's timing was always correct. Even van Lier's choice of a wife was correct. She was beautiful, an almost Caucasian-looking black woman who had been first runner-up in the Miss Black America contest and whose family was important in California politics. Elective office held no appeal for van Lier, who found it expensive to pursue while offering only limited power. From the beginning he saw that Washington possessed a power structure that stayed in place no matter who was in Congress or the White House. The power in an elective office was obvious, not perennial. Van Lier was a man who always took the long view.

In a town where everybody's sex life was a subject of gossip, he was no exception. Gil van Lier was good-looking, successful, confident, influential and made even more attractive by the exotic factor of his race. Thus, it was impossible for him to avoid whispers. However, he handled that gossip with his usual charm, noting that if he had had as many love affairs as rumored, he would be in a museum. The comment had gotten laughs but it hadn't stopped the talk about him and the women of Washington.

As for flaws, people found him manipulative and genially arrogant. Without saying a word, van Lier could make anyone feel like a pair of brown shoes in a black shoes' world. Burt felt Napoleon could have had van Lier in mind when he said he preferred a general who was lucky to one who was good. Van Lier was both and knew it.

According to press reports, he was working hard to arrange a peace between the white minority and black majority in the African nation of Chindé. He was the one man both sides trusted; up until now van Lier had managed to walk a tightrope between bitter whites and impatient blacks. He had even been able to talk to moderate blacks, black guerrillas and representatives of different tribes, without offending anyone.

If he could arrange a peaceful transition of power from whites to blacks in Chindé, he would do more than stop bloodshed. He would be keeping Soviet and Cuban influence out of at least one African nation, because the absence of fighting removed any excuse for outside troops. A Chindé without war meant a nation friendly to America. Along with friendship, Chindé offered the riches of uranium, diamonds, gold, coffee, all avenues of great profit.

At the moment black and white *were* killing each other in Chindé but not in a full-scale war, a fact credited to van Lier's proposed peace plan. If he could get both sides to accept it, his triumph would be America's, giving it prestige in black Africa. Van Lier's star would shine brighter, rise higher—a star that could turn into a comet months from now at the next presidential convention. Success in Chindé would make van Lier a power in his party, with a say in everything that happened at the convention.

With King Kahlid looking down, Gil van Lier took on the reporters and Burt was forced to admit he did it well.

"Mr. Under-Secretary, we understand you're leaving tonight for some sort of unofficial meeting in New York tomorrow with black African UN delegates. We hear that guerrilla warfere's broken out all over Chindé and you're being asked to stop black African nations from interfering. Would you comment on this please?" The question came from a stocky woman with red hair, a purple pantsuit and an overbite. She stood on tiptoe in an attempt to look over the shoulders of bodyguards in front of her. Her ballpoint pen was poised over the back of an envelope.

Burt watched Gil van Lier give the woman a smile that made her lick her lips. Van Lier said, "Nice to see you again, Mildred." Then his eyes slid away from her. Immediately a babble of voices exploded with a dozen questions at once.

"We hear guerrilla forces have threatened to assassinate you if you return to Chindé."

"Is it true you're flying to Moscow tomorrow to talk the Russians out of interfering in Chindé?"

"Is it true South Africa has hired mercenaries to kill

you rather than see Chindé become another hostile black-ruled nation on its doorstep?"

"What did you and the President talk about two hours ago?"

"Secretary of State Rolland's health is said to be getting worse. Is it true you now run the State Department?"

Van Lier held up his hands. "Gentlemen and ladies of the press, please, please. All I can say at this time is yes, I am going to New York and will be there tomorrow night for the opening of a new Broadway musical produced by a friend of mine—"

The reporters again began shouting questions.

"Is it true Secretary of State Rolland was hospitalized this afternoon for heart trouble and the President has now asked you to—"

Van Lier: "Secretary of State Rolland goes to the hospital whenever he can. His wife does volunteer work in a children's ward and he's very proud of her. I understand he's helping her to raise funds for a new wing—"

"Mr. Under-Secretary, if war's broken out in Chindé, does this mean the Cubans may have taken a more active part in what's going on there?"

Van Lier: "Charlie, you've heard more than I have. Who told you war's broken out in Chindé?"

"Came over the wires out of South Africa. Hasn't hit the papers yet, but it'll be in tomorrow's early editions and on the eleven o'clock news tonight."

"Came out of South Africa did it? Well, I'm sure you heard what you heard." Van Lier smiled down at the beautiful Persian rug beneath his feet then at Mrs. Zachery who quickly smiled back. She obviously enjoyed watching van Lier in action; she was staring at the black diplomat the way high school cheerleaders stared at the Big Man On Campus.

"South Africa," said van Lier. "Heard it there, did you?" And without saying more, he had said it all. A comment on South Africa, on rumors of war, on sources of reporting.

He continued, "I'm sorry to disappoint all of you

ladies and gentlemen who followed me into this rather grand building. There is no war and I advise you to check further. I know that a diplomat has been defined as someone sent abroad to lie for his country, but allow me to point out that I am still in the United States—"

Laughter.

"—so trust me until I get on a plane and land in another time zone."

More laughter.

Renata Zachery beamed. Burt saw her touch Gil van Lier's arm, then quickly take her hand away as though the arm had been hot. She looked around to see if anyone had noticed and then her eyes locked with Burt's. A few seconds later, she smiled at someone else in the crowd.

Van Lier nodded to another reporter madly waving at him.

Covering her mouth with one hand, Monica whispered to Burt, "He is slick."

"Like eggwhite on a door knob."

"I mean he's answered every question and hasn't said a thing. All these people getting excited over some rumor and chasing after him are just wasting their time."

Burt's lips touched her ear. "That's why he's in politics and the rest of us have to work for a living."

Burt noticed something else. If someone asked the beautiful Mrs. Zachery an awkward question, it was Gil van Lier who answered for her. The wife of the vice-president seemed to defer to van Lier, to wait for him to protect her, which he did with charm and wit. It was the Gil van Lier show, with Renata Zachery apparently content to play a supporting role. While neither had planned on running into the press tonight, van Lier hadn't been tricked into giving away secrets or putting his foot in his mouth. He hadn't said a thing that would get him or the administration in trouble.

Renata Zachery stood close to him, almost as if the two of them were tied at the ankle. She has a vulnerable beauty, Burt thought, a beauty that lures men into protecting her and therefore into doing what she wants. Her dark brown hair, cut short, framed a face with prominent cheekbones the envy of every woman in Washington. Her nose was short and upturned, her mouth wide and full. The eyes were her most striking feature, they were a clear blue and slightly Oriental; a stunning combination that caused people to constantly stare at her. She was a small woman, just under five foot four and very thin, which made her look younger than her thirty-two years. She wore a white fur hat, black cloak and black boots and Burt could easily understand the media attention she continually received. She photographed superbly, day or night, in any kind of light, smiling or frowning. And because she was the beautiful wife of a man almost certain to be his party's nominee for President of the United States, Renata Zachery was made for the media. She could no more avoid being gossiped about than she could avoid breathing.

Most of the questions were aimed at van Lier and were about his meeting tomorrow at the UN, the death threats he might have received and whether or not he was running the State Department in place of the ill Jerome Rolland. Only a few questions were aimed at Mrs. Zachery, but with van Lier at her side she had no problem dealing with them.

Burt wondered how much truth there was in what the press was throwing at van Lier. If the secretary of state was actually ill, who else could he possibly trust to run things except van Lier. As for Chindé, anything could happen there when van Lier wasn't on the scene. He could only do so much and any peace he had arranged so far had to be considered fragile. He still had his work cut out for him if he wanted to avoid a race war.

Burt watched a secret service man whisper into a hand radio, then nod his head. "All clear out front," he said aloud. "Let's go."

The ring of bodyguards suddenly got tough. They began pushing their way through the crowd of reporters and curious partygoers, clearing a path for Mrs. Zachery and van Lier. Somebody stepped on Burt's feet, then pushed

Monica back into him and only the crush of people around them prevented both from falling down. A woman reporter, her tape recorder held high overhead with both hands, hurled herself into the mob screaming, "Mrs. Zachery, you never answered my question. I want to know if the White House has asked you to curb your social life because of the upcoming presidential convention. Your husband is supposed to be running and—"

Then the crowd was past Burt and Monica, who hung back and watched everyone race toward the large, dark wooden doors. Gil van Lier had his arm around Renata Zachery and the secret service men were huddled around the both of them. In seconds the crowd was across the room, through the door and out into the now empty lobby, still shouting questions, still demanding answers. Burt watched the crowd bear right, toward the front door. No party tonight for Gil van Lier and his companion. Instead it was race outside to the limousines. Van Lier was too smart to press his luck by continuing questions and answers upstairs at the cocktail party.

Alone in the huge room, Burt and Monica held hands and looked up at King Kahlid's huge portrait. The king, arms folded across his chest, stared down at them as though disapproving of everything he had just seen. Van Lier had conned the American press but not Arabian royalty.

A voice behind him said, "You must leave now."

They turned to see a dark-suited Saudi guard standing at the huge open doors. Burt and Monica walked toward him immediately. He looked as if he would enforce his order.

Monica said, "Did you get anything to write about?"

Burt reached inside his jacket for his notebook and pen. "I should be able to get a few lines out of what just happened. Never been that close to Renata Zachery before. She is one beautiful lady."

They were in the lobby. Through the opened front door they looked out into the night at reporters running for their cars, preparing to follow van Lier and Mrs. Zachery.

Again an idea attempted to worm its way through Burt's brain and into a clear space where it could be examined more closely and at length. The idea was that perhaps Renata Zachery and Gil van Lier were quite fond of each other. *Quite.* Should he make something of it?

Burt rejected the possibility. Even if he was now shaving every day and dressing better, it didn't mean he had to start acting dumb.

In the limousine on the way to the airport, Monica slept in his arms while Burt remembered he had bought two suits in five weeks since coming to work for Monmouth. Before that, he hadn't bought a suit in five years. He also remembered Thoreau's warning—beware of all enterprises that require new clothes.

But as he had done with his thought about Renata Zachery and Gil van Lier, Burt pushed Thoreau aside until it too faded away.

# ■ ■ ■ Seven

Carmine DiNaldi, consigliere to Augustino Bonnetti, spoke in Italian and with a slight stutter. His chin was on his chest and the words seemed aimed at his linked fingers in his lap. A casual listener might have thought that the *consigliere* was drifting into sleep, that he was an old man warmed by the April sun coming through the bakery window, that perhaps his eyelids were as heavy this morning as they became on those nights when he slept twelve hours.

But DiNaldi, a small, calm, sixty-two-year-old man with sparse gray hair, his weak, watery eyes hidden behind thick, pink-tinted glasses, was not drowsy nor did his mind wander at any time. He was the most intelligent and cunning adviser in any of the five New York Mafia families and he spoke gently because he was a man of respect and power. He also knew that the best way to get a man's attention was never to raise your voice.

The *consigliere* and other made men never used the

word Mafia, except as a joke among themselves. He and others would say *the Brotherhood* or *the thing.* Sometimes he would say *our thing,* Cosa Nostra, or *the business,* but he never used the word Mafia.

"Twenty years ago the p-problem started and it's only gotten worse. That's when the newspapers started writin' about us and that's when the public became more aware that we existed and we-we didn't need that. People read newspapers and they got to thinkin', 'why should this b-be? Why-why should those people in *the thing* be runnin' around doin' as they p-please?' What happens next is people started complain' to politicians, to the police and we had to do somethin'. We was forced to react and that meant we pay out a little money, not to mention a little aggravation."

"We-we buy more lawyers, politicians, judges, court clerks, cops and accountants, 'cause the smart thing was to insulate yourself, to protect yourself with as many people up front as you can. I'm goin' to tell you exactly what happened twenty years ago, 'cause you're still a young man and perhaps you are not clear on ev-every-thing."

Richie Sweet chewed the inside of his mouth and kept his breathing even, showing no nerves or fear. He was uptight, but in front of a man like the *consigliere,* you had to show you belonged in his presence. Stay cool, but listen. Don DiNaldi was telling him something and Richie had better hear and hear well. Blame it on that fucking Englishman. Robin Bird Man, Richie called him. Robin Ian D'Arcy, whose gossip column lay on the desk in front of the *consigliere,* next to a tiny white cup of espresso and a saucer of sliced, dried lemon peel. Richie wanted to ice Robin Bird Man. Put two in the back of his head and dump him somewhere in Queens. But there was no use even mentioning this to the *consigliere;* he would never go for it.

For almost two weeks, the Englishman had been dig-ging at the Bonnetti family in his gossip column and if there was one thing Don Bonnetti and Don DiNaldi didn't like, it was seeing their names in the newspapers. And so the *consigliere* had called Richie this morning to meet him alone in the small, plain office in back of Carmine DiNaldi's Mulberry Street bakery, the bakery that carried Richie on its books as a cannolli and bread-maker.

DiNaldi kept his eyes on the linked fingers in his lap. "T-twenty years ago, the national commission it schedules a meetin'. Important meetin', 'cause all the bosses, under-bosses, advisers from all the families across the c-country are gonna be there. Maybe a hundred people. All men of respect, Richie. Important men."

DiNaldi looked across the table at Richie, whom he loved as a son, whom he had selected as his chauffeur-bodyguard over a dozen other *soldati*. Richie had talent, guts and he was loyal. Mariana, DiNaldi's wife, loved the boy too, for she had no children and at sixty, never would. It was easy to like Richie. He was good-looking, respectful to everyone who outranked him in *the business* and there was a genuine love in him for Mariana, whom he called *mama*. Richie obeyed orders without question and he could be trusted. But he had a temper and the *consigliere* had warned him about it, telling him again and again that it was wiser to be a fox than a bull. And women. Richie craved them, and again the *consigliere* had tried to warn him, to tell him that a man should never allow his passions to rule him, to be the basis for the fire that could burn and destroy him.

"This me-meetin' was about a couple of vital things. That was when we all had to decide if w-we was goin' into narcotics all the way and we also had to deal with one of our p-people who was sellin' m-membership in *the thing* for fifty-thousand dollars each. Doin' it under the table. Like you probably heard, we took care of him."

Richie had heard about how, years ago, the high rank-ing don, who had been secretly selling memberships, was shopping for peaches at a Bronx fruit stand when two hitters put four bullets in his head and disappeared.

Carmine DiNaldi twisted a small piece of lemon peel over his tiny cup of espresso. "Some people thought w-we should have the m-meetin' in Chicago, 'cause we controlled things p-pretty good there. Cops, judges, you know what I mean. But one of the top people in the commission, he s-says we hold it in Appalachia. That's upstate New York."

Richie watched the counselor sip espresso. The commission always had the last word. It had the power of life or death over every man in the thing, whether he was boss or *soldato* and its word was law. The commission was made up of twelve men who represented all twenty-four families across America.

"I was against it," said DiNaldi. "One hundred of our people from around the country and all in one p-place. All you needed was for one thing to g-go wrong and it did. I stayed here in New York and Don Bonnetti he stayed too, on my advice. What happened up there twenty years ago was a state trooper sees a lotta p-people he don't see before, perfect strangers and he gets nosy. Some of our p-people are fancy dressers—silk suits, hundred d-dollar ties, two hundred d-dollar shoes. Trooper sees 'em, he decides to follow one."

DiNaldi smiled, remembering. "The trooper he finds out the house our p-people are at, then he runs out and he sets up a roadblock. He stops more p-people comin' into the house. Next thing you know, more cops, more state troopers. Inside the house, our p-people p-panic. They rush to their cars, they run into the woods and they start throwin' money and guns into the woods. Thousands of dollars, Richie, and it's floatin' around in the woods. 'Course not all the money's stuck on trees or hidin' under bushes. Cops they take more than three hundred grand from our people."

DiNaldi stopped smiling. "Then they begin to look into exactly what kind of business our people are involved in —and what do they find? They learn about our legitimate stuff, the companies we own as fronts. They learn who's got a record and whether or not these people are involved in things like hotels, restaurants, record companies. What happened up there in Appalachin p-proved to the public once and for all that we existed, that we existed on a n-national scale and we didn't need that, Richie. We did not need that. What happened up there m-made it easy to get more money to fight us. Cops, FBI, everybody went runnin' to the t-taxpayer for money to come after *organized crime*."

Both men smiled at the words *organized crime*.

DiNaldi said, "That's wh-when it b-became easy to get a tap put on your phone. Up 'til then, the courts made it difficult for cops to do wire tappin'. B-but after Appalachin, all they had to do was ask. So we had some problems come outta that but the worst p-problem was p-publicity. We got ourselves written about on account of us being up there and the p-press ain't stopped writin' about us yet. What I'm sayin', Richie, is that we ain't the kind of people who have anythin' to gain by gettin' our names in the papers. So I ask you, what am I gonna do about you and Mr. D-D'Arcy?"

Richie shrugged his shoulders. The *consigliere* probably knew what had happened at the gambling club, so the smart thing was to tell the truth and not make it worse. Fucking D'Arcy. He was screwing Johnnie and she had told Richie about it. Johnnie was more than a piece of ass. She was fan-fucking-tastic and Richie ought to know because he had had more women than any dude on two feet. Johnnie was the best, a disease in a man's blood, something that you couldn't cut yourself loose from any more than you could cut out your insides.

Richie said, "I dumped the Englishman over at Mario's and since then he's had a hard-on for me."

"I think he's savin' his hard-ons for that little t-tramp."

Richie looked down at the floor.

The *consigliere* pulled D'Arcy's column toward him. "This m-mornin', Mr. D-D'Arcy, he writes that this comin' weekend there is goin' to be an important d-dinner, out in Queens for Judge Shallcross, who is retirin' after fourteen years with the State Supreme Court. S-says here that Judge Shallcross served the b-bench with a m-monumental lack of d-distinction and is endin' his career on a similar n-note. Says here the dinner is bein' catered by Golden Seas Caterin' of Manhattan, which is owned by Stanson Realty, also of Manhattan."

Richie shifted in his chair, eyes still down on the floor. He ground his teeth until his jaw ached and imagined D'Arcy hanging naked on a meathook dripping wet and Richie jamming the cattle prod . . .

Carmine DiNaldi sighed, leaned back in his chair and linked his fingers in his lap. Better to deal with the problem while it was small rather than wait until it grew larger and got out of control. Mr. D'Arcy probably got his information from the attorney general's office. But the glare of publicity was going to make trouble. Only a little bit of trouble and not for long, but it was the *consigliere*'s responsibility to avoid all trouble wherever possible. A conflict of any sort was a last resort, for conflict reduced your options.

"Richie," said the *consigliere,* "Mr. D-D'Arcy, he don't come out and say we are tied in with Judge Shallcross or any of the people who were invited to the d-dinner. Of course, some of these p-people are our friends but that's another story. What Mr. D-D'Arcy does is link our family to Stanson Realty and then he ties a string from Stanson Realty to Golden Seas Caterin'. If you read this here column you'll see that he also mentions names of some people invited to this dinner. Now when they read this here column, believe m-me when I tell you they ain't gonna go near this dinner. And it won't stop there. Golden Seas will p-probably lose business and maybe some more newspaper people they come pokin' around. Cops you can forget about. Nothin' they can do 'cause Golden Seas is legitimate. It's run like a b-business oughta be run. No problem there."

Carmine DiNaldi looked at his wristwatch. "We are always under surveillance, b-bein' watched, and we gotta be careful. Now this mornin' I'm gonna have to take the time to work on this little matter. This phone's gonna ring and nobody's gonna have much to say. I'm gonna listen, then you and me we go outside and we call from a public phone which we know ain't tapped and then we talk to these very n-nervous friends of ours. They are gonna say 'what's happenin' with the dinner' and 'maybe I shouldn't show up.' People scare easy, Richie. The last thing th-they want is for the newspapers to find out they know us."

Richie looked up. "Or that they take our money, right?"

"Yes, they take our money, Richie. But for that, m-mostly what we get is they leave us a-alone. Oh, once in a while, we get a favor. But what helps us m-most is when they leave us alone, when they let us do what we w-want. Nobody goes to the mattresses with the family b-but the family. Remember that. Comes times to fight, to bleed, to die, we do that alone. You got no judges, cops, p-politicians to help you then. I think this b-business with Mr. D-D'Arcy is gettin' outta hand. Lotta noise over a small thing. I'm talkin' 'bout this Johnnie. She's no good. She's not the girl for a nice boy like you."

Richie wiped his palms on his thighs. The *consigliere* was like his father. He had given Richie the oath, had been his sponsor, had brought him into *the Brotherhood* and that meant that Richie had clout, a little juice when he needed it. Richie paid attention when Di Naldi spoke.

"See Richie, she's from a f-family that only sees m-money as a way of doin' what's obvious. They d-don't look ahead, those people. She's a cheap girl and this D-D'Arcy, he's too involved over her. He's more her kind. Them two, what's b-between them is like what is between two animals. I d-don't expect a young man like you to be like m-me. I been m-married to Mariana for thirty-four years and I ain't never even looked at another woman. M-maybe it's part of my discipline, maybe it's because I don't trust anybody, I dunno. M-Mariana, she's a good woman and that's what a real nice boy like you needs. Somebody like Mariana; but where you find a woman like that today? You want p-pretty girls with no bras-sieres—"

The telephone rang. Richie blinked.

Carmine DiNaldi picked it up, listened for several seconds, then said, "I call you back. Ten minutes." He hung up and sighed. "It's started. That was a court clerk. He just read Mr. D-D'Arcy's little gossip column. What was I sayin'? Oh, yeah. D'Arcy, he's more for Johnnie than you. He d-don't care what he says about p-people. The vice-p-president's wife, the wife of a dead President, D'Arcy he just don't care. This Johnnie, she d-don't care either. So let them be with each other. And Richie—"

*"Si, mi padre."*

"D-don't you or anybody else go near D-D'Arcy. We can't take on the p-press. We are always gonna lose. 'Specially today after all that Watergate stuff started 'em snooping again, these reporters stickin' their nose everywhere it don't b-belong. That's why D-D'Arcy is so popular. Everybody likes to read d-dirty things about everybody else. I think the dinner will be canceled and Golden Seas, it gets hurt t-too. I think we will lose some b-business. I know you gotta temper and you young people today, you always want to strike back. But this time, you do nothin'. Leave that Johnnie alone. Then D-D'Arcy, he'll leave us alone."

An angry Richie nodded slowly in agreement. But he thought of Johnnie's warm and naked flesh pressed against his, her open, hot, wet mouth sliding down his body and the softness of her long white-yellow hair brushing across his bare thighs and he thought of her doing all of this to D'Arcy.

Richie hated the Englishman and Richie, a Sicilian, never forgot a hatred.

"Leave her alone," said the *consigliere*.

Richie jerked his head up. It was as though the tiny, gray man with the weak, watery eyes could read his mind.

*"Si, mi padre."*

But Richie's demanding sensuality could not forget that Johnnie was the first woman whose sensuality matched his, nor could Richie forget that D'Arcy had forced him, a *made man*, to back down.

The telephone rang again and again, as the *consigliere* said it would.

## New York City

Gypsy was frightened. He was within inches of getting caught and if that happened Simon would immediately cut off any connection with him, killing all of Gypsy's dreams about big money. Not only had he been charging Simon ridiculously high fees, but Gypsy had come to depend on the excitement and mystery in the wiretapping he was doing for him. It was Gypsy's fantasy that he was involved in something that could reach to the White House. So, if it turned out successfully for Simon and his people, Gypsy would be remembered as the man partially responsible. For the first time in his life Gypsy saw himself having real power.

At first Gypsy pretended he hadn't heard his name being called, but when the plainclothes cop laughed and yelled out, "I'm talking to you, you gimpy old bastard!" it was time to stop pretending and start running. With a white-knuckled grip on the new Vuitton suitcase that he had purchased especially for tonight's bug job, Gypsy began walking as fast as his limp allowed. When his name was called out again, he broke into an awkward trot.

The crowd saved him, for he was surrounded by men, women and children who filled the sidewalk and spilled out into the street where traffic had stalled and backed up for blocks in all directions. The crowd was between him and the police and above the babble of talk around him he heard his name being called again. Tonight, a plainclothes cop named Ralph Fingers, a detective sergeant who worked on several court-ordered wiretaps with Gypsy in the past, had spotted him, yelling out, "Let's see what you're carrying in that suitcase!"

Fingers and a large part of New York's police force were in front of the Hotel Alexandria on Park Avenue, where Gypsy was to have done another bug job for Simon. But there wasn't a chance of Gypsy getting to the hotel's front door, let alone making it twenty-eight stories to the roof where he had planned to dangle a microphone 150 feet down the side of the building to record the conversation in a thousand-dollar-a-day penthouse suite. This morning in a quick meeting at Gypsy's apartment on Bleecker Street in the Village, Simon had given him only the barest of details as usual, mentioning the penthouse and adding that security prevented anyone from getting inside to bug the room and phones. With no more than a few hours' notice and no way to get inside the penthouse, could Gypsy bug the room? He could. It would cost extra but he could do it.

But Simon hadn't told him about the men in topcoats and brush haircuts who carried automatic rifles and hand radios, who blocked every entrance to the hotel and were making it hard for even registered guests to get inside. Simon hadn't told him about the dozens of New York cops who were helping the men with rifles, and who had the hotel surrounded from Lexington Avenue to Park Avenue and were inside as well as on the roof and even if Gypsy had managed to make his way through this small army and get to the roof, he could easily have been shot to death. Simon hadn't told him that this security was for the President and vice-president of the United States, who with their wives, were staying tonight at the Alexandria on Park Avenue and 56th Street before delivering separate speeches tomorrow afternoon at the United Nations.

From the beginning, tonight's job had gone badly. Traffic had been so backed up that Gypsy was forced to leave his car in a parking lot on Madison Avenue and walk to the hotel. Getting near the hotel on foot hadn't been easy either; hordes of spectators had gathered for a peek at the President, vice-president and their wives, and though police tried to keep order, groups of chanting demonstrators added tension and numbers to the scene, making the police edgy. To carry a gun around one of these cops, as Gypsy was doing, was a risk he would have thought unbelievably stupid in someone else. Journalists and television crews waved credentials in the air in a vain attempt to force their way past police and secret service men. In the hotel's lobby, people with luggage fought to get outside to the sidewalk; on the sidewalk, people with luggage and reservations fought to get in. Inside or out, the Hotel Alexandria was bedlam and earsplitting noise. It was Gypsy's bad luck to be spotted by a cop he had worked with, a cop with a sadistic sense of humor.

Gypsy limped as fast as he could toward Lexington Avenue, holding tightly to his new suitcase, moving against the flow of the crowd pushing and shoving its way toward Park Avenue, toward the entrance of the Alexandria. They wanted to see the President, a madness that Gypsy could not understand, for he saw no profit in it, no immediate pleasure, no tangible gain. At the corner, he turned right and continued hurrying down Lexington.

On Lexington Avenue, Gypsy didn't slow down until he covered three blocks, until there was a distance and a lot of people between him and Detective Sergeant Ralph Fingers. At 53rd Street he stopped to breathe deeply and look over his shoulder and when he saw just a mass of bodies, he began to relax. He crossed the corner, weaving his way between cars, holding the suitcase high, asking himself again and again why Simon hadn't known about any of this.

The Lexington YWCA was in the middle of the block and in front of its entrance, he stopped to catch his breath again, wiping sweat fron his forehead with the palm of his hand, rather than dirty the new orange silk handkerchief he had purchased especially for tonight. With a clean suit, new handkerchief and a new suitcase, he had expected no trouble in walking into the Alexandria. How was he to know he wouldn't get as far as the elevator.

In the Y lobby, a toothy young black woman sitting behind a huge semicircle of a reception desk directed him to the class he was looking for.

In the elevator, Gypsy's fear began to ease, and anger took its place. He thought of how he was going to tear into Simon tomorrow morning, Simon who was usually so precise, so organized and on top of things. Gypsy was going to insist on less secrecy, on more concrete details, on specifics. Gypsy, a careful man, didn't like taking jobs without time to plan.

Whoever had been in the penthouse had had to move to accommodate the President, which meant Gypsy's target was either in another room or in another hotel. If Simon had sent Gypsy out to bug the President and vice-president of the United States with all of those guns keeping them company, Simon was a schmuck. To do a job on them would involve time and the most careful preparation imaginable. Right now it didn't matter because Gypsy wasn't going near the Hotel Alexandria. He was going home and relax and tomorrow he was going to come down on Simon for almost getting him into a deep hole.

Gypsy was thirsty. All the running and pushing his way through crowds had given him a thirst. Looking up and down the hall, he finally spotted a Coke machine and started toward it. He began slipping dimes into the machine. He drank three Cokes and wished he had some brown sugar to make them sweeter.

As he was about to throw away the empty cups, he noticed a newspaper left on a wooden folding chair beside the Coke machine. The headline mentioned the surprise visit to New York by the President and vice-president and their wives. Gypsy frowned as he read, suddenly positive that Simon hadn't known about the visit after all. As Gypsy continued to read, a thought wormed its way into his brain and he reached inside his jacket for a ballpoint pen. When he came to a name, he underlined it and continued to read. Again he underlined something, this time an entire small paragraph.

He was absorbed in what he was doing and didn't see the beautiful Chinese dance teacher until she tugged on his newspaper and smiled at him. "Such a surprise to see you," she said. "A most pleasant surprise. How long are you staying?"

104

He reached for her hand. "Not long. Got work to do . . . Well?"

She smiled, a hand going to her face to smooth the straight black hair over a hideous scar on her right cheek. "I listened and you were right. You always are."

He grinned and squeezed her hand. Next to him, she had the best ear for sound of anyone he had ever met and she had just admitted that, after listening to a copy of the one-word telephone conversation Gypsy had taped for Simon a few days ago, she agreed with him about the sex of the caller. The caller who had said "Now" and hung up had been female. The Chinese woman's name was Agnes and she was the only human being in the world Gypsy cared about. If Agnes agreed with him about anything on his tapes, it meant he was right.

Leaning forward she gently kissed him on the cheek. "I must return to my class," she said. "Will I see you later?"

His eyes were on the newspaper. "Don't know. I'll call you."

"You seem excited," she said. "Pleased." She smelled of jasmine and warm tea and the jade rings she wore all had string wrapped around the band to keep them from slipping from her tiny fingers.

Gypsy smiled at the newspaper. "Pleased. Yeah, I guess I am."

"Call me." She turned and walked away from him.

Ignoring Agnes, he copied down the underlined name which was that of the American ambassador to the UN, the man who the newspaper said lived in the Hotel Alexandria penthouse. Next Gypsy tore the small paragraph he had been reading from the newspaper, folded it and placed it inside his suit jacket. The paragraph mentioned three men who had been scheduled to meet tonight with the UN ambassador, a meeting that had taken on a new dimension when at the last moment, the President of the United States had decided to attend. Now Gypsy had the names of four men whose conversation he had been hired to bug tonight. The President and the vice-president were not on his list; their appearance had been a surprise even to Simon.

The UN ambassador and three government officials. Four men and one mysterious woman who at the moment didn't have a name. More pieces of the puzzle falling into place.

# ■ ■ ■ Eight

"I can sum up my marriage in a few words," said Burt Anthony. "My wife and I began by loving each other; we ended up by judging each other. Probably the story of most couples, I guess."

"Whose idea was it to get a divorce?"

"Hers."

"Why?" asked Monica Hollander.

"She'd met somebody."

"Who?"

"Associate professor at our college. Arlyn and I married in '68, left school but we still had friends on campus, people we'd met in 'the movement,' as it was called in those days. Arlyn had more contact with them than I did."

"While you ran around being super reporter."

Burt nodded at Monica Hollander who sat across from him in the bathtub. "Something like that. Soon as she told me about the professor, she then had to tell me what was wrong with me. Arlyn wanted to be reasonable, you see."

107

Monica smiled, adjusting her long legs in the tub so that they fitted comfortably on either side of Burt's waist. "Arlyn sounds like a lady who was always looking ahead."

"You are right. Arlyn was caught up in the rhetoric of the sixties. She was excited by the idea of changes on campus, changes in society for blacks, women, gays—"

"Gnomes, poodles, Bulgarians, old ladies without a rubber tip on the end of their canes."

Burt backhanded water at her. "Do not make jokes while gossip columnists are talking about their failed marriages."

"Sorry. You were saying?"

"I was agreeing with you that Arlyn always looked ahead. She wouldn't leave me without first having somewhere else to go. Even without her telling me I knew there was another guy. One day I came home after being away a week or so on a story and I looked at her and I just knew. There's always a certain drama going down in these situations. Neither one speaks to the other. No eye contact. And Arlyn, my nervous little Arlyn was acting like she'd planted dynamite somewhere in the house and couldn't wait to haul ass through the front door. I knew. But Jesus, it hurt like hell when she told me."

"What did you do then?"

"Cried. Screamed at her. Threw a few things. Broke a few things. Cried some more."

Monica sipped white wine. "You said she told you what was wrong with you."

Burt leaned out of the tub and reached down to the floor for the plate containing the remains of a Big Mac. "Did she ever. Said I was thoughtless, which wasn't true. I was always thinking. But not about her, obviously. She also said I was *obsessed* with my reporting and that it had turned me into an occasional husband."

"Which of course was not what she wanted."

"Amen. She also didn't like my two sisters or my mother and father, for that matter. She considered my family *politically incorrect*." Burt picked a slice of pickle from his Big Mac and held it between his fingers. "Politically incorrect. Arlyn enjoyed laying that on people."

"What was politically incorrect about your family, may I ask?"

"Let's see. My two sisters were in their early teens, so they were Beatles freaks and couldn't care less about politics, social changes or old ladies minus rubber tips. Arlyn tried to convert them to one cause or another but my sisters laughed at her. My father had fought in World War II, so he was in favor of fighting in Vietnam. Got to stop the commie pinko bastards before they get to Glendale, that sort of thing. My mother? Well, she kept quiet and smiled a lot and maybe she knew more than all of us. Want my pickle?"

Monica grinned and winked. "I had your pickle, remember?"

"Oh, that was *you* back there in the bedroom."

She splashed water on him with both hands.

"Hey!" Burt held his hands high. "You're getting my Big Mac all soggy!'

"For a minute there," said Monica, "I was on your side. Now I don't know."

"Just for that, you can't have my pickle."

"Sure about that?"

"Okay, you talked me into it. Back into the bedroom."

"Burt, love, you have work to do. It's almost midnight and you're supposed to be at one disco opening, two disco parties and you still haven't shown up at that new restaurant across from Lincoln Center. You promised you would. The screening invitations are just piling up on your desk. What's the matter, you have something against seeing new movies in the comfort of lush screening rooms?"

"You have something against my pickle?"

"I have never seen a man who freezes Big Macs by the dozen, then pops them into a microwave oven—"

"Exactly three minutes each. You should have seen Monmouth's face when I told him I wanted a microwave. At first he thought I meant *shortwave* and that I was going to monitor foreign broadcasts so that I could pick up items

**109**

for my column. What's Un-American about freezing Big Macs so that you can have one whenever the urge hits you and speaking of urges—"

He reached for her. Splashing water on him, Monica shrieked and leaped from the tub.

Later, she sat dressed on the bed watching Burt as he stood in front of the mirror and carefully combed his hair. In another room, the telephone rang almost without stopping as tipsters and informants attempted to reach Burt with gossip or personal pleas for a mention in the column. The hate calls were coming in, too, from screwballs who thought Burt was a degenerate for daring to print certain items. The answering service would take all messages and later this morning Burt could decide which were usable and which were to be ignored.

Monica lit her third cigarette. She was becoming attached to Burt, which wasn't part of the job and a danger, because there was something she hadn't told him. *Couldn't tell him.* Harold Monmouth had ordered her to do more than promote Burt's column and help him find his way around New York nightlife. He had ordered her to report daily on how Burt prepared the column, how he gathered his material. Monmouth wanted to know what mistakes, if any, were being committed and hidden.

It had been easy to say *I'll do it.* She hadn't known Burt then. She hadn't listened to him talk about the stories he had written. She hadn't yet laughed with him at the trouble he had gotten himself into and she hadn't yet come to respect him as a man who cared about something besides himself. Now it was too late to tell Monmouth that sleeping with somebody, then revealing his secrets, was a shitty thing to do. Such a change of heart could also be expensive; it could cost Monica her job.

Tonight for the first time, she had read the two stories that had been laminated, framed and hung on the wall over Burt's desk. They were the two stories on Robert Kennedy written in 1968 within hours of Bobby's assassination that had started Burt on his way to becoming a prominent reporter. Monica could see why people had read them and wept. Arlyn the ex-wife had. That's how she and Burt had met. Arlyn had read the stories, cried for almost two days, then fallen in love with the man who had written them.

Had Monica been a tense, confused kid on a sixties' college campus, she too would have read those stories and cried. And she would have wanted to meet the angry, frightened, idealistic young man who had written them and who wanted to write more stories about an America gone absurdly murderous. But ten years ago, Monica was still yearning to be an actress, to be Katharine Hepburn and make Cary Grant laugh. In less than two years of trying in New York, she had learned that the professional theater was ruthless, fag-dominated and impatient with anything less than glossy professionalism. Monica didn't have the talent or persistence to deal with the constant rejection that went with life in the theater.

It took less time to learn she also wasn't a reporter. Public relations turned out to be the path of least resistance and she found that many of the people in it had come to the field the same way she had. They were in it because they couldn't do anything else, a qualification which didn't prevent many in the business from making a good living. Public relations offered an attractive lifestyle of parties, expensive lunches and dinner paid for by clients and a cornucopia of invitations to openings, screenings, and affairs with a better class of men than one could meet working at Macy's. Monica had had her share of this particular Manhattan smorgasbord, coming to depend on it for whatever meaning existed in her life.

Burt Anthony had started out to be a fun assignment for her, a breathing space between her last romantic disappointment and whatever lay further down life's great highway. Burt wasn't married, he wasn't gay, he didn't tie her to the bed and beat her while wearing her underwear and wedgies. If she failed to have an orgasm, he took it calmly and blamed neither himself nor her. When she

**111**

did, he kissed her eyes, held her to him and said nothing, allowing her to decide what was to be said and done in that private moment.

Burt was becoming fond of her, too. Monica stubbed out her cigarette and reached for another. What the hell was she going to do about him? About herself, for that matter. She was betraying him and the more she thought about it, the worse she felt.

"Thank you," said Burt.

Monica blinked, then looked at his reflection in the mirror. "Thank me? For what?"

He turned to face her. "For making everything easier. New York can be a hard city and it would have been tough for me to get the column going if you hadn't helped."

"Burt, I didn't do a thing, believe me." Except tell Monmouth every goddam thing you told me.

"You've been where I could see you and touch you and taste you and that's a big thing. Let's face it: a lot of people want to get next to me because I have the column. I'm on every first night list, every screening list. I get free records, books, restaurant meals if I want them. No discotheque or nightclub in town gives me a check no matter how many people I come in with. Press agents bombard me with invitations, along with their rotten copy and a week doesn't go by that some tacky girl singer or aging starlet won't drop a hint that if I mention her name in the column and help make her a star, she'll run over here and drop her pants."

Burt gently took Monica's face between his hands. "Monica, a gossip columnist lives like a goddam emperor. But you know something? All this is coming my way for one reason and one reason only. Because I have that column and because people feel I can do them some good. The truth is, I can't trust a soul. Not one ever-lovin' soul. I'm not loved and adored because I'm a prince of a fella. They're coming through the windows and the cracks in the floor because they think I can help them get it by printing their stupid, fucking names. If offerings are being laid out at my feet and they are, it's only because of the column. I'm not dumb enough to think I'm loved for my sweetness of soul. And I just want to tell you that it's nice having you around. It's nice having one person who puts her arms around me because she's, well maybe a little horny and nothing more. With you a pat on the back doesn't mean you're feeling around for the right spot to shove in the knife. It's nice to have somebody I can talk to—hey, you're crying."

He leaned over and kissed her tears, tasting the salt, then held her head against his chest. "Okay, okay. I'll back off. It's the Italian in me." He looked down at Monica's mascara-streaked face. "Just wanted you to know you are appreciated. And that's as heavy as I'm going to get . . . Well, time to go out and do some night crawling. I'm sorry if I upset you."

She wiped away the tears with her fingertips.

"Don't worry about it. God, the mascara. I bet I look like a zebra." Monica wanted to hide. She wanted to tell Burt to save his words for somebody else. She wanted to tell Monmouth to get another fink to spy on Burt.

All she said was, "You don't know anything about me."

"Know your boobs float in the bathtub."

"About your bathtub, it's too small."

"Keeps out the riffraff."

She stood up, digging in her purse for a handkerchief. "I—I just can't think of anything clever right now. If something occurs to me at five this morning, which it probably will, I'll give you a call."

He put an arm around her. "You're my number-one adviser on life in the big city."

She turned her back to him and squeezed tears from her eyes. Two things ran through her mind, neither of which she could tell Burt. The first was the word *shitty*. The second was that she didn't want to lose her job and maybe the only difference between either thought was one of degree, not of kind. Adviser. Who the hell was she to give advice on anything.

■ ■ ■ Nine

The drink in Burt Anthony's hand would have cost him five dollars had he not been a gossip columnist and the recipient of a free membership in Angelique Bernhard's *50/West*, the most popular discotheque in Manhattan. Burt wasn't there to watch Angelique's waiters, all beautiful young men in multicolored leotards. Nor had he come to stare at the six bartenders who were blond weightlifters and wore cowboy boots, sequin-studded jock straps and makeup complete with green eye shadow and pink blush on their cheeks.

Leaving Monica alone in his apartment, with a dinner they'd ordered from the local Chinese restaurant, Burt had hurried out to chase down a tip that Renata Zachery was in Manhattan dancing the night away at *50/West* with several men, one of whom was Gil van Lier. In the week since he'd returned from Washington, Burt had remained under the gun from Monmouth. In six weeks, Burt had written thirty columns, most of which he thought were good and which Monmouth thought were merely adequate. Burt was finding it harder and harder to sleep nights. It was his opinion versus the little Englishman's and the little Englishman had the last word because he signed the cheeks.

Burt finished his second Scotch and water and looked around for the bartender. The bar was mobbed and Burt thought to hell with having another drink and turned back to watch the dance floor.

He couldn't think with all the noise around him, with music booming from giant speakers hanging high on every wall and screeching whistles in the mouths of dancers whose eyes seemed to be pinwheeling in their heads. Find Renata Zachery. Find her and get an item, any item. Check with Angelique's photographer and see if he'd taken pictures of Renata Zachery and any of the men. One with her and Gil van Lier would be best.

Angelique Bernhard. Burt wanted to kick her skinny ass. She was thin and middle-aged, a blond snob of a Frenchwoman who'd been in New York only two months and was growing rich by making her West 50th Street discotheque inaccessible. Tonight she'd refused to tell Burt if Renata Zachery was or had been in the club, claiming that it was not polite to discuss her customers. Of course, he was free to go inside and look around for himself, but he had to understand that Angelique was not about to discuss the private life of a woman of such eminence as zee wife of zee vice-president of zee United States. The thin Frenchwoman had smiled, knowing that Burt had no choice but to accept her explanation and no choice but to write about *50/West* because every night it drew more celebrities and big names than any club in town.

Even with membership cards costing $900 a year, there was a waiting list of over seven thousand people anxious to get them. A glass of orange juice at *50/West* cost five dollars and dinner for two averaged $120. Angelique was also getting away with charging four dollars for a glass of water. She or her lover, a muscular, sometime German soccer player, stood guard at the door, backed by three

**115**

beefy bouncers and together they were the final word on admittance. Burt couldn't understand why people stood in the street at three in the morning and cried because Angelique wouldn't let them inside, but cry they did. Was it human nature that made them do it or was it something that happened if you stayed in New York long enough. Would he wind up crying if Harold Monmouth fired him?

Three of Angelique's bartenders denied ever having seen Renata Zachery. A Marilyn Monroe lookalike, who couldn't have been over seventeen and who was barefoot and bra-less in a green toga, told Burt *yes*, she'd seen Renata Zachery in the ladies' room. Bullshit, said her date, a paunchy man in a shiny toupee and business suit and who was three times her age. He smiled gently as he whispered to Burt that the girl was stoned on pills she'd just bought from a bartender and couldn't remember her own name. A pony-tailed waiter on roller skates said *yes* Renata Zachery had been in tonight, then suddenly corrected himself and said *no* before skating away, a tray of empty glasses delicately balanced on a slim hand held high over his head.

Two more people also said she'd been there tonight and maybe was still somewhere in the mob and a black man in a white fur hat, white fur cape, red long johns and green platform shoes that glowed in the dark, overheard Burt questioning someone else and volunteered that he didn't give a shit who was here because, as he shouted, inexplicably *everything was everything*. That's easy for you to say, mumbled Burt before easing away from him. Where the hell was Renata Zachery and her party of borrowed men?

Finding anybody in a crowd that size was impossible, especially when the staff had orders to keep quiet about who was on the premises. In addition to three rooms for private parties, there was a huge balcony ringing the dance floor that allowed patrons to sit at tables and drink and get high while staring down at the writhing mass of bodies below. Burt found the lighting eye damaging; it ranged from too dark to even darker, which didn't help when you were searching for someone.

Around him were famed actors and actresses, superstar sports heroes and a four-million-dollar-a-year rock star. He spotted an Italian film director and two American authors who'd punched one another out on television but who now carried on a serious, thoughtful conversation in the midst of the noise around them. The governor of New Jersey and a retinue of dark-suited men pushed their way past Burt but goddam it, where the hell was Renata Zachery?

The dance floor was a collection of freaky looks, the ultra-sensual and the merely bizarre, an atmosphere encouraged by Angelique who preferred her patrons to *dress*, which meant that the more outlandish you looked when you presented yourself at the front door, the better your chances of getting past Angelique. The rule didn't apply to the famous or to the powerful, of course, but it was strictly enforced in regard to everyone else. Burt, growing more annoyed at having been pulled away from a quiet dinner with Monica to pursue a phony tip, was now upstairs in the balcony where it was somewhat quieter.

He checked all of the tables. No Renata Zachery. No Gil van Lier. Tomorrow he was going to take care of the press agent who had tipped him. That clown was dead, no more copy from him. No more pleas over the telephone about how badly he needed a mention to keep his client happy.

Burt was staring down at what the press had termed *50/West*'s "coat of arms"—two large crossed coke spoons made of gray cardboard surrounded by paper replicas of known amphetamines and barbituates—when he heard someone say, "Dear me, he does appear rather lost and undone, a stranger in a strange land."

Burt turned to face the voice, which came from somewhere near his right elbow. Robin Ian D'Arcy sat grinning at him. A young and stunningly beautiful blond girl with

**117**

long hair sat at the tiny table with him. D'Arcy lifted a glass in greeting. "Welcome pilgrim and tarry awhile. Miss Johnnie Gelb, may I present my esteemed competitor Burt Anthony. Burt Anthony, Johnnie Gelb."

Jesus. The night was complete. Now all Burt needed to do was jump off the balcony and break a leg. But then D'Arcy would still have the last word because he would probably use the item in his column. Burt had appeared on a radio show the week before with D'Arcy and the Englishman had done his best to make him look foolish. Burt had barely managed to hold his own, an achievement that hadn't impressed Monmouth who wanted winners.

Ignoring D'Arcy's invitation to sit, Burt leaned against the balcony, arms folded across his chest, growing angrier by the second. D'Arcy, sitting so calmly and obviously enjoying himself, symbolized everything that had gone wrong since Burt had arrived in New York. Burt wanted to zap somebody, to strike out and who was a more deserving target than Mr. D.

Offering a cigarette to Burt, who refused, D'Arcy said, "You and I both seem out of place in this madhouse, if I may say so. Then again, our trade requires that we both mingle. Sure you won't have a chair? It's the one thing in this bloody place you can get free. That and a blasted headache."

Instead of sitting, Burt said, "How come you're not out buying photographs from our nursing homes instead of sitting around watching spaced-out freaks work up a sweat?"

D'Arcy wagged a finger at him. "Now, now. Musn't be nasty. Didn't you get all of this out of your system last week?" He paused, bringing a thin, black cigarette to his small mouth before adding, "Or try to."

Burt turned toward him. "Yeah, last week we talked about Helen Carleton and those photographs somebody took of her in that nursing home and how they made her look pathetic and how you printed them. And this week you're still dumping on her in your column."

118

D'Arcy reached for the remains of a gin and tonic. "My, aren't we touchy tonight."

"A lot of people in this country love Helen Carleton."

"The woman's a drunkard, dear boy."

"She's also the widow of a former President of the United States."

"Which does not make her a candidate for the first vacancy in the Holy Trinity. Cahn't I order you a drink or something?"

D'Arcy placed a hand on Johnnie's thigh. Young Anthony was breathing fire tonight, oozing righteous indignation from every pore. The way he was carrying on, you'd think someone had eaten his favority puppy.

"Shove the drink. Mind telling me why you keep runing garbage on Helen Carleton? The woman's sick, half out of her head from booze and pills. Did you have to print those photographs showing her strapped to a bed and looking like a truck hit her?"

"Someone wanted to sell those particular photographs and I wanted to buy." D'Arcy shrugged. "Oh, do renounce this evangelic train of thought and come sit down. Johnnie and I have been observing a perfectly abominable couple who've been amusing themselves on the dance floor by . . ."

"You've got your eyes closed to everything, which means you don't hear a damn word anybody says." Burt wanted to punch the smirk from D'Arcy's face, drive it down his throat, to get the better of him one time, *one time*.

"Hmmmm," said D'Arcy, frowning and tapping his pointed chin with a long forefinger. "Methinks Mr. Anthony has a problem. You are amongst the prancing yahoos for a reason and could that reason have anything to do with a certain rather prominent lady? Could it be that you have been searching high and low for this certain lady and have failed to find her and thus feel frustrated, deprived, dare I say it, perhaps even *depraved?*"

D'Arcy and Johnnie laughed and Burt closed his eyes,

**119**

shook his head and wondered it if might not be a good idea to throw D'Arcy off the balcony. If anybody knew whether or not Renata Zachery was here, it was D'Arcy and he was the one person Burt couldn't ask.

"Is there anything I can help you with?" asked D'Arcy, looking down at the backs of his hands as though inspecting his fingernails for impurities. Young Anthony was certainly laboring under a heavy cross these days. Harold Monmouth was not a patient man. When displeased with something or someone, he quickly sent the offensive item into oblivion, then moved on to other matters without a backward glance.

Burt inhaled the harsh sweetness of marijuana floating out of the darkness. At the base of the wall, several feet away, two women and a man lay on huge blue pillows and fondled and kissed each other. One woman had a hand inside the man's fly as she leaned across his body to stick her tongue in the other woman's mouth.

"I see no reason why we cahn't tolerate each other," said D'Arcy. "I don't feel threatened by you in any way. You have your job to do, I have mine. Let me say I bear you no ill will and—"

"Jesus, if I didn't know better I'd swear you have a warm heart beating under that silk shirt. Why is it that whenever we appear together on a radio or television show you've got your knife out, but when we bump into each other casually, you seem occasionally human?" Burt asked.

D'Arcy snapped his fingers and as if by magic, a waiter appeared out of the darkness. "Gin and tonic again, please. And white wine for the lady." Burt ordered a Scotch.

D'Arcy said, "In answer to your question regarding my behavior toward you at various times, let me say that I'm a professional and fulfill my contract to the letter. Self-promotion is a part of that contract, which means that given the opportunity I promote myself."

"At my expense."

"My dear fellow, but of course. A public conflict with my esteemed rival is of much more value to me than say, a conflict with a butcher over rancid meat, or even heated words with my landlord. One fights one's own. In any case, even soldiers in opposing armies have an occasional truce, though tonight I detect in you a rather tense and somber mood. Has dear Harold bitten you in the throat?"

The waiter, a painfully thin black youth in a silver leotard with silver sprinkles in his hair, returned with the drinks. D'Arcy tipped him five dollars, then watched him mince into the darkness. "I must say the black people in your country are a most surly lot. One gets the feeling that most of them would prefer to see us whites staked out over an anthill under a burning sun, our eyelids sliced off to prevent sleep."

Johnnie playfully pushed D'Arcy's shoulder. "Oh, Robin, that's gross."

"Yes, quite." He looked up at Burt Anthony who sipped his Scotch and scowled.

"If you're in such a good mood, mind telling me if Renata Zachery's here or been here and gone or what." The words were out before Burt could stop them.

D'Arcy stopped laughing. His eyes narrowed and for several seconds he studied Anthony's face carefully. Then he sighed and reached for his drink.

"Dear boy, if I told you then we'd both know, wouldn't we? Don't you find this place perfectly repulsive? Who was it that said all our troubles stem from our unwillingness to stay quietly in our rooms? I've come to believe that it's true that you Americans will pay money for the privilege of being uncomfortable."

Burt slammed his chair down. "Was she with Gil van Lier?"

"Was who with whom, dear boy?"

"Renata Zachery."

"Oh, dear, I wish you'd stop hounding that poor woman and let her live her life in peace." D'Arcy leaned his head to one side, enjoying himself. "Isn't that what you said to me last week when we shared a microphone on the radio show hosted by that rather abominable fat man who insists on thinking he's Orson Welles? Now if I am to leave the poor woman alone, then so should you."

"She's supposed to have come in here with three men, plus secret service." Burt's voice was low, hard, determined.

"Read my column tomorrow."

D'Arcy squeezed Johnnie's hand. Tonight she was with him and he was at peace with the world, which was why he didn't scorch Anthony's behind and send him screaming out into the night.

"Reading my column," he continued, "might improve your approach toward gossip, though I've enjoyed some of your work. You're an excellent writer, if you don't mind my saying so."

Closing his eyes, Burt let his head flop back on his neck. He exhaled for a long time. The noise and smell of grass in *50/West* must be turning his brain into guacamole. When he spoke, his own voice seemed to be coming at him from a room far at the end of a long corridor. "I'll find out what I have to know. Find it out my own way."

"Delighted to hear it, old boy. Self-effort is commendable. One must pay one's dues in this world."

Burt closed one eye and focused the other one on D'Arcy, who was blurred and fading into the darkness. Johnnie—what the hell kind of name was that for a girl—clung to D'Arcy's arm and stared at Burt with a wet, open mouth. She reminded him of those women in ancient Rome who sat in the colosseum and literally had orgasms while the gladiators sliced each other into bleeding strips. Johnnie probably got her kicks watching D'Arcy drown kittens.

Burt looked down at the almost empty glass resting in a hand on his thigh. What did D'Arcy know about the dues Burt had paid? What did he know about the price he'd paid all his life to be his own man?

He looked up at D'Arcy. "I've paid the price. Paid it all my life. Don't give *me* any shit about dues."

D'Arcy leaned forward, a forefinger aimed at Burt's chest. "You don't *stop* paying, friend, and that's what you haven't learned yet. You think because you've bled in the past, the troubled times are now over or should be. Since when does life owe you or anybody else one bloody thing? So you've paid the price, have you? Well, what about the price one must pay for money?"

"What about it?"

"Freedom is the price paid for money! I'm not talking about the fact that you now wear Harold Monmouth's collar. I'm talking about freedom in other areas as well. For example, when you learn that anyone who writes for money had better write what the public wants to read, you are no longer free to write merely what you want to read."

Burt pushed his finger away. "I know that."

"You think you know it. I don't believe it's quite settled into your brain as yet. You are aware of it, but you haven't fully realized this fact. When you do, my drunken friend, it will be reflected in your column and I might yet have a rival worthy of being called a rival."

"Drunk? Who's drunk?" Burt tried to move his legs. They felt as if someone had tied them to the chair. "Man, I'm as straight as, as—"

"I don't think you should drink any more." D'Arcy's voice was soothing. "You've had three since you sat down and God knows how many before."

"Three?" shrieked Burt. He didn't remember ordering three drinks. "You sure?"

D'Arcy smiled. "I try to be. Makes for better reporting, I'm told."

"Ren-Ren-Renata Z-Z-Z-Z." Burt frowned, shook his head to clear the dust from his brain and said, "Zenata Rackery. She been in here tonight?"

Johnnie howled. D'Arcy's smile was almost warm. "Probably. She any relation to Renata Zachery?"

Burt didn't care anymore about being cool, about controlling himself. It took all of his energy to stand up and he had to hold on to the chair, but his anger gave him

**123**

purpose and direction and when he'd gotten to his feet all he could think of was how hard he'd worked in his life with nothing to show for it and how badly he wanted this job and how D'Arcy was laughing at him, showing off in front of his blond bimbo and Burt yelled "Goddam it!" and hurled his Scotch and water at D'Arcy.

Burt stumbled, put off balance by his throwing motion and now he was hanging over the balcony, looking down at the crowded dance floor. Behind him he heard D'Arcy say, "Dear me. It would have been so much better to have a waiter come up rather than drop the empty glass down to him."

Burt felt a hand on the back of his jacket as someone pulled him back and gently guided him down to a sitting position on the floor. Had someone pulled a pillow case over Burt's head? Now he could see, well, see a little. He breathed through his open mouth, chest rising and falling.

He felt someone near and looked up to see D'Arcy hovering over him. "You'll be relieved to know I wasn't hit," said D'Arcy. "There have been no repercussions from downstairs, so perhaps you were lucky down there as well. I won't print any of this, not because I'm kind but because it would only make you notorious and therefore create curiosity in the minds of the reading public. So you'll understand my reluctance to publicize you. However, I do suggest you curb your liquor intake in future or drink out of paper cups to lessen the danger to us all."

D'Arcy stepped away. "May I suggest you crawl away from here before Mademoiselle Bernhard sends someone to see just who's turning her premises into a launching pad for guided missiles. *Ciao*."

And D'Arcy was gone. Along with Johnnie what's-her-name of the wet lips. Burt never did find out her last name, but then again, he hadn't found out much of anything tonight. He stood up and staggered toward the stairs. If he remembered correctly, they were over there somewhere. If he remembered correctly, D'Arcy said he wasn't going to write about Burt throwing the drink and getting drunk and sitting on the floor. Didn't want to make Burt famous or some shit like that.

Even when you lose, you lose.

When the cab stopped in front of Burt's apartment building, the cab driver and the doorman had to wake him up and help him inside.

# ■ ■ ■ Ten

Burt wanted to sleep, to close his eyes and keep them closed for a long time. But someone at the front door wasn't buying that. The caller was insistent; he rang and banged, banged and rang. Burt swung his feet to the floor and sat on the edge of the bed, hands covering his eyes to keep out the world. Maybe the building was on fire. Maybe the Russians were in the Bronx. Maybe a Jehovah's Witness was out there in the hall with an armful of pamphlets and an intense determination to save Burt's soul from Big-Apple wickedness.

He blinked until his eyes cleared and he could see his clock radio. Five minutes to eight. Sun starting to come up. *Sun starting to come up?* Burt got very angry in a hurry.

"Who is it?"

"Doorman."

"Doorman? Are you crazy? What the hell's wrong with

you? I left orders never to be disturbed before eleven o'clock!"

"It's important."

"Important? Who told you it was important?"

"I have something for you, Mr. Anthony. He said it was important and that you were expecting it, to wake you because you were expecting me to bring—"

On his feet now and wide awake, an enraged Burt grabbed a robe and hurried to the front door. Who had the nerve to send a doorman up this early and get Burt out of bed when he'd barely had four hours sleep. Who—

Burt stopped with a hand outstretched, just inches from the doorknob. Harold Monmouth. Closing his eyes, Burt nodded his head. Harold Monmouth would do it.

Forcing himself to appear calm, Burt opened the door. The doorman was a tall, middle-aged Yugoslav with a small head, long neck and a thick handlebar moustache. He wore a red cap and a long red and blue coat buttoned to the neck. Some tenants called him "The Count" because he always gave the impression of being an impoverished nobleman forced to associate with his inferiors. He stood in the doorway, the brown manila envelope balanced gently on his fingertips as though presenting his credentials at court. The Count looked pleased to have gotten Burt out of bed.

"For you, Mr. Anthony, sir."

Handing Burt the envelope, he then bowed his head once, backing away before turning and walking down the deserted hall. The Count saw no reason to mention the twenty dollars he'd received for taking the envelope upstairs. The gentleman who'd given him the money had insisted Mr. Anthony wouldn't be asleep, that he was expecting the envelope and would be quite delighted to receive it. Just in case Mr. Anthony was in the shower, said the giver of the twenty dollars, be sure to ring the bell and knock on his door until Mr. Anthony opens up.

Shutting the front door slowly and holding the envelope as though it were about to explode, Burt saw his name printed neatly on the front, no return adress, no indication of what was inside.

He opened it.

Inside were pages from the *Journal-Herald* and clipped to them was a small sheet of memo paper with the name *Harold Monmouth* printed at the top and the words "For Your Information" hastily scrawled under it. Under that, and printed in black letters were the words *call me immediately*. No signature.

Burt didn't want to look at anything else in the envelope; he wanted to rip it to shreds and flush it down the toilet. His legs were shaky, as though he'd run too far and too fast. His head was about to float away and he never got this lighter-than-air feeling unless he was an inch from being scared.

He watched his fingers unfold the three sheets of newspaper as though the fingers belonged to someone else. Sheet number one was the front page of the *Journal-Herald*, with a three-column photograph of Renata Zachery and Gil van Lier on the dance floor at *50/West*. Just below the photograph was a box with the headline, "Tourists Catch a Slow One," referring to the dancing couple. Underneath the head was D'Arcy's byline and a paragraph detailing Renata Zachery's evening in New York in the company of two men, the husbands of friends. When Gil van Lier had joined the party, the two borrowed spouses had disappeared, leaving him and Mrs. Zachery with three secret service men.

The second sheet was a continuation from the first page. It mentioned that van Lier, with meetings today in New York and Washington over the tense situation in Chindé, still found time last night to put aside weighty matters and relax by dancing with the beautiful wife of the vice-president.

The third and last sheet was D'Arcy's column, which contained among other items, three mentions of Mrs. Zachery, each circled in red pencil by Harold Monmouth.

Burt sat staring at the telephone for a full five minutes before finally dialing Monmouth's number. As he listened to the dial tone, Burt closed his eyes and wondered if Monmouth ever slept or did he spend all of his time sucking blood from the people who worked for him.

"Monmouth here."

"Burt Anthony. I got your envelope." Burt chewed the inside of his mouth and waited.

"Yes, well I thought we'd start the day by straightening out a few matters."

"Like what?"

"Like why you ran nothing on Mrs. Zachery's pub-crawling even though you were in attendance last night at *50/West*. I have your column for today in front of me and there isn't a line on her or van Lier."

"I was in *50/West*, yes, but I didn't see Mrs. Zachery so I didn't print anything on her. Didn't see van Lier either. As far as I was concerned, there was no story."

Monmouth exhaled into Burt's ear. "I see. Then you're saying Mrs. Zachery isn't newsworthy."

"That's not what I'm saying. I'm saying I'm a journalist and accuracy is important to me." Burt made a fist and gently tapped the table again and again.

"If you don't mind," said Monmouth with exaggerated politeness, "I'd like to know why you and D'Arcy can both be in the same place and only one of you emerge with any decent copy."

"I—I walked every inch of *50/West* and didn't see Mrs. Zachery or van Lier."

Monmouth erupted. "Then you had bloody well start looking more carefully, because they were definitely there! And D'Arcy's got himself a front page out of it, while you and I have a fistful of excuses. You were tipped to go down to the club and you did and you came out of the place with *nothing*. Nothing is not exactly why I am paying you one thousand dollars a week."

Burt looked at the ceiling. "They must have left before I got there. I asked around but nobody knew for sure if Renata Zachery and van Lier had been in. Or, if they knew, they weren't talking."

"Perhaps you should have asked D'Arcy," said Monmouth dryly.

Burt almost said, *I did,* but stopped himself in time.

Monmouth said, "I have a breakfast meeting in ten minutes. Nothing you've told me just now constitutes a satisfactory explanation. And the column you've submitted today fails to sustain my interest. I've ordered a messenger to be at your apartment exactly one-half hour from now. I strongly suggest you have another column with more substantial material waiting for him when he arrives. If we delay the press run by twenty minutes or so, we could still manage to make all the editions with your new column."

He slammed down the phone. A rigid Burt sat with the dial tone droning in his ear. His neck was damp with perspiration, his shoulders knotted with tension and his aching stomach felt as though it had been run through a paper shredder.

Thirty minutes to write another column. He stood up, exhaled and shook his head vigorously to clear it. To loosen up, he ran in place for a few seconds, touched his toes and reached for the ceiling several times. Would be nice to have a drink, something to calm his nerves. But early-morning drinking on an empty stomach was a mistake even when you found plenty of reasons for doing it.

Instead of a small drink, Burt forced himself to down a half glass of milk, a tiny square of cheese and most of a slice of whole wheat toast. Something to settle his stomach. Food instead of liquor. He was going to try and hang onto this job without crawling into the bottle. Three columns in twenty-four hours and at least one of them was ending up in the wastebasket.

Monmouth's hanging up the phone like that was scary; it reminded Burt how easy it would be to get fired. Just a finger on the dial, a few words into the mouthpiece and Burt's dreams were yesterday's news and he was back buying gas by the half gallon and saving dimes to get his typewriter out of hock.

He opened his desk drawer and pulled out a half page

he'd written on Terry Earle, a story he'd had reservations about using and had laid aside for the past two days. Terry was a brilliant comedienne, an attractive and very inventive young woman who was the hottest name in comedy at the moment. She'd just signed to write, direct and star in three movies for a major studio and was also negotiating with a television network for a series of specials. Two comedy albums had sold over a million copies each and there was talk of Terry doing a one-woman show on Broadway this fall, if she could find the time. Terry Earle was also a lesbian.

Through police contacts, Burt had learned that Terry had picked up two lesbians at a gay bar in the Village and brought them back to her hotel. During the course of the evening one of the lesbians had fallen from a window to her death. Not only had police ruled the girl's death an accident, but had done their best to keep all news away from the press; Terry Earle had a vulnerability that made everyone want to protect her. The woman's death had shaken the highly strung and emotional Terry, who was now in an Arizona sanitarium being treated for nerves. As far as the public knew she was on a fat farm trying to lose weight for an upcoming movie.

Burt hadn't printed the story because the death had been officially ruled an accident and he suspected that any public airing of the story might be harmful to Terry Earle's career. Since the comedienne faced no criminal charges, what would be the point of making her live through it all again? Terry's lesbianism, only whispered about in show business, would become public knowledge. Terry wouldn't be able to make an appearance without some reference being made to her sex life or to the death of the young girl she had brought back to her hotel room. Burt had written the story, then tossed it in his desk. There were limits, he told himself.

But now he was in trouble. Sorry, Terry. He began retyping the story. It would be his lead. When he finished it, he looked through the copy received from press agents and checked off several items on Renata Zachery. Almost a dozen press agents had sent in reports that she had been seen eating in restaurants they represented. Other press agents had sent copy claiming she was coming to the premiere of their Broadway show or multimillion-dollar films. Pathetic attempts for a plug.

The item Burt chose to print was probably no more tangible than a handful of smoke but he was desperate and Harold Monmouth was leaning on him. Proving the truth of the item was as easy as nailing soup to the wall, but Burt wanted to keep his job, so he made it his second story. The item came from a publishing house which claimed that it was ready to pay Renata Zachery two million dollars for hard and soft cover rights to her life story—no doubt to counteract the rumors that the publishing house was losing money and laying off employees by the handful. The word was that the publisher was having no luck finding a buyer for his company and he obviously thought a line in a gossip column would prop up his stock and keep the creditors at arm's length and maybe, just maybe, catch somebody rich and dumb enough to take the company off the publisher's hands.

From me to you, thought Burt. He began typing. Suddenly he stopped. He was writing junk, sure, but that's not what bothered him. He frowned, combed the furrows in his forehead, then chewed his thumbnail. He snapped his fingers. Goddam it, of course! How did Monmouth know Burt had been at *50/West* last night? Who the hell told him?

Burt stood up and softly said, "Who told him?"

What's more, Monmouth knew he had been drunk. It was in his voice, it was there between the lines.

Suddenly Burt felt cold. Wrapping both arms around himself he began pacing back and forth. Someone was spying on him for Monmouth. Was he being followed everywhere he went? No. Not even Monmouth would go in for something that heavy. Burt shivered again. Too spooky to think about. Was his telephone tapped, his apartment bugged? Maybe. Had the doorman been paid off? Possibly. But none of the doormen knew Burt's whereabouts when he left the apartment. True, one of them had helped him out of the cab this morning, but Burt was too drunk to say anything. And the doorman could not have known where Burt had come from or that he and D'Arcy had been in the same place at the same time.

But somebody had known and that somebody had told Monmouth. Burt stopped pacing. No time to think about that now. Less than fifteen minutes before the messenger arrived. Get back to the typewriter and start producing a column.

Twice while he was typing he stopped and looked over his shoulder, on edge and nervously alert, as though someone were in the room with him. In a way, the Englishman *was* in the room with him and Burt didn't like it. Worse, he hadn't the vaguest idea what to do about it.

## Maryland

The woman put one booted foot out of the car onto the gravel driveway, stopped as though she'd forgotten something, then withdrew the foot and slammed the car door. Through powerful binoculars Gypsy watched her start the engine again and slowly drive forward into an open garage to park beside a gray Mercedes with Washington, D.C., plates. The license number was already in Gypsy's notebook. Turning off the engine the woman stepped from the car and walked from the garage, stopping with her back to the huge, sprawling, ranch-style house behind her. She looked at her car, a dark blue Rambler, then at the narrow gravel road leading from the house to the main road she had driven along. Gypsy knew she was trying to decide if the car could still be seen from the main road. Her face turned toward the elm trees with their spring buds and fragile, pale green leaves, elm trees that dotted the hilly, open countryside surrounding the expensive house.

Focusing the heavy binoculars, Gypsy enlarged the pic-

**133**

ture and almost bit his tongue in his excitement at recognizing the woman. Her head was covered with a silk scarf and her beautiful face almost hidden by oversized dark glasses, but Gypsy knew her. The entire world knew her. Today she wore beige leather jacket, culottes, gloves, with dark brown leather boots. Goddam. It definitely was her! A tan round leather bag hung from her left shoulder and she gripped the strap with both hands as she looked around once more to see if she had been followed or was being observed. Gypsy clinched one fist in triumph. He was on to something big.

Less than two hundred feet away at the top of a low hill half hidden by elm trees, he lay stomach down in wet grass watching her. When she had finished scanning the countryside she turned and quickly walked to the house, up several steps and across a porch. Without knocking or using a key, she opened the door and disappeared inside. Shifting to a sitting position, Gypsy took the binoculars from his eyes and brushed grass and twigs from the front of his rumpled raincoat. He couldn't get closer to the house without being seen. There was a three-car garage, tennis court, empty swimming pool, guest cottage, empty stable and even a large dog house, but all were too close to the main house to risk using. Gypsy was forced to work this job in the open, hidden by a few trees and a knoll soaked by three days of rain.

The house would be occupied, Simon had warned, so forget about getting inside and planting bugs. Work from the outside. Get there at three in the afternoon and stay until dark. Last night in a heavy rain, Gypsy had driven down from New York, checked into a Washington hotel and by noon today had rented a car with Maryland plates and talked with Simon about the job. It meant driving eight miles to Great Falls, Maryland, one of several suburbs favored by government workers who could afford expensive homes. As usual Simon had mentioned no names. Well, Gypsy had a surprise for Simon. The lady who had just gone inside the house had a name and face known to millions.

Following directions, Gypsy had found the proper mailbox then continued driving past it, parking his car in a deserted picnic area completely out of sight of the house. Carrying his battered brown suitcase and eating a Hershey bar, he had walked across the soggy ground and now looked down on the house he was to bug.

Placing the binoculars inside his suitcase, he removed a microphone resembling a long metal stick, a microphone so powerful that just by pointing it you could pick up a conversation a few hundred feet away. Somewhere in the house a dog barked as Gypsy wired the microphone to a recorder lying in the suitcase next to his .22.

Laying the microphone across his lap he removed earphones from the suitcase and slipped them on his head, carefully adjusting them before connecting a single wire from the earphones to the recorder. Leaning over the suitcase he fingered two dials on the recorder and listened and when static crackled in his ear, he frowned and looked up at the sky. The clouds were blacker now. Christ, he thought, not again. Three straight days of rain in New York and Washington and now more on the way. Sometimes the rain affected his bad leg, tightening the knee joint and causing the flesh near the break to burn as though the bare skin was pressed against a hot radiator. If it stormed this afternoon, Gypsy would have to grab his equipment and run because the rain would hide all sound and ruin his microphone and recorder.

Picking up his binoculars again he trained them on the house and focused for the proper distance, scanning the house until he found a window not covered by shades or curtains. He wanted the famous and beautiful woman to start talking because whatever she had to say had to involve a man. A man who was one of the four names Gypsy had come across the day he had run into trouble at the Hotel Alexandria. A man who wasn't her husband. She was married to someone well-known in his own right and whatever Gypsy got on tape today was going to be used against the woman by Simon's senator. Simon seemed pleased with what Gypsy had done for him so far, even

**135**

though he continued treating the wiretapper as though he were a distant nigger relative. That was going to change the second Gypsy learned all about the senator's plans. Either Simon's senator would hand over a larger share of the pie or Gypsy was going to lay a cute move of his own on everybody involved.

He didn't need to swallow a computer to figure out that the bugging he was doing for Simon's senator was connected to something heavy and that the one person who couldn't lose in all of this was Gypsy. As he now saw it, they couldn't drop him if they wanted to. All Gypsy had to do was tell them he knew the identity of the woman he'd just seen and that he also had tapes of recent conversations with Simon, who while still careful not to put anything on paper, had let a few facts slip in recent meetings with the wiretapper. It was because of Simon's snotty attitude toward him that Gypsy had taken to wearing a wire recorder taped to his chest during their meetings on the chance Simon would say something that could eventually be profitable. With these tapes and the knowledge of the woman's identity, Gypsy now had enough to sell to someone else. The person or persons Simon's senator was out to get, for instance.

If certain people ever learned that the esteemed Senator Aaron Paul Banner of Virginia had put a wiretapper on this particular woman, the senator would be in the worst trouble of his life, particularly since a recent poll had shown him to be his party's strongest and most popular presidential candidate. Barring a scandal or death, Banner would lead his party in an attempt to win the White House in November. He had a lot to lose if he didn't give Gypsy a bigger piece of the pie.

On his stomach again, Gypsy peered through the binoculars, shifting his gaze from window to window, the sound of the barking dog loud in his earphones. The wiretapper saw portions of furniture, the arm of a plaid easy chair, a high wooden stool, a desk lamp on the end of a desk and the lower half of a woman's body as she walked past a window, palms up as though pleading. The barking

**136**

dog and static electricity from the impending rain were drowning out some of the talk going on in the house. Too bad about that because with his years of experience, Gypsy knew that what he was trying to listen to was more important than any tap he had done for Simon up until now. Piss on the rain and piss on that dog who wouldn't stop barking and who was jamming Gypsy's reception almost as effectively as the best debugging device on the market.

But he heard the woman say, ". . . hard for me to get away, to have time to myself. I'll have you know it's not easy to fool our nation's secret service." Gypsy grinned. If anybody could fool the nation's secret service, at least for a few hours, it's you, lady. The wiretapper saw a pair of arms set down a tray containing two drinks and then the arms withdrew. He was almost positive the arms were black, probably those of a servant and that the silence now in the room was for the servant's benefit. The sooner the servant left, the sooner the talk would begin again. It did.

"I can get away next week," said the woman. "He's flying to Paris and might make a stopover in Rome. I'll have at least three days but we must be careful."

"Aren't we always?" said a man whom Gypsy hadn't yet seen.

"I'll meet you in New York again. Thursday."

"Make appointments with other people," said the unseen man. "Let's use all the cover we can. It's no problem for me to 'accidentally' meet you when you're with somebody else. The problem is to get you away from them and to be alone with you."

"I love you," she said. "Oh, God, why does it have to be so hard for us to see each other. Why can't the universe give us a break and just leave us alone. Oh, Bill."

"There's no way the world is going to leave either one of us alone," said the man. "You know it, we both know it. Why don't you stop wasting time and come over here . . ."

The dog began barking and the static electricity seemed to answer the animal and suddenly the conversation

**137**

inside the house was buried under this unwanted noise. Gypsy clenched his right fist in frustration and anger. Christ, he was so close and now the dog and the weather . . .

The front door opened and the dog ran out, a large tan and black German shepherd who leaped across the porch and down the stairs and spun around in circles on the gravel driveway. The front door closed and there was no sound in the house except for soft music. Bingo, thought Gypsy, certain that the woman and the man she had been talking to were heading for the bedroom. Now that would be something to get on tape. One of the most famous women in the world in the hay with a man she called Bill, a man she loved, a man who wasn't her husband.

The dog attacked Gypsy before he could turn and defend himself. The wiretapper had been concentrating on the house, listening to it and watching it, his mind now thoroughly absorbed by the thought of the woman stripped naked for a man she wasn't married to and Gypsy had been within seconds of deciding to sneak closer to the house. It would have been risky but definitely worth it.

His mind had dismissed the dog. The energetic German shepherd had loped around to the other side of the house which to Gypsy's mind had been the same as evaporating from the face of the earth. Only the woman mattered now because she was going to be the best thing that ever happened to him.

When the dog's fangs tore into the back of his hand and wrist Gypsy yelled, pushing at the animal with his arms, kicking at it with both legs and sending the dog backwards in the air, a piece of Gypsy's bloodstained raincoat dangling from the animal's mouth. Landing on its side the dog leaped up immediately, its fur now darkened by falling rain. But the wet grass was to slippery for its claws and it collapsed twice before being able to dig its claws deep enough into the ground to make another charge. Gypsy, his large face wet with rain and his own tears, grabbed the .22 from his suitcase and fired without aiming.

Stopping abruptly, the dog yelped with pain then bared its fangs. In the heavy rain it barked loudly, thrusting its head forward with each bark and trembling with a savage hatred of Gypsy. The fur on the dog's skull was now flattened and made shiny by the gray rain. A dark stain appeared in the tan hair on its chest as it swayed, eyes glazed but still bright with a desire to hurt Gypsy who still feared the dog, not knowing it was mortally wounded and too weak to charge. In a desperate act of courage, the dying dog stood on wobbly legs in the heavy rain and barked a warning to the house, a warning that went unheard in the thunderstorm. Gypsy pulled the trigger again and again, unaware that he had fired all of the bullets and was now jerking the trigger on an empty gun.

# ■ ■ ■ Eleven

The croupier spun the roulette wheel, then sent the tiny ivory ball spinning in the opposite direction as he called out, "No more bets, ladies and gentlemen. No more bets, please." As the ball clattered across the numbered compartments of the moving wheel, Johnnie gently eased in behind Robin, taking care not to disturb him and only when the ball stopped bouncing and settled in double zero did she touch him, laying a hand on the back of his neck. Without taking his eyes off the wheel, D'Arcy brought her hand to his lips and kissed the palm.

"How much have you lost?" she asked.

"Little over a thousand since you flitted off to the loo. If memory serves me correctly, which it usually does in moments of sadness and distress, I've lost close to fifteen hundred altogether."

Irritated at losing but not yet ready to abandon the table, D'Arcy dropped three pearl-gray chips worth twenty-five dollars each on number fourteen, red, then leaned back in his chair, reaching for Johnnie's hand now on his shoulder. Suddenly he felt the wet warmth as she took his thumb in her mouth. Closing his eyes, he pressed his knees tightly together and picked up a chip from the table, squeezing it with all his strength. Taking a deep breath and holding it, he exhaled, giving himself up to the sexual heat now burning his body and mind. Johnnie was the swiftest sexual turn-on he had ever met.

"Twenty-three, odd," said a voice filled with professional indifference. D'Arcy opened his eyes to see his chips and those of other losers being raked in by the round-faced, catatonic-looking croupier. America giveth, America taketh away. A portion of D'Arcy's excellent salary was now in other hands, other pockets. Two women at the table, having played it safe with one ten-dollar chip on odd, collected their meager winnings, flashing weak, smug grins at each other. Having wagered little, thought D'Arcy, you two crones have been spared excessive emotional involvement. And thus, you have missed the point of gambling. The thrill is in the risk and in nothing else. Winning and losing are mere artifacts. To walk the sharp edge of the sword in your bare feet is everything; to cut your feet and bleed is a trifle to be dismissed.

Suddenly D'Arcy felt Johnnie's warm breath in his ear. His skin tingled. He closed his eyes and shivered. "Play odd," she whispered. "Just this once, okay?"

She watched him open his eyes as though awakening from a deep sleep then lean forward and casually drop four twenty-five-dollar chips one by one on odd. As the wheel spun, Johnnie placed her head on his shoulder, stroked his arm and wondered what Robin would say if he knew what she had done tonight in the short time she was out of his sight. When she left she had headed toward the ladies' room. But then Johnnie had accidentally run into Richie Sweet and together they had managed to have one incredible fuck in the elevator. Thinking about it excited her and she gripped D'Arcy's arm tighter. He patted her hand, believing her to be as involved with the turning of the wheel as he was. He had no idea that her thoughts were somewhere else. . . .

A plainclothes New York detective with burn scars on the backs of both hands had gotten Johnnie and Robin into the illegal gambling club, a triplex in a Gramercy Park building of fading elegance. The huge apartment was used as a casino three nights a week. An old couple, a blind dentist and his wife, rented it out for gambling at a thousand dollars a night. During those nights, the couple would check into a hotel at the end of the block. When they returned three days later the apartment would have been cleaned and left exactly as it was on the morning they vacated it.

Once inside the casino, the detective, described by D'Arcy as "a source reliable, anonymous, vindictive and useful," ignored them and attached himself to a crap table. There he gambled with fifty-dollar bills in amounts never seen by most policemen in their entire lives.

Johnnie knew about Robin's gambling. He did it a couple of times a week, never seeming to mind if he won or lost. Johnnie had gambled a few times but didn't care for it. Too much dependence on luck, on a power that belonged to someone besides yourself. To depend on luck was to admit there was something in the world with power over you. That wasn't for Johnnie. Sex was her power; as long as she had it, she didn't need anybody.

As Robin played roulette, Johnnie stood at his side and silently watched and when watching wasn't enough, she looked around for something to chip away at the boredom. All she saw was dead faces, faces belonging to people who were dead to everything except gambling. Men, women. Nothing but dead faces. So she decided to go to the john and play with her makeup. Tonight she wore red eye shadow the same color as a silk dress Robin had given her. She wore black boots and four different kinds of perfume and a red headband held her long platinum hair in place. She wore neither bra nor panties, preferring the feel of the silk against her bare skin.

To get to the ladies room, she had to pass the bar and walk up a small flight of stairs to the second floor. At the bar, men turned on their high stools to watch her. They lifted their eyes from their drinks or ignored the women they were with to stare at Johnnie, which made her feel good. Lifting her head higher, she slowed down her walk, aware that she was being watched. When someone suddenly grabbed her wrist, she was annoyed that some jerk would dare to interrupt her "walk."

She turned to see Richie.

Her heart jumped and her tongue circled her pink lips. Her smile was confident. At the bar, men watched the two of them and Johnnie knew that's what Richie wanted, too. He wanted them to know he was good enough to stop this beautiful woman in her tracks, good enough to get her to stand still and look at him. He had his game going, she had hers and it excited her to realize it. She wasn't bored anymore.

Richie kept his grip on her wrist. When he spoke, his nostrils flared and he didn't hide his sarcasm. "You're here with bird man."

"You mean Robin?" Johnnie's eyes held his. Richie was jealous. Good-looking Richie who gave all the women hot pants, who made men afraid of him, was jealous of Robin. And he wanted Johnnie, who remembered what it was like to have him between her legs. How long had it been since they had screwed?

He tightened his grip on her wrist, sending pain up her arm. The pain made her breathe faster, because she knew it meant Richie wanted her. She made no attempt to stop the pain, because she wanted him too. Now.

Richie wanted her, but he was also angry at her. She was seeing bird man, who Richie wanted to hurt but had been told to leave alone. Now all he could do was watch and think of what it was like to have Johnnie's bare ass in his hands and her under him with her legs wrapped tight around his thighs and her head shaking wildly when the orgasm started. He remembered her mouth cruising his naked body like he was some kind of delicacy and she hadn't eaten for a month. Shit, did he ever remember that. That's what made it worse, knowing that the Englishman was riding Johnnie now. Anger, ego and sexual longing were all one huge flame burning Richie's ass and he couldn't think straight.

He was here for business reasons, to meet a man and collect five thousand dollars from each table and bring the money back to Carmine DiNaldi. But right now all he wanted to do was slap Johnnie until she begged him to stop and then he wanted to bury his face in her crotch and drown in her juices.

If he and Johnnie said any words to each other tonight, Richie didn't know what they were. All he knew was they were walking up the stairs hand in hand and were on the landing when an elevator stopped, its doors opened, and two couples got out. Then he and Johnnie were in the elevator, one of two leading from the triplex down to the lobby. Richie closed the doors by pulling down a long bar that went across them; the elevator was operated by a large brass handle. As he stared, Johnnie lifted up her dress. "Start," she whispered.

Richie's eyes were glued to her pubic hairs.

Dimly, he heard her say, "Start the elevator, Richie."

"What? I mean, where we going?"

"Nowhere. Start it. Go down a couple of floors then stop."

She pulled the dress over her head, dropping it on the floor over her tiny purse. She stood naked in black knee boots and the erection in Richie's pants was so huge, so sudden, that it was painful. His mouth was dry and his palms damp and he felt as he did the first time seconds before they had made it together. There was something about Johnnie that made you want her so badly that you would do anything to have her. Richie had never met a broad like her.

"You can't. I mean we can't—" Richie stopped. To do it in an elevator with all those people out there in the club was fucking insane. He had never done anything like this before in his life. But he saw Johnnie's naked body and

144

saw the brightness in her eyes and he knew she was serious. She wanted to get laid right here in an elevator.

Johnnie thought of Robin sitting at the roulette table waiting for her to come back to him and the excitement of it all was enough to make her scream with uncontrollable joy.

Richie took a step toward her. "You're goddam crazy! We can't do it here. I mean—" The second he said the words he knew he was lying because he wanted her so much, he would have done it in a church aisle during a funeral.

Frowning and biting his lip, Richie backed over to the elevator control and with shaking hands, moved the brass handle to down. The elevator jerked into life, stopped, then started again. His head light with nerves, Richie brought the elevator to a stop, then turned to see Johnnie with a hand between her legs, fingers digging into her cunt and she started to grind her hips. With her other hand, she beckoned him closer.

"Now," she whispered. "Now, now, now."

He ran to her, jamming his opened mouth down hard on hers, bumping teeth and mixing spit, tongue to tongue and feeling her hand fumbling with his zipper. She leaped up, wrapping both legs around his waist. He backed her into an elevator wall as he fumbled with his pants. And then he slid into her, pushing hard into the delicious wetness, pushing hard, gripping the thin wooden railing that ran waist high around the inside of the elevator, pushing, pushing, pushing. Johnnie closed her eyes, head back, fingernails digging into Richie's shoulders, feeling him hard and hot inside of her.

She thought of the people only a few feet above them, vaguely heard the tape-recorded music and hum of voices, thought of Robin expecting her back any second and she moved against Richie harder, harder and felt the ecstasy begin to trickle into her groin, crawl up the base of her spine and grip her brain with fingers of electrical velvet. The orgasm increased in intensity, in speed.

"Oh, God! Oh, God!"

Richie quickly placed a hand over her mouth to keep her quiet. And with her back in the elevator corner, she squirmed, twisted, jerked, her tongue and teeth against his palm and then her teeth were tearing into his flesh, a delicious pain. The salty taste of Richie's blood seemed to increase Johnnie's sexual frenzy. Her response only inflated Richie's ego more and soon he blended into the thrill she felt. Her nails dug painfully into his shoulder and her teeth ripped skin from his palm as she stiffened, jerked and moaned against his hand now wet with her saliva and his own blood. Then Richie came, digging his feet hard into the elevator floor, pushing Johnnie into the corner with all his strength, holding her there for the seconds of incredible pleasure.

Then they were both on the floor breathing loudly, drenched with perspiration and Richie was on his knees before her as though in adoration. He knelt with his chin on his chest, pants and black bikini underwear around his ankles and unable to remember when he had had such a great fuck. Incredible. There wasn't a woman alive like Johnnie.

She sat in the corner of the elevator, head back, hair damp with perspiration and half covering her face. Her eyes were closed and she breathed through her open mouth, hands palms up and resting on her bare thighs. As the exquisite pleasure of her orgasm receded she thought of her friend Maxine who had always said that the best fucking was done in public places where you risked being discovered. You had to take the chance, otherwise where was the fun. Maxine did it in the cockpits of airplanes thirty thousand feet in the air, in public telephone booths, on stairways in courthouses, in the back seats of movie theaters, in taxis, in museums.

Slowly getting to her feet, Johnnie reached out for the railing to steady her wobbly legs. Richie was still at her feet as though praying to her. She looked down at him and moved her lips in a smile that had no warmth in it

146

and wasn't meant to. She had proven her point and that's all that mattered.

"Zip me up, Richie."

Silently standing and before pulling up his pants and underwear, he did as she demanded. Both spent a few minutes brushing dust from their clothing. The brief ride back to the casino was a quiet one; when the elevator door opened, Johnnie stepped into the casino without looking back at Richie. He had played his role and she had no more use for him tonight. The boredom was gone and she felt like being with Robin again. First she had to repair her makeup and see if her hair was all right. Then it was back to Robin.

Richie watched her disappear into the ladies' room. Just like that. He gives her the greatest fuck she has ever had and just like that she turns her back on him and walks away. Probably thinking about bird man. Maybe she wasn't; maybe she was so knocked out by Richie's throwing the meat to her that she couldn't say anything. Yeah, maybe that was it. At the top of the stairs, Richie looked down at the guys lining the bar. They had seen Johnnie with him and even though she had just walked away, hell they were hip enough to know that Richie had racked up a few points.

What they didn't know was just how many points. Even the bitch herself is so played out she can't talk. Didn't that say something about Richie? Didn't that say he was a better man than bird man any day of the week? Tonight he had put the horns on bird man's head and so he could afford to hate him an inch less. But he still hated him and wouldn't forget that skinny, funny-talking son of a bitch.

D'Arcy's delight was mild, a restrained exuberance, he would call it. He was winning at roulette. Almost four thousand dollars. Johnnie was calling his bets, shifting his chips from black to red, from odd to even and having her own string of good luck. Which was the reason for his diluted pleasure. The luck was hers, the decisions were hers, eliminating complete participation for D'Arcy. Still, if it pleased her then D'Arcy could tolerate it this once. Whatever made Johnnie happy when they were together could only work in D'Arcy's favor.

Earlier she hadn't seemed interested in playing or even watching him play. But since she had returned from the loo, she had taken an unexpected delight in roulette, clapping her hands when they won and looking more beautiful than she had all night. Whatever she was doing to him was being accomplished with a witchcraft that eliminated his ability to reason where she was concerned. He had become Johnnie's victim. If she hurt him, she also had the power to cure him. Later tonight he would have Johnnie's flesh pressed against his and that would be the most valuable of all prizes. He was bored with watching her gamble; gambling only interested him if he was doing it. And the evening was late. He wanted Johnnie in bed.

He looked down at the pile of chips. Should be over five thousand dollars there. Almost two thousand of it was his original stake. One last thrill.

He placed a hand on Johnnie's arm, preventing her from pushing more chips onto the numbers. D'Arcy said to the croupier, "What's my limit?"

"For you, Mr. D'Arcy, none at all." The house knew a loser when it saw one.

"Splendid."

D'Arcy tossed three chips across the table to the croupier, who nodded his thanks, tapped each one on the table as though testing it for strength then held it high overhead before dropping it in his shirt pocket. Tapping and holding up the chip was for the benefit of spotters, the silent, unseen men working for the house and watching for cheats on either side of the table; it meant the chip was a tip from a patron, not an attempt by a dealer to cut himself in as a silent partner.

Pushing the rest of his chips forward, D'Arcy stood up and took Johnnie's elbow, slowly guiding her away from the table as though he had already lost. "On twenty, if you please. All of them. That's the lady's age."

Johnnie's eyes widened. "Robin, you're crazy! You know how much money that is?" Her heart started to pound the way it had back in the elevator with Richie.

There were whispers around them, as people stared at D'Arcy. Some players told the croupier they too wanted number twenty and others held their chips tightly in their hands, too frightened to go near the wheel on this particular spin. D'Arcy sensed their hesitation and enjoyed it, but not as much as he enjoyed the disbelief and excitement in Johnnie's beautiful face because everything she felt at this moment was in reaction to him. For this single space in time, no man but D'Arcy existed for her. No Richie, no pickups in department stores, no rock singers, no Venezuelan boxers. Just D'Arcy. His recklessness, his total unconcern for logic and custom had swept her away on a tidal wave of defiance. Defiance was the only thing Johnnie could understand, the only thing she would submit to.

As the wheel spun they stood and silently looked at each other. D'Arcy had Johnnie and he felt the thrill of gambling surging through every inch of his skin and there was nothing else the gods could bestow upon him tonight. He fixed his eyes and soul upon Johnnie's beauty. Camus was right. Women are all we know of paradise on earth.

"Twenty-one, red, odd." For the first time in a long while, the croupier's voice lost some of its boredom. He blinked three times before looking across the table at D'Arcy and Johnnie, who still stared at each other. Other gamblers looked at the couple, who then put their arms around each other and walked away.

D'Arcy kissed her cheek. "Next year's birthday, love."

As the elevator took them down to the lobby, D'Arcy and Johnnie kissed deeply and D'Arcy could feel her growing sexual urgency. Her hand caressed his body, brushing across his fly, lingering for a second before moving higher. D'Arcy wanted her more than ever before and not even the presence of three other people in the elevator bothered him. It wasn't the sort of thing he would have

149

done in England, this public *snogging*, but Johnnie was a fever in him and D'Arcy knew neither right nor wrong.

He didn't know he was in the same elevator that Johnnie and Richie had used less than a half-hour ago and that this thought, as much as anything else, was causing her present passion.

# ■ ■ ■ Twelve

When the taxi stopped on the corner of Eighth Avenue and 38th Street, Burt, sitting alone in the back seat, opened the curb-side door and Action Jackson slid in beside him. At 6'5" and 260 pounds, Jackson took up a lot of room, which left Dave Tiegs, who had been waiting on the corner with him, no choice but to squeeze himself in the front seat with the driver. Action Jackson was a huge, bearded black man with a high voice and several silver spoons twisted into bracelets on each of his thick wrists. He worked as a security guard at the *Journal-Herald* and he was going to tell Burt why the paper had refused to print two of Robin Ian D'Arcy's columns. This wasn't the biggest story Burt had worked on since coming to New York, but terms of pleasing Harold Monmouth, it was one of the most important.

Ordinarily Burt wouldn't give a damn about D'Arcy's columns being yanked. But with his own ass on the line, Burt suddenly found out that he cared a hell of a lot about

**151**

those two missing columns. D'Arcy had run substitutes, but it was those two pulled columns that interested Burt and would surely interest Monmouth if D'Arcy came out looking bad.

Until six months ago, Jackson had been a plainclothes detective on the police force. Currently he was on suspension while being investigated on charges that he had robbed a dope dealer of cocaine and money before arresting him. Dave Tiegs, who had spent nights riding around Manhattan in a squad car with Jackson, had warned Burt not to mention the suspension. Jackson regarded it as a very sensitive subject and since he looked big enough to drive holes in Burt's skull with his thumbs, Burt was going to find it easy to skip any mention of Action Jackson's official troubles.

On 40th Street, the cab stopped for a red light. "Turn right on 42nd," said Jackson in a voice much too small for his huge body. "Just want to check out what's happenin'."

Open a vein and he'll bleed cop blue, thought Burt as he studied Jackson who stared out of the window at the Port Authority Bus Terminal. "Ain't nothin' good happenin' in that place," said Jackson, his back to Burt. "Runaways come in off the hound and the pimps hit on them before them kids know what city they're in."

"What's the hound?" asked Burt.

"Greyhound. Runaways never fly planes. No bread. You never find pimps hangin' round airports. Always find 'em at bus terminals." Jackson rapped on the plastic protective shield between him and the driver. "Turn right on 42nd. Got to see what's goin' on."

Burt had seen 42nd Street and could do without seeing it again. It was an armpit, worse than anything he had ever seen in Los Angeles, or even San Diego, a navy town. It was as bad as Tijuana and Juarez, two of Mexico's raunchiest border towns. Forty-Second Street was porn movie houses, pizza joints, massage parlors, army surplus stores, boy prostitutes waiting in doorways, porn book shops, overflowing trash cans, cheap clothing stores, penny arcades, record shops with music exploding through loud-speakers. It was neon wrapped around filth and the red bearded white man Burt noticed near a subway entrance, who stood on a wooden crate and pounded a bible with his fist while he shouted about redemption in the blood of the lamb, wasn't going to make any difference.

Action Jackson coolly watched it all from the cab, alert eyes seeing things Burt probably missed. Finally, he turned to Burt. "You want to know 'bout D'Arcy."

Burt nodded.

Jackson said, "Dave here says you're righteous."

"I try to be." Burt tried to hold Jackson's gaze. It wasn't easy. As a big man and a cop, Jackson was used to staring people down.

Dave Tiegs had given Jackson fifty dollars, calling it a "loan," though the both of them knew better. Burt had promised Dave the fifty back and fifty more as a bonus if Jackson's information turned out to be usable.

"*Alll*right," squeaked Jackson, hands on his knees. "Here's what's happenin'. Week ago, the truck drivers who deliver the paper were told to wait. Paper wasn't going out the usual time. Some kind of delay. This meant extra work for everybody. Printers had to wait around, then work late and naturally the security guards had more to do. Turns out the paper decided at the last minute to pull one of your boy D'Arcy's columns. They got scared and said they weren't going to run it.

"I hear tell that one of the lawyers calls up and says back off. Cool it. Don't print this particular column, because there was a good chance of bad things happenin' if the column ever sees the light of day. Paper was all ready to go to press, then we get the word to stand by. We wait while somebody gets one of D'Arcy's substitute columns and puts that in this nice little hole we got on page ten. Word is the column that got everybody uptight had somethin' in it about senator helpin' a company to get a government contract, then gettin' a kickback for his trouble. Paper didn't want to take a chance so they listened to the lawyer. I wasn't all that interested so I didn't pay too much attention about why. I hear, though, that D'Arcy's information maybe couldn't stand up. His source wasn't all that strong; some society dame in D.C. Man didn't have enough proof to suit his editors and their lawyers. Somebody also tells me the senator found out about the column and threatened to sue the paper's ass off, which is why we had all this last-minute shit 'bout not runnin' it."

The cab stopped for a red light at the corner of 42nd Street and Sixth Avenue. Burt was so elated at the news he was getting from Action Jackson that he could have danced naked in Bryant Park.

D'Arcy's column yanked. Right on.

"What about the second column?" asked Burt.

Jackson threw up his large hands in resignation, letting them flop down on his muscular thighs. "Man just had an attitude, know what I mean? Wanted to have his own way. Writes another column 'bout the same senator and tries to get *that* one printed. Same thing happens. Paper's lawyers say don't run the fuckin' thing and we all sit around again while everybody argues in the conference room. In the end the man who owns the store always has the last word. They yank your boy D'Arcy's column a second time. Same reason. Nobody believes he knows what he's talkin' about. Or maybe they just too scared to write about them people down in Washington. Anyway, the column don't run."

Burt held his breath. "Know the senator's name?"

"Yeah. Danziger."

Burt exhaled. Bingo.

Jackson adjusted his dark glasses and straightened his black leather cap. Couple of white boys getting excited over something which never got printed. Didn't make much sense. D'Arcy is the one who should be excited since he's the one who lost out. Tiegs and his friend didn't have much to holler about, but they looked like they wanted to holler just the same. Hard to figure what people had going around in their minds.

Burt knew about Senator Adam T. Danziger. Not too

154

long ago, the senator from Florida had appeared at the White House to witness the President sign an important bill. Danziger had wanted to make sure the folks back home saw him prominently featured in all of the photographs and television newscasts taken of the signing, so he'd gotten to the White House early and stationed himself directly behind the President's chair.

However, the majority whip, a senator even more important than Danziger, had wanted to be photographed behind the President. The whip asked Danziger to move to the side. The Florida senator refused. The whip asked again and again Danziger refused. The whip pushed Danziger, who pushed back. The whip then got some help at pushing and pulling Danziger from behind the President's chair, but Danziger held on with both hands and finally the whip and his associates gave up. Danziger was photographed with a white-knuckle grip on the chair, a grim expression on his fleshy face as the President signed the bill.

Danziger could be determined; if anybody could make trouble for the *Journal-Herald,* he could.

"You goin' to put somethin' in the paper about D'Arcy?" asked Jackson.

Burt nodded slowly. "Oh, yes. Count on it."

"Sounds like you plannin' to stick it to the dude."

Burt grinned.

Jackson said, "D'Arcy ain't no pussy. He's tough. You gonna bring it to him, bring it to him good, understand?"

Burt nodded again. "I understand. Believe me, I understand. Look, I owe you one. If there's anything I can do, you know where to reach me."

Jackson snorted. "I got some bad shit goin' down. Ain't nobody can help me but God and I ain't even sure he's heard about my troubles yet. Wasn't for bad luck, wouldn't have no luck at all."

"I know the feeling," said Burt. "I've been there."

As Dave Tiegs directed the driver to turn down Lexington Avenue, Burt wrote down his home telephone number and gave it to Action Jackson. It was a reporter's reflex.

Keep in touch with your sources and let them know where they can find you. Action Jackson was the kind of man Burt would like to know better, but there was no time for that now. A few months ago Burt would have looked into Jackson's problem with that drug bust and satisfied himself about who was lying or telling the truth. It would have been a challenge to come up with a story that would either hang Jackson or get him off the hook and back on the force. But Burt had no time for social work or charity cases at the moment, he was more interested in getting himself off the hook. The rest of the world would have to wait.

He said to Jackson, "Where can I get in touch with you?"

"Through Dave. Don't call me at the paper. This job ain't much but I need it to get me over 'til this other thing gets straightened out. Don't know how long that's goin' take. Nothin' I can do but sweat it out."

Burt rapped on the protective shield to get Dave Tiegs' attention. "Tell the driver to stop at the corner. We're getting out." Tiegs nodded and touched the driver's sleeve.

Burt looked at Jackson. "Like I said, I owe you one."

The big black man snorted. "You wouldn't have any juice downtown, would you?" He assumed Burt knew about his trouble but the request for help was made casually. Jackson had been around long enough to know that you really couldn't expect too much from the human race.

Burt decided to be upfront with Action Jackson. There was something about the black man that inspired one to be intensely truthful. "I'm new in town. Still feeling my way around and connecting slowly. Dave can tell you that. But if I come across anything or anybody that can help you, I'll pass it on. You have my word."

Jackson sighed, huge fists resting on his knees, "Money's runnin' low. Me and my family might have to move out of our apartment and in with my wife's relatives. Hate doin' that. Means we got to board the kids out and split up the family. Tough on the kids. Anyway, might be hard for you to find me at home. Got me a second job.

Bouncer in a discotheque. Check with Dave here. He can get through to me there without causin' a fuss."

Burt extended his hand.

Jackson stared at it for a few seconds, then casually took it. His grip was gentle. He had nothing to prove by crushing bones and knew it. Burt appreciated that.

"Later," said Burt.

Jackson moved a corner of his mouth as he pocketed the two folded twenty-dollar bills Burt had slipped him. "Later, my man."

On the corner of Lexington and 38th, Burt and Dave Tiegs watched the cab pull away with Action Jackson inside. Closing his notebook, Burt slipped it inside his jacket. It was almost one in the afternoon and Lexington was still jammed with people pouring out of offices and hurrying to lunch. Burt said, "I'd hate to be the man Jackson caught kicking his mother."

"That's called a death wish," said Tiegs in his raspy voice. He wiped his leaky nose with the back of his hand. "Him and me sorta met that way. Few years back I was coming out of a subway station over on Seventh Avenue and these two bozos jumped me. Couple of junkies lookin' to get well. Action comes running out of his squad car like his ass is in flames and he has himself a time and a half. Junkies got knives but Action he don't care. Never pulls his piece. Just uses his hands and feet. The man does good work, believe me. Never bothered to book them. Left them there on the street. Once in a while, we trade off information. Like he'll hear about a bust that has big names in it. Lawyers can keep a thing like that quiet sometimes. Maybe I'll come across something he might like to know."

Dave Tiegs spat at a trash can and missed. "Know something? I enjoyed riding around with him in that squad car at night. Different city at night. Nighttime hides all the shit, the things that you really don't want to see. You got your squirrels at night, the kind of people that make you want to cross the street when you see them coming, but I still dig it better than I do the daytime. If I got to pick me a man to stand between me and the animals in this town, I'd just as soon go with Action. Somebody's got to clean up the human garbage and who else is willin' to do it except the cops."

Burt looked at Dave Tiegs. Tiegs was over fifty, a lump of a man with a nose covered in red veins and a thin-lipped mouth twisted far to the right as though in imitation of an old-time movie gangster. His voice was harsh, irritating and fascinating at the same time. Burt wondered what had happened to make Tiegs' vocal cords produce a sound like that. He also wondered if Tiegs was the one who was spying on him for Monmouth. Tiegs did his job well; he collected information and passed it on to Burt, a service he could easily do for Harold Monmouth.

"Monmouth still bitching?" asked Tiegs as he and Burt walked toward Park Avenue.

"Yeah."

Tiegs shook his head. "Man's hard to please. The column's good. Getting better. Tougher, tighter. You're doing an ace job."

Burt smiled. *An ace job.* Love those oldiest but goodies. "You and my mother think so. Monmouth has his own opinion."

Burt and Tiegs separated to let a teen-age girl and a Great Dane walk between them. Tiegs said, "Jesus, ain't nobody ever gonna be Walter Winchell no more. Monmouth oughta be happy with what he's got."

"You ever meet Winchell?"

"Shit, yeah. He was the biggest this business ever saw. He invented the gossip column back in the thirties. First man to do three dot stuff. You know, three dots between every item, that kind of shit. You would not believe how big Winchell and his gossip column was in this town.

"Winchell was the first guy I ever sent stuff to," Dave continued. "He had to have it first and it had to be typed neatly. You sent him sloppy copy and he threw it away without even reading it. You sent him an item that bounced, somethin' that turned out to be wrong, you were dead. I mean dead. He wouldn't go near your stuff for a long time and in those days, Winchell was just about the only game in town for a press agent. Without him, you might as well be livin' in Iowa and writing on bathroom walls. Some people he helped, some he hurt."

Burt said, "Anybody ever hurt him?"

"Couple people tried. But he knew where all the bodies was buried. He knew cops, J. Edgar Hoover, senators, hookers, he knew everybody. The man was a superstar. He'd cut your throat if he had to, but with all the clout he had, not many people could get to him. One guy kinda got to him, you might say. Winchell once printed somethin' the guy didn't like and the guy breaks into Winchell's dentist's office and steals Winchell's plates."

Burt laughed. "Wonder if D'Arcy has false teeth."

"He's got sharp teeth, tell you that much. You headin' back to write this up?" Dave Tiegs knew how important the D'Arcy story was.

Burt nodded. "It's tomorrow's lead."

"Thought it might be."

The two men stopped on the corner for a red light. Traffic was heavy and the smell of gas fumes was everywhere.

Burt said, "You sure about Jackson?"

Dave Tiegs spat on the sidewalk before answering. "Man's too big to lie. He don't have to be nice to nobody. He's straight. Never hung me up before. Besides, if you go down with this one, so do I. I'm the guy that fed you the information, remember? I'll be hurtin' if it bounces."

Burt smiled at Dave. "Check with me before you make your rounds tonight. If you've got something strong, I'll use it tomorrow along with this. You ever talk to Monmouth at all?"

Tiegs wrinkled his nose as though smelling something bad. "What for? He ain't writin' the column, you are. Besides, he don't like me that much."

"Why doesn't he like you?"

"Hey, don't get me wrong. He ain't come out and say he don't like me but you can tell these things, you know?

He's an Englishman, a real proper guy with fingerbowls on his table and clean underwear every day of the week. I get the feeling he thinks I pick my nose and lick my fingers afterwards. Him and me we talk a couple times before he hired me to work for you, but that's been about it. I go down to the paper once a week to pick up my check, since I don't trust the mail. Ain't seen him once in the two months I been working for you."

Burt forced another smile. "I guess you two wouldn't have much to talk about."

Dave Tiegs shrugged and looked across Park Avenue. "See that hotel over there?" He pointed and Burt nodded. "A hooker's working a convention that came in yesterday, except she ain't a hooker. It's a he, a transvestite who's tryin' to earn money for a sex-change operation. Wonder what all them dentists would say if they really knew who they were drilling?"

Burt laughed and as he and Dave Tiegs shook hands in farewell, the raspy-voiced man said, "Guess the moral of the story is you got to know who you're screwing."

"Or who's screwing you."

"Yeah, that too. Check you out later."

In the cab taking him back to his West End apartment, Burt wondered if Dave Tiegs had been trying to tell him something. *You got to know who you're screwing.*

All Burt could do was wait and find out.

At noon the next day, Burt sat alone in his kitchen drinking herb tea when the telephone rang, Burt knew who it was and he took his time answering it.

"Hello, Burt. Burt?"

"Speaking."

"Monmouth here. Just wanted you to know how pleased I am with today's column. Extremely pleased.

"That's the sort of thing I've been expecting from you all along. I knew you could do it, I knew it." Monmouth sounded exuberant. Burt could imagine the little Englishman's eyes gleaming like polished glass. A thought to make

Burt sleep easier at night. But only for a short time. Monmouth never stopped wanting.

Monmouth said, "Of course you realize D'Arcy won't like this and he'll come after you. One way or another, he'll come after you."

"The thought has crossed my mind."

Burt scratched his crotch and yawned. He'd gotten up early this morning to grab a copy of the *Examiner-World* and read today's column. Maybe he could take a short nap before his secretary got there. Molly was due at one. She would turn on the phones and take messages from the service and type them for Burt to read.

Somehow Burt wasn't as happy as he had expected to be when Monmouth called. Everything he had done in the past twenty-four hours had been to please the man he worked for, not himself. Going after D'Arcy wasn't something Burt would have done ordinarily. D'Arcy's columns had been pulled, not printed. The man hadn't been proved inaccurate.

"Oh, by the way," said Monmouth cheerily, "did you see the front page?"

"No. Haven't been up that long," Burt lied. "Glanced at the column and was sipping some tea." He wondered if Monica had read the column. She was supposed to call him this afternoon about getting the two of them into a screening of Francis Ford Coppola's new movie that Coppola himself was hosting.

"Check the front page," said Monmouth. "Daresay your story had some small hand in that. Well, must run. Again, well done. I'm much pleased." He hung up without waiting for Burt's reply.

Burt stared at the receiver in his hand. "Glad you're glad. Call again."

Back in the kitchen he turned on the radio, fiddled with the dial until he found an all-news station, then reached for the newspaper. Let's hear it for Action Jackson and Dave Tiegs, who talked straight and gave Burt the kind of story that was going to keep him in new jeans and sneakers for a while. Dave couldn't be making telephone calls to Monmouth behind Burt's back. Christ, today was no day to be paranoid. Today was a day for dancing in the streets and worshiping the sun and rolling around on Monica's shiny silk sheets.

Maybe Monmouth was getting his information from Burt's secretary Molly, a quiet Irish girl, with a thin, pale face, blood-red hair and a bored voice that seemed to keep most people who telephoned Burt at an arm's distance. Molly was lean as a broom handle, plain looking with braces on most of her teeth and she worked faster than anyone Burt had ever seen. No matter what he gave her to do, it was done with incredible speed, letter perfect and not so much as a comma out of place.

Molly had no interest in anything except work and Catholicism. Occasionally she'd take home a record album for her sister's children, but other than that, Molly showed no extreme signs of life. Burt wondered if she got her kicks by spying on him for Monmouth.

Front page, front page. Ah, yes. Right where it should be. Up front. Monmouth had said something about Burt having a hand in . . .

It was at the bottom, far right, with a small photograph, a Hollywood dateline and the story was credited to a wire service. Earlier, Burt, anxious to see his own column, had turned the page in a hurry and, consequently, he had missed the story on Terry Earle.

She was in intensive care in a Los Angeles hospital, having tried to kill herself with a massive overdose of sleeping pills. A secretary had found her on the bathroom floor and immediately called an ambulance. The story quoted her manager Calvin Amos as saying Terry had been extremely depressed ever since the story about the death of that girl in New York had gotten out. The story, which had first appeared in a New York gossip column, had also been picked up by other columnists, magazines, weekly scandal sheets, all of which combined to keep the story alive for the past ten days. Calvin Amos never mentioned the word lesbian. He didn't have to. Burt had done it for him.

162

The story also contained a quote from a hospital spokesman who said Terry Earle's chance of surviving her suicide attempt was fifty-fifty. Touch and go all the way for the gifted and unstable comedienne.

*Daresay your story had some small hand in that.*

Sick to his stomach, Burt threw the newspaper against the kitchen wall and hung his head. On the radio the announcer began reading the same story, adding only that Terry Earle's condition was guarded and she was being attended twenty-four hours around the clock. The announcer was reading a brief history of Terry Earle's career when Burt got up from the table and still in his shorts, walked barefoot into the living room and found a half bottle of Scotch. Drinking directly from the bottle, Burt felt the warmth explode in his stomach, and because the announcer's voice seemed to get louder and louder, Burt drank some more.

Later he vaguely remembered crying, though he wasn't sure he had. And if he had cried, was it for Terry Earle or for himself? He did remember making his way to his desk, the bottle of Scotch still in his hand and he was probably drunk when he sat down to write a letter to Terry Earle telling her he was sorry for what he had done to her. But he never finished the letter. He stopped to drink some more and stare at the sign on his desk, a quote from Theodore Roosevelt: *God save you from the werewolf and your heart's desire.*

A drunken Burt passed out at his desk and dreamed a frightening dream of being torn apart by a huge werewolf as Terry Earle and Harold Monmouth held hands and laughed.

# ■ ■ ■ Thirteen

## New York City

**Killing the German shepherd had been the turning** point; it had brought about the full flowering of Gypsy's obsession to learn everything about Senator Banner's plans for the famous woman and her mysterious lover. Emptying the silenced .22 into the dog was Gypsy's admission fee; he figured it entitled him to know all the details of this operation and one way or another he was going to learn them. As for the dead dog, Gypsy had loaded it into his car and on the way back from Maryland had dumped it in New Jersey. The gray-haired wiretapper now shuddered as he recalled lifting the still warm and bleeding body of the German shepherd from the trunk of the car and throwing it into a rain-filled ditch.

At the moment he was watching Agnes who sat across from him at a small table in her kitchen, her eyes closed as she listened for the second time to a telephone conversation he had taped a few hours ago. Gypsy was eating chocolate cupcakes and drinking from an opened can of pineapple slices, swallowing the thick, sweet syrup in large gulps. But now he waited, can poised before his mouth. The section of the tape he wanted Agnes to pay particular attention to was coming up. As the voices of the man and woman came from the small recorder, Gypsy held his breath.

A few seconds later he said, "Well?"

Agnes opened her eyes. " 'G.' She is saying 'G.' Without a copy of the Maryland tape it's impossible to compare her two conversations. But I'm sure she said 'G.' "

Gypsy turned off the recorder. "It's the same woman, take my word for it. Down in Maryland when I heard her voice I thought she said 'B.' 'I love you, Bill,' she said. But I'm thinking maybe I heard wrong. Static electricity and the dog barking screwed up my reception. Simon's got the only copy of the Maryland tape."

Gypsy slammed the table with the palm of his hand. "That's got to be it. I just heard wrong. All this time I'm thinking the man's name begins with a B and it really begins with a G."

He watched Agnes leave the table and walk to the oven where she was broiling two steaks for him. After turning over both steaks, she wiped her hands on a large, damp sponge and left the kitchen. Seconds later she returned with a newspaper folded to a gossip column and without a word she handed the newspaper to him. Gypsy, whose reading was limited to sports pages or an occasional pornographic novel, eyed the newspaper then looked at Agnes as she opened the refrigerator.

Gypsy snorted. "So?"

"So read it." Agnes looked into the refrigerator.

Eyes on the gossip column, Gypsy reached for the opened can of pineapple and suddenly he was reading faster and his grip tightened around the can. Unaware the can had begun to bend, he finished reading then looked up to see a smiling Agnes holding a plate of steaming, over-cooked steak in each hand. As she set the steaks in front of him, Gypsy snatched both of her hands, kissed the palms and squeezed her hands in his. His eyes were bright with excitement.

"Yes, indeed," he murmured. "Oh, yes, indeed."

He read the column once more, not hurrying this time and nodding his head over and over. It was here in his hand, in black and white and all he had to do was read it.

Agnes sat down. "Now read the front page."

Gypsy unfolded the newspaper, thumbing the corners until he found it. The headlines told the story. The vice-president had declared himself for the presidency and the story beneath the headlines said he had his party's nomination all but sewn up. A smiling Gypsy closed his eyes, letting his head flop back on his shoulders. Of course. Suddenly all of the pieces of Senator Aaron Paul Banner's puzzle were fitting into place, all of the pieces except one. A very important one.

Agnes used the back of a teaspoon to spread melting butter over Gypsy's steaks. "It was all over the news tonight," she said. "It was the lead story on every channel. Everybody seems to feel it will be him or Banner as our next President. All the polls give the vice-president a slight edge over Banner."

Gypsy bounced the heel of his hand off his forehead. Schmuck. Senator Banner had known the vice-president was going to be his opponent and he had made plans to handle this situation in his own special way. Banner was two jumps ahead of everybody, which was why his aide Neil Knightly—"Simon"—had hired Gypsy. Banner knew that his party's presidential nomination was his any time he wanted it and that the vice-president was the one man who might beat him in the November election. More important than either of these two facts was Banner's having somehow learned that the vice-president's wife was having an affair, an affair that could ruin her husband's political career and give America its biggest scandal since Watergate.

Laying the paper aside and ignoring the steaks, Gypsy frowned and began chewing a corner of his mouth. Twelve hours ago he had walked up five flights of stairs to avoid meeting anyone in the luxury apartment building on East 72nd Street. It was the second time Simon had ordered him to bug that duplex, a twelve-room apartment belonging to a couple named Parton who traveled a great deal and allowed friends to use the place while they were away. This is where Gypsy had heard the one-word conversation "Now."

Again Gypsy had bugged three telephones as instructed, in addition to placing a bug under the bed in each of two bedrooms. In a large living room, he had placed a bug inside of the television set as well as one behind a large painting of a horse that hung over the fireplace. With a little luck Gypsy could pick up the missing piece of the puzzle—the name of the woman's lover.

Later, as Gypsy sat in his car and listened, a man inside the apartment dialed the phone.

"Yes?" The woman who answered at the other end was anxious. Gypsy noticed she had picked up the phone on the first ring.

"Sorry I couldn't call earlier," said the man. "I haven't had a free moment all day. So much is going on and it's all bad, I'm afraid."

"If the bad news has to do with us, I don't want to hear it."

"It has nothing to do with us. Rolland's condition is worse. He's in the hospital and they're bringing in a heart specialist from Cleveland to take a look at him. It looks like I'll have to fly to Israel in his place."

"Damn," said the woman. "So I'm not going to see you tonight."

"No." The man sounded exhausted. "The trouble in Africa is coming to a boil, too. Another problem that just won't go away. We're trying to work out something with the UN, some sort of peace-keeping force, perhaps, but as usual it's a question of money and who'll be in

**167**

charge. The President wants me to go over there but he prefers an invitation first, an invitation from both sides, from whites and blacks. Meanwhile whites ambushed and killed a dozen blacks there this morning and we're still waiting to hear if the dead blacks were really terrorists as the whites claim or just civilians who happened to be in the wrong place at the wrong time."

"You'll end up in Africa again," she said. "Why does it always have to be you?"

"Because I'm the best."

"Who's in the apartment with you?"

The man chuckled. "You don't miss much do you. I told you, I'm trying to sound out a few people on their willingness to go for a peace-keeping force for our little African troublespot. You're hearing UN delegates from seven different countries and at the moment they're eating a couple hundred dollars of very expensive delicatessen food that I have to pay for."

"I bought a new dress today," said the woman. "It was especially for you. I had planned to wear it when we went dancing."

"Save it," the man said. "I'll get to see you in it."

"You should see me when I'm not wearing it." She giggled.

"I think about that often enough."

Silence. Then the woman said, "You're starting something you won't be able to finish. I'm ready to jump into a cab right now and drive over there."

"Just a minute," the man said. He sounded impatient and the sound level went down, meaning he had just covered the receiver with his hand. When the sound returned, he was talking to a third party. "Yes, yes, I know what he wants but he always begins by asking for more than he'll eventually settle for. Let me finish talking here, then I'll come inside with you and we'll talk to him." A door opened and several voices could be heard in the background until the door closed.

The man said to the woman, "I can't talk to you now.

All hell is breaking loose in the next room and I've got to go in there before they start throwing food at each other. At the moment it's going to be tough to even see you tomorrow. I've got meetings here in town and I'm sure I'll have to fly down to Washington for a briefing with Rolland at the hospital before I leave for Israel and Rome. The President's due to call here any second. If there was a way I could see you before—"

"Find a way." The woman was definite about it. Gypsy could almost see her stomping her foot for emphasis. Her voice was a whisper. "I love you and I have to see you, that's all there is to it."

"Only ten blocks between us and it might as well be ten thousand miles." The man sighed. Then he said, "Wait a minute. You said you bought a dress."

"The most expensive thing I've bought in three years. I've been back twice to have it fitted correctly. The designer's anxious to have me seen in it, but he's so nervous working around me he almost swallowed a mouthful of pins."

"That's it," said the man. "The dress. That's your excuse for getting out tomorrow. You'll have to set up an appointment with your designer and let everybody know you're going there but you're actually going somewhere else."

"Where?"

"Where do you think? I'll explain. Tomorrow I might have some time between the morning UN session and when I leave for Washington in the afternoon. If you can manage to cut yourself loose from the secret service—how many do you have?"

"Two," said the woman. "It won't be easy but I've done it before. By now they expect something like that from me and they won't be surprised. They won't like it because it makes them look stupid, but they won't be surprised."

"Listen carefully. Let them escort you to the designer's showroom—"

"He works out of his penthouse on East 68th Street, just around the corner from you."

"Good. Once you're there, there's one place you'll be alone and that's in the changing room. Then you'll have to sneak out without anyone seeing you and I'll be waiting out front in a taxi. No limousine."

"Oh 'G', it sounds great. I know it'll work, I know it will."

"One more thing," said the man. "Cover your face when you get in the cab and keep it covered. Dark glasses, scarf, ski mask, anything but keep it covered. I'll call you from the UN and that'll be your signal to leave for your appointment with the designer. Make it for, let's say, one thirty and plan to stay there for at least half an hour. At precisely two o'clock, find a way to get out without the secret service knowing. I'll wait exactly ten minutes, no more. If you're not there by two-ten I'll know you're not coming. I just hope nothing comes up to stop us from getting together."

"It won't, it won't. Oh, I'm so excited."

"We'll come back here," said the man. "There's always a doorman downstairs but we'll get around that. I'll send him out to the cab to pick up a package or something while you're sneaking in."

"It sounds perfect," she said. She was cheerful, pleased at getting her way.

"Wish I could settle all my problems this easily," the man said. "I've got to go." Gypsy thought the man sounded cool, controlled and very, very confident.

"You do that," the woman said, "but save some of that energy for tomorrow afternoon. And 'G'—?"

"Yes?"

"Don't let anything spoil tomorrow for us, okay?"

"I'll do the best I can. Don't I usually?"

"No complaints on that score. Tomorrow."

"Tomorrow." There was a click as each hung up.

And my bugs are already in place, thought Gypsy as he rubbed his hands together. Tomorrow. Immediately

170

his car radio was filled with a torrent of voices from the living room bugs. Turning the sound down, he leaned back in the front seat and narrowed his eyes. His orders were to monitor the tap until 11:30 tonight but after that, he was going to see Agnes because he needed her precise ear. Tonight he had heard the woman say G, not B.

# ■ ■ ■ Fourteen

**D'Arcy uncapped a quart bottle of Perrier water,** dropped two aspirins into the fizzing liquid and held the bottle up to the kitchen light to watch the aspirins dissolve. Setting the bottle in the kitchen sink, he uncapped a second bottle and again dropped aspirin in it. Then with a bottle in each hand he walked from the kitchen into his large living room where he poured the Perrier water and melted aspirins on his plants. Every third week. D'Arcy watered all of his plants with this combination of room temperature Perrier water and the strongest aspirins he could buy. He believed it gave his plants health and long life, helping them to produce oxygen and purify the air around him. When he had finished, D'Arcy filled a small bowl with lukewarm water, taking it and a box of tissues back to the living room where he spent a half-hour carefully dusting leaves on his plants and planning his next attack on Richie Sweet and the Augustino Bonnetti family.

Johnnie had told D'Arcy about the episode in the elevator at the illegal gambling casino. Someone had to pay for that and Richie Sweet, along with his odious collection of thugs and hoodlums, was elected. D'Arcy's pain was going to become a public airing of one of the Bonnetti family's little secrets. Richie sows, Richie reaps and weeps. On the mantelpiece over the fireplace, an enamel and gold Louis XIV clock chimed the hour in delicate, harplike tones. It was almost 9:30 at night and D'Arcy was staying home to write several exact and powerful paragraphs meant to be annoying if not damaging to Mr. A. Bonnetti.

Dear Johnnie, she was so lovely and bewitching that D'Arcy could not consider life without her. He needed her as Baudelaire said all lovers needed each other. Love, said that doomed poet, was irritating because it was a crime requiring an accomplice. D'Arcy's love for Johnnie was a crime against himself but he could not stop nor did he choose to. His honesty gave him only the strength to admit what he was doing, not the strength to do anything about it.

When he had finished tending to his plants, D'Arcy selected a recording of songs written by King Henry the Eighth, placed it on the stereo, then opened a bottle of champagne. At his typewriter, D'Arcy, in a black-and-white-striped dressing gown, drank champagne and filed his nails and when he had finished two glasses, he was ready to write. He wrote for the next hour, intensely, with total concentration on what he wanted to say and when he had finished, he was physically exhausted from the effort. Sipping more champagne, he read what he had written, smiling and nodding in approval.

"You've done well, dear boy," he said of himself. "Damn well."

After reading Robin Ian D'Arcy's column, Carmine DiNaldi removed his thick, pink-tinted glasses, then used the fingertips of both hands to rub his tired eyes. His eyes weren't strong anymore and he needed more rest with each passing year. A man definitely paid a tax for the use of the body God gave him. Disease was tax and so was old age and death. The *consigliere,* who sat alone in the small office in back of his Mulberry Street bakery, reached for a small cup of espresso coffee sitting on the edge of his desk. He took two sips of the bitter, unsweetened coffee then placed the cup and saucer back on the desk. The cup was his favorite, given to him forty years ago by his wife on their wedding day. He never allowed anyone else to touch it, use it or even wash it. The *consigliere* did all of that himself.

D'Arcy had attacked the family again in his gossip column, something he usually did when Richie came near that young girl Johnnie, the one who lived her life as an animal in heat. But Richie had been ordered to leave her alone. Had he disobeyed?

The *consigliere* believed that disobedience to the brotherhood was never to be tolerated, for it was a risk to everyone. Disobedience was to be handled firmly, immediately. Only those men who did exactly as they were told were of any use to the brotherhood. Carmine DiNaldi had always obeyed and that was how he had come to grow in power and influence. Now he too demanded obedience and loyalty, but he had also come to learn that changing times meant changing ways. The modern young men of the seventies were independent, not as quick to obey as their fathers and grandfathers had been. Today's young man too often thought for himself, cared only for himself. He would question a decision by the old ones as easily as he would let his hair grow long. Carmine DiNaldi preferred the old ways, the old days, when no questions were asked and an order was accepted as law. That's why a few years ago he had been one of the first important men in the brotherhood to send to Italy for *greenies,* greenhorns, those tough youth from the harsh south, from Sicily, where there was nothing to look forward to but soul-destroying poverty and an early death.

The *greenies* obeyed because they did not want to go back to Sicily where the land was heated by a merciless

**174**

sun and a man was old and dried up at thirty. In America, a *greenie* was completely dependent on those who brought him over from the old country. He had not been brought up in the free and easy American style, with its lack of discipline and hard training. From a precarious existence in a dirt-poor Sicilian village to employment by the brotherhood in New York was the chance of a lifetime and a *greenie* would kill for it. Those brought over by the brotherhood would sometimes have to kill.

Carmine DiNaldi smuggled his *greenies* into America through Canada. They would jump ship in Toronto and be met by someone who would then bring them across the border into the United States. In America they would be put to work in restaurants, dry cleaners, pizza parlors and construction companies owned by the family. All of these illegal aliens were thrifty and saved their money with a miserliness that was almost comical. Some had wives and fiancées back in the old country and would quickly seek the don's permission to bring them over. Those aliens who didn't move up into the family as soldiers remained hard and willing workers in legitimate family businesses.

A few days ago Richie had driven up to Toronto to bring back three men coming in on a freighter sailing out of Morocco. Had Richie been in New York this morning, the *consigliere* would have asked him about three paragraphs in D'Arcy's column, paragraphs on the smuggling of illegal aliens and its relation to a narcotics bust made in Montreal six months ago.

D'Arcy had written of the arrest of an illegal alien, an Italian restaurant worker living in Montreal for three years and married to a Canadian woman. The Italian who had originally jumped ship had also managed to bring over six relatives illegally, four of whom were still in Canada, two of whom were in New York. The restaurant worker had been arrested on a tip received by Canadian immigration authorities. To avoid deportation and separation from his wife and children, the Italian had told authorities that he and his relatives dealt in small amounts

175

of narcotics from time to time, which they shipped to New York for sale. In New York they were in contact with other illegals to form a petty narcotics operation. The worker was willing to betray his narcotics ring if immigration would not send him back to Sicily. American federal drug enforcement soon became interested in the case and the trail they followed led to Italian illegals suspected of having been smuggled into America by Carmine DiNaldi and the Bonnetti family.

The sudden and suspicious disappearance of two Italian illegals connected with Bonnetti, wrote D'Arcy, had meant an end to the case. But the investigation had brought Canadian police and federal law too close to the Bonnetti family. Carmine DiNaldi correctly guessed that D'Arcy's source for this story was probably a contact at Drug Enforcement Administration. The columnist had finished by writing that the Bonnetti family continued to smuggle in illegal aliens for use in both its legitimate and illegitimate enterprises. Such a practice, said D'Arcy, increased the criminal population at a time when no such increase was needed. He wondered why American immigration officials had not paid regular visits to the Bonnetti family businesses. He also wondered if New York's congressmen could not be tougher in enforcing immigration laws in an already overpopulated city.

Carmine DiNaldi twisted a piece of lemon peel over his steaming cup of espresso. When Richie returned to New York tonight with the *greenies,* the *consigliere* would ask him about this story in the Englishman's gossip column. Meanwhile, Carmine DiNaldi would sit quietly and sip espresso from the little cup his wife had given him on their wedding day and think of what he himself would say to Don Bonnetti about what D'Arcy had written.

### ■ ■ ■ Fifteen

Shortly before eight a.m., Burt Anthony stepped from the elevator in the Hay-Adams Hotel and yawned as he walked across the empty lobby. At the front desk he handed his room key to the clerk, who bowed and smiled as though he had just been presented with an award. The bowing and smiling were in keeping with the hotel's standing as one of Washington, D.C.'s best, known for its fine service, good taste and eighteenth-century furniture. The city's movers and shakers ate in the hotel's dining room, surrounded by wood paneling which had been lovingly waxed and hand rubbed. Burt looked at his watch. Two minutes to eight. Forget breakfast. By eight he was supposed to be in front of the Jefferson Memorial at the Tidal Basin for a meeting with Hoyt Pathy, whose telephone call ten minutes ago had yanked Burt from a sound sleep. Pathy claimed to be sitting on a story that would end up as a front-page headline.

The phone call hadn't awakened Monica, but it had

been enough to get Burt, with just three hours of sleep, out of bed, into his clothes and rushing down the hall toward an elevator. A hastily scrawled note to Monica told her where he was going.

Now he hurried across the hotel lobby, passing a pair of congressmen deep in conversation and on their way to the dining room for a breakfast meeting, a widespread custom in Washington. As he ran Burt patted his pockets to make sure he had his wallet, notebook and two ballpoint pens. On the sidewalk, he yawned again as he waited for the doorman to get him a taxi. Directly across from the eight-story hotel was Lafayette Park, quiet and empty at this hour of the day. Walk through it and you were at the White House, where Burt knew another breakfast meeting was taking place, this one between the President, vice-president and Gil van Lier, who had suddenly become the most talked-about man in America. The handsome black diplomat was the reason Burt and Monica had come to Washington. Yesterday they had arrived in town, along with scores of other reporters, for a press conference hosted by Vice-President Richard Zachery, who had introduced Gil van Lier as acting secretary of state, the temporary replacement for Secretary of State Jerome Rolland now hospitalized with heart trouble.

Van Lier had suddenly been recalled from Chindé in Africa, where he had been trying to arrange a peaceful transfer of power from the white minority to the black majority without excessive bloodshed. Black guerrillas and whites had clashed and only van Lier's negotiating had kept the fighting from getting worse. Burt didn't have to be a diplomat to know that if the conflict between whites and blacks in Chindé escalated, it could draw the participation of other nations and Chindé's problems might never be solved. Though small, the African country was rich in diamonds, coffee, oil, uranium and was strategically located in regard to larger African countries. If van Lier were successful in securing a nonviolent takeover by the black majority, he would be scoring a coup for the United

**178**

States while eliminating another potential African trouble-spot.

In the taxi Burt flopped back against the seat. Gossip, rumor or hard news. What did Hoyt Pathy have to offer at eight in the morning? Pathy, a good source, was once nationally known in the civil rights and peace movements, and now, at thirty-three, was a special assistant to a Colorado senator. Today Pathy was very much a part of the establishment he had once opposed. Before he had come to Washington, Pathy wouldn't have cared who saw him talking to Burt or other reporters. In those days Pathy craved media exposure, promoting himself with the aggressiveness of a Hollywood starlet on the make. Today Pathy, married with children, was a team player who didn't make waves. As part of the power structure he now had something to lose and didn't want to lose it. Pathy had always wanted power, thought Burt. He had chased it all his life and now had it, which meant Pathy had become somebody Burt would have to watch carefully. And trust less. Pathy, former radical and revolutionary, still used the press. But now he didn't want to be caught at it.

The Jefferson Memorial was on the south shore of the Tidal Basin, just minutes from the hotel. After paying the cab driver, Burt stood on the sidewalk and stared at the cherry trees lining the Tidal Basin which were now in full bloom. He heard his name being called, and turned to see Hoyt Pathy behind the wheel of a tan Buick with Virginia license plates, face half hidden by dark glasses. Walking over to the car, Burt opened the door on the passenger side. There were two large manila envelopes on the seat and he had to move them before he could sit. As Burt slammed the car door, Hoyt Pathy quickly pulled away from the curb and sped past parked tourist buses, his face knotted with worry.

"Was it something I said?" asked Burt jokingly. Pathy hadn't bothered to say good morning.

Hoyt Pathy continued to drive in silence, turning down 12th Street and going two blocks before stopping for a red

**179**

light. When the traffic light turned green, he slid his foot off the brake reluctantly and shook his head sadly. Something was bothering him and Burt had the impression Pathy was debating whether to talk about it.

Pathy was slim, with a nose too small for his round face and he now combed his hair sideways to hide a bald spot. Burt noticed he had put on weight; flesh was starting to hang beneath Pathy's jaw and a small paunch was pushing its way over his belt. He wore a suit and tie, something Burt hadn't seen Pathy wear even to the funerals of murdered civil rights' workers. There were lines around Pathy's eyes and mouth and he looked like a man aging faster than he should. It was Burt's guess that Hoyt Pathy had gotten what he wanted out of life but it was costing him more than he had ever thought it would.

"Heard you were in town to watch van Lier shinny up the greasy pole of success," Pathy said. He spat out of the car window.

"Isn't everybody? You don't sound happy about it. I thought van Lier was the fair-haired boy in this town? The miracle worker. Gil van Lucky and Super Spade and all that."

Hoyt Pathy reached up to adjust the rear-view mirror and for a few seconds, Burt wondered if Pathy was checking to see if he were being followed. "Van Lier's a prick," said Pathy. "What did you really come down here for?"

"The press conference," said Burt. "For the time being, the country has the first black secretary of state in its history. That's news to a few people. What did you think I was down here for?" He watched Pathy carefully.

Again Pathy drove silently, turning left on 12th Street and onto Pennsylvania Avenue. When he was within sight of the White House, he pulled over to the curb, turned off the ignition and leaned back in his seat, eyes on the White House.

"Are you being straight with me?" he asked. "You really just came down here for the press conference and nothing else?"

"What else is there? You called me, remember? Something tells me it concerns van Lier. Right now I don't think you can knock the man. He's capable, confident as hell and he's got the respect of top people in Europe, Asia, South America and Africa. They say he's the one man in the entire State Department who can hold American foreign policy together until Rolland gets back on his feet."

"Rolland's dying," said Pathy. "He's finished."

"Is that gossip or hard news?"

"It'll be gossip if *you* print it. But I'm telling you it's true and you never heard it from me. Everybody knows Rolland's a dead man but the President's not about to come out and say so. If he did, some delicate negotiations might just collapse. So the President lies and pretends that Rolland's going to pull through and meanwhile van Lier minds the store until the President can think of something."

Burt shifted until he was facing Pathy, who continued staring at the White House. "Sounds as if you don't like van Lier," said Burt. "Give the man credit, he's keeping the lid on Chindé. If it wasn't for him a lot of people, black and white, would be dead. From where I sit van Lier's the only chance for peace that country has."

Hoyt Pathy lit a cigarette, then took it from his mouth and stared at it. "I've quit these damn things three times this year. You think van Lier's bringing peace to Chindé? Two days ago a plane landed at an Air Force base in New Jersey. There were twelve dead bodies on that plane and the official story is they died when a 707 crashed in Africa while carrying medical supplies to a village hit by a flash flood. When I say official story I mean that's the story given to wives, families, relatives. There's been no story released to the press and I doubt if there ever will be. Twelve dead GIs."

Pathy looked at Burt. "They didn't die in any plane crash. They died fighting in Chindé as mercenaries with the permission, encouragement and knowledge of the American government. Van Lier, the great peacemaker, knows all about it. He's in on it."

Burt said softly, "Do you know what you're saying?"

"I'm saying America is heading for another Vietnam. I'm saying if Russia or Cuba knew about this, they'd have troops in Chindé before the sun went down and then you would really have one hell of a fucking mess. Christ, even the Chinese would send people there. I'm telling you that American troops are fighting in Africa with the knowledge and connivance of the American government. God, talk about *déjà vu*."

He blew smoke toward the White House. "And van Lier sits over there with the President and Zachery and everybody thinks he's the greatest thing since sliced bread. He's like everybody else. A hypocrite."

Burt touched the manila envelope sitting on his lap. "What's in these envelopes?"

Again, Pathy spat a tobacco strand through the car window. "Courtesy of a civilian pilot involved in this shitty Chindé business. He was hired by a certain agency of the United States government to fly a 707 out of Puerto Rico by way of the Canary Islands then on to Chindé. Carried the GIs, their supplies and he also took a few photographs and kept notes. Sort of a half-assed diary. If you're wondering how I got my hands on this stuff, it was brought to Kinsolving by the pilot who thought we could help him get paid. The pilot also thought he could get a few bucks for an arm he lost. That certain agency welched on both the pilot's fee and helping him with medical expenses."

Burt turned the envelopes over in his hand. Foster Kinsolving was the Colorado senator that Pathy worked for, a slow-talking giant of a man with a talent for attaching himself to issues minutes before they became popular. He rarely took chances, yet somehow had emerged as a courageous congressman from the West, a man untainted by politics. Senator Kinsolving had carefully nurtured his image as an independent and a representative of the common man, but Burt thought him more expert at enlightened self-interest than at serving the public. Senator

Kinsolving and Hoyt Pathy hadn't found each other by accident.

"Hoyt, you're telling me van Lier's pushing peace and at the same time sending American troops into Africa to kill?"

"That's exactly what I'm telling you."

Burt shook his head. "Can't be. It doesn't make sense."

Pathy lit another cigarette and inhaled deeply. "Doesn't it? You've heard the rationale before. Kill enough people and sooner or later you run out of people to kill and then you have peace. Pressure one side, back them into a corner and make them accept your terms. Vietnam started that way. A few American so-called advisers to fire some shots at the bad guys and the war would be over in twenty minutes. Took a little longer, didn't it. Took sixty thousand dead GIs and we still lost."

"*Déjà vu,* you said."

Pathy nodded. "I get the shakes thinking about it. And yesterday when I saw van Lier with that Ronald Romance smile of his that gives every female reporter in this town wet pants, Jesus, I just went fucking bananas."

Burt chuckled. "Didn't you once tell me 'black is beautiful'?"

"It was," said Hoyt Pathy. "Then."

Burt saw Pathy's eyes glaze over as though seeing the past and a better time. "Sounds like you're disillusioned."

"Hang in there. Your turn will come."

Burt's smile was quick, automatic and more a reflex than anything.

Hoyt Pathy looked at him. "You were a damn good reporter once and now you're writing about discotheques, Hollywood cocaine parties, lesbian comediennes and congressmen who fuck their secretaries on top of the desk during lunch-hour. Yeah, I know what you think of me. It's in your face. I didn't sell out, Burt. I grew up and there's a difference. On the outside I had nothing: no power, no influence, no position. I'm on the inside now and I get more done with one phone call than I could by marching in the street for years, not to mention I haven't had my skull bent by a cop's club in years. Fact is, when I say to the cops in this town 'squat and shit,' they squat, they shit and I like it, pal. I like it."

I know you do, thought Burt. "I wasn't putting you down, Hoyt," he lied. "I was wondering why you wanted to make trouble for van Lier. Especially now."

Pathy sighed, removed his dark glasses and rubbed his eyes. The lines around them were deeper than Burt had first noticed and there were even deeper lines between his eyebrows. The man obviously did a lot of frowning. "Pollution gets worse this time of year," said Pathy. "Damn tourists with their cars, buses. The exhaust fumes will kill you, I'm telling you."

He looked at Burt. "Old habits are hard to break," he said. "Once a do-gooder, always a do-gooder. Every now and then I get an itch, something makes me want to go after the big guys, after the establishment. Call it one of my few acts of unadulterated purity. Call it a longing for the good old days of *us* versus *them*. Call it whatever the fuck you want. You've got a story, unless you're less of a reporter and only a gossip-mongerer these days. Washington's the gossip capital of the world, they tell me."

Burt eyed the envelopes on his lap. Pathy tapped the manila envelope with his dark glasses. "Open them."

Burt did. And flinched. The first envelope contained eight by ten black and white photographs, enlarged and grainy and definitely not the work of a professional. But they were clear enough. Too clear. The top one showed a young white man lying on his back in a dirt road. He wore battle fatigues, a short military haircut and there was a bullet hole in his forehead the size of an egg. His jaw and neck were black with large flies. Burt closed his eyes and turned his head to the side.

"Are they all like this?" he asked.

"Most are. There's one or two of the plane and a couple of the guys when they were alive. But you've got more dead men in your hands than you have live ones."

Burt quickly shuffled through the photographs. Pathy

was right. At least seven of the photographs featured dead men in grotesque positions, bodies partially mutilated and disfigured by gunfire, rockets or mortar shells; the men lay in poses made possible only by the total absence of life in their flesh.

Burt looked at Pathy. "These could be Europeans, even Latins, especially the black ones. There are no names, dogtags, nothing to identify them as American GIs."

"True," said Pathy. "But when you publish these photographs, the American relatives and survivors will take it from there. They'll know, pal. They will definitely know."

"You claim these deaths were explained away by saying the men had died in a plane crash. You don't need twenty/twenty vision to see the bullet holes or a foot blown off or this stomach open and the intestines hanging out. Jesus, whoever took these must be a morbid bastard. How did anybody convince relatives these men died in a plane crash? One look tells you they didn't."

"Ah," said Pathy. "One look, the man says. Except that no one was allowed to look. The bodies were all delivered back to the States and to the relatives in sealed coffins. Now in case somebody did open a coffin, well that little matter was taken care of as well. According to the pilot, and he's got it written in that other envelope there, the order came down to use a flamethrower on the corpses"—

"Jesus—"

—"and make them look as if they had really died in a plane that crashed, then burned and exploded."

"Van Lier ordered that?"

Pathy shrugged. "I don't think so. Sounds like something only a military mind could come up with. But he knows American troops are fighting in Chindé. He has to. Nothing goes on in that country without his knowing about it. The man is willing to kill for peace, which makes him dangerous."

Burt opened the other envelope. It contained the type of notebook used by grade-school children, a small, cheap notebook approximately four by five inches. Burt began reading. The pilot had written of preparations made at the Puerto Rican airbase for the long flight to Africa and described the plane, which wasn't the best and the cargo he would be carrying. The pilot had his misgivings about the mission but apparently he needed the money. He didn't trust the men who had hired him and he was angry because he had been able to obtain only a small advance on his salary, not the large advance he had been counting on. Furthermore, he and all of the men connected with his flight—GIs and ground crew—were segregated on the base, forced to keep themselves in a restricted area surrounded by armed guards day and night. The pilot had not been allowed to telephone his family before takeoff, which seemed to bother him more than anything else.

If the diary were genuine, if the dead men in these photographs were American soldiers, Burt had a story bigger than anything he had ever worked on as a reporter or gossip columnist. The back of his neck turned cold and the excitement of what this might mean to him caused his throat to constrict. There would be more work to do on this story. Everything would have to be checked out and he would begin with Gil van Lier, the man who knew more about Chindé than anyone else. A story like this could begin as gossip or even rumor but it had to end up as hard news. The diary and photographs were only the beginning.

Once this story saw print Congress, the American public and world opinion would all be screaming. Burt felt his adrenaline flow faster and he closed the notebook, making a fist around it, establishing possession. He was a reporter, hungry for the truth and ready to do anything to get it.

He forced himself to be calm. "It needs work. I'll have to talk with the pilot, check him out. Somehow I'll have to come up with the names of the men in these photographs and trace their movements from this country to Africa."

"You could save time," said Pathy, "by getting to van Lier. Show him these pictures and see what he says."

A warning went off in Burt's head and to give himself time to think about it, he looked down at his lap and shuffled the photographs without really seeing any of the dead men. After carefully slipping the photographs and notebook into one envelope, Burt placed it between his thighs on the car seat and looked at Pathy.

"I'll have to come back to you for information, contacts."

Pathy nodded once. "You know where to reach me. Whatever's necessary to help you expose van Lier will be done."

The warning in Burt's head was louder now. "A question," he said. "Why does Foster Kinsolving want to ruin Gil van Lier?"

Pathy licked his lips. A hand went to his dark glasses, then slid down to stroke his tie. The gestures of a man trying to decide which lie to use, thought Burt.

"I don't know what you mean," said Pathy. "I gave you a story. Isn't that enough?"

"I don't mind being used, Hoyt. I just want to know why."

Pathy leaned away from Burt, looked out the car window, then looked through the windshield at the White House once more.

Burt said, "You said it, Hoyt. I'm a good reporter and when I start digging, I could just as easily find it out on my own."

Pathy stuck an arm out of the car and began nervously tapping the top of the car. He pursed his lips and tapped and finally he sighed for long seconds while looking straight ahead.

"Kinsolving knows Rolland's going to die. And he knows van Lier's riding high at the moment. The feeling is that van Lier could end up as the permanent secretary of state. Kinsolving wants that job himself."

Burt smiled and shook his head. "Rolland's not in his grave and everybody is busy dividing up the man's worldly goods. You're in a shitty business, Hoyt."

"It's been called fascinatingly unpleasant."

"I'm sure van Lier has his faults," said Burt, "but he's

**187**

also trying to keep Chindé from exploding. I'm not defending the use of American troops in that country. But as long as you've got black and white fighting there, you've got a chance of foreign intervention that could get out of hand and maybe, just maybe lead to something inconvenient. Like world war three, for example. In the long run, I think van Lier really does want peace."

Pathy said, "So give van Lier points for pouring oil on troubled waters even if he does it by killing people. Don't you find that a bit hypocritical?"

"No more hypocritical than Foster Kinsolving."

Hoyt Pathy shrugged, turning his hands palms up. "If you stand still in this town, people run over you on their way to wherever it is they are running to. You move up or you move out. Kinsolving wants his, that's all. It's an election year, remember? Anything can happen."

Burt leaned closer to Pathy. "Let's have the whole story, Hoyt."

Pathy frowned at him, then looked away. Both of his hands were on the steering wheel, squeezing it tightly. "Jesus, what are you, a fucking mind reader?"

"You're not that hard to read," said Burt. "You're jumpy as hell. And that question about why did I really come down to Washington, I mean, who's kidding who? I'll buy Kinsolving's ambition, that he's always thinking ahead for Foster Kinsolving, that he stands around with a straw in his mouth, digs his bare toe in cow shit and says 'aw shucks.' I'll buy the fact that he'd rather be secretary of state than see a black man in the job."

"He's not the only one in this town who feels that way," said Pathy. "Washington's a southern city, even if it does have a black mayor and a huge black population. The whites who work here have a southern attitude toward blacks, which isn't the most enlightened and it's the whites who control the power and money."

"Do you feel that way, Hoyt?" asked Burt.

Pathy shrugged. "The truth is I don't give a shit one way or another. There are no saints in this town and that includes Gil van Lier. If he does become secretary of state, I mean permanently, he'll have a lot of enemies."

"Because he'll make changes," said Burt.

"A new broom sweeps clean. People know he'll bring in more black faces, younger faces. Nobody likes changes, Burt. Nobody."

Burt placed an arm along the top of the car seat. Hoyt Pathy was continuing to hold back on him and Burt was tired of it. "I'm still waiting. You've dropped a few remarks that need clarifying."

"Such as?"

"Such as mentioning this is an election year and saying it in a voice you might have used to tell me there's a bomb under the hood of this car. You also said 'anything can happen.' What did you mean? Is van Lier planning to run for vice-president? Is that what's bothering your friend Kinsolving? Also, I'd like to know what you think I came down here for?"

Burt watched Hoyt Pathy swallow, then run a finger around the inside of his shirt collar. Pathy was uncomfortable and it had nothing to do with the heat or too many tourists in Washington or leaving the house without breakfast. Hoyt Pathy, yesterday's peace marcher and flower child, was today's survivor and he now had to choose his words more carefully.

Pathy spoke to his reflection in the car windshield. "Renata Zachery is in love with Gil van Lier. The two of them are having an affair. If that ever gets out, this whole country could fall apart."

"Do you know what you're saying?" Burt almost shouted at him.

Hoyt Pathy looked at him. "I'm saying that the wife of the man who could be the next President of the United States is getting her brains fucked out by the man who was just named acting secretary of state, who also happens to be black. And before you tell me I'm crazy, that this is just another piece of Washington gossip, I'll tell you that it's not."

Pathy's voice dropped to a whisper. "I've got no proof I can give you, but I'm hearing it from people I trust, people who know what they're talking about and Burt, these people are scared, man. *They are scared."*

"Why?" Burt cleared his throat. His voice had emerged as a squeak. Renata Zachery and Gil van Lier were occasional dinner and dancing partners but that was all. Or was it?

"You've got a national election coming up," said Pathy, "and Richard Zachery is the man to beat. He's leading in the polls and has the President's blessing, which means the party and the money boys are behind him. If you want to place a bet in November on whose ass sits in the White House next, put your money on Zachery. But if the country learns his wife is having an affair with a black man, doesn't matter which black man, well the country's not that liberal, man. It just isn't, that's all. You'll have the press making trouble and you'll have people calling Renata Zachery everything from nigger lover to slut. Her husband's career won't be able to stand it."

Burt held up both hands in a stop signal. "Wait a minute. What you've just said about the election depends on your being right about Renata Zachery and Gil van Lier."

Hoyt Pathy angrily jabbed a forefinger in Burt's chest. "Do you think I'd tell you this if I wasn't sure?"

Burt pushed the finger aside. "You've admitted you have no proof."

"That's right. But I've given you tips in the past without proof and you've done pretty well with them, pal. That's one of the advantages and disadvantages concerning gossip, in case you haven't noticed. You don't always have the proof and you can still be right. I'm telling you this comes from people who are so heavy, I'm not about to drop names. There's *mucho* talk around of what could happen if this affair becomes public. For sure Zachery would be finished in politics and you'd have an entirely new team running the country, people with their own ideas about what's right for America."

Burt rubbed the back of his neck and stared at the dashboard clock which read 8:30. He felt as if he had been in the car for hours. No wonder Hoyt Pathy was uptight and about to leap out of his skin.

"Burt, a lot of people won't touch this one. The repercussions could be enormous. I hear things, you know? Some people wouldn't mind it coming out, but other people, man, they would kill, I mean kill, to keep this thing buried deep. There's a lot at stake. Power, money, ego like you wouldn't believe. The man who sits in the White House has more power than anybody else on the face of the globe. He can hand out billions of dollars and he can push a button and half of the world ends up as a pile of charred rags and ashes. I'm telling you some men would do anything to be in a position like that."

Burt looked at Pathy. "Does Kinsolving know?"

Pathy nodded slowly. "He does. And he doesn't want to touch it. He wants van Lier out of the way, but he'd rather do it with the business of the American troops in Chindé. He can't bring up the troop thing himself because he doesn't want to step on anybody's toes. He doesn't want to make waves."

Burt said, "You mean it might be the President's idea or someone with more power than Kinsolving?"

Pathy shrugged. "In this town it doesn't matter whether you win or lose, so long as you win. You're right. If Kinsolving tries to be a crusader and makes the wrong enemies, he could hurt himself. So naturally he doesn't want to be the one who points the finger at van Lier and Renata Zachery. You know that the messenger who brings bad news to the king gets his head cut off."

"Cutting Kinsolving's head off won't be easy," said Burt. "He doesn't stick it out far enough. And that's what you think brought me here?"

Pathy snorted. He'd taken off his dark glasses again and Burt noticed there was a slight nervous tic in Pathy's left eye. "Mr. Anthony, sir, I think *that* is a big enough story to bring a reporter back from the grave. I just want to make sure that you weren't tying it to Kinsolving. He's planning to be one of Gil van Lier's sponsors. After Rolland dies, I mean. This is off the record, right?"

Burt frowned and smiled. "I guess so. You mean when van Lier's nominated for secretary of state—"

"After Rolland dies."

"If Rolland dies. When van Lier's nominated, Kinsolving, who doesn't want him to get the job, who's passing on information that could destroy van Lier, is going to nominate the man for secretary of state?"

"Why not? If you can't beat 'em, join 'em. Kinsolving wants to be on the winning side, no matter what happens. Meanwhile he'll work behind the scenes to secure, let us say, an entirely different outcome after the election if at all possible."

Burt shook his head and turned away from Hoyt Pathy. "I don't believe it."

"Believe it. And before you start moralizing and telling me again what a shitty business I'm in, ask yourself one question: How big a man would you be if you could prove Renata Zachery and Gil van Lier were having an affair?"

Burt looked down at his lap and said nothing.

Hoyt Pathy, who knew the answer, said, "That's what I thought. We all have something to gain from this one, pal, you as much as the rest of us. Like I said, keep me and Kinsolving out of it. I don't give a shit what you do with van Lier. Look, I know the man could get hurt in this whole thing but that's how it goes. If you and I don't do it, somebody else will. Somebody else will pick up all the prizes and we'll be sitting home watching it on the eleven o'clock news. I'm handing you something, pal. Take it and run with it. Do us both some good."

Burt slowly stroked the envelope with his thumb, and thought about what Hoyt Pathy had just said. It meant ruining Zachery and van Lier and almost certainly ruining others as well, because if van Lier was having an affair with Renata Zachery, the fallout was going to be tremendous. The man who could prove this would have the decisive say in who became President in November. If Burt was that man, if he was the reporter who broke the Renata Zachery–van Lier story . . . Burt closed his eyes and let the excitement warm every inch of his body . . . he could write his own ticket.

Burt opened his eyes. "You'll hear from me. And you have my word: nothing on you or Kinsolving. I always protect my sources."

Pathy reached for the ignition key. "That may be, pal, but on something like this, you'll definitely be hearing from a few people who might insist you tell them who whispered in your ear. Van Lier could end up in front of a congressional committee on this African business and I can tell you for sure, if the President ever finds out about van Lier and Zachery's wife, God help us all. You'll be getting telephone calls at all hours of the night and your doorbell won't stop ringing. I have telephone numbers on van Lier, if you want them. Private numbers, home, office here, apartment in New York that belongs to one of our UN people."

Burt reached inside his jacket for his notebook and a ballpoint pen.

Back at the hotel Burt checked his mailbox behind the checkout desk and found no messages. Upstairs in his room Monica was in the shower and after greeting her, Burt checked his note pad and picked up the telephone. He tried unsuccessfully to reach Gil van Lier. When Monica came out of the shower, Burt grabbed her hand, dragged her over to the bed and told her of his meeting with Hoyt Pathy. When he finished, Monica opened her eyes as wide as she could.

"If you can prove it," she said, "you've got it made! You can name your price and the world will pay it. Monmouth will adopt you and blow in your ear. God, what a story! My mouth is watering already."

**Arlington, Virginia.
2:10 a.m.**

Senator Aaron Banner sat in a rocking chair in his booklined study and sipped from a pewter mug of warm milk and brandy. On his lap was a typed list containing the

**193**

names of ten senators. In the next forty-eight hours, Banner intended to convince at least six of them to join him in inflicting a serious defeat upon the President of the United States.

In vetoing a bill Banner had worked on for the past seven months, the President had done more than stop one billion dollars from being allocated for a space platform capable of firing atomic warheads at any country in the world from a distance of fifty miles up in the sky. He had issued a challenge welcomed by Banner in this presidential election year. That challenge was made more intense by the fact that the House of Representatives had just over-ridden the President's veto by the necessary two-thirds majority and Washington, as well as the nation, now watched to see if Banner could manipulate the Senate into doing the same. If he could, then the space platform bill automatically became law and both the President and vice-president would have suffered a major defeat at the hands of Aaron Banner, the man who intended to replace them in the White House.

With his party's convention scheduled for August, Banner didn't want to accept the presidential nomination with the smell of an important defeat clinging to him. To lose on the space platform bill was to create the impression in some minds that Banner would also lose in November. Before going to bed tonight, he would select the senators who owed him favors or soon would. Aaron Banner was a methodical, disciplined man who had achieved all by hard work and persistence. He understood the United States Senate better than any man in either house of Congress. He knew its rules, habits and traditions, its protocol and potential and he knew how to go about piling up the political IOU's needed to achieve anything on Capitol Hill. Banner's deliberate approach to politics and his soft-spoken Virginia drawl masked a shrewd as well as intelligent mind. To friend and foe alike he was thoughtful and courteous, observing the tradition of good manners demanded by the Senate of the one hundred men elected to sit in its marble and mahogany chamber. He served his constituency well and at fifty-six, was in his third six-year term in Congress.

It was late and when the telephone rang, Banner looked up in mild shock. The telephone was in a bottom drawer of a large antique desk across the room and in front of a ground-floor bay window looking out at a two-hundred-year-old oak tree. It was a plain black phone with an unlisted number known to less than a dozen people in all of Washington. It rang only on occasions of extreme urgency. There was always the chance it would ring tonight regarding the gathering of votes needed to defeat the President, but Aaron Banner had not expected that to happen. Placing the pewter mug on a nearby end table Banner stood up, frowned and stared toward the ringing telephone for a few seconds. Then slowly crossing the room, he walked behind the desk, lifted up the blotter and found the tiny key that opened the drawer. Carefully removing the ringing phone, he sat it down on the desk before lifting the receiver.

"This is Senator Banner."

Someone at the other end took a deep breath before answering. "This, this is Gypsy."

"Who?" Banner's mind, working swiftly, knew exactly who Gypsy was. A cold rage began to creep into the Virginia senator.

"Gypsy. From New York. You hired me to do a special job for you. Just wanted you to know I came up with something special tonight and I think we are going to have to talk, you and me. What I got is what you need to blow that other guy right out of the water and put you where you want to be."

Banner closed his eyes. "I'm afraid you have the wrong number. I suggest you dial the operator and seek her help in gettin' the proper party."

"Have it your way, Senator. But think on this: tomorrow your assistant, Neil Knightly, is supposed to meet me in New York and collect a certain tape. When he shows he had better be holding big because he ain't getting this particular tape for the usual price. The tab has gone up. I want fifty thousand in cash. That's in U.S. dollars and you got a bargain. This tape is going to make you number one with a bullet, if you get my meaning."

Banner's jaw was rigid. A vein throbbed in the smooth pink flesh on his forehead. "I am afraid, Mr. Gypsy, that you have the wrong number. There is nothin' I can do for you and I suggest you take your grievance elsewhere."

"You called the tune, Senator. That's the last thing I want to do. Go elsewhere, I mean. But if you force me I will and I'm betting the other side would like to get their hands on what I've got right here in front of me. Bet they'd also like to know who hired me to get it, too. Look, Senator, I'm not a hard guy to get along with. I don't think of myself as a greedy man. But what's to stop you from dumping me after you get this tape? I just want to make sure I get mine. I mean after all, I did good work for you and you're heading for big things and I don't see no reason why you and me can't work together in the future. There's always a need for my services. You ought to know that. I—"

Banner leaned forward, his face grim and unsmiling as though he were addressing an enemy seated directly across from him. "Good night, sir."

Banner hung up. Then removing the receiver, he dialed a number with a cold precision, his eyelids sliding down to almost hide his pale blue eyes. While the phone rang at the other end, Banner sat unmoving in a high-backed, dark brown leather chair. Then— "Neil? Get over here right away. Don't ask questions, just get over here and don't ring the bell. I don't want to wake Roseanne. The front door will be unlocked."

Placing the receiver gently back on the hook, Banner stared at the telephone for a long time. He had been through too many crises to allow his anger to cloud his judgment and cause him to make a wrong decision in the heat of rage. Revenge, as he had learned, was a dish best served cold. Somehow that conniving New York wiretapper had obtained this unlisted number and was now indulging himself in a bit of blackmail. Worse, the fellow saw himself as a continuing associate, someone entitled to remain close to the seat of power, occupied by Aaron Paul Banner, for years to come. Banner had not come this far and planned so carefully to allow himself to be overtaken that easily.

Banner planned to see that the news of Renata Zachery's affair broke in a New York gossip column, in a city where the media was powerful and concentrated, where such a story would be picked up by press from all over the world. In Washington, a journalist might ignore rumors of Renata Zachery's affair with a black diplomat, dismissing it as "mere gossip," refusing to investigate it. There were reporters who out of loyalty to the President or vice-president might kill the story even knowing it to be true. Should a reporter from a major newspaper be interested in pursuing the story, he'd have to spend time and money investigating it and also produce enough corroborating witnesses to satisfy a discriminating editor and publisher. The gossip columnist Banner had in mind had no such drawbacks or scruples.

Also, Aaron Banner did not want to break the story in Washington and risk its being traced back to him. Instead he planned to have Clare Chandler take the tapes to New York and hand them over to Robin Ian D'Arcy.

This telephone call from Gypsy the over-reacher was not going to interfere with Banner's plans. He had plans for Gypsy, too. Banner was still sitting behind his huge antique desk thinking of how he was going to deal with Gypsy when he heard Neil's car out front. Walking from behind his desk, Banner was halfway toward the door of his study when the special telephone rang again. He stopped, stared toward it but did not answer it. His answer would come later and Gypsy would not like it.

# ■ ■ ■ Sixteen

Whenever he visited Washington D'Arcy stayed with Clare Noel Chandler in her grand and sprawling colonial-style home in Mount Vernon, Virginia, on land that had once been part of the ancestral estate of George Washington. D'Arcy had a room to himself. He slept alone in a four-poster bed that had once been the property of Lawrence Washington, George's half brother and the man responsible for having named the family acreage after Admiral Edward Vernon, Lawrence's commander in the British navy. Even though George Washington's manor house was less than two miles from Clare Chandler's property, D'Arcy had no desire to visit it. He found American history boring, obsessed with self-praise and totally oblivious to moral consequences.

This morning D'Arcy had just plugged an electric typewriter into the wall and was about to begin writing from the notes he had taken the night before when there was a knock on his bedroom door.

"Yes?"

"Robin, it's Clare. May I come in? It's important."

"Yes."

When Clare said something was important, it was. What's more it would take an event of some magnitude to get her out of bed before noon; she was a woman who enjoyed her sleep. Now she entered his room quickly, as though being chased, looking alarmed and on edge. Leaning against the door she closed her eyes and opened her mouth. When she let her arms flop to her side, her robe opened and D'Arcy could see a nude body that despite being fifty and several pounds overweight was appealingly voluptuous.

"Rolland's dead," she said. "Neil Knightly just phoned and he says all hell's broken loose. Rolland died in his sleep early this morning and the President's planning to nominate Gil van Lier as *permanent* secretary of state."

D'Arcy's pale blond eyebrows crawled slowly up his forehead. Clare took a step toward him, then stopped and whispered. "Robin, can you imagine what would happen if they knew about van Lier and Renata Zachery?"

"Trouble," said a smiling D'Arcy.

"The first black secretary of state in our history. Dear God, what will become of us?"

"He'll probably inject a sense of rhythm into your foreign policy, I should think."

There was genuine horror in her face. "Robin, I'm not joking. I'm talking about him and Renata, about what will happen when people find out about the two of them. Van Lier will have to resign and God above, how will that look to the rest of the world."

Since this news meant that D'Arcy would be exploiting Clare more than ever before, he put an arm around her shoulders and guided her over to the four-poster bed. He wanted Clare to calm down and answer some questions, because whoever broke the story on the Zachery-van Lier affair in this presidential election year, would bring America a turmoil it would not soon forget.

D'Arcy stroked her hair. "Tell me about this telephone

**199**

call. Who told you about Rolland's death and van Lier's replacing him?"

"Neil Knightly. You've met him. He's Senator Aaron Banner's assistant."

"Ah, yes. Mr. Knightly's eyes never stop blinking, if I recall correctly. And this Senator Banner, isn't he the one the newspapers have predicted will run again Richard Zachery for the presidency in November?"

Eyes on the floor, Clare Chandler slowly nodded her head.

D'Arcy began to massage her shoulders. "That was considerate of Mr. Knightly," he said, "to keep you abreast of what's going on."

She closed her eyes, enjoying the touch of his fingers. "Being the first to pass on gossip makes people feel important. You ought to know that."

"I also know it would be a big help to Mr. Knightly's employer, Senator Banner, if the world were informed of this little romance between Mrs. Zachery and Mr. van Lier."

"What are you saying?"

"I'm saying it was thoughtful of Mr. Knightly to telephone you so early this morning particularly since at the moment I happen to be your house guest."

She turned to look at him. "Robin, it's true, I'm sure it is. Why would Neil lie? If he says Rolland's dead, I'm sure it's so and I'm sure the President's picked van Lier to replace him. What are you driving at?"

"We both agree this affair could end Richard Zachery's career, correct?"

"Yes."

"Meaning, Banner wins the presidency."

"Look, don't blame any of this on Aaron. I know him quite well and I can assure you it wasn't his idea that Renata Zachery sneak around and make a slut of herself. She was always common, completely lacking any class and self-respect. I tried to tell Richard that before he married her but no, he had to have her, he had to marry her. Don't you ever print this but I, I offered Richard an 'arrangement.' I told him if he married me, I wouldn't make a fuss if he continued seeing Renata Zachery, so long as he was discreet about it. If he felt he needed her that much, we could marry and he could still have his fling. Sooner or later it would have ended and I would have had him to myself. I would have been the wife of the vice-president. God, how I hate her! I could see her dead this minute."

D'Arcy watched an angry Clare close her eyes as though she were seeing Renata Zachery's corpse being lowered into the ground. In the past two days Clare had taken D'Arcy to seven Washington parties, where he had gathered enough gossip to fill four notebooks, enough copy for a week of columns. At a cocktail party for an Ethiopian prince said to be a relative of the late Emperor Haile Selassie, Renata Zachery had put in a quick solo appear- before hurriedly leaving. Clare had told D'Arcy that Renata Zachery's hasty departure meant she was on her way to meet Gil van Lier, her lover. And D'Arcy had witnessed a nasty little scene between the two women, which proved that Clare Chandler hated Renata Zachery enough to do something about it when the opportunity arose.

The Ethiopian prince, a stocky, middle-aged black man with a chest full of medals, had taken a fancy to Clare and spent much of the evening following her around, ignoring D'Arcy who found the prince's ardor for the taller Clare amusing. Politicians, journalists and assorted social climbers anxious to meet the prince had pushed through the crowd to his side and to each the prince had insisted on saying something flattering about Clare's beauty, charm and money. While she had no intention of returning with the prince to his hotel room, as he had requested several times, D'Arcy noticed Clare enjoyed being the center of attention. She and the prince were photographed together several times and those who couldn't get his ear asked Clare about the three hundred million dollars the prince was supposed to have on deposit in Swiss banks.

D'Arcy had whispered to her, "I think he wants to buy you. If he offers me a bolt of red cloth and three cows, I think we might do a deal."

Clare turned from the prince whose thigh was pressed against hers and spoke to D'Arcy from the corner of her mouth. "Red's not my color, darling, and besides, I'm only trying to assist the hostess. Her husband wants to sell the prince a few tractors."

"Ah," whispered D'Arcy. "So that explains the plague of locusts now surrounding us. Everyone wants to take a bite out of our prince, who it appears wants to take a bite out of you."

"American women are extremely healthy," said the smiling prince, attempting to recapture Clare's attention. "They exercise, swallow handfuls of vitamins and their skins are absolutely fascinating. So pink, so fair even as in the Bible, where it is written that women bathed in the milk of an ass, you know."

Before Clare or D'Arcy could comment, there was a stir in the crowd and some of the people near the prince turned toward the entrance where flashbulbs popped and voices cried, "one more, just one more." D'Arcy felt Clare's hand clutch his arm, her fingernails digging through his coat sleeve and into his flesh. He turned to see her face quickly become hard and unsmiling, the lean nostrils flaring.

"Who?" he whispered.

"Mrs. Zachery," said Clare Chandler with cold precision and D'Arcy knew Clare did not like having the spotlight shift from her to the vice-president's wife. Which is exactly what happened whenever the two women were in the same room. In taking Richard Zachery away from Clare Chandler, Renata Zachery had done more than merely deprive her of a husband. She had prevented Clare Chandler from becoming undisputed queen of Washington society. In Washington, a proper position on the social ladder was the very breath of life and Clare Chandler could not forget what might have been hers.

"We have a visitor of some note," said the prince standing on tiptoe. "Why do your reporters insist on taking so many pictures?"

"I can't imagine," muttered Clare.

As the prince leaned to his right to allow someone to whisper in his ear, D'Arcy said to Clare, "How can you be sure it's her? I cahn't see a bloody thing in this mob."

"It's her, I can assure you."

"You don't sound happy to see her."

Clare looked at him quickly, then turned back toward the flashbulbs and commotion, the hatred firm in her face.

The prince touched her arm. "I do believe she's heading this way. Perhaps you can introduce me to Mrs. Zachery?"

D'Arcy watched Clare give the prince a look of contempt, then quickly force a smile and keep it in place, saying nothing and D'Arcy grinned, enjoying the play. And then the mob surrounding Renata Zachery pushed its way through the crowd and she and the prince were face to face. Flashbulbs continued to go off and D'Arcy found himself shoved closer to Clare, the prince and Mrs. Zachery.

Renata Zachery was breathtakingly lovely. She wore a simple green and white dress and D'Arcy thought she had one of the most beautiful smiles he'd ever seen. Men crowded around her and she handled them skillfully, a touch on the cheek for one, a smile for another, a small wave to someone else. Photographers pushed against the secret service men with her and worked their cameras with relentless frenzy, capturing her every move. She was a small, extremely attractive woman and D'Arcy couldn't take his eyes from her.

Twice she called a photographer by name and each man waved and grinned at her, obviously pleased to have been noticed. Renata Zachery was clearly aware of the occasion, of being the center of all eyes but D'Arcy felt a genuine warmth coming from the woman. She seemed to enjoy the attention yet was somewhat frightened by it, which is why men competed with each other to protect her, pushing back the crowd to give her room. Each protector she rewarded with her vulnerable smile, which

**203**

D'Arcy observed actually made one man blush like a schoolboy.

"Mrs. Zachery, Mrs. Zachery," shrieked a small male reporter. "Do you plan to aid your husband in his upcoming presidential campaign?"

"I plan to set the alarm," she said, "to see that he makes his planes on time."

Laughter.

"Mrs. Zachery, is it true you've raised two million for your husband's campaign?"

"I don't know," she said, "is it?"

Laughter.

D'Arcy caught her eye, smiled and nodded once and she smiled and nodded back before quickly turning her beautiful face to someone else in the crowd, giving D'Arcy a good look at her left profile. A polite little flirt, he thought. Restless, searching and in revolt against growing old and having to live a life prescribed for her by Washington protocol and her husband's status. But she's good copy and we're all feeding off her. We're at her feet, which gives her a superior position and makes one wonder if she is actually as fragile as she looks. Could she be a tough little beauty, an iron butterfly?

By now the prince had turned his attention to her, ignoring a jealous Clare who watched as he bowed then kissed Renata Zachery's hand, holding onto it seconds longer than was necessary. Like many men in Washington he had fallen under her spell and other women were forgotten. Photographers directed the two of them to stand closer together and Clare was shoved backward, bumping into D'Arcy. That's when Renata Zachery called out, "Clare, how are you? You look marvelous."

Clare smiled with her lips but not with her eyes. "Thank you," she said and returned no compliments of her own. Instead she hesitated only seconds before pushing through people between her and the prince. Sensing he shouldn't miss what was about to happen next, D'Arcy quickly followed Clare in time to see her grab the prince by his elbow and edge herself between him and Renata Zachery.

Holding his breath, D'Arcy saw Clare, her back to Renata Zachery, give the prince a large smile then turned to look over her shoulder at the vice-president's wife and say, "You don't mind, do you? There are some people I'd like him to meet."

D'Arcy wondered if he was the only one who heard Clare mutter from behind clenched teeth, "I'm sure you won't mind. After all, you spend so much time with *his* type."

D'Arcy, who rarely felt embarrassed, was embarrassed now as he watched the smile instantly fade from Renata Zachery's face and her jaw drop with shock as though she'd been struck in the face. There was hurt and fear in her eyes and there was something else in them, too. There was the awareness that Clare *knew*. Then D'Arcy saw Renata Zachery's mouth close and her jaw tense as though she were biting down on something hard and D'Arcy saw her fight for control and win. The smile came back and she turned to a man who held a foam-wrapped microphone inches from her face.

"How's your book doing, Phil?" she said.

"Fine, Mrs. Zachery. Did you get the copy I sent you?"

"My secretary has it. She won't let me read it. She says it's excellent and she just can't put it down. Next time send two, will you?"

"You got it." The reporter beamed and D'Arcy snorted in admiration. There was more than a little bit of iron in the butterfly. Renata Zachery had been hit hard by Clare's remark, but somehow the vice-president's wife hadn't let it floor her. Renata Zachery was more than good looks and lightweight charm. Richard Zachery had chosen well. As for Clare she had all but pushed the prince away from the vice-president's wife, continuing to push him through the crowd until they had reached a pair of Arabs. Quickly making introductions, Clare held onto the prince's arm, physically preventing him from returning to Renata Zachery. It had all happened so fast that only the most observant in the crowd had seen the entire drama.

D'Arcy, however, was among the most observant. Never

before had he ever seen Clare be this bitchy in front of others and for a few seconds it made him sympathetic towards Renata Zachery, a feeling he was confident wouldn't last too long. As the vice-president's wife disappeared into the crowd he turned to look at Clare; she was smiling triumphantly at him.

*His type*, thought D'Arcy now, as he got off the four-poster bed and began pacing back and forth in front of a silent Clare, who continued staring at the highly polished wooden floor.

D'Arcy stopped pacing. "You said Neil Knightly telephoned you with the news of van Lier's appointment. And Knightly works for this Senator Banner. How does Banner feel about van Lier?"

"Despises him."

"Uppity nigger, that sort of thing?"

"He'll definitely vote against van Lier's confirmation if that's what you mean. I can tell you that Aaron Banner will do everything possible to prevent Gil van Lier from becoming secretary of state and he won't be working alone."

"I see."

"What are you driving at?"

D'Arcy looked toward the window, at the early-morning sun that was beginning to warm the room. As if talking to himself he said, "I do so love scandal. I thank God for it every day of my life. Three cheers for the hostility the human race so gleefully inflicts upon itself."

Turning to Clare he said, "Can you tell me how this congressional business works regarding van Lier's appointment?"

"Well, it starts with the President saying he wants him in the job but Congress has to vote on him."

"Meaning Congress can vote him out, so to speak. Deny him the position."

"Yes."

"Ah," said D'Arcy rubbing his hands together. "Now we have something. I'd like you to get me a list of van

Lier's supporters in Congress as well as his detractors. Just the important ones, mind you."

Clare nodded. "That's easy enough. One thing I can tell you is that Aaron Banner heads the list of van Lier's enemies."

D'Arcy didn't seem surprised to hear that.

# ■ ■ ■ Seventeen

Burt turned from his desk in time to see Molly walking back to hers while pointing over her shoulder. When he looked in the direction of Molly's bony forefinger, Burt grinned. Standing in the middle of the room was a pretty girl in her early twenties, with frizzy blond hair and large breasts that pushed hard against a form-fitting white T-shirt containing the name of a new discotheque about to open on the East Side. She also wore brief denim shorts, black shoes with spiked heels and was bare-legged. The innocence of her sexuality was fading fast and turning into something coarser, harder. But she was attractive and that's why she was here. She had Burt's complete attention along with Molly's Roman Catholic resentment.

The girl threw her arms up in the air and struck a model-showbiz pose. Left leg in front of the right to slim the hips, knees slightly bent and mouth open in an exaggerated and meaningless smile.

"Hi!" she squealed. "I'm Bonnie and I'm your invitation to *Babylon*, the ultimate in disco experience!"

Crossing her arms at the waist she gripped the T-shirt then pulled it up and over her head. She wore nothing under it. Her breasts were huge with large brown nipples and written in lipstick across them and her stomach was the name of the discotheque, its opening date and telephone number.

"It's free!" she squealed as she unbuttoned the shorts and slipped out of them to stand naked in black, high heel shoes.

Burt suddenly remembered Molly. The woman looked quickly at the girl then turned away, stammering into the telephone. "I'm, I'm sorry, w-would you please repeat that?" Burt grinned. Then Bonnie waved at him, coyly placed both hands over her pubic hair and slowly wet her lips with the tip of a very pink tongue. What some people wouldn't do to save on postage. He felt himself getting aroused, a hell of a thing to do in front of prudish Molly and he crossed his legs to keep his erection from rising higher. Bonnie squealed, then stuck her thumb in her mouth and moved her head back and forth.

When she spoke her voice was a bad imitation of Marilyn Monroe at her breathless best and Burt could only hope Bonnie was putting him on.

"We really want you, Mr. Anthony," she said. "We really do. Please say you'll come, Mr. Anthony, sir. Please say you'll come."

In about three seconds, thought Burt. All over my new pants.

*"Mr. Anthony, sir."* Molly spat the words at him. When Burt looked at her, she was putting the caller on hold and slamming the receiver down on the hook, keeping her face turned away from Bonnie.

"On four," said Molly. And as if to punish Burt for whatever lewd thoughts he had been thinking, she refused to tell him who the caller was. She returned to her typewriter, fingers speeding across the keys faster than ever.

Burt tore his eyes from Bonnie and turned around in his chair, his back to her. *It's free.* Not while Molly was in the room.

He picked up the receiver and pressed down four. "Burt Anthony."

"Cortes Arnold. I'm calling on behalf of Mr. van Lier. He wonders if you could meet him today. He realizes this is short notice but as you know, Mr. van Lier is an extremely busy man. He's scheduled to fly to Africa tonight and he has a few briefings lined up before he leaves. Would it be convenient for you to leave now and meet him? He's in New York today, on East 72nd Street and—"

The voice was as soothing as that of a nurse comforting a sick child and the politeness in it was firm, practiced, professionally adept and detached. It was a voice used to power and certain what to do with it and that certainly made it secure enough to be gracious in a remote and removed way. Whoever owned the voice was a skillful diplomat.

Burt took a few seconds to breathe. His heart jumped and threatened to push its way through his rib cage. Gil van Lier had gotten Burt's message after all. A week of telephone calls to van Lier in Washington and New York and nothing to show for it until today. In the satisfaction he now felt, Burt slowly pounded the desk with a clenched fist and closed his eyes. He was going to see Gil van Lier. Face to face.

"Mr. Anthony?"

"I'm here. Yes, today would be fine. May I have the address, please?"

Arnold gave it to him, speaking slowly, precisely and repeating it once more and adding, "Fine, then we'll be expecting you."

"Yes," said Burt. He bit a knuckle on his fist to keep from saying more. He didn't want Arnold to know how eager he was.

Placing the receiver back on the hook, Burt kept his hand on it and dropped his chin on his chest. Van Lier had agreed to see him. Van Lier, who was waiting for Congress to confirm him as the first black secretary of state, who had divided Washington into strong pro and con camps over his ability to hold down that position, who was on the covers of *Time, Newsweek* and *U.S. News and World Report*, and who was now the subject of hundreds of news stories worldwide. Van Lier, who was rumored to be a candidate for vice-president on the ticket headed by Richard Zachery, who was rumored to have been offered any ambassadorship he wanted providing he stepped down from the job as secretary of state. The hottest news subject in America had agreed to see Burt Anthony because Burt had backed him into a corner by threatening to write the story of how twelve American GIs had died in Africa. Right or wrong, complete or incomplete, the story, along with publication of the photographs of the dead Americans, would have harmed van Lier and his peace efforts in Chindé. That's what Burt had written in a short note, giving van Lier one week to reply. The black diplomat had waited exactly one week before contacting Burt.

Ignoring the naked Bonnie, Burt rushed over to Molly who looked up at him and said, "Was that who it was supposed to be?"

Burt nodded, his arm around her thin shoulders. "It was. Take down this address. I'm on my way over there now. I'll check with you before leaving there. Don't tell anybody where I've gone and I mean anybody."

"Anybody?"

"That includes Monmouth."

"Anybody." The question mark was missing this time. Molly had her orders and would act on them.

Peering past Burt, Molly sneaked a quick look at Bonnie whose smile was still in place. "What about her?"

Burt turned to look at the naked girl. She did have great tits. The *Babylon* discotheque would not soon be forgotten. He wondered what he would have done if Molly hadn't been here and van Lier's office hadn't called.

"Get dressed," Burt said to Bonnie. "I have to leave. Tell your boss he's got his plug."

"Ooooo," said Bonnie in an orgasmic sigh. "He'll be soooo pleased. I'm so glad you'll be there."

But Burt was already on his way toward the front door.

The elevator stopped and Burt stepped off to be immediately stopped by a pair of secret service men who searched him and spoke into a hand radio to announce that Burt Anthony was in the hall and now about to enter Gil van Lier's apartment. At the front door one of the secret service men rang the buzzer, his eyes on Burt who held his gaze and didn't look away. When the door opened, a guard inside looked at Burt then at the guard behind him who nodded to confirm that this was indeed the real Burt Anthony. If van Lier could find a way to carry on an affair with Renata Zachery, while surrounded by his and hers secret service agents, thought Burt, he deserved to be secretary of state.

"Mr. Anthony? I'm Cortes Arnold." A slim, immaculately dressed Latin man walked across the huge living room, his arm outstretched. He had dark hair, a thin moustache and smelled of a heavy, sweet cologne. He wore rimless blue-tinted glasses and his dark suit was tailored and neatly pressed. He reminded Burt of a maître d' in a high-class restaurant, a man paid to please the public but who didn't particularly care to. Something in his manner, however, said he was more than he seemed to be. He had a calm that was exasperating and he openly studied Burt while they shook hands. For a man who didn't weigh over a hundred and fifty pounds, Arnold had a strong handshake.

"Mr. van Lier is in the other room," he said in a voice with a slight Spanish accent. "He barely hangs up the telephone when it begins to ring again."

"Since I've spoken only to you," said Burt, "maybe you can tell me what Mr. van Lier wants to see me about."

"Sorry," said a very cool Cortes Arnold, who didn't appear sorry at all. "Mr. van Lier does have a few secrets from me. May I get you a drink or is it too early?"

"I can wait."

"Please take a seat," said Arnold. "I'll tell him you're here." And then he walked across wall-to-wall carpeting and through a door, closing it noiselessly behind him, leaving Burt alone with one secret service, who stood arms folded across his chest, back to the door, his eyes trained on Burt. Something about the guard reminded Burt of a truth he had learned in years of reporting: real power came equipped with muscle, which meant it could hurt you in a variety of ways.

Seating himself on a beige leather couch in front of the fireplace, Burt stared at a huge painting of a horse that hung on the wall directly in front of him. The painting, though recent, was fairly good and the frame alone worth a few thousand dollars. Somehow Burt had the feeling that the people who owned the painting also owned the horse. As with everything else in the room the painting smelled of old money. The apartment was decorated in the restrained, inoffensive taste of people who have absolutely nothing to prove and no one to impress. As usual, van Lier was moving in the best of circles.

A door opened and the black diplomat entered the living room. He seemed exhausted and he was frowning, but the tall van Lier was still one of the handsomest men Burt had ever seen. He was unshaven, his eyes puffy and bloodshot but all it did was make him appear more interesting. His shirt sleeves were rolled up and he wore a pair of casual tan pants and scuffed black boots. His brown arms were corded with muscle and on his right wrist he wore several thin silver bracelets. His wristwatch was thin, tasteful, expensive. His waist was flat and there was gray at his temples and in his sideburns. All the man has going for him, thought Burt, is brains, good looks and power. Other than that he's got nothing. Burt, who was almost six feet tall, guessed that van Lier was at least four inches taller.

They shook hands in silence and eyed each other, a ritual Burt had gone through hundreds of times as a reporter and which he knew was the equivalent of boxers cautiously circling each other in the early rounds of a fight before really going to work. The secret service man took a pair of dark glasses from inside his jacket, put them on and stepped outside into the hall, closing the door behind him. Which leaves us without a referee, thought Burt.

Motioning Burt to sit down, van Lier said, "Coffee okay?"

Burt removed his notebook and pen. "Tea's better."

Van Lier flopped down at the opposite end of the leather couch and covered both eyes with his hands. "I've only had five hours' sleep in the past two days. I'm looking forward to traveling again. At least I can sleep on the plane. Of course, some people claim the State Department's always asleep, in the air or on the ground."

Burt didn't want to smile but he found himself doing so.

A door opened and Cortes Arnold entered carrying a tray with cups, saucers, sugar, two small metal pitchers and a tiny glass pitcher of milk. On a saucer beside one cup were two teabags and a slice of lemon, causing Burt to wonder if Cortes Arnold had ESP or had merely been eavesdropping, since the Latin had appeared without having been summoned and complete with tray. Perhaps that was a major function of Mr. Arnold, to anticipate. As he poured hot water into Burt's cup, Arnold spoke briefly in Spanish to van Lier who snapped his fingers as though he'd forgotten something. Van Lier said *gracias* and continued speaking in Spanish. Cortes Arnold listened, looked quickly at Burt then back at van Lier before leaving the room.

The man said *gracias*, thought Burt, wondering why van Lier had glanced at his watch and held that private little conversation in Spanish.

Now it seemed to be van Lier's turn to anticipate. "Cortes was asking me if I wanted to take any calls while you and I talked. I told him only if it was urgent."

"I take it he also works for the State Department?"

"Cortes works for me. I should say he works for me within the State Department. He's a specialist in Latin American affairs, speaks two more languages than I do

214

and at one time he owned more than twenty thousand acres of land in Cuba. But that was before Castro took over. Strangely enough he and Castro are still in touch."

"Which is an advantage to you," said Burt.

"Which is an advantage to me, yes."

Burt stirred his tea. "I get the feeling Cortes is quite protective where you're concerned."

Van Lier smiled. "He's loyal, if that's what you mean. I'm responsible for his being in America and for his working at the State Department. That reminds me: there's something on television I want to see, if it's all right with you. It'll only take a minute or so."

"Sure."

Standing up, van Lier looked at his watch as he walked to a large television set and turned it on. After he selected the proper channel, he stood looking down at the set, ignoring Burt who watched him carefully. When the picture came on Burt saw a broadcaster in shirt sleeves standing in the clearing of an African village and signing off, giving his name and the station call letters. "Damn!" muttered van Lier as though angered at having just missed something important. Burt noticed the sound was being kept low as if van Lier didn't want anyone else to hear. On-screen the picture shifted to a female broadcaster speaking into the camera and while it was impossible to hear everything she said, Burt heard a few words. ". . . *last night . . . when the final casualty count . . . a tragedy for peace . . . the United States will . . .*"

Van Lier concentrated on the screen, his back to Burt. Commercials and more news followed and when Burt was about to abandon looking at van Lier looking at television he saw the black diplomat shift his weight from one leg to another and then Renata Zachery's beautiful face filled the screen. The vice-president's wife was in New York. Along with the mayor, politicians and several theatrical celebrities she was attending the ceremonies surrounding the opening of a new legitimate theater on West 43rd Street. Burt leaned forward, eyes darting from the screen to van Lier and back to the screen again. Mrs.

Zachery was lovely and vivacious and dominated the group of well-known faces standing on either side of her. Holding a pair of golden scissors overhead in one hand she turned and waved in all directions, acknowledging applause and cheers from a crowd gathered to watch the ribbon cutting. Anxious to hear what was being said and even more anxious to see van Lier's face, Burt stood up and softly walked toward the television set, taking care not to disturb the black diplomat.

"I love the theater and I love New York!" shouted Renata Zachery. "And let me tell you, the country needs both!" Her next words were drowned out by applause and cheers from dignitaries and people in front of the theater. Then stepping forward she cut the ribbon—not once but twice—ending up with several inches of ribbon in one hand. As the clapping and shouts continued, she walked over to a ten-year-old child actress, tied the ribbon around the child's blond hair, then handed her the scissors, which the smiling child clutched to her chest as though it were the most wonderful doll in the world. The crowd went wild and the mayor stepped forward, frantically applauding and then the camera closed in on Renata Zachery as she leaned over to hug the child.

Burt saw a small smile start and fade at a corner of van Lier's mouth. His face softened, relaxed and the worry and fatigue magically disappeared. He gently reached out and touched the television set, and Burt held his breath. Suddenly van Lier stiffened, aware of Burt's presence and the softness went out of his face as he bent down to turn off the set. Looking quickly at Burt, he smiled. Burt's mind raced to define the look he'd just seen. Had van Lier been afraid he just revealed something he desperately wanted kept secret? Had Burt witnessed a man admit his love for a woman he had no right to love? Burt was suddenly sure that the conversation in Spanish between van Lier and Cortes Arnold had been about Renata Zachery's appearance on television.

Van Lier led the way back to the couch. "Well, let me start by saying I received your message, Mr. Anthony, or should I say messages. You don't give up easily. I also received some photographs from you."

He sat down and began to study Burt, but said nothing more.

Burt broke the silence by saying, "The photographs were of dead American soldiers killed fighting as mercenaries in Chindé."

"So you said. You also said if I didn't agree to see you you'd print some sort of story about how they died."

"If I'm wrong you don't have a problem," said Burt. "But you wouldn't have agreed to see me if there was nothing to the story, so let's talk about Chindé."

Van Lier's smile was smooth, practiced and he used it easily. "Let's talk about Chindé." He waited, letting Burt make the early moves. Gil van Lucky was a counterpuncher, thought Burt, with all the moves of Muhammed Ali in his prime. He wants to see what cards I'm holding before he commits himself to anything.

"Mr. Secretary," said Burt, "I was against the Vietnam War from the time I inhaled teargas on a college campus until the last body count came out of Saigon in 1973. I knew too many guys who went over there only to come back in a green rubber bag. And I know too many guys who came back without a face or eyes or hands, so you can say I'm very down on anything that could mean another Vietnam. I could have printed the information I have on American troops in Africa but I wanted to hear your side of the story."

Van Lier leaned back, hands behind his head and shook his head sadly, as though Burt had just failed at a small but important task. "Mr. Anthony, you aren't here to get my side of the story. You are here to help me hang myself. You are here to get me to admit something damaging and newsworthy, which you will then rush out to print in bold, black headlines and feel good about."

Burt blinked. Score one for Mr. Secretary's insight into the motives of your everyday ambitious reporter.

Van Lier flashed his magnetic smile. "Nothing is that simple, is it?"

Despite not wanting to, Burt found himself smiling back. "No, it isn't."

And then as van Lier leaned forward glancing at the television set with sad eyes, Burt frowned, wondering if he was beginning to feel sorry for the man. When the silence had gone on for long seconds, Burt said, "The public has a right to know the truth, Mr. Secretary."

Van Lier looked at him. "Truth has been described as kindness and it was added that where the two diverge and collide, kindness should override the truth."

"In that case," said Burt, "truth becomes a handicap and that's something I can't accept."

"If I can return to Chindé as secretary of state," said van Lier, "I have a chance to ease the fighting there. There's an outside chance I might even stop it altogether. But if the fighting escalates, there could be foreign intervention, of which I'm sure you're aware. The presence of a high American official at the bargaining table is bound to bring pressure on everyone to come to an agreement. I need your help, Burt. I need your cooperation."

Burt had been nervous, but now he found himself calmer. He could deal with van Lier because the man was going to ask him to lie, to cover up and not write a story and that would be the same as admitting American troops were fighting on African soil. All Burt had to do was sit and wait because sooner or later, Gil van Lier would say something that could be used against him.

"Why do you need my help, Mr. Secretary?"

"To save my life."

"To save your career, you mean. They are one and the same, right?"

"No, they are not. Saving my life means exactly that. Unless you help me, I'm going to be assassinated. Not character assassination, though there's enough of that aimed at me these days. I'm talking about being dead."

Perhaps Burt imagined it but he thought he saw a small smile begin at the corner of Gil van Lier's mouth then disappear as if the black diplomat knew *he* now had the upper hand. Burt was now at a disadvantage and could

218

only wait for Gil van Lier's next move. If this talk about assassination was a performance, van Lier was an effective actor. Burt studied the black man's handsome, tired face and could find no indication he was lying, which when all was said and done didn't prove a goddam thing.

Van Lier continued, "My future credibility with you rests on my telling the truth and I assure you I am. Unless you help me and we both know what I mean by that, I'll be dead within two days."

# ■ ■ ■ Eighteen

**While Burt talked with Gil van Lier the** telephone rang continuously, bringing Cortes Arnold into the room with folded notes which he slipped to van Lier. The diplomat glanced at them, shook his head *no* and handed the notes back to Cortes Arnold, who slipped them into a jacket pocket. This process was repeated several times, with one exception. Van Lier looked at one note, immediately stood up and headed for a room where he could take the telephone call. The small slip of paper he left behind on the couch was only a few feet away from Burt, but Cortes Arnold was anticipating again. With a quick grace the Cuban reached the couch in one step, pounced on the note and methodically tore it into small pieces that also went into a side pocket.

While van Lier was taking the call, Burt welcomed the chance to be alone. The diplomat was too effective, too good at talking you into doing what he wanted. There was a lot of style in van Lier and conviction enough to match it. He was gifted with a talent for convincing others to share his beliefs.

When van Lier returned to the room he said, "There was something on television just now."

Burt almost said *I saw her, too*, but he kept quiet and played van Lier's waiting game.

"I missed most of the newscast," said the diplomat. "Caught the tail end of it. Some people were killed last night in Chindé, at least eight, maybe more. We're still trying to find out exactly how many. In any case, it's touched me directly. It's the reason my life's in danger."

"Really?"

"Why don't you begin by calling your paper," said van Lier. "They'll confirm a lot of what I'm about to tell you. I want to repeat that if I lie to you during our first meeting, my credibility with you is bound to suffer for a long time, wouldn't you say?"

"I'd say that, yes."

"Understood. I've been on the telephone with Africa and Washington since five this morning. Things are about to explode over there which is why I'm flying to Chindé as soon as I can. Robert Mswamba, the black leader I've been working with for the past few months, the most moderate and reasonable man in the country—" Van Lier choked, swallowed and shook his head. "He was murdered last night. Whoever killed him also killed his wife, three children and at least three of his lieutenants. He was a very good friend of mine. A very good friend."

Burt sat up straight on the couch.

Van Lier's bloodshot eyes held his. "We're not sure who killed him but we have an idea. Nothing you can print, so excuse me if I sidestep any questions on that just now. It could even have been his own people. Some of the blacks aren't interested in any peaceful solutions with whites, which is understandable from their point of view. They want justice, which to them is synonymous with revenge and Robert Mswamba would have prevented them from having it. It's inevitable that blacks take over, so the hardliners among them say why compromise."

Van Lier stood up, his back to Burt. "The murders could also have been committed by the anti-guerrilla force of the white minority government. This force has a reputation for brutality and makes no secret of its intention to kill as many blacks as possible before any settlement is reached. There are some blacks in this force; they're still the best trackers, and we do know it was blacks who actually killed Robert Mswamba."

Turning, the diplomat walked over to Burt and looked down at him. "I want you to understand what's going on in Africa and what could happen in Chindé if total war breaks out. I'm going to tell you how my friend, his family and his friends died. Robert Mswamba and his wife Sylvia, both dear friends of mine, had their eyes gouged out. Their daughters, neither one of them over fifteen, were raped and the son was beheaded. The lieutenants had an ear or parts of flesh sliced from their bodies and the flesh was cooked and they were forced to eat it. Afterward, they were shot to death. Mr. and Mrs. Mswamba and their two daughters were hacked to death by machetes. All of them, men, women, children, had their hands hacked off and the hands are missing. Now this isn't the worst example of African warfare I've seen or heard of. Some things have happened over there which you would swear were impossible, but you'd be wrong. It's happening all over Africa every day of the week."

Van Lier blinked tears from his eyes and looked at the ceiling. "I thought we had a chance over there. Christ, I thought I could pull it off."

He looked at Burt. "A message was left near Robert Mswamba's body. It said that I was next and if I ever again set foot in Chindé, I'd never leave the country alive."

Burt whispered, "And you're going back?"

"As soon as I can."

Van Lier was quiet before saying, "If you follow through on your threat to publish a story that American troops are fighting over there, I'm a dead man. No amount

222

of security and bodyguards can keep you alive if someone wants you dead badly enough. You and I both know that."

To get away from van Lier's eyes and persuasive voice, Burt stood up and took a few steps toward the fireplace. His plan had been to back van Lier into a corner but instead it was Burt who suddenly found himself between a rock and a hard place. Van Lier was probably telling the truth and that's what was ripping Burt apart inside. Exposing van Lier was one thing: helping to assassinate him was another.

Behind Burt's back, van Lier spoke softly, slowly. "I'm going back. I'll be dealing with factions now more militant than ever, that are more determined to stay away from all compromise. The whites' position will harden because they won't want to be slaughtered like Robert Mswamba. Blacks, when they aren't fighting among themselves, will blame the whites for Mswamba's death, which in turn will make whites dig in their heels to resist blacks bent on revenge. If the fighting gets worse, Cuba and Russia will choose sides and that means more troops, more guns, more deaths."

For the first time since their meeting van Lier used his name. "Burt, the wrong story right now is a death sentence, for whites, for blacks, for me. It's not the first time my life's been threatened but if certain people in Chindé felt I'd betrayed them they'd make it their business to kill me. The odds against me are tough enough. I'd be grateful if you didn't make them any tougher."

When Burt spoke his eyes were on the portrait of the horse over the fireplace. "Mr. Secretary, are American troops fighting in Chindé?"

"Burt, there are always Americans fighting in Africa as mercenaries. No one can do anything about that."

Burt turned to face him. "I'm talking about Chindé. I'm talking about twelve dead GIs whose bodies were brought back to Leslie Air Force Base in New Jersey."

"I know you want a straight answer but I can't give you one. I will say something off the record."

"Off the record."

There was strength in van Lier's voice as he pointed a finger at Burt. "My off-the-record answer: give me time. Let me go to Chindé. Let me try to stop the fighting and if I'm lucky, if I can bring about a peaceful changeover of power from white to black, then I'll answer all of your questions. By then the fighting will have stopped, I hope, and any negative story about me shouldn't make much difference. At the moment it makes one hell of a difference and before you say I conned you into accepting an off-the-record comment, let me say I haven't lied to you. Have I?"

"No. But you've played fast and loose when it comes to direct answers. Pinning you down is like trying to catch light in a thimble. All right, let's say I put this story on hold for a while. What then?"

"Then maybe I can stay alive. And help whites and blacks in Chindé to stay alive."

Burt shrugged. He had come for a story and now he was going away with nothing. He would telephone the *Examiner-World* to check on the Robert Mswamba murder even though instinct told him van Lier was telling the truth. But for how long? Burt had always avoided all cooperation with public officials, refusing to trust them, seeing them only as adversaries and targets. But now he stood in front of Gil van Lier, the first man to make Burt even consider throwing aside that all-important attitude of distrust. And if Burt did lower his guard was he doing it to help van Lier or himself? After all, wouldn't it be to Burt's advantage to be on good terms with van Lier, one of the best news sources in the world?

The diplomat was giving Burt his full attention, watching his every move with a full intensity that Burt found unnerving. It was as though van Lier were trying to will him into doing as he asked. Which is why when a door opened and Cortes Arnold again entered the room with a folded note between manicured fingers, van Lier barely suppressed his annoyance at being interrupted at this particular moment. Reading the note, van Lier said, "Tell her I'll call back."

"It's the third time she's called," Arnold said, touching his rimless, blue-tinted glasses, a gesture that gave Burt the impression the Cuban was showing his disapproval of something. Van Lier immediately replied in Spanish and Arnold nodded. Burt realized that if van Lier hadn't been caught unawares he wouldn't have spoken to the Cuban in English. And if the Cuban hadn't been annoyed he wouldn't have answered in English. Both men, however, had recovered quickly enough.

Van Lier waved the Cuban away and Arnold started across the room, but before the Cuban had taken two steps, van Lier said, "Cortes?" The Cuban stopped and turned. The diplomat spoke to him in Spanish and Burt, listening carefully, caught the words *un momento*.

Arnold continued across the room, van Lier turned and grinned at Burt. "Reporters," he explained. "Each one wants an exclusive interview and each one wants it yesterday."

Reaching inside his jacket for his notebook, Burt brought his eyes up to meet van Lier's. "Is that a reporter on the phone? She seems determined."

Van Lier's smile was guarded. "Have you ever known a woman who wasn't determined?"

"Some are more determined than others, Mr. Secretary. I remember reading that in Paris a woman once dressed up as a maid and tried to get into your hotel room."

"She claimed she had a message for the world and I was the one to bring it to the American people. Speaking of messages, I'm going to have to excuse myself for a minute and take that phone call."

Burt watched van Lier carefully. "I suppose, Mr. Secretary, that a man in the public eye encounters a lot of women?"

"I do encounter a lot of women," said van Lier slowly. "The only way to avoid human contact is to become a recluse, which would be a drawback in my line of work."

225

Burt took a deep breath and plunged forward. "You're in the gossip columns a great deal. Didn't you come in for a bit of criticism for having attended a diplomatic reception in New York only hours after you attended Jerome Rolland's funeral?"

"I did," said van Lier. "And in the company of Renata Zachery, as you know. What the gossips didn't add was that this was done with the knowledge and approval of the White House. The Israeli prime minister and defense minister and their wives had arrived in New York that day and expected to meet Secretary Rolland. They couldn't cancel their trip nor was it diplomatically proper that they be greeted by anyone less than the secretary of state. Mrs. Zachery was with me in an official capacity. She represented the White House and the Israeli officials understood and accepted this. I had to attend White House briefings and a UN meeting so I was only able to stay at the reception for a few minutes. Mrs. Zachery spent most of the evening with the Israelis. Did you read in the gossip columns that within an hour after leaving the party I was on a plane back to Washington for an emergency meeting with the President?"

Burt shook his head. "No, I didn't."

Van Lier yawned and stretched. "We create our own world, Burt. There are some who see a rope and think it's a snake. I'm not complaining, but every now and then you wish someone would tell the truth."

"I've said the same thing myself, Mr. Secretary. Usually about public figures."

Van Lier's smile was dazzling. "Touché."

He looked over his shoulder at the closed door.

*It is her,* thought Burt. And there's nothing he'd like more than to turn his back on me and go running to the phone. I can't see him killed in Chindé and he certainly won't let me walk into the room and listen while he talks to *her.*

"Does it bother you, Mr. Secretary, to be in the gossip columns so often? It's not the usual place for high-ranking members of the State Department to be found."

"Burt, some people are more interested in my private life than in my public career. Not much I can do about it. Frankly, I'd rather not see that happen but it comes with the territory."

"Speaking of reading things not to your liking," said Burt, "what was your reaction to hearing about the German model who swallowed a bottle of sleeping pills and tried to kill herself, allegedly over you?"

Van Lier's face hardened and he clenched his fists at his side. "Last year's news, Burt." He smiled and slowly rubbed his flat stomach. "Haven't had breakfast or lunch. Can't keep going on coffee. I understand you've won a few journalism awards. You didn't do that by dealing in boutique journalism, did you? I think it's better we stick to issues rather than innuendo and personalities."

"Mr. Secretary, I came here to discuss the issue of American troops fighting in Chindé, which you have refused to talk about and which you want me to avoid until you've been able to bring about a peace there. I'm more than willing to discuss *that* issue but you're not. It seems I have to save your life by cooperating, as you put it, and I'm willing to do just that. But only for a very, very short time and that time comes to an end the second I think you're lying to me. If I ever find out you're doing a number on me, then all bets are off. Meanwhile you say keep innuendo and personalities out of it. Mr. Secretary, you're not just a personality, you're a public figure and being a target goes with the job, as you've already pointed out. In your position you don't have a private life or for that matter, any right to one. Whatever you do in public or private is done in the name of the American government and good or bad, the American government's stuck with it. You're fair game and anybody who can stick a pin in your balloon is going to do it."

Van Lier said, "Does that include you?"

"Yes. The difference is I'm not in a hurry, at least not at the moment. But sticking pins in peoples' balloons is my job. That's how I won those awards you just mentioned."

"There are people who'd rather not see me become secretary of state. I think we both know why."

"Race?"

"Nothing new about that, is there? Did you know I've been offered the opportunity to run for senator, with a war chest of two million dollars behind me, providing I resign my present position?"

"Which state and who made the offer?"

"Burt, if I told you that I'd have another war on my hands. I need those people who made the offer and I need them to back me as secretary of state. Give me time and I'll win them over. I usually do."

"Washington's leading political columnist predicts mass resignations from the State Department if you're confirmed. He says people won't want to work under you."

"That particular columnist," said van Lier, "has called me twice this morning for news. We've been invited to the same dinner party next week at the Spanish Embassy. He has to please his publisher, which means taking a few shots at me now and then. We both understand how the game is played. I know how newspaper publishers can be."

He looked at Burt. "I really have to go," said van Lier. "I'd appreciate whatever you could do, at least for the next few days. After that, I suppose I have no right to expect anything. Robert Mswamba's funeral is the day after tomorrow and there's been some talk about my not showing up. Security thinks it might be better if I stay away. That won't be easy. He was my friend and I'd arranged for his son to come to America and attend school here. The boy was my godchild."

Burt looked up from his notebook. "Just a couple of things before you leave, Mr. Secretary."

"Yes?"

"You have various social engagements you must attend in connection with your work?"

"Yes."

"Why doesn't your wife make more public appearances? You've escorted other women to these social functions. I've mentioned Mrs. Zachery—"

"My wife does make appearances with me. But we also have children and they require most of her time and energy. She is also a private person who resents being in the spotlight."

"You seem to juggle quite a few things at one time, Mr. Secretary. Your career, family, an active social life. Does it ever seem as though you've extended yourself too far?"

Van Lier's smile was tight, his eyes totally unsmiling. "You mean give them an inch and they'll take a mile?"

"I mean have you ever thought that it could all prove to be too much for you eventually? Rolland overworked himself and now he's dead."

"Is there something I'm doing that you feel I shouldn't be doing?" asked van Lier with mild sarcasm.

Burt kept writing in his notebook as he answered. "If there is, Mr. Secretary, you'll read about it." Burt looked up. "Sooner or later."

Burt put his notebook back inside his jacket. "That's the one thing I want to make clear. You've put me on the spot about those dead GIs, even though I think we both know there is something to that story. I can't write anything I know will cause your death. But that only makes me more determined not to be played cheap, so I'm telling you I'm still a journalist, which means I'm not letting go of anything. Like I said, if you're doing something you shouldn't be doing you'll read it sooner or later."

Burt took a deep breath, then added. "No matter what or *who* it may involve."

"Who?" Van Lier arched one eyebrow.

"Yes, Mr. Secretary. *Who*."

They stared at each other while telephones rang in other rooms. He knows I know about Renata Zachery, thought Burt. He's too smart, too instinctive, too *knowing* not to know.

Van Lier frowned, gently chewed the inside of his lip and his gaze seemed to turn inward as though making a serious evaluation of something.

"I expect you'll be keeping tabs on me pretty closely," said van Lier.

"Yes."

"Fine." Van Lier walked over to Burt, extended his hand and gave him that dazzling smile, a smile filled with confidence and defiance. And then van Lier had turned and was hurrying toward a closed door, which opened seconds before he got there. Cortes Arnold held the door open for van Lier, closed it behind him and walked over to Burt, taking his elbow and propelling him toward the front door.

"You have our telephone numbers," said Arnold.

Burt freed his arm, a gesture which made the Cuban flinch. "I'm good at this," said Burt. "Walking, I mean. Tell Mr. van Lier I sure as hell do have his number. Tell him I said that."

Outside on the street, Burt hurried to a drugstore on Madison Avenue and in a public telephone booth, spoke to the city room of the *Examiner-World*. Van Lier had told the truth about everything that had happened in Chindé yesterday, including the death threat to himself. Burt was relieved that he hadn't been made a fool of by van Lier but worried that sooner or later he would be. He had told van Lier he wouldn't publish anything for a while, but he hadn't promised to permanently avoid van Lier's troubles and he certainly hadn't promised not to keep digging into them. What's more, Burt planned to write the story as he went along, to have it ready for publication any time.

# ■ ■ ■ Nineteen

## New York City

Yesterday Gypsy had recorded an afternoon meeting in Manhattan between Gil van Lier and Renata Zachery and what he had overheard had made him bold enough to go directly to Aaron Banner and demand a lot of money. Through connections at the telephone company in New York, Gypsy was able to get any unlisted number he wanted and Banner's number was no exception. On the phone Banner had been cool, all ice and in total control of himself, admitting nothing, promising nothing and not once raising his voice when Gypsy had asked for very big bucks.

But Gypsy had done some fast thinking and decided the senator had been putting on a good act, that despite what Banner had said he did want this particular tape. He couldn't afford to have Gypsy turn it over to Richard Zachery. If that were to happen Banner would lose all chance of becoming President. Gypsy's conclusion: Banner would pay. What's more he would be forced to admit he needed Gypsy to work for him in the future. As for Neil Knightly, when that snotty little bastard with the blinking eyes showed up he'd better be carrying fifty thousand dollars because that's how much the tape would cost. Fifty big ones. Take it or leave it and Gypsy was betting Banner would take it.

Twenty-four hours after talking with Aaron Banner, Gypsy sat in his Greenwich Village apartment and lied to Neil Knightly who stood looking down at him. "You got my word this here tape I'm going to play for you is the only copy," said Gypsy, who had two copies of it hidden under the kitchen floor. "Understand, I'm just trying to make a living. I figure I can work with you people again, so why should I want to mess up a good thing? We both know the senator can always use a guy like me, especially if the senator goes all the way to the top. Know what I'm saying?"

Neil Knightly pointed to the cassette recorder sitting on a small coffee table only inches from Gypsy's knees. "Skip the bullshit, shall we? Let's hear the tape."

"What about the money?"

"What about it?"

"Last night I told Banner—"

"I know what you told Senator Banner, friend. Now let's hear the tape, if you don't mind. The only reason I'm here is to make sure you've got something to sell. You'll pardon us if we don't take your word for anything."

Gypsy shrugged, palms upturned. "You want it, you got it."

Taking the folded newspaper containing the silenced .22 from his lap, Gypsy placed it on the couch within easy reach. Then he leaned forward and pressed down the *play* button on the cassette.

"You're not going to hear much at the beginning," he said. "The bugs are always live, always ready to pick up and what you're going to hear now is nothing, just a lot of quiet. When I cut the tape I left a minute or so of dead air at the beginning just in case somebody besides us gets hold of this thing and plays it. Usually when people hear nothing they turn the thing off."

Expecting to be commended for his foresight Gypsy looked up at Neil who stared stonily at the cassette, ignoring Gypsy completely. This was his second visit to Gypsy's apartment; it was the first time Gypsy felt a need to be on guard against him. Which was the reason for the hidden gun. Because he had backed Banner into a corner, Gypsy wanted today's meeting to be on his own turf, where he felt better able to defend himself and where he could, of course, easily tape any conversation.

This afternoon Neil stood holding a worn briefcase under his left arm, hands folded in front of him, refusing to sit and ignoring Gypsy's offer of a drink. He also kept his gray topcoat on, making it clear he intended to spend as little time as possible with Gypsy.

"I didn't see the two of them go inside," said Gypsy. "Couldn't get a parking space near the front of the building, which was just as well since I've already worked that building for you a few times and there's always the chance somebody might spot me. I was around the corner and— here it comes. You can hear the key in the lock and the two of them laughing—"

"If you shut up," said Neil, "I could hear everything."

"Yeah. Sure."

The two men watched the recorder in silence, with Gypsy occasionally looking up to see if Neil's bony face softened, relaxed or showed any reaction to what he was hearing. It didn't.

From the recorder came the sounds of Gil van Lier and Renata Zachery laughing and the front door opening and closing, then Renata Zachery said, "Oh, God, I can't stop laughing! Gil, I haven't had this much fun in years, in years."

"You can unmask now if you want to. In case you haven't noticed we're inside the apartment."

Her voice became slightly muffled as though her mouth were covered. "I vish to remain mysterious a little longer, if you don't mind. Oh, Gil, this is fun! Now I know how Arab women feel. Keep your face covered and walk behind the man at all times. I was too busy hiding behind you to hear what you told the doorman."

"I told him nothing," said van Lier. "Sometimes the less you say, the better. You were with me and that's all he had to know."

"I've been mysterious enough for one day. Did I tell you I've missed you?" Renata Zachery literally purred.

"Yes. Now come here and show me."

There was silence as they kissed for a long time. A small moan escaped Renata Zachery, who then murmured, "Yes. Oh, yes."

Van Lier's voice came from deep within his throat. "I don't want to rush you or anything, but . . ."

"You wouldn't by any chance be trying to get me into the bedroom, I hope?"

"Me? Now why would I do a thing like that?"

"That's the trouble with you diplomats, all talk and no action."

"No action, the lady says." In the silence they kissed again. Finally she said in a small voice, "Would you believe I'm so happy I'm about to cry. Oh, Gil . . ."

More dead air.

Then van Lier said, "Before I forget, there are a couple of packages for you in the closet. Your 'shopping,' complete with receipts. These are the things you bought today while out on your own. Wouldn't look good if you returned empty-handed. Oh, you've got to make those calls right away."

"I don't want to move. I want to stand here just like this, the two of us holding each other and nothing and no one between us."

"I said you've got to make those calls. Now scoot. Call your designer and the people you're staying with before someone gets the national guard out looking for you. Tell them you're shopping on your own and everything's fine. Tell them you'll be home before dinner and not to worry."

"I want to hold you."

"Use the phone in the upstairs bedroom. I've got to make a couple of calls myself. I'll use the phone down here."

"Don't be too long," she said. "You're the one who said we don't have much time. I forgot to ask, you're not expecting anyone are you?"

"Only Cortes. But he won't come until I call him so that gives us an hour. Washington thinks I'm at the UN; the UN thinks I'm off to a secret meeting of some kind, so I'm hard to pin down. Can't stay away too long, though."

"Does Cortes know about us?" Renata asked.

"Cortes knows a lot of things."

"I see. Did you tell him?"

"You know better. Besides, I didn't have to."

There were a few seconds of dead air. Then she said, "Oh, well, no sense worrying about that. By the way, where are your secret service men?"

Van Lier chuckled. "Remember that secret meeting I just mentioned? Well, I ordered my guards to back off for a while, to leave me on my own. I told them I was getting together with some very sensitive blacks from the UN and Washington, something unofficial but nevertheless very important. No white faces allowed, I said. It's the new era of diplomacy, I told them. They believed me. Actually there is such a meeting, but it's set for tonight. So I'm pretty well covered."

"Aren't there any black secret service men?"

"A few," said van Lier. "But they look so straight that they might as well be white. You know I'm not officially secretary of state yet so at the moment there's some disagreement on just how much protection I should have. Being black helps, let me say. Nobody wants to offend me so they let me do things my way, at least up to a point. Cortes told the guards he knows where I am at all times and speaking of time, we're running short so why don't you make those phone calls like I told you to?"

"Aye, aye, sir."

Seconds later she was telephoning her designer and the apartment where she was staying. Each time she began by saying, "This is Mrs. Richard Zachery . . ." And at the beginning of his three quick telephone calls, two of which were long distance to Washington, Gil van Lier also indentified himself by name. There was now no doubt as to whom the voices on the tape belonged.

Renata called out, "Gil, where's the shower?"

"Which one? There're three."

"Any one."

"Behind you in the bedroom."

"What do I have to do to get you to join me?"

"You just did it," said van Lier. "I'm on my way up there right now."

There were sounds of him hurrying up the stairs and the couple kissed once more before moving into the shower and out of range of the bedroom listening device. The powerful bugs, however, picked up the sounds of running water, laughter and muffled conversation and once the tape clearly recorded Renata Zachery squealing then shouting, "That was *cold* water! Ohhhhh!"

And then the two of them were once more in range of the bedroom bugs.

"Beautiful room," Renata said. "Beautiful, beautiful bed. Oh, Gil, can you hold me like this for just a little while. Please?"

"If you want."

"Just stand here," she said. "Don't go in yet. I want to stay here in the doorway and look at the bed. Am I too heavy for you to carry?"

"No."

"Do you carry all of your women to bed in your arms? Don't answer. I don't want to hear about your other women."

"There aren't any others," van Lier said.

"You always know the right words. Do you really mean that?"

"Yes."

"Gil?"

"Yes?"

"Love me. Please, please, love me." It was the voice of

a sad, little girl and the sound of it was almost heartbreaking.

And then they were on the bed and she was whispering his name again and again, first slowly, then faster and there was a long sigh from her and silence before she started to moan, her audible rhythms indicating that van Lier was a patient, skillful lover. Each time when it seemed she was on the verge of orgasm, van Lier would somehow slow her down and then the moment came when she could no longer hold back nor did she want to and she called his name rapidly, *"GilGilGilGil!"* and the long cry of ecstasy that followed came from a deep and hidden place within her.

After a short silence she sighed and whispered, "I love you, I love you" and nothing was heard until she said, "Oh, God, oh, God!" and desire was again heavy in her voice as van Lier once more began to bring her to ecstasy. There were sharp moans from the both of them and she hurriedly whispered, "Don't stop! Oh, God, don't stop!" and once more she cried out at the indescribable joy electrifying her body and mind and while she grew quiet immediately after, van Lier continued.

There were sounds of bedsprings moving rhythmically, steadily and short grunts of pleasure from him until he whispered, "Baby, oh, baby!" and then his rhythm took on a special speed, a private urgency and now she was calling his name, drawing him swiftly toward the pleasure she had just known and suddenly he groaned loudly, reaching his climax and after long seconds had passed, he too was quiet.

Renata whispered, "I'm glad I decided to see my designer today."

"And go shopping. Don't forget, you went shopping."

"Did I spend much?"

Van Lier chuckled. "No more than usual. Don't you read the newspapers? You're supposed to be the worst spendthrift since the invention of the credit card."

"I love this apartment," she said. "It's big, it's beautiful and most of all it's quiet. I get so tired of having someone

237

around me all the time. In Washington everyone seems to be staring at me and I don't like it."

"Lovely ladies always get stared at."

"Ummm, that feels good. Don't stop. A little more to the right, near the base of the spine. Ummm, yes. Anyone ever tell you you have magic fingers?"

The telephone rang, stopping all conversation.

After a short silence van Lier said, "Forget it."

"Why? It could be important."

"It's not. All calls go to my UN office first. Cortes is there. If something's urgent, he'll call me here with a prearranged signal. He'll let the phone ring once, hang up, repeat, then immediately call again and I'll know it's him."

"Clever. You broke one of your rules today, you know."

"Which one?"

"No presents," she said. "We're not supposed to give each other presents or send letters or carry photographs of one another. Today you went shopping for me and I consider that a present, even though technically it's not."

"Consider it a present," he said. "You know why I made that rule—"

"I'm not complaining. You said we had to be careful, that we couldn't do things that would—"

"It's hard enough for you to get away by yourself. Frankly, if you weren't Renata Zachery, Washington rebel, you wouldn't be able to do it. People expect you to do something crazy every now and then. But if we start sending each other perfumed letters and flowers and knitted sweaters, Christ!"

"Please darling, don't get upset. Sometimes when I'm not with you I wish I had something of yours to cling to, to look at and be reminded of you. I'm a woman, Gil, and I need love. I need romance and everything that goes with it. Richard has his own world and there's very little room in it for me. His friends, his associates are all in politics and that's all they ever talk about. Politics, politics, politics. They get their jollies from power and a woman is only an afterthought with them. Gil, I'm alive. Alive. I

238

need someone to hold me, to tell me I'm beautiful, to see me as a woman, not as two points in a political poll. Gil, what do I do if he wants me to go with him on his campaign?"

"You go. You're his wife."

"But, but it means you and I will be apart."

"No," said van Lier softly. "It just means it'll be harder for us to get together. Remember what I told you: I don't have problems. I only have opportunities."

The telephone rang again.

Van Lier chuckled. "Hey, hey. Calm down. Don't be so jumpy."

"Don't be so jumpy, he says. Easy for you to say. You're always cool. You like problems, you enjoy intrigue, confrontations—"

"Opportunities."

"Opportunities. Can't you unplug that phone?"

"It'll stop ringing. Unplug it or take it off the hook and you'll have a few people curious about what's going on over here, curious enough to pay us a visit and we don't want that. Relax. The doctor will take care of you."

"Doctor?"

"That's me," said van Lier. "They call me doctor 'cause I make 'em feel so good."

"By them," said Renata Zachery, "I take it you mean women?"

"Aren't you curious about what you bought while shopping today?"

"Notice how cleverly he changes the subject. Yes, I'm curious. What did I buy today?"

"The best. A dress, a blouse and a skirt, from some very impressive shops."

"What's the dress like?" she asked.

"Ankle length, a very pale lavender, sleeveless and high neck. Should look great. It's your color."

"Sounds fantastic. Maybe I'll wear the dress next week. Washington's having one of the biggest events of the year, a benefit performance by the Bolshoi Ballet. Top tickets are a thousand dollars each and I'll have you know I'm the honorary chairman or chairperson. It's next Saturday night. Will you be in town then?"

"No."

"I forgot. Africa?"

"Yes."

There was disappointment in her voice. "Just thought I'd ask. They tell me I'm leader of what is supposed to be Washington society."

"You photograph well," said van Lier.

"Seems to be the only qualification necessary. Actually, I'm the winner by default. Our dear President's dear wife, religious fanatic and 'born again' Christian that she is, prefers to stay home in the White House at night reading her bible. I don't think anyone's seen her in public in months. If she ever smiled her face would crack. Every time the two of them invite me to a White House screening of a movie, it's either Disney or some piece of crap about a family living in the wilderness with bears and chipmunks. God, what a dull, dull woman she is!"

"You two seem to get along."

"Ha!" Renata said. "Credit my husband with that. He's asked me to behave myself around her and I try to. His career, you know. Let's say the President's wife and I have an understanding. We're polite to each other and neither of us throws rocks when we meet, but there's no love lost, believe me. I know she disapproves of me, my clothes, how I live my life, the fact that I won't stay home and try to get my two spoiled stepchildren to love me. Gil, I've tried everything with those kids short of opening a vein and letting them use my blood to fingerpaint with. But nothing seems to work. They resent me for having married their father, for having taken their mother's place and I don't think they'll ever accept me."

"Sometimes we forget how cruel kids can be."

"These two aren't about to let me forget. Richard wants to be President and the kids want their dead mother back and that leaves me very much alone in my own home. What's more, not a week goes by that I'm not criticized for

240

something. The press is on me, the women's clubs in Washington are on me. If I didn't have you to turn to, I don't know what I would do."

"Why don't you stop talking and come over here."

As the telephone rang, they began to make love again with a greater abandon than before, their passion forever imprisoned on the tape, forever condemning them. And when there was nothing more to hear, Neil Knightly exhaled for a long time, his eyes on the recorder. Without a word, he tossed the briefcase at Gypsy, making no attempt to hide the fact that the gesture was one of contempt.

A wide-eyed Gypsy looked first at the briefcase then at Neil, who leaned down and picked up the small recorder. "You don't have to count it," said Neil. "It's all there."

Gypsy looked down at the suitcase. His voice was barely audible.

"How much?"

"Exactly what you asked for." Neil's eyes were on the recorder he now held in both hands.

Gypsy, heart in his throat, gingerly picked at the worn briefcase, slowly unbuckling a flap and peering into the case. He saw green. Nothing but. He closed his eyes, opened them wide and looked at the money again. He wanted to sing, to shout, to dance around the room. He wanted to tell the world. Gypsy had found the biggest score of his life and he had never been happier.

"You'll hear from us," said Neil, who walked across the room, opened the front door and left the apartment. He didn't bother closing the door behind him.

Gypsy let his head flop back against the couch and breathed through his open mouth. He was dizzy with excitement and fear and for a long time he sat on the couch clutching the briefcase full of money to his burly chest.

■ ■ ■ **Twenty**

Clare Chandler was late and D'Arcy didn't like it. Annoyed, he waited alone in her study, sipping his third gin and tonic while idly thumbing through a first edition of Grimm's Fairy Tales, one of the hundreds of rare books owned by Clare. Neither the chauffeur who had met D'Arcy at Dulles Airport nor the butler who had served him drinks and a light lunch at the house would say where she was. The chauffeur had offered the only comment, passing on Mrs. Chandler's apologies for not being there. Something important had come up and she would meet Mr. D'Arcy as soon as possible.

D'Arcy, in Washington to gather news on Gil van Lier's nomination as secretary of state, was curious about what was important enough to send Clare running off hither and yon. He was also becoming increasingly irritated that she wasn't here to tell him about it.

He slammed the book shut, dropped it on a nearby

table and reached for the remainder of his drink. He was stalking the biggest story of his career and in no mood to cool his heels. While D'Arcy was wasting time staring at shelves of books, someone else could very well be poking in secret places in search of that very same story. Where in the name of the Queen Mother was Clare, the bloody cow. D'Arcy needed her contacts more than ever. The rumors surrounding van Lier's nomination were growing daily and had to be weighed, balanced, then accepted or discarded.

Was it true that when van Lier was confirmed he planned to recommend to the President that *all* major American ambassadors be recalled and replaced? Was it true that he planned to fire a minimum of eight hundred State Department employees? Had the Cuban government, holding out promises of future goodwill, secretly contacted Washington to urge van Lier's confirmation? Had Richard Zachery promised cabinet posts (after he was elected President) to important congressmen in return for their support of Gil van Lier? Was South Africa spending a million dollars to finance a secret lobby in Congress against van Lier?

D'Arcy rolled his empty glass between the palms of his hands. Truth and falsehood were so interwoven in the tapestry called life that even God with a microscope couldn't tell the difference. D'Arcy looked at the telephone. Perhaps he should make a few more calls. He had already spoken to several of his local gossip contacts, coming up with a half-dozen items and passing them on to his assistants in New York for tomorrow's column. D'Arcy hadn't brought up Gil van Lier's name. He listened and took notes, but van Lier was a subject he preferred discussing only with Clare Chandler. D'Arcy didn't want to alert anyone to the fact that his interest in the black diplomat went deeper than the man's political career. If D'Arcy had a fear of anything at this point it was having someone else break the news of *the affair* before he did.

D'Arcy was headed toward the telephone when the

study door burst open and a breathless Clare Chandler rushed into the room.

"Robin, Robin, please forgive me. I'm sorry I'm late. It was totally unavoidable. You already have a drink. Good."

She was in his arms, cheek brushing his and kissing the air in the traditional greeting found in those circles she'd frequented all her life. Clare Chandler smelled of expensive perfume which D'Arcy knew she occasionally had sent to her from Paris by diplomatic pouch, her way of avoiding customs duty. She collapsed in D'Arcy's still warm chair, slipping off her shoes and sighing. "God, they just wouldn't let me leave. I kept telling them I had someone coming from New York, but they ignored me. They kept on talking and talking and talking."

There was a knock at the study door.

"My drink," she said breathlessly. "Robin, would you?"

"Why not? It's the absolute high point of my day carrying alcohol across this room. I'm getting good at it."

"Dear Robin, I'm sorry I kept you waiting. I simply couldn't get away. Wait until you hear my news. I really do need that drink."

D'Arcy opened the door and took a vodka gimlet on a small silver tray from a servant, then slammed the door in his face and brought the drink to Clare. With a ravenous expression, she reached for the glass with two hands and drained half of it in one gulp.

Letting her head flop back against the leather chair, she exhaled.

D'Arcy stroked the side of his long nose with one finger and waited.

Clare's eyes were closed and she rubbed the back of her neck with one hand. "Adam Danziger," she said.

D'Arcy froze.

"He and Deirdre, she's his wife," said Clare, "they called me a half-hour before I was about to leave to meet you at the airport. They had to see me. Absolutely had to see me. Couldn't postpone it, couldn't do it another time. It had to be now, so what could I do? They're both old friends and, before you say anything, I know you don't like him."

"All he ever did," said D'Arcy, "was threaten my paper with a ten-million-dollar lawsuit if it printed my columns on his taking kickbacks from contracts in his home state of Florida. The bastard is up to his addled brain in bribes, payoffs and filthy money."

"Oh, Robin, come on. You admitted there wasn't enough proof, otherwise you'd have published the column."

"And furthermore," said D'Arcy, "he beats his whores to a pulp and sends them to the hospital looking like war casualties. He's done that three times in the past year."

"And so have a few others in this town. If you impeached every congressman who slapped a slut, you'd have plenty of empty chairs up on Capitol Hill."

"I said he beat them, not slapped them. There's a difference, dear heart, and yes, I don't like your Adam Danziger and I haven't forgotten him, I can assure you."

"Robin, my head's aching. Don't shout at me, please."

"What about Danziger?"

"There's a benefit performance next week at the Kennedy Center for the Performing Arts. It'll feature the Bolshoi Ballet and it's just about the biggest event of the social season so far. Everybody's going and if you don't have a ticket, you don't dare show your face. It's quite a plum to be a member of the sponsoring committee, but the biggest plum of all is the chairmanship. Deirdre Danziger had her heart set on it. She was told she had it, that her name would be on the letterhead and she'd be photographed by the newspapers, that she'd meet the dance troupe at the Russian Embassy, be photographed with the Russian ambassador, the whole bit. The dancers are presenting the chairman with an honorary membership in their troupe and you have to know Deirdre to realize how much this would have meant to her. She's a frustrated ballerina and—"

"How old is she?"

"Fifty-six. Why?"

D'Arcy sneered. "Rather long in the tooth to be leaping about in a tutu, isn't she?"

"Robin, please."

"Sorry. Do continue. I find this tale of yours mesmerizing."

"She wanted that chairmanship," said Clare. "These sort of things matter a great deal in this town. Anyway, she didn't get it. Renata Zachery got it instead. The powers that be felt she would ensure a better turnout, that she'd draw more money as well as press coverage. Tickets are a thousand dollars, some of them anyway. Renata, as they say, is box office. Well, Deirdre was crushed and she asked me if I could do anything, if I could pull a few strings and use my influence to get her named chairman instead. I tried, God I tried, but Mrs. Zachery has her coterie of admirers and I didn't get very far."

"Is this what took you so long?" asked D'Arcy.

"Robin, she's my friend and so is Adam. I had to listen, I had to try to help them. Deirdre's very social and she'd already told a lot of people she was going to be honorary chairman."

"And now she feels like a fool."

"Yes, she does. And Adam's angry because he thinks it's a slap at him. He was a madman, cursing and carrying on and insisting that I do something, anything, to get Deirdre the chairmanship. I couldn't. I tried but I couldn't."

Clare looked at D'Arcy. "And then he said something else. He said Renata would pay for what she'd done to Dierdre. Somehow he thinks Renata did it deliberately. I disagree. Renata doesn't give a damn what happens in this town. She simply was offered the position and took it."

"What did Danziger say?"

"He said Renata was going to be sorry. Danziger said the pendulum swings both ways and one day he'd be riding high enough, as he put it, to piss on Renata Zachery and her jungle bunny."

D'Arcy cocked one pale, blond eyebrow. "He said that?"

246

Clare Chandler paused with the remainder of her drink in front of her lips. "Did he ever."

"Did he mention van Lier?"

"He didn't mention any name, but that's who he meant." She drank, eyes closed in the temporary contentment alcohol gave her.

"Danziger's a senator," said D'Arcy. "He's on a few important committees. How much higher can he go?"

Clare Chandler daintily bit a stuffed olive in half. "Lots. Aaron Banner's considering him as a running mate. And he's already set to give the keynote speech at the nominating convention."

"Vice-President Adam T. Danziger. I suppose it has as much a ring to it as anything else the electoral process can produce. Banner and Danziger. My, my."

Clare took a deep breath, exhaled and shook her head. "I said I had some news for you." She looked at D'Arcy and after a few seconds she said, "Adam lost his temper over this business with Deirdre and Renata Zachery and I guess he said a few things to me he didn't mean to. He said *they* were tapping phones, that when they were finished Renata Zachery and her jig would be so embarrassed, they'd kill themselves. Those were his exact words. They'd be so embarrassed they'd kill themselves."

D'Arcy was at her side, his eyes bright with attention. "Go on, love."

"I've never seen him this angry before. He swore the whole country would hear about it one of these days. As he put it, there's no way she can get out of this one. They had it on tape and she was going to be one very sorry lady. Adam has a temper, you know, and he can really get worked up."

"There are a few bruised tarts who couldn't agree with you more. Did he say who's doing this taping, who has these recordings?"

"No. Frankly, I became a little nervous at hearing all of this. The last thing I want to do is get involved in something I shouldn't. I'm thinking of calling Aaron and telling him what Adam said, about the tapes I mean. Between

247

you and me I don't give a damn what happens to Renata Zachery. They can bury her alive and upside down for all I care."

D'Arcy gently took her hands in his. "You haven't called Aaron Banner yet?"

"No."

"Don't."

"Why not?"

D'Arcy kissed her fingertips, his green eyes on her face. "Because, dear heart, something tells me he already knows about these tapes. I'd hazard a guess that your Senator Banner is the man responsible for this wiretapping."

"Aaron? *No.*" Clare eyed D'Arcy as though she'd never seen him before.

D'Arcy was on his feet, pacing and running a hand through his hair. "Your defense of your important friends is commendable, but I do believe it's misplaced. To begin with, your Mr. Danziger said *they*. He said *they* had the tapes."

"Yes, but—"

"Meaning he's not alone in this sordid little business. Meaning he did not decide on his own to go forth and spy on Mrs. Zachery and her dusky lover. He'd be absolutely stupid to do that, to risk his chance at higher office. While I'm no admirer of the man, I do give him credit for not being enamored of political suicide. No, your Mr. Danziger is a number-two man, a lieutenant, not a captain. He takes orders, he listens, he obeys and that's why he is in line to be a heartbeat away from the presidency, as you people put it. He does what Aaron Banner tells him to do. *They*, my precious. Banner and Danziger. A twosome to set the mind a-pondering. And Banner is in charge. If anyone's calling the shots on this wiretapping business it's he, because he has the most to gain."

"You really think he'd go that far?"

"Dear Clare, *please!* You've been in this town long enough to know how far its inhabitants would go for power. They'd do anything for it and do it twice over. Watergate proved there's no such thing as *too far.*"

Clare bit her lip. "Robin, I really think I should call Aaron."

D'Arcy was again at her side, taking her hand and kissing it, then stroking it while he talked. "Dear one, don't even think such thoughts. Mentioning the tapes to him will constitute a warning and forewarned is forearmed. Those tapes will become even more inaccessible and I don't need that. I must learn more about them. If God is kind I'll even get to hear them. The last thing we need is for Banner to know I'm aware of what he's up to. Now, let us discuss how we go about learning more of Mr. B's interest in wiretapping."

D'Arcy gazed at the ceiling. "We can eliminate the CIA, FBI and all government agencies. Banner doesn't have the power to command them. Not yet anyway and besides, it's doubtful an agency would officially accept such a job. No, I'm afraid we can assume Banner's procured an independent for this task, someone who'll keep quiet, someone preferably unknown around town. But who?"

"There's a man who could help us find out," said Clare.

"That's my precious. Who?"

"Bob Michaelson. He owns a security agency that furnishes burglar alarms, bodyguards, guard dogs to some of the biggest people in town. When my last husband was alive, Bob had the contract to take care of the security for all his plants. After Charles died I recommended to the board of directors that Bob be kept on and he's been very grateful ever since."

D'Arcy smiled. "He owes you." He loved using American expressions.

"Yes."

D'Arcy pointed to the telephone. "Ask him if Banner's hired anyone to do a bug job for him. No. Ask if, if Banner—and add the names of three more top congressmen or government officials—ask if these four men have hired Michaelson or anyone else for a bug job. Let us use diversion where we can. Toss in those other names to keep

249

Michaelson off balance. Banner's important and important men lead such a fishbowl existence."

"Any three men plus Banner?"

"Top drawer only."

Clare stood up and took one step toward the telephone before stopping. "Aaron wouldn't do this sort of thing himself. He'd turn it over to Neil Knightly."

"The resident dirty trickster is he?"

"You might say that."

D'Arcy rubbed his hands together in satisfaction. "Mention Mr. Knightly's name to Michaelson as well. Get on with it. Onward and upward. Huzzah and excelsior and all that."

Clare reached Michaelson, who told her he'd ask around and get right back to her. Forty-five minutes later, Michaelson called back. He himself wasn't working with any of the names mentioned by Clare, nor was any other agency in town. Michaelson guessed that an independent might be working for the four men but he doubted it. Michaelson knew every competent wiretapper in town and none of them were involved with the names Clare had mentioned. If these men were using a wiretapper at the present time, it was someone from out of town.

"What's next?" Clare asked D'Arcy.

"Neil Knightly. Don't call him. Just find out where he is at the moment."

Clare did.

"New York," she said.

A thoughtful D'Arcy tapped his thin mouth with a forefinger. "And so are Renata Zachery and Gil van Lier. All three in New York at the same time."

Gently brushing Clare Chandler's cheek with the back of his hand, D'Arcy said, "And so, I might add, is our unknown wiretapper, the man whom Aaron Banner has hired to hand him the presidency."

# ■ ■ ■ Twenty-One

Courage, Monica Hollander reminded herself, was grace under pressure. Therefore the trick to controlling her fear this afternoon would be to appear as graceful as possible. Harold Monmouth, gracious and well-mannered, met her just inside the door of the *Examiner-World* conference room and after Monica returned his smile she quickly willed her hand not to shake as she extended it to meet his. She wanted a cigarette but thought it best to ignore her screaming nerves until she was seated and had finished informing Monmouth that she couldn't spy on Burt Anthony any longer. After that she *knew* she would need a cigarette. And possibly a new job.

Gently touching her elbow the publisher guided her to a chair at the near end of a long table. He sat down beside her and crossed his legs. "Terribly nice to see you again, Monica. You've been keeping busy with our gossip columnist and there hasn't been the opportunity to get together as often as I would prefer. Well now, what's so important that you couldn't tell me over the telephone?"

Monica waited as Monmouth quickly looked at his pocket watch, decided how many minutes he could spare her, then slipped the watch back into his vest pocket. Taking a deep breath, she was about to speak when she saw Denis Radd at the far end of the conference table. He was in his shirt sleeves and a hand was balled into a fist as he hunched over a telephone speaking in a low voice to someone at the other end of the line. The beefy, red-faced editor was fighting hard to control his anger.

Monica had wanted to talk with Monmouth alone. Yet somehow the presence of a third party in the room didn't upset her as much as she thought it would. She had come this far and fear or no fear she would find the strength to say what she had wanted to say for some time.

"Don't mind Denis," said Monmouth. "A slight problem to be ironed out downstairs. We've just fired an institution."

"His being here doesn't bother me. Who did you fire?"

Monmouth chuckled, stretching his legs out in front of him. "Sargent Alexander, the columnist. Manhattan's own man about Manhattan, as he enjoys referring to himself. He's been scribbling his fey little columns on this city for more than twenty years. We've decided to let him go and now there's some sort of backlash among his supporters on the staff. His union is also making resentful noises in my direction. But not to worry. There are times when I have difficulty convincing American unions that this paper is my property and that I am free to do with it as I please. Denis can handle the matter. Now, what is it you want to talk about?"

"I want to talk to you about Burt Anthony."

"Yes." The publisher smiled and waited patiently for her to continue and in that instant Monica sensed he knew why she was here.

"I can't continue spying on him for you," she said. "I find it distasteful. It's turning into one of the hardest things I've ever had to do and I don't like it. The sooner I stop doing it, the better I'll feel."

"I see. You're in love with Burt Anthony, of course."

Monica lit a cigarette and said nothing, making sure she kept her eyes on Monmouth's face. *Grace under pressure.* Nobody ever said it was easy.

"As I suspected," said Monmouth. He waited for her to react to what he'd said, and when she didn't he continued. "Association breeds attachment and your past few weeks of association with Mr. Anthony have resulted in an attachment that has now taken its toll upon your job."

The words were out before she could stop them. "That's not true. I *am* doing my job and doing it well. Burt's gotten at least as much coverage as D'Arcy. You have the clips to prove it. Magazines, wire services, television and radio appearances, you name it and I'll show you where I've placed Burt Anthony."

"Agreed," said a smiling Monmouth. "The cuttings are piled high on my desk and the name of Burt Anthony is included in each and every one. But let's acknowledge one rule. I and I alone define your job. I'm the one who must be satisfied, who determines what your job entails and the sole judge as to whether or not you've done well. You've produced press cuttings on Burt Anthony, but that's not all I expect you to produce. I'm paying for more and I expect more."

"Mr. Monmouth, obviously this bothers me more than it does you. A lot more, in fact. But it does bother me and eventually it's going to affect my relationship with Burt as a client, to say nothing of my relationship with him in any other capacity. I didn't know it would come to this, that I'd get to the point where I couldn't look him in the face. But that's what's happened. Literally I cannot look the man in the face and I realize it's as much my fault for agreeing to spy in the first place as it is your fault for asking me."

"You feel you're hurting him," said Monmouth.

Monica nodded.

The publisher leaned forward, a forefinger aimed at her. "Has it ever occurred to you that all life on this planet is at the expense of someone or something else? We slaughter animals to eat their flesh and wear their skins. Trees are cut down for firewood, shelter and I might add, for newspapers. Wars are waged and men killed so that other men might live. Buildings are demolished so that buildings may be erected. No intelligent person would deny the necessity for any of this and yet destruction lies at the core of everything I've just told you. Life harms life and only because of this does life continue. It happens a thousand times a day at all levels of existence and no one thinks twice about it."

He pulled his chair closer to her, his voice that of a firm, all-knowing father. "Exploitation is the order of things and I know what I'm talking about. Not a year goes by that I don't have to explain my position exactly in these terms to both my detractors and my competitors. This isn't something you have to like, but you must accept it. The law of the jungle, as it's commonly called, may sound offensive and to use your word, distasteful. But it's reality. Monica, people are hurt every day on this planet and to concern yourself about it unnecessarily is rather juvenile, I would say. Life will go on and the price to be paid for this must and will be paid."

She waited until she had finished lighting her second cigarette. Out of the corner of her eye she saw Denis Radd slam the telephone down, mutter an obscenity then dial again.

She said, "Mr. Monmouth, I stopped being an infant a long time ago. And while it may not show, I've been through a few wars of my own, particularly in the theater and in journalism. People play rough in both fields and I have scars to prove it. I was young and a woman and neither fact prevented me from getting hurt. However, I've seen enough to know that life doesn't have to be dirty pool all the time and that's what should be added to this discussion. You're telling me dirty pool is the only way and I disagree."

Monmouth leaned away from her, again folding his hands in his lap. "Let us say you've come to disagree after having fallen in love. The cleansing effect of passion, so to speak."

254

Monica nervously reached for the ashtray. "Mr. Monmouth, with all due respect, how I came to see the right and wrong of it doesn't matter."

"Oh, but it does matter, Monica."

"Why?"

"Because you, like Burt Anthony, accepted all conditions of employment when you came to work for me whether you both knew it or not."

"Looks as though you're defining Burt's job for him the same way you're defining mine."

"Precisely."

"I see." Ignoring her pounding heart Monica added, "You wouldn't be making up the rules for the both of us as you go along, would you?"

Throwing his head back, Monmouth chuckled. "Ah, Monica. I do like you. I genuinely like you. Like all American women you're so energetic and you work at a pace that is exhausting to watch. I admire your independence and contrary to what you might think, I do not find it to my advantage to crush the spirit of my employees. People who cannot stand up to me cannot stand up for me. But the fact remains that I and I alone am the final authority regarding the performance of those in my employ. The success of the *Examiner-World* is of paramount importance in my life and nothing must be allowed to prevent that success. When I say nothing, I mean precisely that."

Monica saw Monmouth quickly turn toward the sound of Denis Radd pounding the table with the flat of his hand and shouting, "No, no, no!" into the telephone. Neither Radd nor Monica would ever be as determined as Harold Monmouth and Monica knew why. Weeks ago she had gone out for drinks with a pair of English reporters who had just arrived in America to begin jobs on the *Examiner-World*. They had told her about Harold Monmouth, who was born poor and a Jew in class-ridden, anti-Semitic England and how hard he had worked to become wealthy and influential; about his continuing attempts to use that wealth to buy acceptance from the aristocracy.

Monmouth had been determined to gain recognition for himself and his wife and it was this intense social climbing that became a welcomed target for Robin Ian D'Arcy, who had used his London gossip column to brutally savage the publisher. D'Arcy had even accused Monmouth's beloved wife of being a "jerrybag," an epithet applied to English women who'd slept with German soldiers in World War II during the Nazi occupation of the English Channel Islands of Jersey and Guernsey. D'Arcy's story on Monmouth's attempt to bribe his way onto the honors list in hopes of obtaining a knighthood hadn't personally hurt the publisher as much as the story on his wife's indiscretion as a girl of seventeen. *Jerrybag*. According to the two British reporters that's what thugs hired by Monmouth had repeated the night they'd beaten D'Arcy bloody in front of his London flat.

Monmouth was now determined to beat D'Arcy in New York and this time he was using Burt Anthony to do it.

"Monica?" Monmouth's voice was softly persistent.

She looked at him.

"It must be my way," he said. "With all due respect to you, I have to do things my way. That's why I make a point of paying you an excellent salary. I am paying for the privilege of being the boss. Your job depends on you agreeing to this one condition, that when you work for me you do as I ask. Is that understood?"

"Whatever happened to compromise?"

"It's a word I abandoned a long time ago. As much as I like you and am pleased with your work, I can and will replace you if need be."

She closed her eyes. "And so the hurting goes on."

"I suppose it does, yes."

Taking her cigarette lighter from the table she dropped it into her purse. Another birthday coming up soon and the last thing she needed was to celebrate it with another failure. In the past she had failed to become an actress, a reporter, a woman fulfilled in love. At the moment she had a job that paid very well and Burt Anthony being in her life gave her hope that this time she might even win at love. But those gods who had presented her with both love and money were demanding payment.

"Either or," she said softly.

Monmouth nodded in agreement.

Monica rose to her feet, her courage almost gone. However, there was something else within her. There was anger at having to live her life according to someone else's guidelines and it was this anger that made her look at Monmouth and say, "I thought you might understand. You've been concerned enough about another person to, to—"

Monmouth leaned his head back, his slitted eyes never leaving her face. "To what, Monica?"

He waited.

Monica blinked tears from her eyes and looked down at the floor. At the same time Denis Radd concluded his telephone call and began walking toward them. Monica had her back to the two men and was drying her eyes as the publisher said to Radd, "Monica could use a drink and by the looks of things I think you could use a break yourself. Why don't you two go somewhere now and relax a few minutes over a glass of sherry."

Sure that Monmouth was ordering and not asking him, Denis Radd rubbed the back of his own neck and said, "Think I'll do just that."

A numb Monica said nothing as Radd put an arm around her shoulders. "Let's go, me darlin'. I know a dark and quiet place hereabouts where the food is absolutely filthy and the drinks are dangerous to your health. You'll love it."

Monmouth watched them leave and for several seconds after the door to the conference room closed behind them he continued to stand in place. At one point his eyes went from the door to the empty chair in which Monica had been sitting then back to the door again. He almost smiled.

You're right, he told the absent Monica. I did care enough to have D'Arcy beaten.

Suddenly forcing his mind to deal with more immediate

257

matters, Monmouth looked at his pocket watch again. There was no time to concern himself with what Monica thought.

## New York City

FBI agent Arthur LaChance stuck both hands in his back pockets and slowly walked across his office to stand behind Gypsy's chair and stare at the lined red skin on the back of the wiretapper's neck. When he saw the man squirm and reach back to stroke his neck, LaChance knew he had won that small battle in the war of nerves. LaChance said, "We're pros, you and I. We've been around and we both know how the game is played. It's not easy for you to do what we're talking about, but look at it this way. Somebody's going to take a fall on this one. Somebody's going to jail. It's either you or them but take my word for it, somebody is going down. You can decide who."

LaChance waited. He was trying to convince Gypsy to turn informer, to "roll over," "to do the right thing." Placing a hand on the wiretapper's shoulder, LaChance lowered his voice. "You really don't have a choice, you know. I want to help you if I can, but that means you've got to help me, too. Unless you give me something, I can't very well go in to my people and ask them to give you something. Now that's only fair, right, Dan?"

This was LaChance's third straight day of interrogating Dan Einstein, the best wiretapper in New York if not the entire country. If he didn't get something out of Einstein soon, LaChance's superiors would want to know why the bureau's time was being wasted. Einstein, whose street name was Danny the Jew, was ugly, overweight and gross, with a garbage can for a stomach. He ate enough for six people every day of his life, but his talent for electronic eavesdropping was the best money could buy. Danny the Jew worked for both sides, the law and the wise guys, and he had laughed at the thought of going to jail. He knew too many people to get arrested, he bragged.

Fat Danny wasn't laughing anymore because unless he "flipped" and turned informant, he was going to a federal penitentiary at Atlanta or Lewisburg, where any time he'd do would be hard time.

LaChance looked at the tape recorder on his desk then at the two agents in the room, who were acting as witnesses to the interrogation. The only way to make this case was to get Dan Einstein to inform, Einstein who had done months of wiretapping for the Bonnetti family, a job that meant he knew plenty about the mob. LaChance was doing the best he could to convince Einstein that it was in his own best interest to talk and talk soon. Three days ago LaChance had arrested the wiretapper at the apartment of a Chinese woman, who'd cried as if Einstein was being taken away to be shot. It mystified LaChance that someone as pretty as she would give a rat's ass about a man like Danny the Jew, whose face looked as if it had been combed with a rake.

LaChance wanted information on the Bonnetti family's role in stock frauds, stolen securities and the looting of top Wall Street brokerage houses, all big money crimes, all crimes that could financially cripple numerous investors in the stock market. The boastful Einstein had made a mistake in telling Bonnetti about FBI bugs planted in an East Side restaurant owned by the Mafia leader and now LaChance was squeezing Danny the Jew for that mistake. The FBI agency had told the wiretapper that by warning Bonnetti of federal surveillance he had made himself an accessory before the fact. Making this charge stick wouldn't be easy, but it was all LaChance had and he was going to run with it.

The wiretapper turned in his chair to face LaChance with red-rimmed eyes. So close, so goddam close to scoring big and now this had to happen. Gypsy had made almost $100,000 from Senator Banner and there was more to come. All Gypsy had to do was wait until Gil van Lier returned from Africa and Europe and made his move toward Renata Zachery again. Gypsy was sure he would hear from Banner and Neil Knightly again and the money would start flow once more. That was what Gypsy wanted to be doing. He wanted to be collecting his pot of gold at the end of his personal rainbow instead of sitting in a hard chair at FBI headquarters on East 69th Street and watching his world come apart like some cheap toy. Gypsy had never taken a fall in his life, never spent one night in jail.

LaChance leaned over until his lips almost touched Einstein's ear. "A lawyer can't do it for you this time. Yes, I know you walked a couple of times in the past because we couldn't make anything stick. You played both sides, you made a few bucks. But, my friend, you have impeded a federal investigation and let me tell you we can really go to town on this one."

Gypsy's eyes shimmered behind tears. "You want me to give up some heavy people, LaChance. I haven't finked in my life. If you got a sheet on me, you know that."

LaChance placed an arm around Einstein's shoulders and softened his voice. It was stroke time and LaChance played the game as well as any agent in the bureau. "Dan, let me tell you a little about Atlanta. You've probably heard that it's a hellhole, the worst. You're right. What I bet you don't know about are the killings. Yes, the killings. I'm telling it to you straight, Dan. In the past eighteen months, there's been something like fifteen cons killed inside and there's not a thing we can do to stop it. We both know cons actually rule a prison. The warden and the guards collect their checks and try to stay alive and that's about it.

"Something else about Atlanta, Dan. We've got a lot of crazies there. Guys who are doing two hundred years and four consecutive life terms, the kind of people who have nothing to lose. They flip out all the time, Dan. They'll stick a shiv in your ribs just to get your shoes or because somebody paid them a pack of cigarettes to do it or because somebody wants to get their hands on your pretty little boyfriend. Maybe they'll kill you because you won't take down your pants and be their girlfriend. One more thing, Dan. You've been in here three days and the way people think on the street three days is more than enough time to talk. Wouldn't surprise me if somebody hasn't already decided you've rolled over for us."

Gypsy tried to stand up but LaChance pushed him back down into the chair. Gypsy said, "You kept me here deliberately. You set me up. Three days—"

LaChance kept his voice even. "Dan, I've got a job to do. Come on, we're pros, you and me. We both know how the game is played. One thing I forgot to add. On the street you can eat. Remember that, Dan. Outside you can eat what you want, when you want. Inside it's just not that way. Think on it, Dan. Think on it hard."

Einstein cleared his throat. "I'm thirsty."

"Coffee?" LaChance watched the wiretapper carefully and held his breath. Experience told him that Einstein was on the edge of deciding one way or another. "Coke," said Einstein. "Two. No, make it three and you got any brown sugar?"

One of the agents stood up. "Back in a minute."

And that's when LaChance knew that Dan Einstein had decided to inform against the Bonnetti family. LaChance's eyes took on a hard gleam and he forced himself to stay calm, controlled.

# ■ ■ ■ Twenty-Two

No matter how late he stayed up collecting gossip, Burt managed to be out of bed by noon the next day. On rising he slipped into a sweat shirt and shorts, dialed an all-news station on the radio and ran in place for ten minutes. Then came fifty situps and fifty pushups followed by standing on his head, feet touching the wall for exactly three minutes. Very California, smirked Monica. Your El Lay obsession with geriatrics. Cheaper than therapy, Burt had replied and first-class sublimation if your sex life is down a few points.

By one o'clock he had shaved, showered, eaten breakfast and was waiting when the punctual Molly rang his door-bell. Once at her desk, Molly placed a small gold crucifix to the right of her typewriter and covered it with a rosary of pale blue plastic beads. Having secured God's help for the rest of the day she went to work without another word, first checking the answering service and typing a list of callers. Burt scanned the list, deciding what calls should be returned.

Today's first caller, as usual, had been Harold Monmouth and Burt, wondering what the Englishman wanted to complain about, ordered Molly to get him. No matter how many names were on the list Monmouth's rated number one. Seconds later Molly reported that number one was tied up in conference and would call back later. Grateful for Monmouth's unavailability Burt told Molly to call Hoyt Pathy in Washington. Getting Pathy wasn't easy and while Molly cradled the receiver between her ear and shoulder and typed, Burt dialed Monica's office.

For the past three days he hadn't seen or spoken to Monica and it wasn't from lack of trying. On the surface it seemed as though they were missing each other by just inches. Burt, however, was getting strange vibes, vibes which said Monica was avoiding him. He had no idea why and there was the possibility he was reading into her actions things that weren't there. But she hadn't returned any of his phone calls and most surprising of all, she hadn't acknowledged flowers he had sent her. This time a male voice sounding as if it were holding its nose told Burt that Miss Hollander wasn't in the office and would he care to leave a message. After asking if Monica had arranged any more interviews for him and finding out she hadn't Burt left his name and number and hung up. The vibes were stronger now. A quick check of the list of callers showed Monica's name wasn't there. Bad vibes were now a tight wire around his brain.

"Burt?"

He turned toward Molly.

"I have Hoyt Pathy for you," she said. "On four."

Burt picked up the phone. "Hoyt. What's shaking?"

"Plenty. But I can't talk to you right now."

"Are you alone?"

"No." Pathy was definite about that.

"How do we work it?" asked Burt. "Shall I call back or will you call me?"

"I'll call you. There's somebody you might want to talk to. In fact I'm *sure* you'll want to talk to him. I spoke to him last night and he wants to get together."

"Jesus Christ, can't you even give me a hint?"

"No. I've got people with me," said Pathy. "I'm afraid you'll just have to *wing* it. *Wing* it, good buddy."

Burt frowned, shifting the receiver to another ear. *Wing*. That was the code word, but what was Hoyt Pathy trying to tell him? Burt snapped his fingers. "The pilot. You spoke to the pilot who gave you those photographs and the notebook."

"That seems to be the case," said Pathy with a false calm. "I think it would be better for me to check my figures on this and get back to you. Will you be at this number long?"

"I'm here until I get your call."

"Good." Hoyt Pathy hung up.

Burt slumped in his chair, a hand holding the telephone cord while the receiver dangled and spun around in crazy circles. *Good*. That's all Hoyt Pathy said before hanging up. *Good*. Now all Burt could do was sit tight and feel his stomach lining being eaten away while he waited for Pathy to call again with the biggest story of Burt's life. A face-to-face talk with the pilot would give Burt an eyewitness account of what American troops were secretly doing in Africa. As for van Lier he had arrived in Chindé for Robert Mswamba's funeral and so far was still very much alive. The black leader who had succeeded Mswamba was giving van Lier a hard time and the white minority was busy arming itself against expected black retaliation for Mswamba's death. There had been no meeting of black and white since the funeral; the best van Lier had been able to do was to arrange a meeting between the blacks and himself. For the moment, blacks were in no mood to talk peace with whites.

And then there was van Lier's affair with Renata Zachery. Burt had read clips on the couple from twenty different newspapers and magazines and he had talked to his Washington sources, most of whom had dismissed the affair as "mere gossip." Not everyone had, however. Some were sure the affair was real, but could offer nothing concrete in the way of proof. Proof was Burt's job. He would have to be the one to cart this particular dead horse up the stairs and stuff it in van Lier's bathtub for the world to see.

No one in Washington had mentioned anything about van Lier being involved with American troops in Africa and for that, Burt was extremely grateful. That was his baby, his ladder to climb and the less anyone else knew about it the better. Congress was still holding hearings on van Lier's nomination as secretary of state and the press was printing every conceivable nomination story it could find or invent. When the subject of van Lier's taxes was brought up a quick check revealed that for the past two years he had overpaid his taxes. Even the IRS had fallen into step behind Gil van Lucky, who Burt suspected was clever and farsighted enough to have deliberately overpaid his taxes in case of such an investigation.

Newspapers carried wire service photographs from Chindé showing van Lier surrounded by armed, uniformed guards who stayed close to him from the airport to the funeral. No matter how many people were around him van Lier stood out, his handsome face controlled, his bearing almost regal. Burt, despite working on two stories that could destroy the man, had to admire him for managing to appear indifferent to assassination threats not to mention the potential destruction of his career by scandal. The story Burt was writing on van Lier included the diplomat's evasive quotes during their first interview. They would furnish quite a contrast with whatever else Burt could dig up on the twelve dead GIs. Admiration for van Lier's insistence on being a target in Africa had nothing to do with telling the truth about him. As for Renata Zachery, Burt hadn't forgotten her. But his mind kept shifting to Monica Hollander and when the telephone rang, Burt, hoping it was her, grabbed the receiver before Molly could touch it.

"Hello?" said a male voice. "Burt Anthony, please."

"Hoyt, it's me."

"I'm in a phone booth. Sorry I couldn't talk before, but all calls go through a switchboard. You understand."

"Sure. What's up?"

"Take down this name," said Pathy. "Donald Rettig. Last name's spelled with two tees. He's the pilot and he lives in Camden, New Jersey. Now for the bad news."

"Let's have it."

Hoyt Pathy cleared his throat. "Remember I told you Rettig wanted to get together with you?"

"And now he doesn't. What the hell went down between now and the last time you called, which was less than twenty minutes ago?"

"Rettig called me just after I hung up with you. Said he'd changed his mind and didn't want to see you. Didn't want to see any reporters."

"He say why?"

"No. But I've got a wild guess if you'd care to hear it."

"I care."

"All this time Rettig's big complaint, his one complaint has been money. He wasn't getting what he felt he had coming and he also wasn't getting any medical care for his missing arm. If he's suddenly gone quiet I'd have to say someone probably came up with a few bucks. Nothing else would cool him out, but that's just a guess."

Burt's smile was tight. "Here's another guess. If somebody reached your friend Rettig, it might mean they know he's been talking."

"Holy shit. I never thought of that."

"Hoyt, in my business a little paranoia helps."

"Jesus." Hoyt Pathy's voice was higher, his breathing louder. "What the hell am I going to do? Man, I don't need this."

"Need what?"

"Creepy crawlies on my case. The FBI, CIA or whoever is doing black bag jobs these days. People tapping my phones, following me around, checking my tax records, my bank records—"

"Hoyt," said Burt deliberately, "climb down off the ceiling. I'm only guessing. Look, the sixties are over. Your job's safe. Nixon's out in San Clemente working on his memoirs and the rest of his gang is off somewhere talking to *their* agents about book deals. Nothing to worry about. Probably somebody acting on his own approached Rettig and gave him money."

Hoyt Pathy sounded only a little less intense. "It's different now, Burt. You've got to understand that. I'm into a different game now. It's called respectability. It's called winning."

"I do understand it, Hoyt. Maybe that's my trouble. I understand it too well because I'm into a different game, too, and I wonder about it. I wonder about it a whole lot. Now let's talk about Donald Rettig. Where does he live?"

"What do you have in mind?"

Burt reached for a pencil. "I'm going to see him. Surprise visit. And before you tell me again that he's changed his mind, don't bother. I've gone through this before. Once I get my foot in the door he'll talk to me. I'll make him talk to me."

"He lives in Camden, so you might end up driving a long way for nothing."

"Hoyt, if Rettig's changed his mind because van Lier's throwing money at him, then I want to know. Van Lier's asked me to put this thing on the back burner, to give him a few days grace while he tries to stop the killing in Chindé. Well if he's sneaking around behind my back and trying to cover up during our little truce, now that's a no-no and all bets are off. What's Rettig's address?"

Hoyt Pathy told him, then added, "This item might have a little something to do with van Lier. Word is that Renata Zachery and her husband are now sleeping in separate bedrooms. She's also supposed to have another small problem. She's said to be pregnant and talk is it might not be by her husband. Burt, you still there?"

"Yes."

"Why are you so quiet all of a sudden?"

"Thinking over what you just told me about Renata Zachery. It sounds good, but how can I run with it? It's rumor, innuendo—"

"It's gossip and that's how you make your living. Anyway, it's up to you whether you use it or not. I think the bit about separate bedrooms is firm. My source on that is good. The other thing, well, I don't know. I heard it and I'm just passing it on. You take it from there. You really going to see Rettig?"

"Soon as I hang up. Don't worry. Your name doesn't figure in any of this. You're my own Deep Throat and I'm not about to share you with the world."

Hoyt Pathy didn't sound reassured. He sounded like a man who wished he had never gotten involved. "Man, if they're tapping my phones—"

"Hoyt, call in an electronics expert and have him clean your office. If there're any bugs around I'm sure he'll find them."

"Yeah. I'll do that."

After hanging up, Burt wondered whether or not he should do the same thing. Instead he dialed Monica again and again was told she wasn't in the office and hadn't left word when she would return. Burt, on his way out of his apartment to see Donald Rettig, knew something was wrong there and when he returned to New York the first order of business was to find out what.

It came as a shock to him that he didn't want to lose her.

A tired Richie Sweet stepped into his East 55th Street apartment with a shopping bag in each hand, kicked the door shut behind him, then turned and double locked it. He yawned as he leaned against the door for support and removed his shoes. Dropping the shoes into one of the shopping bags, he stretched and yawned again, then picked up the shopping bags and in his stocking feet walked across a living room floor that had been covered wall to wall with a rug of white Llama fur. The fur's curly appearance made the floor seem hidden by an ankle high, swirling white mist. Joe Namath had once owned a rug like it and when Richie had heard that, he knew he had to have one, too. To protect the rug, anyone entering

Richie's apartment was asked to remove his shoes and place them on the floor of a closet near the front door.

Setting one shopping bag on a coffee table made of blue glass and gleaming chrome, Richie continued into the kitchen. There he opened the refrigerator door and emptied a second shopping bag.

Richie bit into an apple and still carrying the shopping bag, left the kitchen. In his bedroom he took a slim package of laundered shirts from the shopping bag, unwrapped them and placed the shirts neatly in a drawer. Next he undressed, carefully hanging up his clothes before slipping into a knee-length robe of green silk trimmed in black velvet. Richie was a neat, careful man. His apartment was tidy, with nothing out of place and so was his life, a lesson he had learned from Carmine DiNaldi. The closest thing to a loose end was Johnnie, and Richie was keeping away from that bitch as though she had the clap.

Dropping the apple core into a wastebasket he walked into the living room, turned on the stereo and yawned. He had been busy all day, working on a very important hit that was to go down soon. There could be no mistakes with this one. It meant too much to the family and therefore to Richie. He looked at his watch. Almost nine o'clock and he hadn't had dinner. Time to *mangiare*. When he had adjusted the volume on the stereo, Richie walked back to the coffee table and flopped down on a black leather couch in front of it. He usually kept the stereo tuned to a soft music station, something to help him relax. For a few seconds he closed his eyes and listened to the theme from *Gone With The Wind*. He had never seen the movie and didn't care to. The movie was too old, too out of touch for him. He had no interest in watching four hours of broads in hoop skirts, guys waltzing and niggers sweating, but the music was nice.

He pulled the shopping bag on the coffee table toward him and took out the two guns. They were brand new and wrapped in a khaki-colored towel, a pair of .32 Smith and Wessons from a shipment recently stolen at Kennedy

269

Airport. Only a new gun was ever used on a hit, used once then thrown away. A hitter would no more borrow a gun or kill with a used gun than he would invite the FBI along to watch him blow somebody away. A weapon with a past history was easily traced. Guys had been killed for selling used guns.

From the bag Richie also removed his shoes, a newspaper and a bottle of red wine, which he kissed before setting it down on the coffee table. Nothing like good old Dago Red. Mother's milk to a ginzo. Next he took out a copy of *Playboy* magazine and flipped it open to look at the $2,500 in cash he had placed inside the centerfold. Right between your legs, baby. My favorite bank. The money was from a small loan shark operation the *consigliere* had given Richie permission to work on the side. Though setting up the hit, Richie had found time to collect installments and interest owed him by two people.

The rest of the articles were left in the shopping bag: fake license plates for cars to be used on the hit; bullets and silencers for the .32s. After dinner Richie would test the guns and silencers by firing a few shots into his pillows. With his special silencers he could shoot off a gun in a crowd and no one would hear a sound. Richie and Sal Abruzzo had been assigned to kill Dan Einstein. Carmine DiNaldi wanted the wiretapper burned before the week was out and there could be no mistakes on this one. Einstein had *flipped*. He had turned FBI informant to save himself from prison.

The *consigliere* had learned about Dan Einstein because an FBI man had talked to a New York City detective who liked to gamble. The detective had talked to Carmine DiNaldi and that conversation had sealed the wiretapper's doom. Einstein was playing hard to get, giving the FBI only bits and pieces at a time and insisting that he, Einstein, stay on the street and out of custody. Richie knew the game Einstein was playing: get all you can from the FBI and give them nothing. Sooner or later, however, the game had to end and the FBI was bound to win. When they had convinced Einstein that prison was unavoidable, the wiretapper would go out of his way to tell the feds everything he knew.

Carmine DiNaldi wanted Einstein taken care of before he led the FBI to Wallace Barstow, a banker who handled mob money. Should the FBI ever come down on Barstow, the banker would fall apart faster than tissue paper in the rain: he would be useless to the family which would have to find another way to dispose of six million dollars in stolen securities and find another banker to help on future deals. If the *consigliere* wanted Einstein dead, Einstein was dead. A couple of days more and Richie and Sal Abruzzo would know enough about Einstein to pick the best time and place to ice him.

In the kitchen Richie placed fettucine in boiling water and was preparing to melt the butter for the sauce when the doorbell rang. Richie jerked his head toward the sound as though it were a gunshot. He wasn't expecting anybody and what's more the doorman downstairs hadn't buzzed him. What the hell was Richie paying $750 a month for if any asshole could walk into the building? Wiping his hands on a damp sponge, he walked into the living room, looked quickly at the guns on the coffee table, then at the front door.

"Yeah?" he said irritably.

The flat sound of the front door buzzer was his only answer.

Richie angrily threw the sponge down on the white Llama rug and ran to the door. "Who the hell is it?"

This time someone placed a finger on the buzzer and kept it there. Son of a bitch. At the door he squinted through the peephole and softly said, "Holy shit."

*Johnnie.* She stood in front of Richie's door in a white dress, no bra and that long, platinum blond hair that Richie wanted to eat by the handful. She was calmly smoking a cigarette, a pair of high-heel shoes with thin gold straps dangling from the fingers of one hand. Richie felt cold sweat trickle down his spine. He closed his eyes and shook his head. Jesus.

"Open up," she said. "I know you're in there."

She sounded high. She had admitted doing every drug there was and a few Richie had never even heard of. She stepped forward and pressed the buzzer again.

"Richeeee!"

Christ, she definitely was on something. Richie turned his back to the door, leaned against it and took a deep breath. Every time he came near her, something happened. All he could think about was getting into her. Johnnie brought out a craziness in him that no other woman could. But she was bad news. The *consigliere* had said so.

"Richie, if you don't open the door, I'm going to take off my clothes and stand out here in the hall and ring your bell—"

Crazy bitch.

"I mean it, Richie."

"What do you want, Johnnie?"

"I want to come in."

"You can't."

"Richie, I said I want to come in."

"I got somebody in here."

"You're lying, Richie. The doorman said you just came in and you were by yourself. Are you going to open this door or not?"

Richie clenched his fists at his side, digging manicured nails into the palms of his hands. He thought of Johnnie's bare legs wrapped around his waist and her ass grinding under him and how she always said, "fuck me, fuck me" just before she came. And he thought of the *consigliere*. Johnnie rang the buzzer again and screamed his name. Somewhere in the hall, an apartment door opened, then closed quickly. A tenant had looked out and hadn't like what he or she had seen and speedily backed off.

Richie wanted Johnnie and he wanted her to go away. He wanted to fuck her brains loose and he wanted to stay alive. "Johnnie? Johnnie? Stop with the bell, okay?"

272

"You going to open this door?"

"If you don't get the fuck away from here, I'm going to kick your ass, I'm telling you."

"You do that and I'll bring a cop back."

She would. She was crazy enough and doped up enough to do anything.

"Just for a minute, Richie," she pleaded. "I got stood up tonight. Nobody stands me up. I got stood up, Richie. Let me in for a minute, then I'll leave. I promise."

Richie closed his eyes. "Just for a minute, Johnnie. I got somewhere to go. Business."

"Okay, okay. I understand. Business. I'll leave right away."

"I got to put on some clothes," said Richie, his eyes on the guns. "Be right with you."

He ran to the coffee table, scooped up the guns, put them in a shopping bag, then grabbed the bag and ran into the bedroom to hide it on the top shelf of a closet and as far against the wall as possible. Then he ran into the kitchen, turned off the heat under the fettucine, sprinted back to the door and opened it. Johnnie had tears in her eyes. "Stood me up," she mumbled. "Bastard stood me up. Nobody stands me up. No fucking body."

She staggered into his apartment, tossed her shoes over her shoulder and continued staggering to the couch, where she turned, fell backward and sagged, tears rolling down her cheeks. "Stood me up."

"Who?"

"Works in show business. Some kind of agent. Big man. Very, very important man. He's ten years older than my father. I met him Sunday at some dumb discotheque and he took me out to East Hampton for a couple of days. We were supposed to go to a dinner party tonight, but he never showed. Didn't call, didn't show his face."

She opened her purse.

"You look wired," said Richie. "What are you on?"

"I'm on the couch." She giggled. "On. The. Couch."

She patted the couch. "Come. Sit down. I won't bite

273

you, I promise. Said I'd leave, didn't I? I know you've been avoiding me. I never hear from you anymore. Why's that, Richie?"

"Don't jerk me around, Johnnie," said Richie. "You know why."

"I know why." She nodded her head as if to confirm she had said the right words. "Yes, I know why." She looked up at Richie. "Robin."

"Robin."

She shrugged, placed a cigarette in her mouth and looked far into the distance. "Robin." Her mind struggled to deal with the name and what it meant to her. "I know Robin." She smiled at Richie. "I know Robin."

"Finish that cigarette, Johnnie, then split."

"Whatever you say, Richie." She lit the cigarette and inhaled. Richie watched her take the cigarette out of her mouth, then place it back between her lips and he thought how it felt to have his cock in her and the way she groaned when—

He felt the erection under his robe.

"Have a cigarette with me, Richie." She tilted her head to one side and smiled. "Please?"

He cleared his throat and nodded his head. "One. Then you go out that door."

"I promise."

She took a single cigarette from her purse, handed it to him and their fingers brushed.

The first thing Richie remembered was laughing like hell, laughing until his chest ached and kicking off the sheet and looking over at Johnnie who lay naked beside him in his circular bed. Then they were both laughing, lying on their backs and pointing up at the mirrored ceiling in Richie's bedroom. "Hog," said Johnnie and they both laughed some more. She was telling Richie the different names for the drug they had just been smoking. She had given Richie a joint sprayed with PCP, called "Angel Dust" on the street. It was a stronger drug than

274

heroin and LSD. It was so pleasant that Richie had wanted to cry. He felt so powerful that he knew he could fly around the room if he tried. Fucking Johnnie had been a dream, a wild dream in wild colors and when he had come, it had lasted for hours, man, lasted for hours.

"It's also called 'goon,'" said Johnnie and Richie thought he would laugh until he peed. He had done a little cocaine in the past, not much and occasionally he smoked a little weed. Never any hard stuff, because the family had no use for junkies. Richie had never touched heroin and never would. Tonight all he had done was take the joint from Johnnie, light up and the world had disappeared. But when it had returned, it was too much. He and Johnnie had fucked like rabbits and it had never been better. Then they both had started talking at once and Richie had told her a lot of things, most of which he couldn't remember. He did remember telling her about the FBI, because Johnnie had laughed when he called them "The Feebs," which is what everybody on the street called the FBI. Goddam feebs. Why would he mention them? Dan Einstein. Yeah, Dan Einstein. The feebs wanted him and so did the family. Einstein was hiding out, trying to avoid getting blown away but it wouldn't do him any good. Richie already knew where he was and Richie and Sal Abruzzo were going to burn Danny the Jew. Johnnie had laughed and repeated "Danny the Jew, Danny the Jew" and then Richie had repeated it and then the two of them were like children with a nursery rhyme. "Dannythejewdannythejewdannythejew."

And then Johnnie was sucking Richie's cock and tickling his balls and his fingers were lost in her white gold hair. Dannythejewdannythejew. . . .

When Richie woke up, he was alone in the circular bed. He opened his eyes wide and prayed that it had all been a dream, a nightmare, for in his mind's eye he saw the wrinkled face of the *consigliere*. Sitting on the edge of the bed, Richie worked saliva into his dry mouth. His tongue felt thick and covered with hair. Maybe it had all been a dream. He had to piss. Somehow he made it to the bathroom and when he had finished pissing, he turned to wash his hands in the sink and froze. Written on the bathroom mirror were the words, "Danny the Jew and me and you. Johnnie."

Richie hung his head and felt the bitter taste of bile at the back of his throat and when his stomach began to heave, he vomited into the bowl, and for the first time in his life saw himself as a dead man.

# ■ ■ ■ Twenty-Three

The sign, Rettig: Knock. Bell Not Work had been crudely printed on a piece of brown wrapping paper and hung from the knob of a screen door. Burt knocked, then shaded his eyes and peered through the rusted screen and into the small, one-story house. Inside he saw a dog's rubber bone dotted with teeth marks and a large toy robot lying on its side in a narrow hallway leading from the front door to the back of the house. He smelled ammonia and fried chicken and heard a brassy musical fanfare announcing the beginning of an afternoon television talk show. Somewhere in the back of the house a large dog began barking and wouldn't stop.

Burt was about to knock again when he heard slippers slapping against the hallway's bare wooden floor. Still squinting he watched a wide-shouldered, stocky woman come toward him out of the darkness wearing a quilted pink robe, her head covered in large rollers made of perforated plastic. She held a spatula in one hand and used the other to keep the robe closed at the neck. A long time ago she had been pretty.

Stopping a few feet from the screen door she said, "Yes?" The word came with an added hiss, as though the woman were European.

"My name is Burt Anthony and I'd like to talk with Donald Rettig."

"Is he expecting you, Mr. Anthony?"

"No, ma'am, he isn't. Are you Mrs. Rettig?"

"Yah. I am Mrs. Rettig."

*Yah.* European, Burt thought.

"May I please come in, Mrs. Rettig? It's very important that that I talk with your husband."

She pulled the pink robe tighter around her throat with both hands as though the garment were a shield. The large dog kept barking until a male voice in the house yelled, "Cory, shut the hell up will you?" The dog immediately stopped.

Burt reached for the screen door, opened it slowly and gave Mrs. Rettig his widest smile. A sudden move would alarm this woman who seemed the type to scare easily. Considering her husband's problems she had reason to be jumpy. Burt, however, had driven almost two hours to meet Donald Rettig and had no intention of being stopped on the doorstep. He had to get inside.

"I'm a reporter, Mrs. Rettig and—"

She snapped her head toward the back of the house, shouting, "Donald? Please come. Please come, Donald. It is a *reporter.*" In her panic the word *reporter* sounded radioactive and when she again looked at Burt he noticed she held the spatula in a white-knuckled grip.

The alarm in Mrs. Rettig's voice brought her husband hurrying to her side and only after seeing she was unharmed did he turn toward Burt. However, he first gently moved his wife behind him. Donald Rettig was a small, balding man between forty and fifty years old. This afternoon he was unshaven and barefoot and the empty right sleeve of his shirt was folded in half and pinned to his shoulder by its cuff. Despite his size, he gave the impression of being tough. Rettig, his left hand held behind him as though he were hiding something, looked past Burt, saw he was alone, then concentrated his attention on the reporter and waited.

"I'm Burt Anthony and I didn't mean to upset your wife. I'm a reporter and I'd like to speak with you. We have a mutual acquaintance, Hoyt Pathy—"

"I've already told Mr. Pathy I didn't want to talk to you or any reporter. Told him that just a couple of hours ago. You're wasting your time, Mr. Anthony." Rettig's voice was soft, with the flat broad $A$'s of a man born and raised in New England.

"Hear me out," said Burt. "Give me a minute. I know, let's say I'm guessing, that you've recently been paid off, that you've received all or part of the money you had coming. Now if this is true then you got paid only because somebody's afraid you'd talk to me. In a way you've got me to thank for getting paid. I think it might be a good idea if you learned how you could make more money. I said *more* money, Mr. Rettig."

Rettig blinked then began chewing the inside of his mouth.

Burt took one step forward and stopped. "I mean it when I say I can show you a way to get more than you've been paid so far. It's also important that you protect yourself, Mr. Rettig. Somebody tried to screw you and they only eased up when they thought you were going to talk to the press. Ask yourself what's to stop them from changing their minds and quit paying you, maybe even causing trouble for you in the future. If you're smart you'll hear me out, because I can help you."

Rettig stopped chewing the inside of his mouth. "And I suppose you're only doing this out of the goodness of your heart."

Burt shook his head. "We both know I'm not. I plan on getting mine out of this. I'm putting together a story on Chindé and it could be the biggest thing I've ever worked on. I'm offering you a trade. We help each other. I get what I want, you get what you need."

Rettig looked at his wife, then at Burt. After a few seconds of silence, the little pilot stepped aside and jerked his head toward the back of the house. Burt exhaled and stepped forward, doing his best to ignore the gun Rettig held in a left hand now dangling casually at his side. In a living room containing plain, cheap furniture and dominated by a huge color television set, Burt sat in a sagging easy chair and watched Donald Rettig lay the short-barreled .32 pistol beside a bowl of goldfish on a small end table. When the pilot sat down on the couch his left hand was only inches away from the gun.

His wife turned off the television and said, "I see to the chicken, Donald, then I come back." She hurried from the room, slippers dragging across a worn rug whose green color was fading into scattered patches of beige threads.

Rettig scratched his blue jaw. "Your dime, Mr. Anthony. Start talking."

"Before I do, what's with the gun?"

Rettig looked at the .32, then at Burt. "I don't like surprises and when you work for people in politics, and I'm talking about people the world over, sometimes you get surprises. A couple of times lately my wife and I have noticed a certain car driving slowly past the house. We could be imagining things, but I don't think so. Nobody got out of the car and nobody's threatened us, but like I said, I don't like surprises. By the way, you have any identification?"

Burt showed Rettig his press card and the little pilot nodded. Then leaning forward in his chair to escape a particularly sharp spring Burt said, "I hate to alarm you but you're probably wise to stay alert. You're involved with people who can play rough."

"What do you know about the people I'm involved with?"

"Since we both know about Hoyt Pathy, I guess I'm not revealing a source when I mention his name. I know what he's told me and I have your notebook and photographs."

Rettig touched his empty right sleeve. "Then you already know a lot."

"Not enough. By the way, some of the people involved in this thing are probably more afraid of me than they are of you."

"And why's that?"

"You know why. A major news story on Chindé could raise hell with both Congress and the American public because neither wants another Vietnam. This is an election year, in case you've forgotten. A story about what's really going on in Chindé could put some people out of office and other people in."

The little pilot's smile was cynical, bitter. "Having a big lip in my line of work isn't good for business or your health. I've flown some hairy missions in the past thirty years and always kept my mouth shut. But I'm missing an arm and I'm missing some money and I figure now is as good a time as any to break my silence."

"I couldn't agree more. That's why you'd be wise to cover yourself and at the same time, get what you're owed. Not just a part of it. *All* of it."

Rettig fished a pack of cigarettes from his shirt pocket, shook one free and took it gently between his teeth. After lighting it, he said, "I'm listening, Mr. Anthony."

"You're protected when we both know what you know. Once you've talked to me then you're not in this alone anymore. It won't matter how many cars drive past your house because it won't make any sense to lean on you. They'll have to shut me up as well, which won't be easy. I have a big New York paper behind me and that's a lot of muscle. But you, Mr. Rettig, you're alone. As long as you're the only one with your knowledge, you've got a problem. I think you already know this, otherwise you wouldn't be carrying a gun."

Rettig eyed his goldfish. "Been a pilot since I was seventeen. That's thirty years ago and during that time I've flown for almost every government on the face of the earth and a few that don't even exist anymore. I did the dirty stuff, the quiet stuff, the stuff that never sees the light of day. I'm good, Mr. Anthony. Well, let's say I used to be good. I survived where a lot of pilots didn't. You need a talent for survival and since I'm sitting here talking to you, I suppose that proves I have it. I've learned to take care of number one, because no one else does. I don't like having one arm, but I guess that's how the wheel turns and it turned bad on me this one time. Took me quite a few hours just to print that sign on the screen door. Not used to being left-handed, but I guess I'll have to learn. No complaints, Mr. Anthony. My people never brought me up that way. But I was brought up to expect a day's pay for a day's work, so that's why I went to Senator Kinsolving. Figured him to be a man of the people and all. Figured he'd help, I just want to get piad for what I did. Just give me what I've got coming, nothing more. So far I've been thrown crumbs, a few dollars to keep me quiet. A bone to a dog, so to speak. You said something about money. Mind telling me how?"

"Not at all," said Burt. "There's a very important man involved in all of this. He's a high government official and I can't mention his name. But he's got his own reasons for not wanting any of this in the newspapers. For the moment I've got his ear and if I ask him to give you money he will."

"Just like that."

"Just like that. The last thing this man wants is to be linked with American mercenaries in Chindé. He'll pay to keep you quiet, whether for a week or a year. How much have you been paid so far?"

Rettig blew smoke at the ceiling and watched it float higher. Then his sad eyes met Burt's gaze. "Eight hundred dollars."

"How much are you owed?"

"A lot. My contract was for six months at five thousand dollars a month with a ten-thousand-dollar bonus on completion of the contract. I'd flown four months but only collected one month's salary. The people who hired me were also supposed to have taken out an insurance policy for me and paid the premiums, which is customary for mercenaries. I found out they didn't. I've gotten some medical treatment, but I need more and they're hedging on that. They've bought me an artificial arm, but it costs money to have somebody teach me to use it."

"Mr. Rettig, I can get you every dime you've got coming and I can get it with one phone call."

Rettig said nothing for a long time. Then—"You'll pardon me, Mr. Anthony, if I don't get my hopes up."

"I'll make the call from here before I leave."

What Burt had in mind might be called blackmail in some circles. If van Lier went down because of American mercenaries in Chindé he would drag Richard Zachery's presidential hopes with him and that was why Donald Rettig would get his money. It was the price van Lier would have to pay for Burt's temporary silence.

"If you can get me my money with one phone call," said Donald Rettig, "I think it'll be time to run to the window and look for three wise men from the East."

"Watch me," said Burt. "About the eight hundred dollars. Who gave it to you?"

"It came to me in the usual fashion. A cut out. A false front, a phony business. This one was the Alladin Travel Agency in Washington, D.C., which listed me as a travel consultant. My contact was a man called Brian Catherine, who I've worked with in the past. He's a civilian but everybody knows he's connected with the government. My guess is he's some sort of go-between, a link between official agencies and the outside people hired for that quiet, dirty stuff I told you about."

"Who do you think is behind Alladin?"

"Your guess is as good as mine. CIA, Army Intelligence, national security, who knows. But take my word for it. Alladin's a cut out."

"There must have been officers in charge of the mercenaries," said Burt. "You mentioned one in your notebook, a man called Madonna. Were there any others?"

"Yes there were. Lieutenant Colonel Madonna was the

one who gave most of the orders. He was the one who wouldn't let me telephone my wife from Puerto Rico. Madonna was the nervous type. Never relaxed, always worried about security. Ah, Captain Rubin, Major Quarry, Major Hapstein and let's see, there was Captain Fontaine. He died the first night we were in Africa. That's all I can think of at the moment."

As Burt wrote in his notebook the Great Dane trotted over to him and began sniffing his shoes and ankles. Mrs. Rettig followed the dog into the room, taking a seat on the couch beside her husband.

"Cory," said Donald Rettig to the dog, "over here. My wife feels I need protection, Mr. Anthony, so she brought Coriolanus in from the yard."

"Coriolanus?"

"My wife used to be an actress in East Germany. Did quite a bit of Shakespeare, opera, even a few movies. We met when I flew some people from East to West Germany some years back."

Mrs. Rettig looked at her husband and her face softened. "I fell in love with him that night in the plane. The police they shot at him and he laughed and I fell in love with him."

Rettig smiled at her. "You krauts never could shoot straight. That's why you lost the war."

She stood up. "Time for your medication."

"Let me talk to Mr. Anthony a little longer."

"You take your pills while you talk." She looked at Burt for sympathy. "The pain bothers him and he wakes up in the middle of the night and he tries not to scream. A brave man, but he doesn't always take his pills like he should."

"I'll take the pills, I promise."

When his wife had left the room Rettig said, "She's got a good voice. Could have been a great singer. Somehow it never worked out for her, for us. We've got each other but not much else, as you can see."

"You've got a lot, Mr. Rettig."

"Used to be me taking care of her. She's been sick a lot—pneumonia, virus, tumor in her stomach. We couldn't have kids, so we adopted a daughter and wouldn't you know, she's healthy as hell, that kid. Twelve years old and strong as a moose. Guess it's my wife's turn to take care of me and Jody."

"Would it bother you to tell me how you lost your arm?"

Rettig began patting the Great Dane. "No. Things were going bad for us in Chindé and what happened was our base got overrun. We thought the enemy was fifty miles away and it turned out they were only fifty yards away. That's a hell of a difference. They were on us before we could get out of bed and it was all I could do to stay alive. My tent was hit by mortar fire and everyone in it was killed except me. My arm felt like it was in flames, but I managed to make it to the plane. Don't ask me how I got it off the ground or even landed it. Somehow I did. By the time I finally reached a hospital, the arm was infected. African doctors aren't the best in the world, which didn't help me any. Facilities over there are pretty bad, too. Maybe all that crawling around in the dirt trying to get to the plane and my arm bleeding and all brought on the infection. They told me they had no choice but to cut it off. I was unconscious at the time so I didn't have a vote."

"After that particular action where did your plane land?"

Rettig reached for another cigarette. "In what we refer to as a neutral African nation, one supposedly not involved in any of this shit. I think we, by we I mean the American government, are paying them to let us use their country as a base of some kind. At least this is what I heard over there."

"Which country is that?"

When Rettig told him, Burt whistled. "That's a surprise," said Burt.

"I'd say so," said Rettig.

"I'm guessing you fought on the side of the black rebels who are trying to take over Chindé."

"It's dumb for the U.S. to back anyone else. It's the blacks' turn now, whether anybody likes it or not. Chindé is rich and whoever ends up running it will be sitting on a lot of money. That's usually the bottom line in any kind of mercenary action. You're fighting for oil, diamonds, gold, uranium or military bases. Do you know that two American oil companies are giving the black rebels money?"

"No."

Rettig told him the name of the companies and added, "You can guess what they're after."

Mrs. Rettig returned with a tray containing four bottles of pills and a glass of water and as Burt watched, the little pilot began taking his medication.

Rettig whispered something to his wife, who shook her head and said, "*Nein.* I watch, you go to sleep. Don't worry. I watch out for her."

"Our daughter Jody," said the pilot. "She's due home from school and I like to sit out front and keep an eye out for her."

"That car you told me about?" said Burt.

Rettig nodded, then swallowed more pills. "These things are supposed to kill the pain. I keep hoping maybe they'll make my arm grow back."

Burt stood up. "May I use your phone?"

Mrs. Rettig pointed. "Over there near the bookcase."

Burt looked in his address book, found the number he wanted and dialed. When the phone was picked up at the other end, he said, "This is Burt Anthony and I want you to pass on a message to the man you work for. Donald Rettig, the man who flew American GIs into Chindé, has some money coming. He's owed five months' salary at five thousand a month and he's got a ten-thousand-dollar bonus coming for a total of thirty-five thousand dollars. That's thirty-five thousand dollars. He's also getting some static about medical treatment and insurance. You tell

286

your boss to take care of this. Get Rettig all the money he's got coming and see that he gets the medical treatment. No more nickel-and-dime stuff like somebody's been doing. Tell your boss I said I'd appreciate it if he takes care of this right away, say in the next twenty-four hours. What your boss gets in return is at least another week of silence from me. Seven days from today. If Rettig doesn't have his money by tomorrow, I go into print the next day."

Burt hung up without waiting for Cortes Arnold to reply.

"Just like that," said Donald Rettig. But his tone was less cynical and there was admiration in his eyes.

"Just like that."

"You're connected with somebody heavy."

"Whether I like it or not. Call me in New York tomorrow and let me know if you receive the money. I'll be straight with you. If we pull this off it'll just be a one-shot. We won't be able to go to the well again. The man I'm dealing with will either make a counter move or he'll draw the line at being hit twice. Sooner or later I'll have to print something and by then who knows what will happen. If you're to get your money, you've got to get it soon."

Rettig's voice was starting to slur with the effects of the medication. "Appreciate your being straight with me. Startin' to nod out. Sorry I won't be able to talk to you much longer."

"You did fine, Mr. Rettig."

"Don."

"Don." Burt wanted to shake the pilot's hand, but hesitated. He watched Mrs. Rettig gently stroke her husband's brow and whisper, "I look for Jody, I look."

And then her husband was asleep in her arms.

Burt silently stared at them and wondered when he had last met a couple he had felt as much instant affection for as he did these two. They had so little and yet in each other they had so much. A one-armed man and a German actress who had both run out of dreams. But they loved each other and Burt wondered if that didn't make them winners after all.

Outside in his car Burt was about to pull away from in front of the Rettig's home when he saw the girl. She was thin, with blond hair and clutched school books to her chest. He saw something else, too. A car was slowly cruising parallel to the girl, who apparently hadn't noticed it. Burt's first instinct was to drive away, to avoid getting involved. But he thought of the Rettigs embracing each other and he thought of all the broken promises they had lived through and he said, "Hell," and got out of his car.

At the same time the cruising car stopped and a door opened and someone in the car called out to the girl and she stopped, her eyes widening in fear and surprise. Burt ran toward her. "Jody! Jody!"

She turned to Burt, who ran faster. "Jody! Jody!"

The car door slammed shut and with squealing tires, the driver sped off.

When Burt reached the girl, she was rigid with fear.

Dropping to one knee, he spoke softly. "Jody, it's all right. I know your parents. Come on, let's walk to your house. We're only going to your house. See it's just over there. Look, I'll start walking and you follow me over there."

Behind him, Burt heard the screen door slam and he turned to see a frightened Mrs. Rettig come running toward him screaming Jody's name.

Burt pointed to Mrs. Rettig, and said to Jody, "See? That's your mother. It's all right. It's all right."

When the girl began to weep, Burt took her in his arms and stroked her hair. The car might have been driven by a crazy, a child molester. Or it might have been driven by someone willing to use Donald Rettig's daughter to keep the pilot from talking about Chindé.

Mrs. Rettig took her trembling daughter in her arms and both wept. With her face hidden by Jody's blond hair, Mrs. Rettig reached for Burt's hand and clutched it in a desperate, fearful gratitude.

288

Burt's throat tightened and he followed them back to the house in silence.

After seating herself at Burt's desk, Monica reached in her purse and removed her address book. "Molly? What line can I use?"

Molly, a phone to her ear and typing swiftly as always, kept her back to Monica and yelled, "Three."

"Thanks. Sorry Burt's not back yet. I'll leave the information on his television date with you. D'Arcy may also be on that show, so tell Burt to be prepared."

Lying is easy, she thought. It is also sickening. It is admitting you can't cope with the situation, which is the truth, an odd word to use at this time. Her visit to Burt's office was not a surprise as she had pretended to Molly. It was planned and had taken place only after Monica had made sure Burt was still away from his apartment. Monica loved Burt, but the idea of giving up her job for love was too scary to deal with; at the moment it was easier to betray Burt behind his back than do it face to face. Avoiding him hadn't been the answer, because Monmouth had pushed her for some sort of report on Burt as soon as possible. When Monica's secretary had telephoned Burt to tell him about the upcoming television appearance only to learn he wasn't in his office, Monica had acted on impulse. Now she was going through the notes on Burt's desk, to see if she could find something, *anything*, to tell Monmouth.

She dialed her own office, her excuse for sitting at the desk. Molly's back was still turned when leaning forward, Monica fingered pieces of paper scattered over Burt's cluttered desk. She found his typed list of calls to be returned, saw her name doodled and circled at the top and she panicked. She was about to abandon her scheme and run from the apartment, but fear kept her rooted to the chair. It took all of her willpower to make her search appear casual, while sneaking furtive glances at Molly.

When her own secretary Jimmy came on the line, she forced herself to sound relaxed.

"Jimmy, I'm at Burt's . . ."

Monica glanced at a slip of paper she held in her hand and the words *Renata Zachery pregnant* seemed to leap off the paper to hit her in the face. She inhaled sharply.

Jimmy said, "Monica, what's wrong?"

"Nothing, Jimmy. Nothing at all. Any messages for me?"

Monica read faster, ignoring Jimmy's voice in her ear.

# ■ ■ ■ Twenty-Four

After he toweled his wet head once more, Burt slipped into a robe and hurried from the bathroom toward the front door of his apartment where the newspapers would be waiting outside in the hall. Over breakfast he would check his column and D'Arcy's to see how each had done today in the gossip wars. Perhaps he would make a quick telephone call to the Rettigs, a very grateful family since Burt had scared the car away from their daughter a few days before. Accepting their gratitude had meant staying for dinner and taking time away from his work, but it had been worth it. Burt had their trust and he also had additional information from Donald Rettig, with a promise of the pilot's complete cooperation in the future. Burt had decided he might as well use all the clout he had with Gil van Lier and try to get the black diplomat to call off the dogs of war who had almost harmed the twelve-year-old girl. He didn't want to believe van Lier was involved with that, but anything was possible.

Burt was due in Washington later, where he would be one of thousands at a Richard Zachery fund raiser, an all-star show featuring dozens of celebrities who had pledged themselves to raise one million dollars for Zachery's presidential campaign. Once in Washington he could also look into the mysterious Brian Catherine and the Alladin Travel Agency. But first he would have to knock out a column in a hurry for tomorrow's paper. The column had to be in before he went poking around D.C. to learn just how well Gil van Lier was doing in his attempt to become secretary of state.

Burt picked up the newspapers from the hall, slammed his door and unfolded the *Examiner-World* and froze. Running across the very top of the paper in boldface type was the headline: RENATA ZACHERY PREGNANT? SEE THE BURT ANTHONY COLUMN, PAGE SIX. A numb Burt turned to page six and the numbness gave way to anger as he read the four-column lead—*First Lady In Waiting Said To Be Waiting.* Directly under that was the item—*Renata Zachery, much talked about wife of Vice-President Richard Zachery, has an excellent chance of becoming the nation's new first lady this fall and if this happens, there may also be another first. The thirtyish Mrs. Zachery is said to be expecting and if true, her first child might be a White House baby.*

Enraged, Burt crushed the newspaper and threw it to the floor without reading the rest of his column. He hadn't written one damn word about Renata Zachery being pregnant. Someone else had, someone who had added those words to his column without Burt's knowledge or permission.

An angry Burt dialed Denis Radd at the *Examiner-World.*

"Radd here."

"What the hell's going on down there? Somebody's screwing around with my column—"

"You'll have to take that up with Mr. Monmouth. Now if you don't mind I've got a newspaper to run."

"Radd, you see every line of type that goes into the *Examiner-World*. You know what's happening and now I want you to tell me."

"Laddie buck, you seem to be hard of hearing. I said you have to take that up with Mr. Monmouth. Now I've got a dozen other calls to take and there's scores of people hanging around my desk waiting to be told what to do. I've already told *you* what to do and now I suggest you hop to it."

Radd hung up.

Burt gave himself a few seconds to calm down, then dialed Monmouth. The publisher was in conference and couldn't be disturbed. Burt slammed down the phone. How did that item on Renata Zachery end up in his column when Burt had decided not to use it, considering it just another rumor whirling around the most glamorous, talked-about woman in the world. He'd left it on his desk—

Burt snapped his fingers, then dialed again.

"Molly? It's Burt."

"Yes? Is anything wrong? I'm on my way to mass then I'll be coming into work."

"Nothing's wrong, Molly. Jesus, something *is* wrong. Have you seen today's column?"

Molly inhaled. "No. I usually buy the paper at the subway and read it on the way in."

"There's an item on Renata Zachery in my column and I'd like to know how it got there. I *didn't* write it and I *didn't* give it to you to type."

"You did give me something on her for the column," said Molly. "You wrote about a concert she attended."

Burt chopped the air with the side of his hand. "I know, I know. But I didn't write *anything* about her being pregnant."

"No. I would have remembered something like that. No, you didn't."

"Then who the hell could have written it? I got the item from Hoyt Pathy and I copied it down and left it on my desk and I was going to forget about it. It looks as if somebody got to my desk, found it and—Molly are you sure you didn't accidentally—"

Molly's voice was soft and weak with hurt. "I would never do a thing like that. I never have."

"I'm sorry, Molly. I know you wouldn't. I'm really sorry."

"I never sit at your desk. Never. I didn't think it was wrong to let Miss Hollander sit there."

"Monica?" Burt felt a sudden chill.

"She dropped by to visit you the other day when you were in New Jersey and she sat down at your desk to make a few phone calls. Remember the message about the television show she's arranged for you next week?"

Burt closed his eyes. "I think I've *finally* gotten the message, Molly."

"I'll be in right after mass, okay?"

"Fine, Molly. See you then."

Burt hung up and stared at the phone. He didn't bother telephoning Monica, because he knew she wouldn't take his calls. He walked into his small kitchen, sat down at the table and stared at the sun now pushing its way higher into the sky. The discovery of her betrayal paralyzed him with an unspeakable pain and he sat in the chair for a long time.

# ■ ■ ■ Twenty-Five

D'Arcy walked over to a full-length mirror and held the dark blue tie against the pink shirt he wore. Satisfied with the match of colors, he turned up his shirt collar and placed the tie around his neck, pausing to smile into the mirror at the pair of FBI agents standing behind him in the doorway of Clare Chandler's bedroom. Tonight the agents had driven from Washington to Mount Vernon to talk with D'Arcy about what he had written on Dan Einstein. It was the opinion of the FBI that D'Arcy had placed the wiretapper's life in danger by letting the public know of the race between the FBI and the Bonnetti family to see who got their hands on Dan Einstein first.

D'Arcy, of course, had not intended to attack Einstein. The columnist had been after Richie Sweet, knowing that Augustino Bonnetti wouldn't like it. D'Arcy had written it after Johnnie had told him of her visit to Richie's apartment and what the two of them had done in Richie's round bed under a mirrored ceiling. But why tell the FBI everything? Why tell them anything?

His tie tied, D'Arcy walked back to the dresser for a pair of pearl-studded gold links. Incurring the wrath of the FBI was of no concern to him. Offending them was a pleasure and besides, Clare Chandler could easily prevent them from doing him any harm. Her influence was astonishing and in recognition of this fact, D'Arcy had reversed himself and taken to sleeping with her on his trips to Washington. This slap-and-tickle was a therapeutic necessity, benefiting D'Arcy's ambitions as well as Clare's healthy libido.

Her nerves needed soothing, for she feared the power games she suspected were now gathering around Renata Zachery and Gil van Lier, power games that could harm Clare Chandler as well as the lovers in question. Self-interest dictated that D'Arcy use his sexual favors as a calming influence on her and he did so without hesitation. Had anything ever been achieved without hard labor?

While no longer a schoolgirl, Clare Chandler was in possession of a formidable appetite. She lacked the fulfilling and appealing depravity of Johnnie Gelb, but between the sheets Clare manifested outrageous energy. The excessive friction in and around D'Arcy's pubic area from a night's coupling with her had resulted in a bothersome rash. Her gratitude at these moments, however, was a thing D'Arcy willingly turned to his advantage.

Tonight she and D'Arcy were to drive into Washington to attend a fund-raising gala designed to fatten Richard Zachery's presidential campaign coffers. Tickets were obscenely high priced, but Clare Chandler had received hers without cost and delivered by chauffeur-driven limousine. As for the FBI now lurking in the bedroom doorway while D'Arcy dressed, well, he had broken no law. He was free to print whatever he wanted to, or to be more precise, whatever he could get away with. He had agreed to see the FBI at his convenience and out of curiosity.

He found the two men from the legendary law enforcement agency to be amazingly ordinary, in no way the supermen they appeared to be in movies. They had the bland, vapid faces D'Arcy had come to associate with the American heartland, a place whose terminal boredom he imagined could be relieved only by such natural disasters as tornados and dust storms. The FBI agents were coolly polite, no doubt a concession to being in the home of Clare Chandler. They were well aware of who she was.

When D'Arcy had put on his jacket he again checked his cufflinks then looked into the mirror and patted his hair. He turned to look at the FBI agents. "You claim," said D'Arcy, "that my column has jeopardized Dan Einstein's life. But I think that your convincing Einstein to turn informant is the sole cause of his present dilemma. Had he not agreed to betray his associates, I doubt if he would be on the run now. I fail to see how it solves anything to blame me for actions set in motion by you."

The smaller agent coughed into his fist. "Sir, we were just doing our job. We're in the business of law enforcement. It's our job to secure informants, to work with them in obtaining intelligence that will aid us in bringing major criminals into a federal courtroom. We were doing our job and following a prescribed procedure. However, you've severely damaged that case. If Dan Einstein hasn't read your column, he's certainly heard about it and that means he's found himself a hole to crawl into. We'd like to know where you obtained your information and we'd like your assurance you won't publish such information again."

D'Arcy sneered. "*You* want. Well, you are not going to get. I shall not tell you anything concerning my sources, nor shall I make you any such promise as you suggested. You and I both know I don't have to."

The tall agent spoke for the first time. He had obviously grown a moustache to strengthen a weak face. "We could do it the hard way."

The second the words passed his lips, he knew he had made a mistake. He quickly looked away and didn't see the other agent glare at him. "Mr. D'Arcy," said the shorter agent, "we have no intention of making trouble for you. We'd simply like to have your voluntary cooperation, that's all."

"In return for what?" said D'Arcy, folding his arms across his chest.

"Sir?"

"As you Americans put it, what's in it for me?"

"I don't understand."

"Try."

In the silence, the man toyed with his hat and looked at the huge four-poster bed in the room.

"I'm not sure I know what you're suggesting, Mr. D'Arcy," said the shorter agent, "but I do know you've harmed our investigation and it would be appreciated by the bureau if you were to stay in contact with us in the future—"

"Censorship, you mean."

"Not censorship, sir." The shorter agent's mouth tightened. He was finding it hard to hold onto his temper. "We would appreciate it, that's all." The words came through clenched teeth.

"I see." Turning his back to the agents again, D'Arcy walked to the dresser, found a purple pocket handkerchief and after folding it, stuffed it into his breast pocket. He thought of Johnnie and Richie Sweet in bed together.

Spinning around, he strode briskly across the bedroom, toward the FBI agents, who parted to let him through the doorway. Without turning to face the agents, a suddenly angry D'Arcy snapped, "If you two bright lights of anti-crime aren't trying to censor me, you have asked an exceedingly foolish question of a gossip columnist. I am no more interested in your approval of what I write than I am in eating mud and bark. Dan Einstein is *your* problem. Gossip is *mine*."

And then he was on the stairs and hurrying to meet Clare Chandler, who waited for him in the study. All thoughts of FBI agents were pushed out of his head. D'Arcy would take his revenge when needed and if Einstein had problems, credit the FBI with bringing them on. At the moment, D'Arcy wanted to get into Washington and continue his search for information that would put an end to the public career of Richard Zachery.

At the bottom of the staircase D'Arcy shouted, "Clare? Clare?"

As he helped Clare into her evening cape, D'Arcy looked back to see the pair of agents standing at the top of the winding staircase. Neither man attempted to hide the hostility he felt toward the Englishman. D'Arcy grinned and waved at them. "Do drop in again when I'm dressing," he said. "Next time we'll exchange underwear. *Ciao.*"

The applause could be heard in the lobby where Burt leaned against a wall and stared out into the night at the floodlit Washington Monument. He had had his fill of stale jokes, overamplified singing and dull dramatic readings all in honor of Richard Zachery, who hadn't even appeared at his own fund raiser. The vice-president was stuck at an airport in Vermont, where his plane had developed mechanical trouble during his tour of the state to raise money.

Burt cringed as he heard an aging comedienne in the auditorium shout hysterically into a microphone—"Victory! Zachery! Victory! Zachery! Come on everybody, let's all get VZ! Let's all get infected by this glorious disease! VZ! VZ! VZ!" She did her best to get the crowd to pick up the chant. Closing his eyes in disgust a depressed Burt shoved his hands deeper into his pockets and wished he could hide. Monica. She haunted him like a persistent ghost.

The surprise was that he hadn't known how much he loved her until now, for there couldn't be this much pain without love. When he returned to New York he had a meeting scheduled with Monmouth to talk about what the publisher called "our little disagreement." Burt also planned to find Monica and ask *why*. He wasn't surprised that Monmouth would spy on him because the publisher hadn't become rich by trusting anyone. All Burt wanted to know was why had Monica become a part of the

Englishman's "dirty tricks," especially after leading Burt to believe she cared for him. Welcome to the big city, Mr. Anthony, and watch your back at all times.

"I think the word is *boring*."

Burt looked up to see D'Arcy standing in front of him. Lighting a long, thin black cigarette, the Englishman said, "I suppose this is all part of your wonderful American political process, but given the choice I think I'd rather be sitting in a dentist's chair."

Burt folded his arms across his chest. "You could have stayed home and shoved puppies into a microwave oven."

"And miss this extravaganza?" D'Arcy lifted his eyebrows in mock horror. "Along with all you others standing about, I thought I might come out here and enjoy some fresh air. I've about had it with watching the glamorous ancients strain their hardened arteries for the greater glory of Richard Zachery. You look rather peaked, dear boy. Are you coming down with the vapors?"

Burt shook his head. "Just one of those things, and it only hurts when I laugh."

"Ah. An affair of the heart."

Burt looked at him and said nothing. He refused D'Arcy's offer of a cigarette with a shake of his head.

"I've left a guest inside," said D'Arcy. "She seems fascinated with the entertainment. Small minds to small things and all that. Well, I must say you're learning to play the game much better. Your headline today on Mrs. Zachery's um, 'pregnancy.' Stroke of genius, dear boy. Untrue, of course. Wish I'd thought of that myself."

"Don't worry, you will."

D'Arcy chuckled. "You're probably right. Oh, my congratulations on telling one and all about my two columns being shunted aside. Jolly good, that. I'm not without a certain amount of grace, you know."

"If you say so."

D'Arcy blew a spear of blue smoke at the lobby ceiling. "But you do worry me, dear boy. Indeed you do. This business about the pregnancy smacks of a certain despera-

300

tion. It's almost as if you've decided to play harder without quite knowing how, if you don't mind my saying so. I'd say that Harold the Horrible is pressing you for results. He's quite insatiable in that area, you know."

"Really?" Burt snorted. "That's news to me."

"Oh, he is, believe me. Nothing you do will ever be enough for him. He'll begin by demanding your heart on a plate. After that he'll start getting nasty. I have a proposition for you."

"Sorry, I only go out with girls."

"Well, more's the pity. You really should try diversifying yourself in all areas. Anyway this is a business proposition, dear boy. Now you and I are both quite interested in a certain story involving a certain lady and her lover, who is a high government official. I'm told you've been asking questions about her and I know you're intelligent enough to have found out I'm doing the same. Let's face it, this affair I'm talking about can only end badly. I can see no hope for these star-crossed lovers, but why dwell on that. What does interest me very much is becoming the first man to report that affair as a reality. It's my dream and I want it quite badly. I'll do anything to be the first and that's why I want you to back off."

D'Arcy held up one hand. "Wait. I do not say this lightly. It's my not so humble opinion that you will not last long with Monmouth. At the most you'll finish out your six-month contract then crawl off somewhere to lick your wounds. You'll have little to show for the experience and you'll need a bit of something set aside. So here's my proposition: you continue digging into their affair, but turn over all your information on that particular item to me. Not for the fun of it, dear boy. You do it for fifty thousand dollars."

Burt pushed himself away from the wall and stood up straight. "You're offering me fifty thousand dollars to work for you?"

"That is the American way, isn't it? Money, I mean."

"Christ, you've got one big set of balls."

"Dear me, *it's offended*. Do I have to point out that the reason you went to work for Harold Monmouth, dare I say it, is money?"

Burt looked down at the floor. "Fifty thousand."

"Approximately your yearly salary," said D'Arcy. "And in cash, if you prefer, unbeknownst to the tax collector, of course. I guarantee you a first payment within days, if you agree." D'Arcy thought of Clare Chandler's checkbook and smiled.

Burt looked at him. "The Renata Zachery–Gil van Lier story means that much to you?"

D'Arcy nodded. "We both know what that story means."

"You're worried about me, aren't you? Worried I just might make it, that I might put it all together and beat you. The stories on your columns and Renata Zachery's pregnancy have you shook up."

"Monmouth—"

"Monmouth my ass. You keep throwing Monmouth at me as though he's God. I'm not worried about him— so cut the games."

"Oh?" D'Arcy arched an eyebrow. "I think you should ask yourself if you can afford to refuse my offer."

"The question is, can I afford to take it."

D'Arcy gently smacked himself in the forehead with the heel of his hand. "Do mine eyes deceive me or did I just see an attack of ethics, followed closely by an avalanche of morals?"

"I've won more than a dozen awards for reporting," said Burt. "How many have you won?"

D'Arcy's smile was faint as he dropped his cigarette on the floor and crushed it. "Touché. Then the answer, I take it, is negative."

"You take it correctly."

"Disheartening to say the least. It's not every day that I attempt bribery on such a massive scale and am rejected. What *is* the world coming to? Sure you don't want to think it over?"

"D'Arcy—" Burt began as if he might explode with fury.

D'Arcy clapped his hands together. "Oh, well, cahn't blame a man for trying. By the way, is there anything *you'd* care to talk about? You do seem somber and brooding this evening, rather Byronic if I may say so. Did someone die?"

"Something, not someone."

"Oh, dear, oh, dear. I would say passion has disappointed you, as it must disappoint us all. Passion's death brings bitter wisdom, but one rarely hears three cheers for bitter wisdom these days."

For the first time since their meeting tonight, Burt smiled. "What do you do when passion disappoints?"

D'Arcy aimed his pointed chin at Burt. "I shall tell you what I do, dear boy. I destroy. Well, I must be getting back. If you should change your mind about my offer, you know where to find me."

D'Arcy fluttered his fingers at Burt and quickly smiled in farewell before walking away.

*Destroy.* Burt wanted to destroy Harold Monmouth and Monica Hollander, which didn't stop him from loving Monica. Inside the auditorium a famous male folksinger tuned up his guitar and made bad puns, chasing more people in evening dress into the lobby, where they stood around in small groups and ignored each other while looking for celebrities. Burt, in no mood to talk with anyone else, walked outside to the street. May was almost over and so was his third month with Monmouth. If Burt somehow managed to complete the entire six months of his contract, he would certainly need some time to think before doing anything else. D'Arcy's fifty thousand would buy a lot of time. Why not sell out? Take the money and run. No one else around Burt was showing any large amounts of integrity, so why the hell should he be any different?

"Mr. Anthony?"

Burt flinched. There were two of them, both dressed

neatly and wearing short hair along with bland faces. One brought a hand radio to his mouth and said, "We've found him."

Both stood uncomfortably close to Burt who began to panic.

The one with the radio said, "Please come with us, Mr. Anthony. Someone wants to talk with you."

"Tell me who and I'll tell you if I want to talk with someone." Burt hoped he sounded calmer than he felt. Was somebody leaning on him? He suddenly remembered what had almost happened to Jody Rettig.

Radio man said, "It's Mr. van Lier, Mr. Anthony. He'd appreciate it if you found time to speak to him."

"Right now?"

"Yes, sir, right now."

Burt, his heart still pumping too fast, took a breath of cool night air and followed radio man down the auditorium steps toward a line of limousines parked at the curb. The second man waited then fell into step behind Burt as though expecting him to try and run away. At the second limousine radio man opened the back door and when Burt had stepped inside, the man slammed the door and walked several feet away where he stood with his back to the car.

A grim Gil van Lier stared straight ahead as though he were alone in the car. Burt noticed there was no driver.

"I thought you were still in Africa," said Burt.

Van Lier kept his eyes on the empty driver's seat. "I don't like being threatened, Mr. Anthony."

"You mean the business of getting Mr. Rettig the money he's owed?"

"I don't like being threatened by reporters."

"That wasn't a threat, it was a promise."

Van Lier looked at him. "What goes around, comes around. You ever hear that before?"

Burt smiled. "Now *that's* a threat."

"I can't stop you from smearing me," said van Lier, "but I can find a way to let you know how much I dislike it."

"The other day I saw a car pull up beside a twelve-year-old girl but I scared the car off before anything could happen. I don't have to smear you. All I have to do is tell the truth and when grown men try to harm a twelve-year-old girl, the truth can hurt."

"What the hell are you talking about?"

Burt told him.

"I had nothing to do with it," said van Lier. "You think I'd be crazy enough to do something like that?"

"Why should one twelve-year-old girl be an obstacle? People in your position have eliminated large numbers of twelve-year-old girls in the past. Isn't that what Vietnam was all about? Isn't that what Chindé is all about? Up that body count and the bastards will beg for peace. After what almost happened to Jody Rettig I don't give a rat's ass about what you like or don't like, *Mr. Secretary*."

"I'm not confirmed yet," said van Lier, "and I don't make war on twelve-year-old girls. Is that what got you all hot and bothered?"

Burt shook his head. "It helped. The truth is I'm using what I've got to get what I want. You've asked me to give you time, to cool it on writing anything about Chindé. Fine. But it occurred to me that you were getting off cheap, that you weren't giving me enough in exchange. So I asked for something in return. It's as simple as that. All you had to do was see that Donald Rettig got the money he had coming, nothing more. By the way, did you do that?"

Van Lier frowned. "Did you mention my name to Rettig?"

"No. Any reason why I should?"

Van Lier sneered. "Well, you haven't exactly let grass grow under your feet since you arrived in town today. I understand you've been inquiring about travel agencies and a certain Brian Catherine."

Burt had also given Hoyt Pathy the names of the army officers mentioned by Donald Rettig, among other things to be checked out. But he saw no reason to discuss that with van Lier.

"Brian Catherine's got a nasty reputation," said Burt. "He's supposed to have had a hand in American dirty tricks in a dozen countries. People have linked him to everything from attempts on Fidel Castro's life to being a torture instructor for the secret police in Brazil and Chile. I wouldn't put it past him to try and harm Jody Rettig."

"And you're here in Washington to link me with Brian Catherine?"

"Not really. If it happens, it happens. At first I thought there might be a link between you two, in an indirect sort of way. But from what I've been able to learn, Catherine is an independent, something of a crazy who's hard to control."

"You'll find that's true of many people in a certain line of work."

"I'm talking about espionage, along with mercenary actions and other things that no one wants to talk about in this town."

"Sometimes," said van Lier, "an organization can't control its field agents and this is especially true when you hire independents. Many things happen that people at the top can't foresee or prevent."

"Brian Catherine drew up the contract for Donald Rettig to fly troops to Chindé and he's Rettig's payoff man. You're involved in Chindé and I don't mean just the peace talks. How are they going by the way?"

Van Lier shrugged. "When the jet lag's disappeared, I'll let you know. I came here straight from the airport. Let's say we've still got a chance over there. Do you intend to link me with Brian Catherine?"

"A while back I asked you a question. I asked if Donald Rettig has received his money."

Van Lier grinned. "Call Rettig."

"I will. You know what else Rettig told me? He said that the Pentagon sometimes gives its army officers a special leave of absence and then these officers go to Africa, as well as other countries, where they become heads of security for American businesses. Rettig says some of these businesses are really fronts for American espionage. I'm getting a list of these so-called businesses. I'm only guessing but I wouldn't be surprised if some of those officers who served in Chindé with American GIs were involved with these companies at one time."

"What else have you learned while I've been away?"

Burt shrugged. "No sense in boring you with all the details. I did learn which military hospital treated Rettig and I'm about to learn the base where you're keeping GIs on alert for a sudden flight to Chindé."

Van Lier nodded. "It's always nice to return home."

"I've heard that," said Burt. "East, west, home's best."

Van Lier closed his eyes and sank back against the seat. "I'm tired."

"And irritable."

The diplomat smiled at him. "You noticed?"

Burt smiled back.

"It was rough over there," said van Lier. "Someone took a shot at me, which did nothing for my nerves. We decided to keep that quiet but you can print it if you want to. I lost a lot of sleep trying to get both sides to at least sit down and talk and to make matters worse, I ate something in Chindé that hasn't decided whether or not to agree with me. Not to open up a Pandora's Box or anything, but I hear you're also asking questions about my private life as well. A friend called Cortes and told him to tell me that. Or warn me, I should say."

"You've got some loyal friends," said Burt. "I've learned that much. If you're wondering what your personal life has to do with being nominated for secretary of state, the answer is everything. The office is one of the highest in the land. You're even in line for the presidency, of which I'm sure you're aware. Because of that position, you're news in every way, like it or not."

"I like it not, but it comes with the job. Let me ask you this: are you looking into that part of my life as a reporter or as a gossip writer?"

The question was as much of a surprise to Burt as a punch in the throat and it caught him off balance. Sensing this, van Lier said, "It's never easy, is it? Trying to decide who and what you are, I mean. We have that in common, you and I. What are we, who are we and why does it matter? But in the end it does matter, doesn't it?"

Burt looked away. Van Lier's voice was soft, almost that of a friend, of someone who cared and the last thing Burt wanted to believe was that a man he might have to destroy cared about him. Van Lier could use a few friends himself. He was the subject of more rumors than anyone else in Washington. There was talk that the State Department would resign en masse if he became its head and another rumor had the President now backing down and begging van Lier to withdraw voluntarily, rather than create a white backlash against the President's party in November. A few senators were supposed to have placed a high price on their vote of confirmation, a price the President wasn't willing to pay for van Lier. There had even been a rumor that van Lier planned to tell the President that he wouldn't return to Chindé unless confirmed as secretary of state. This would be embarrassing to America not just in Africa but worldwide. It would indicate that the nation wasn't committed to peace enough to appoint its most able diplomat because he happened to be black.

Van Lier began to talk and Burt listened. The diplomat spoke of himself, his family and the fishbowl existence of his life since Jerome Rolland's death. Van Lier had to be on guard every day: his vigilance ran from minute to minute and he dare not let down his guard, for his every action reflected not merely on himself but on the President as well as the nation. The same is true of you, he said to Burt, perhaps in a different way. A story, any story by you, right or wrong, can hurt someone other than myself.

Burt watched van Lier nervously toy with a handkerchief. It was small, feminine, definitely not a man's handkerchief.

"Richard Zachery's one of my most important supporters," said van Lier. "He's out on a limb for me, especially now."

"Since we're on the subject," said Burt, his eyes on van Lier, "I guess you could say that in an election year, some people might try to attack Zachery through his wife."

"I wouldn't like to see her hurt. She's a nice lady."

And that's what this is all about, thought Burt. We've reached the bottom line, which is don't hurt Renata Zachery. Someone must have warned him that I'm getting closer. Van Lier and D'Arcy. I've got them both worried. Maybe Monmouth ought to talk with them to find out how well I'm doing. It suddenly hit Burt that if anyone was harming Renata Zachery at the moment, it was van Lier.

"Mrs. Zachery does deserve some consideration," said Burt. "I'll do the best I can. Her friends ought to do the same."

Van Lier sighed. "So you're giving me another week."

"Providing Rettig got his money. If not, who knows? I hear Cubans are already fighting in Chindé. Did they kill the GIs?"

"Ask Castro. Tell him I said to sit down and talk with you. Bring plenty of ice cream with you. Fidel loves the stuff. I'm serious. If you want to talk with him I'll have Cortes arrange it."

"Is that a bribe?"

Van Lier's smile was wide. "You can't bribe a man, Burt. Didn't you know that? You can only meet his price."

The two men talked for a few minutes more and despite his earlier irritability van Lier couldn't have been more charming and interesting. Burt knew he was being stroked, that he was being drawn closer to the diplomat for reasons that were far from purely social, but it didn't lessen his admiration for the skill with which it was being done. And when they shook hands in farewell both of them were laughing over nothing in particular. Burt, who had been depressed and tense, was reluctant to leave the diplomat. It was the small handkerchief in van Lier's hands that gave Burt the idea.

He left the limousine, walked up the stairs leading into the auditorium and once inside, doubled back, making sure he could see the limousine but that no one in it could see him. In the auditorium behind him a choir of black teen-agers had reached the final stanza of "You'll Never Walk Alone."

Burt saw her. It was dark and her face was covered, but he knew who she was. She stepped from a limousine parked behind the one Gil van Lier now sat in alone and she ran the few feet to his car, opened the back door and got in. She had been only a few feet away. The guards near van Lier's limousine acted as if they had seen nothing.

Burt, however, *had* seen Renata Zachery.

Minutes later he telephoned Donald Rettig and learned that yesterday a messenger had delivered thirty-five thousand dollars in cash.

And with that money Gil van Lier had purchased a few more days of secrecy about what Burt had just witnessed.

# ■ ■ ■ Twenty-Six

Sal Abruzzo folded his newspaper and placed it under his left arm, the signal that he had spotted Dan Einstein returning to the hotel. Abruzzo, whistling softly and tunelessly between his teeth, turned in the doorway and walked into the lobby of the rundown hotel and past Richie Sweet, who sat with a group of shabbily dressed men watching a televised wrestling match. As Abruzzo entered, Richie stepped over the legs of a snoring, fat black man sitting beside him and casually strolled toward a staircase near the registration desk. He ignored Abruzzo now standing in front of the elevator. Sal was to get on the elevator with Einstein and stay close to him when the wiretapper got off on the second floor. Richie would be waiting and together, he and Sal would kill Einstein in the wiretapper's rented room.

On the second floor, a slightly out of breath Richie cracked the Exit door and waited. He heard a man shuffle slowly down the hall toward the toilet and the sounds of a baseball game on a transistor radio came from the room next to the stairs. Richie's nostrils flared in disgust at the smells around him. Piss, cheap wine and the sour odors of food cooked on ten-dollar hotplates. Einstein was hiding in a transient hotel in Queens, a garbage dump for old men waiting to die. Well, the wait was over for Danny the Jew. Richie heard the elevator cable jerk and the old car creak as it began its ascent and he wondered what Einstein would say if he knew who Sal was. The wiretapper knew Richie by sight but he didn't know Sal and that was too bad.

Einstein also hadn't known the men who had been watching him for the past few days and were now acquainted with his every move. The first to spot him a week ago when Einstein had sat alone in a Queens restaurant and eaten two whole chickens and a dozen oysters was the polite, smiling man who owned the restaurant. The proprietor was respected in a community unaware that he was a soldier in the Bonnetti family. The FBI, with its agents and informants, its surveillance of Einstein's apartment as well as the apartment of his Chinese girlfriend, hadn't been able to locate the wiretapper. Once on the street Einstein had disappeared or tried to. In the darkness of the stairway landing it occurred to Richie that if Einstein hadn't eaten so much he might have lived a little longer. Not forever, but a little longer.

The elevator stopped and Einstein, a bag of food in one arm, limped off and headed down the hall toward his room. Sal, pretending to be heading in the opposite direction, let the wiretapper get several feet away. As Einstein crouched in front of his room to insert a key in the lock, Richie jerked open the Exit door and, with Sal at his heels, raced toward Einstein. The wiretapper heard the sound of rushing feet and looked up in panic as Richie crashed into him, sending Einstein hurtling inside onto the floor, his food scattering across the small room. Sal Abruzzo slammed the door shut and stood with his back to it.

Richie waited while a frightened Einstein fumbled around on the floor, found his glasses and put them on.

"How's it going, Danny? Long time, no see."

"Richie? What's, what's going on?"

"That question's already been asked, Danny. Only you haven't been around to give us an answer. Maybe you'll tell us now. What *is* going on?"

"Don't, don't know what you mean." Einstein, in a sitting postion, began to slowly back away from Richie.

"Danny, Danny. Didn't your mother ever tell you it isn't nice to lie? You got popped. Arrested by the FBI and—"

Einstein scrambled to his feet. Perspiration was heavy on his unshaven face. "Look, I know what you're going to say. You're going to say I talked. No way, Richie. I wouldn't turn Judas for nothin'. They tried. Jesus, they fucking tried but they got nothing out of me. They got zilch. I swear it."

Richie pulled a chair toward himself, straddled it and leaned on the back of it. "Street says you turned, Danny."

"Street's full of shit, Richie. You know that. I mean, hey, look you been around. Since when do you take anything you hear on the street seriously. The family's been good to me, so why would I want to hurt them?"

"To keep from going down," said Sal, who placed a finger against one nostril and blew snot on the floor.

Einstein licked his lips. "Hey, they had nothing on me, so why would I have to talk? They were forced to let me go because they couldn't charge me with shit. My lawyer—"

"*Our* lawyer," said Richie, rubbing the back of his neck.

Einstein frowned. "I don't understand."

"*Our* lawyer. We paid him to get you out on bail. Yeah, I know, he's an old friend of yours and you've done some work for him in the past and you thought he heard about your trouble and came to help you out of the goodness of his heart. But he's ours, bought and paid for and he's been ours for a long time."

"I didn't know that."

"Not many people do."

Einstein said, "Richie, you know I wouldn't fink. You know it. The don knows it, the *consigliere* knows it."

Sal Abruzzo cleared his throat. "If you didn't do anything, why you hidin' out in this armpit?"

Einstein shrugged. "I needed time to think, to get my head together. I know what you guys think. You think I ran away because I told the FBI something. I just needed to be by myself, to be somewhere away from everybody, where I could relax. Look, the FBI never placed me in protective custody. They never even assigned me one bodyguard."

"You disappeared before they could," said Richie. "The FBI opened the door because our lawyer forced them to and you just flew away like some little bird. At first we thought you might head out of town, say Mexico or South America."

"I, I have important business here," said Einstein. "Some people, real heavy people—"

"The FBI is sure enough heavy," said Sal.

"No, no," insisted Gypsy. "I'm telling you, you got this all wrong. These people I'm talking about are from Washington and I'm telling you they are well connected. I got a deal going down with them. Look, I'll cut you guys in on it. How's that?"

"Cut us in on what?" said Richie.

"I, I can't go into details but the money's good. Real good."

"How good?" asked Sal.

Einstein cleared his throat. "What if I told you guys I could guarantee you maybe twenty-five thousand each if you let me go. Just let me walk out of here and I promise you twenty-five big ones a piece. Look, I got some money with me. I'll give it to you as a down payment. All you got to do is turn around and walk out that door. Give me some time. I know I can square myself with the don and Carmine. I know it."

"You're some kind of talker, Danny," said Richie. "How much you say you got with you?"

314

"Fifteen thousand."

Sal Abruzzo whistled.

Richie turned and looked at him. "What do you say, Sal. Danny's offering us fifteen thousand. That's all you got, Danny?"

"Except for a couple of hundred walking-around money. What do you say?"

Sal Abruzzo looked down at the floor. "Fifteen's a lot of bread, Richie. I sure could use it."

Richie looked at Einstein. "Let's see the bread, Danny, and maybe we can get together. But you understand this only buys you some time. You're still on the hook and you got to work it out with the man. He's the only one who can make things right for you. All we can do is walk out this room and leave you with the problem."

Einstein sighed. "Don't worry, don't you worry. Like I said, I know the don and Carmine's an old friend of mine. I'm sure I can talk to them and straighten this thing out. You leave that to me. You let old Danny the Jew do his own talking."

Richie stood up. "Let's see the bread."

Einstein's hands were shaking. "Sure, sure. I carry it in a money belt and I never take it off. Even sleep with it. Man would be some kind of jerk to leave anything worth a fuck in this room. Lots of break-ins. Junkies, winos, crazies."

"That's why New York's a fun city," said Sal, easing away from the door and moving over to Einstein's left side. Reaching into the wiretapper's waistband, Abruzzo pulled out the silenced .22 that had been hidden by Einstein's coat.

"Danny, Danny. Tsk, tsk, tsk."

Einstein's eyes pleaded to be believed. "I wasn't going to use it, honest. I ain't no shooter."

Richie grinned and gently laid a hand on his shoulder. "You're a lover, not a fighter. Now let's see the money so we can get out of here."

"Yeah, sure. I really appreciate this, Richie. You won't

be sorry." Opening his coat Einstein unbuttoned his shirt, pulled the money belt from around his waist and held it out to Richie.

"It sure looks fat," said Richie admiringly. "Put it on the table and open it. Let's see what we've got."

"Sure, Richie, whatever you say." Einstein, eager to please, turned and started toward a tiny table against the wall and Richie nodded to Sal, who stepped behind the wiretapper and with a silenced .32 shot him in the back of the neck. Einstein gagged, collapsing on his side, eyes wide in horror and pain. Richie placed a foot against his shoulder, pushed Einstein on his back then leaned over and jammed his silenced .32 in the wiretapper's mouth, pulling the trigger four times. Shooting a man in the mouth was telling the world that the man had talked too much.

Sal Abruzzo stared at the bulging money belt on the floor.

"Don't even think about it," warned Richie, as he tucked the still warm .32 in the small of his back and buttoned his jacket.

Without another word he turned and walked toward the door. Abruzzo followed. Fifteen thousand dollars at their feet and all either man could do was walk away from it. On a contract like that you never touched a dollar belonging to the man you killed. The hit was an execution, not a robbery; it was a warning, not an opportunity for profit.

In the hall the two shooters separated; Sal waited for the elevator and Richie walked downstairs. They would also leave the hotel separately, meeting four blocks away at the car. Before leaving Queens Richie telephoned Carmine DiNaldi at his Mulberry Street bakery and told him the delivery had been made.

The morning after the wiretapper's killing, Carmine DiNaldi sat in the back room of his bakery and said to Richie, "Somebody else has to d-die. The don has spoken on this."

Richie, dizzy with fear, kept his hands behind him, linking the fingers together to prevent his hands from shaking. I'm dead, he thought. I'm cold meat and it's all because of her. Johnnie's dug my grave and D'Arcy the Bird Man helped her.

Richie and the *consigliere* were alone, but there were two soldiers on the other side of the only door to the office and four others scattered around the bakery and what's more, Richie wasn't carrying today. When he had appeared at the bakery a soldier had asked for his piece, saying it was the *consigliere*'s orders, that Mrs. DiNaldi would be arriving soon and Richie was to drive her around while she shopped. Richie had driven her before and this was the *first* time she had ever objected to his being armed.

Now there was nowhere for Richie to run and nowhere to hide. Sweat was hot ice on his spine and he was so filled with the thought of dying that he found it hard to even draw breath. He wondered how long he could stand in front of the *consigliere* before breaking down.

Carmine DiNaldi steepled his fingers under his small chin. "Me and Mariana, we love you, Richie. You coulda b-been my own son. I think that's why I give you the spot as m-my bodyguard. I sorta felt it was like having a m-member of my own family around me all the time. I tell you this so you know that when you do somethin' wrong, it hurts me two ways. It hurts me as *consigliere* and it hurts me as a father. The don he feels that nothin' will stop you from seein' this girl Johnnie Gelb."

*Somebody else has to die.* Richie bowed his head and waited.

"Einstein was important to the FBI," said DiNaldi, "and they will investigate his d-death. Now this girl Johnnie, she can be the thread that connects Einstein to us. I'm sure you know what I'm talkin' about. I'm talkin' about what this D'Arcy writes in his column and I'm talkin' about her knowin' about the contract in advance because you t-told her. You t-told her, Richie. I did

317

everything I could to keep you alive and the don he says, okay—"

Richie bit his lip to keep from blacking out.

"The d-don he says you live, Richie. But Johnnie, she has to die."

Richie blinked tears from his eyes. The tears were not for Johnnie; they were tears of relief.

"You kill her, Richie," said the *consigliere*. "The don says you have three days to settle this problem."

Richie, his head still bowed, nodded to indicate he understood. Three days from now if Johnnie wasn't dead Richie would be.

"Make her disappear," said the *consigliere*. "See that she is not found for a long time. Let p-people believe she is missing, that she is indulging her appetites somewhere, anywhere. Do this, Richie, because I cannot go to the don for you again. Do you understand?"

Richie, not trusting himself to speak, nodded once more.

The *consigliere* arose and walked from behind his desk toward the door. When he reached it he spoke with his back to his bodyguard. "Fix yourself before you go outside. Mariana will be here soon and you d-don't want her to see you like this. Three days, Richie. No more."

In the tiny bathroom near the office, Richie splashed cold water on his face, dried it with paper towels, patted his hair then looked down at his shaking hands. A small, barred window was to his right and he turned toward it, feeling the sun on his face. The sun's heat was delicious and Richie almost opened his mouth to eat it as though it were food from God's hands.

Three days. Good-bye Johnnie. Somebody else has to die.

# ■ ■ ■ Twenty-Seven

An exhausted Monica looked at her face once more in the small hand mirror, then dropped mirror and lipstick in her purse. The dark circles under her eyes could have belonged to a raccoon and there was a tiny line at the corner of her mouth that hadn't been there yesterday. It wasn't a laugh line because lately there hadn't been anything to laugh about; for the past few days she had worked harder than ever, forcing herself to keep busy, anything to avoid thinking about Burt. Sooner or later they would run into each other; the Manhattan world of media was a small one and its participants lived in the same restaurants, theaters, press conferences and too often shared the same ambitions, lovers, hurts. Monica had been able to postpone meeting Burt, but that couldn't go on forever.

It was five o'clock and her desk had a mechanically arranged neatness that would have pleased an engineer and now there was nothing else to do but leave it. In a few minutes she was to meet Harold Monmouth in his office two floors above hers. More work, half necessary, half not. Monmouth had been pleased with the Renata Zachery pregnancy story and quite frank about not caring whether or not it was true. The headline had sold newspapers, the only matter of concern to Harold Monmouth. His praise for what Monica had done did nothing to ease her guilt. And though her job was somewhat more secure as a result of it, Burt's job wasn't. What else was Burt hiding, Monmouth had wanted to know.

After taking one last look around her office, Monica opened the door to leave and almost screamed. Burt stood in front of her. He stepped forward, forcing her to move back into her office and when she did he slammed the door behind him and leaned against it.

"I said to myself, 'self, how's old Monica' and self replied, 'why don't you give her a call?' 'Well self,' I said, 'she's not returning my calls these days.' Self then came up with the perfect solution. 'Drop in and surprise her.' "

Burt folded his arms across his chest. "After all, you've surprised me lately. Anyway, it pays to listen to yourself from time to time. Myself says you've got a few things to tell me. I can't wait to hear them."

"You believe in coming to the point, don't you? Just barge right in and—"

"You have to admit it saves money on telephone calls, not to mention wear and tear on my dialing finger. It also saves you forcing Jimmy to lie and tell me you're not in when we both know you are."

Monica exhaled and looked down at the floor. "What do you want to know?"

"You've been spying on me for Monmouth, haven't you?"

"Yes."

"Why?"

"Monmouth said it was part of my job. He gave me no choice. Either do it or quit."

"And you didn't want to quit."

Monica's eyes glistened as she looked up at him. "Can

320

you give me one reason why I should? I know what you think of me and I suppose you're right from where you stand. But I've worked hard to get this far and now you're asking me to give it all up *for what?* Tell me why I should. I'm listening."

Burt, sure of his position when he'd entered the room, frowned and gnawed at his lower lip. "You want me to say you were right to stab me in the back?"

Tears rolled down Monica's face as she spoke. "Men accuse women of trading up, divorcing one husband to marry a richer one, that sort of thing. Well, in a sense I'm trading up. If I'd had a reason to say no to Monmouth, maybe I'd have said no."

"I don't understand. What the hell, I don't *want* to understand. I came here—"

"To accuse me. You're right. I'm guilty. I spied on you to keep my job, to avoid being fired. I was given no choice in the matter, not by Monmouth, not even by you. I fell in love with you, which only complicated matters and from then on things just seemed to go downhill in their own little way. Love made it hard to stab you in the back, as you put it."

"But somehow you managed."

"Yes. Somehow I managed. And here's something else for you to think about. You just said you didn't come here to understand—"

"That's right, I didn't."

Monica looked away from him. "I was about to say that if you'd only given me a reason to say no to Monmouth, maybe I would have said no. It might have helped if you'd given me a choice."

"What kind of reason and what kind of choice?"

"It's a four-letter word. Love. Burt, you seem to expect something from me, call it a kind of love, a kind of devotion or loyalty but I can't recall your having given any of that to me. Yes, we sleep together and we have an affection for each other. Well, maybe I should use the past tense. I just wonder if you ever planned on giving *me* a commitment of some kind. Have you really, I mean *really* given this matter as much thought as you can? I'm not supposed to betray you. Rule number one, I suppose. Monica gives up everything for Burt just like that. If it costs me, if I lose, if my future is nothing and I'm left without a job, without a lover, well let's not think about that. Let's think about Burt. Is that what you expect the people around you to do?"

"Explanations don't change facts," said Burt. "You helped Monmouth make my life one big pile of shit."

Monica closed her eyes. "Burt, ask yourself who's really responsible? No one forced either one of us to work for Monmouth. We're both over twenty-one and we did it because we wanted to. We did it for the money and that's why we keep on doing it."

She opened her eyes. "You had to have known something about the man. I did and I went right ahead and signed on. I'm not excusing myself for one minute. I did what I did and I'm not proud of it. I wish with all my heart that I could take it back. Whether you believe me or not I regret what happened. Except, except for loving you. That was real and with all the pain, maybe I'd do it again. Maybe. You know why I can't stop talking? Because I'm scared. Just can't shut up. Maybe I don't have the right to point the finger at you, since I haven't been too courageous lately. But I think, I think if either one of us wants somebody to blame maybe we ought to look in the mirror. We're not children, Burt. We're playing different games now, games grown-ups play and sometimes you get hurt. Monmouth's made that very clear to me. You have to expect to get hurt."

"I didn't think you'd be the one to do it," said Burt quietly.

"Neither did I."

They stared at each other in silence. Finally he said, "Monmouth wants to see me. Any idea why?"

"No. And that's the truth. Monmouth doesn't tell me everything."

322

"You tell him everything, though."

Monica flinched as though she'd been struck in the face. "I suppose I have that coming."

Burt looked at the ceiling. "Did you get my flowers?"

"Yes. They were beautiful, thank you. I still have them at home. They're all brown now."

He shrugged. "You're supposed to water and feed them."

"I did. I did everything I could to keep them alive, to make them last."

"Yeah, I guess you did." He looked at the floor. "But they die anyway, even when you don't want them to. That's the sad part. Something's always dying and there's nothing you can do about it."

For the first time in minutes he looked directly at her and each sensed that there was more to be said, more that must be said. But Monica's secretary Jimmy knocked on the door without coming in and said, "You're late. Godzilla won't like that."

And the moment between her and Burt was lost.

Holding the door open for her, Burt said, "I won't keep you. I suppose you're right about the both of us doing what's best for our jobs. Maybe I ought to give that more thought. Maybe I've thought about it too much. I don't know . . ."

His voice trailed off.

Monica turned her back to him, squeezing tears from her eyes with her fingertips. "I'm, I'm going to be late."

She walked to her desk, found the box of tissues in a bottom drawer and when she had dried her eyes she looked at the door, it was open and Burt was gone. Jimmy stood in the doorway, fingering the one gold earring he wore, and watched her.

When Monica began to weep once more, Jimmy crossed the room and gently took her in his arms, stroking her hair. "He's a hunk," said Jimmy with sweet sympathy, "and I suppose if he were mine I'd be crying too. But don't bleed too long over him, doll. You've got work to do. Men. We can't live with them and we can't live without them, but dear God, I'd like to give it a try. One of these days I am really going to give it a try."

Harold Monmouth spoke into the intercom and told his secretary to have Monica Hollander wait. Then he flicked the switch to *off*, folded his hands on his desk and said to Burt, "This won't take long. I'm putting you on notice. Unless you improve your column in one week, you're through. I'm letting you go."

Burt started out of his chair. "You're what?"

"*Sit* down. I said unless your column improves and I mean improves drastically, you're getting the sack. Fired. Terminated."

"I, I have a contract. You can't—"

"I can and I will. As for your contract, there'll be some sort of settlement on that if need be. Should you decide to sue for the full amount, be advised that I've been to court before and I can tell you it is a very expensive proposition, one which usually drags itself out for some time. And time costs money, which I don't think you have and therefore I don't think you will be in any position to fight me for very long."

The anger and fear in Burt made his fight for self-control difficult. When he spoke his voice was a small sound in a throat that was almost closed. "Do you mind telling me what brought all this on?"

"Not at all. Part of it was brought on by the success of the Renata Zachery pregnancy item and headline—"

"Neither of which were written by me."

"Neither of which were written by you and that, I'm afraid, is precisely the point I am trying to make. We scored our biggest sales to date with that item and headline, no thanks to you. Newsstands reported complete sellouts and we ended up printing extra editions. Regardless of what you might think it seems this is the sort of material people want to read. Your column has never been as well read before or since, sad to say."

Burt threw up his hands in disgust. "That item was stolen from my desk and it's inaccurate. I knew the item was false and not worth printing. What about all the denials that have been turning up, denials from the White House, from Mrs. Zachery, Vice-President Zachery, from everybody. Why publish stuff you know is wrong? Sooner or later you're going to get caught and when that happens you'll have trouble getting anyone to believe a word you say."

Leaning back in his chair, Monmouth fingered a tiny, gold penknife on his watch chain. "When I want lectures on morality, I'll contact the Archbishop of Canterbury who happens to be an old acquaintance."

Monmouth slammed his hand down on the desk. *"Results.* That's what I'm paying for and that's what I shall have. D'Arcy's column is delivering readers for his newspaper, but you are not delivering enough readers for me. I'm not getting the results from you that I need."

"What's that supposed to mean?"

"It means the circulation of the *Examiner-World* has improved somewhat since I hired you, but it hasn't improved enough."

"You mean it hasn't improved enough in relation to D'Arcy."

Monmouth snorted. "You Americans have a saying, I believe, that close only counts in horseshoes and hand grenades. I'm not interested in how close you come to D'Arcy. You were hired to surpass him. You were hired to win, which I believe was mentioned to you during our first meeting in California. *Win."*

"Give me time. Why can't I at least have the time I was promised in my contract?"

Monmouth pointed a finger at him. "I'll tell you why. Since D'Arcy writes a better column than you, *his* salesmen have that to point to when they attempt to peddle his column to newspapers throughout America. D'Arcy is the leader, the front runner and everybody likes a winner, do they not? They do. So the newspapers are buying his column and they're not buying yours. Once D'Arcy gets in, it stands to reason that no matter how good *you* are there's no room for you. I'm told by one of my salesmen that I might have to consider cutting the price of your column in order to make it competitive with D'Arcy's. Good Christ, man, I didn't go into business to cut my price! And I certainly didn't come to America to crawl around in D'Arcy's footprints and beg people to buy my wares. I won't have it. I absolutely won't have it!"

Burt closed his eyes, because it made it that much easier to skirt the edge of begging. "I need time. I'm onto something big, very, very big. If it comes through I'll give you a month of front-page headlines."

*"If,"* snapped Monmouth. "I don't have time for *if's.* You've got one week to deliver on your *if's.* I don't care whether it's van Lier and the vice-president's wife or van Lier and the Queen of England or who the bloody hell else you're taking notes on and not writing about. One week. After that you can spend all the time you want with your journalistic integrity or whatever you call it."

"I came here," said Burt patiently, "to tell you I don't like people writing under my byline any more than I like having notes stolen from my desk and used without my permission. I might as well get that in while I'm here."

Looking at his pocket watch, Monmouth said, "You've said it and I've heard it. Now if you'll excuse me I'm supposed to be meeting Miss Hollander. If you can save your job in the next seven days you'll find the rewards as great as I promised they'd be. But frankly I think you have an uphill fight. Gossip is a peculiar sort of journalism and that's something you'd better learn in a hurry."

Burt stood up. "As you yourself remarked, you've said it and I've heard it."

The publisher closed his antique watch with a snap. "I trust your best exceeds what you've put forth so far. Some advice, Anthony: money is always hard earned. When you reach for it, reach hard. Grab hard. There's no other way. In my book the end always justifies the means and it always will."

"I'm working on it."

"On your way out would you please tell Miss Hollander to come in."

In the waiting room outside Monmouth's office, Burt paused and looked down at a seated Monica who was nervously chain smoking. After a few seconds he said, "I suppose he's a nice guy, but I'd have to ask myself if he's worth cloning. He told me to send you in."

Monica nodded then smiled quickly. Standing up she looked at him and when he said nothing more she dropped her eyes and hurried past him.

Burt watched her open the door to Monmouth's office and close it behind her, leaving him to stare at the door until Monmouth's secretary cleared her throat. He loved Monica but he was in no hurry to forgive her and by the time he did, how much love would be left? It was a question that stayed with him for the rest of the day and through a sleepless night.

The cactus plant had been sent to D'Arcy several weeks before by an irate reader who had suggested that D'Arcy's dispostion could be improved by stripping naked and sitting on it. D'Arcy had immediately taken a fancy to the pale green plant with its clusters of needles and had decided to keep it on the floor near his desk where he could observe its harsh ugliness. This afternoon he was watering it when his assistant Fiona answered the telephone and told him the FBI was calling.

"D'Arcy here."

"Agent LaChance of the New York FBI office. We'd like you to come down, if you will, to talk about Dan Einstein. We'd also like to speak to you about a friend of yours, a Miss Johnnie Gelb. Her life's in danger."

D'Arcy slammed down the phone, picked up the plastic container of water and smiled as he resumed watering his cactus plant. Dipping a tissue in the water he began to gently brush its leaves, taking care to avoid the cactus needles. This time the FBI hadn't threatened him. Just some official bore, with a hokey little tale designed to serve the agency's own interest and D'Arcy was having none of it. The telephone rang again and Fiona answered, pursed her lips and placed a hand over the mouthpiece of the receiver.

"Guess who?" she said to D'Arcy.

"The FBI."

Snatching the receiver from Fiona's bejeweled hand, D'Arcy wasted no time in attacking. "You stupid, stupid sod! Your twitish ploy to censor me won't work. Einstein's death is as deplorable as your efforts at keeping him alive. You'd get more done by apprehending his killers than by harassing me. Why don't you stop wasting my time and get on with whatever it is you people do."

"Mr. D'Arcy," said Arthur LaChance, "I started to tell you about a friend of yours, a Miss Johnnie Gelb. She is definitely a target for a mob hit. They intend to kill her as soon as they can. Our informant says the contract's been out on her for at least twenty-four hours and there's a rush on it. We thought perhaps you'd like to help us keep her alive."

"Really?" D'Arcy toyed with an exceptionally long needle on the top leaf of the cactus. "Mr. LaChance, I haven't been in your country very long but I have learned a few things and one of them is that the mob, as you put it, almost never kills women. It's simply not the way they play the game. As for Dan Einstein, well, if you couldn't keep him alive, what makes you think you can keep Miss Gelb alive, assuming you are telling me the truth about the threat to her life."

LaChance cleared his throat. "A couple of things, Mr. D'Arcy. The mob rarely kills women, true. But it *has* killed them. It's killed women who inform, who steal money, who cheat on their husbands. Now it doesn't happen often, I grant you, but it happens. Miss Gelb is in a position to link people to the Einstein killing and these people are willing to kill her to keep out of jail. It's as simple as that. As for Dan Einstein, his lawyer legally got him out of our custody and put him back on the street. Nothing we could do about that. Once he was on the street

Einstein made it clear that unless we stayed away from him there wasn't a chance in the world of his cooperating with us. Frankly we needed him more than he needed us, so we were forced to back off. That's when he disappeared. I should add, Mr. D'Arcy, that I believe the story in your gossip column about Einstein was a factor in his killing."

"Rubbish," snapped D'Arcy. "Who forced Einstein to inform? Who freed him so that his killers had easy access to him? It seems to me that if I were to turn Miss Gelb over to your tender mercies she would not have the longest of life spans."

"Do you know where she is?"

"I do not. Nor would I tell you if I did."

"I see. Did she ever mention a Richie Sweet or a Richard Suitori to you?"

D'Arcy jerked his hand away from the cactus, pricking his finger on a needle.

"Mr. D'Arcy."

"I'm still here. Go on."

"This Richie Sweet is supposed to be the man who did the Einstein killing and we've been led to believe that Miss Gelb can link him to it—"

"Good-bye Mr. LaChance."

D'Arcy abruptly hung up and began sucking blood from his pricked finger, shivering with the sudden and alien feeling which his mind translated as fear and concern for another human being. Behind him telephones rang and his assistants Fiona and Perry did their best to ward off other callers trying to stake their claim on D'Arcy's time and energy.

D'Arcy reached for the telephone. Time to run a quick check on Mr. LaChance. He dialed the number of the FBI office in Manhattan and when the switchboard answered he asked for agent LaChance. Two secretaries and one phony name later (D'Arcy used the name 'Mr. Wales,' hastily borrowed from the heir to Britain's throne), a male voice said, "Yes, Mr. Wales, this is Agent LaChance. May I help you?"

329

Same voice, same bloody voice of a minute ago. D'Arcy slammed the phone down violently, not seeing Fiona flinch at the gesture and stare at him. Years of dealing with liars and pretenders had given D'Arcy an instinct for the truth and he now knew that Agent LaChance was real. And it frightened D'Arcy, for it meant that Johnnie was in trouble.

He dialed again, this time calling Johnnie's answering service and leaving an urgent message for her to call him immediately. He then told Fiona and Perry to either take messages or hold all calls unless they were from Johnnie or Clare Chandler. And in the next two hours an anxious D'Arcy dialed Johnnie's answering service eight times and also canceled two appointments so that he would be in his office should she call.

■ ■ ■ **Twenty-Eight**

The bartender placed a second Scotch and water on the bar in front of Burt, picked up a ten-dollar bill and made change, laying singles and coins beside the drink. Ignoring liquor and money, Burt continued massaging his temples with the fingers of both hands, digging his fingers into his skull as though trying to pull all the torment from his brain. Only five days remained of the week given him by Monmouth. The past forty-eight hours were a blur that had pushed Burt to nervous exhaustion. Forty-eight hours of little sleep, meals eaten on the run and a frenzied effort to complete the story on Gil van Lier's involvement with American troops in Chindé.

Burt was enough of an investigative reporter to insist on proof of any accusations concerning van Lier and Chindé. But when it came to the diplomat's affair with Renata Zachery, the only way Burt could handle that was to lie. Perhaps lie was too strong a word: as a gossip columnist he could describe what he intended to do as taking a chance on not losing a good story. Before he had gone to work for Monmouth, Burt would never have taken such a chance, nor would he have had any respect for a reporter who did.

Van Lier's wheeling and dealing in Chindé, no matter what the reason, was a fact and by tying the alleged affair with Renata Zachery to this story, Burt hoped to convince the public that all of it was true. If the public bought what was happening in Africa why wouldn't it buy the existence of a love affair in Washington's power circles, a love affair that could change the course of the next presidential election?

Burt sipped his Scotch and looked at his notebook. He had just left New Jersey and a very productive second meeting with Donald Rettig, who had identified three snapshots of American army officers given Burt by Hoyt Pathy. Pathy had gotten them through a contact at the Pentagon and Rettig had confirmed their names as well as their presence in Chindé while he was there. Hoyt Pathy had also given Burt the name of a CIA official, now retired, who owned a Maryland real estate company and a Washington travel agency called Alladin. The ex-CIA man supposedly was no longer involved in American espionage, but Donald Rettig had placed him at the Puerto Rican air base where Chindé flights began and he had also placed the man in Chindé on two occasions. Burt had been especially pleased when the ex-CIA man had turned out to be Brian Catherine's brother.

Now it was time for Burt to break his word to van Lier, to deny him the chance to make peace in Chindé. Burt wondered if publishing the story tomorrow or the next day would hurt the Rettigs, who had reported the absence of mysterious cars cruising in front of their home since Burt had gotten in touch with van Lier. Burt hoped the Rettigs wouldn't be harmed but his way of dealing with that was to sip more Scotch and not think about it.

Burt motioned to the bartender, holding up his empty glass for a refill. Monica had given him more than enough to think about. He *had* expected her to love him and ask no questions and to give as much as she could. And he had *not* committed himself to her; he hadn't even thought about it. What's more, Burt the crusader had always expected family, friends, ex-wife and ex-lovers to see the truth as he saw it and accept his version of what the truth really was. To be honest, Burt had expected too much. He had no right to force-feed his ideals into anybody any more than they had the right to do it to him and that was what he had done in his zeal as a man chasing perfection in an imperfect world. Not only did he owe Monica some sort of apology, but he also owed his father one as well. Gary Anthony wasn't a saint; he was just a man fighting to get through one day at a time as best he could and that made him one of billions of other people in the universe. Monica, Burt's father, and so many others had done nothing worse than be born human. But apologies would have to wait until Burt survived the next five days.

As the bartender set another Scotch in front of him, Burt glanced at his watch. He hadn't checked into the office in over an hour. Taking his drink with him, he walked to a telephone booth in the back. He was drinking more than he had in a long time. Now he needed alcohol to get through the day and he needed it every day and the thought of that bothered him.

Molly answered, immediately put him on hold without asking his name and by the time she had come back to him Burt had swallowed the rest of the Scotch, vainly trying to ignore the sickly warmth now oozing throughout his stomach. He made a mental note to eat more and drink less.

"Burt Anthony's office," said Molly. "May I help you?"

"It's me, Molly. What's left of me, anyway."

"Oh, my God, where have you been?"

"You sound worried. What's wrong?"

"I'm not sure. It's Miss Hollander."

Burt shifted in the phone booth, knocking his empty glass to the floor. "What about her?"

"Mother Mary, there go the other phones."

"Forget the other phones. What about Monica?"

"She keeps calling here every five minutes. Says it's very important that she get in touch with you. She sounded quite upset."

"Any idea why she's upset?"

"No. She wouldn't say. She seemed very worried."

Burt took out his notebook. "I'll call her back. Let's have the rest of the messages."

"Okay. Miss Hollander sounded like it was a matter of life or death."

"At the moment, it is." He hadn't told Molly about Monmouth's ultimatum. No sense worrying her, especially if Burt managed to get through the week without being fired.

"Ignore the phones," said Burt. "Give me the messages. I'll call Monica from here."

When he dialed her office, the phone at the other end was picked up at the same time by both Monica and Jimmy. After telling Jimmy to hang up and hold all calls, she said, "I'm glad you called."

"Believe it or not I was planning to. Molly got the impression it was important."

Monica hesitated before saying, "I think it is. Monmouth's planning to hurt you in some way and he's planning to do it soon, real soon. I think he's planning to do it in the next hour. Burt, the man has gone crazy, I mean really crazy."

"Slow down. How's he planning to hurt me and why? Not that I wouldn't put it past him."

"I'm not sure how. Jimmy's going to tell me as soon as he finds out."

"Jimmy? What the hell's Jimmy got to do with this?"

"It's D'Arcy," said Monica. "There's a chain of newspapers in the Midwest, a very important chain called the Montalvo Press. Montalvo owns fifteen newspapers in eight different states and he's been shopping for a gossip column to help boost circulation and draw advertisers. It was between you and D'Arcy."

"Don't tell me," said Burt. "D'Arcy won."

"Burt, it involved a great deal of money and tomorrow when the story's released, Monmouth is going to look bad. He wanted that deal in the worst way and I guess you can say he went about getting it in the worst way. He tried paying off a few people in Montalvo's organization to get them to buy your column instead and it didn't work out. Montalvo's angry and you know who Monmouth is blaming for all this."

"Me."

"I'm sorry," said Monica. "I really am. Monmouth's flipped out. I've never seen him this angry. The word around here is that you're through as of now. Monmouth hasn't said anything to me, but that's what I hear. Now here's the strangest part—Jimmy's having an affair with one of the security guards here, though you can't really call it an affair since Jimmy doesn't really stay with anyone too long. He and this guard had a date today after Jimmy got off from work, but the guard had to cancel. He told Jimmy that he and a couple of the other guards might have to do a rush job on you."

Burt's hand went to his throat. "Me? Are you serious?"

"I'm only telling you what Jimmy told me. Burt, I'm frightened. Would Monmouth really have you beaten?"

"He paid to have D'Arcy leaned on, didn't he? And I've heard a few other stories about Mr. Monmouth that are far from heartwarming. Christ, what do I do now? Do I leave the country, grow a beard, what?"

"Burt, hold on. Jimmy just came in. Hold on, don't go 'way."

Monica covered the receiver with her hand and all Burt heard was a muffled conversation. Somehow he made out the word *bizarre*. Jimmy had just said *bizarre* and then he said *tres bizarre, mon cher*.

And then Monica was back on the phone, as out of

breath as if she'd just been running. The excitement was getting to her. "Thanks, Jimmy. I won't forget it." When Jimmy had left her office and closed the door behind him, Monica's voice dropped down into a whisper. "Burt, you won't believe this! Monmouth's insane, I mean he is really insane."

"I believe it. What's he planning to do to me?"

"He *is* going to do a job on you, but it has nothing to do with having you beaten."

Burt closed his eyes and exhaled. "I guess I should feel relieved, but somehow I don't. Let's have the rest of it."

"Jimmy's friend just called. He told him their date was still on because what they're planning won't take long. They're going to your apartment and they're going to take away all your files, all your notes. They're going to clean the place out of everything that has to do with your column. As soon as Monmouth has his hands on that material, he's going to telephone you and tell you you're fired."

Burt slumped back against the wall of the telephone booth. "That son of a bitch. He's found another way to kill me and he knows it. I've worked my ass off on the Chindé story and he's going to ruin it for me just because he wants to be top dog in the gossip wars. I could strangle him with my bare hands."

"It's my fault," said Monica. "I spied on you and I gave him that item on Renata Zachery and I'm to blame for what he's planning to do to you."

"Don't say that. Monmouth would have found another way to stick it to me. That's his style. You were right about a few things and one of them was I've got no one to blame but myself. You lie down with dogs, you get up with fleas. I joined the team and now I'm paying for it."

"Where are you now?"

"Washington Heights," said Burt. "That's in upper Manhattan near the George Washington bridge. Monica, I've got notes, photographs, Donald Rettig's notebook and God knows what else in my office. Monmouth has more than enough to write some kind of story if he gets those notes. I can't tell you what it's going to do to me to see him break this thing after I've half killed myself trying to put it together."

"Can you get to your office before the guards do? Just take the important stuff and disappear. Write the story for some other publication. You've got the contacts, haven't you?"

Burt shook his head. "I'm too far away to make it in time. Even if I drove with my foot down to the floor I wouldn't get there before Monmouth's goons. And warning Molly wouldn't help either. I'd have to tell her what's going on and convince her to help me and I don't think I could do all of that in time. She's not the type for intrigue. She's just a sweet, hard-working Catholic girl who thought she was being hired as a secretary, not as a mistress of intrigue."

"They have a key to your apartment," said Monica. "Jimmy says Monmouth gave it to them. I suppose Monmouth had it all along."

"It figures. He had no intention of giving me a week. He was going to fire me no matter what I did. Now he'll do his own version of what's happening in Chindé and what's happening with van Lier—Jesus!"

"Burt, if you can't get there in time, maybe I can. Let me leave now and see if I can beat the guards there. I'll get the notes and keep them for you. It's the least I can do. If it wasn't for me, Monmouth wouldn't have—"

"Stay out of it. We're down to the short strokes and Monmouth's playing rough. You think those goons would let you stand between them and what they want? No way. You didn't do a damn thing. The trouble is neither did I. I should have stood up to Monmouth a long time ago, even if it meant blowing this job."

"I'm going to do it, Burt, and you can't stop me."

"Monica, please don't. If anything happened to you—"

"No matter what you say, it's my fault. I told him what you were doing and I told him about your notes. Monmouth thinks you're keeping things from him, that you're

337

sitting on some sort of gossip gold mine which you refuse to print. The least I can do is go to your apartment and see what I can grab."

"I said you don't owe me a thing. I owe you. Now stay out of it. You gave me a few things to think about and suddenly I'm thinking a lot harder than I'd planned to. I'll make out somehow. I always have. You and I've got a few things to talk about."

"Later, perhaps. Right now I've got to leave if I'm going to get to your place before the guards do."

"Monica, please. I appreciate what you're doing but you could get hurt."

"Good-bye," she said. "I love you."

The line went dead and Burt called her name over and over, pounding the walls of the telephone booth with his fist. Then fumbling through his pockets for a dime he quickly dialed Dave Tiegs.

"Hey, Burt," rasped Tiegs, "why so early? It's only three-thirty in the afternoon and I ain't had breakfast yet. What's up?"

"Trouble. I need help. Can you reach Action Jackson?"

"Oh, ho, it's that kind of trouble, is it? Yeah, I can reach him. He works nights and he oughta be home now. Why do you need him?"

"No time to explain. He won't need a gun, but he may have to use a little muscle. It might just be that kind of scene. Monica's walking into something that's hairy, something that involves three guys and I can't handle those kind of numbers. Tell Jax there's a couple of hundred in it for him and I'd like him to drop whatever he's doing and meet me in front of my apartment immediately. That's now, Dave, and give him the address."

"Done," said Tiegs. "Action's your man. I'll do my best to get him there. Can I help?"

"No. I can't drag you into something that might backfire against you in this town. You have a family and you might want to work for Monmouth again."

"Hey, hey," said Tiegs. "What's goin' on here?"

Burt hung up and ran from the bar. It was Monica, not

himself, not his career, but Monica that he thought of as he raced his car downtown toward his apartment.

## Washington, D.C.

Senator Aaron Paul Banner stood at the window of his office and stared at the White House. He knew everything there was to know about the building, which had been designed by an Irishman who'd copied it line for line from a home built for a Dublin duke. George Washington had been the only American President not to live there. But I'll live there, thought Banner, and I'll be President. He would get to be President because of that final tape from the now dead Dan Einstein, the tape of van Lier and Renata Zachery making love in a New York apartment.

Banner, who considered himself a moral man, had no respect for the Zacherys, man or wife. She was trash and he was a weakling who couldn't control her; neither deserved to live in the White House and Banner would see that they didn't. Tomorrow this tape would be in New York and in the hands of Robin Ian D'Arcy who had already come dangerously close to exposing the affair in his column. Dangerously close because earlier exposure wouldn't have been beneficial to Banner.

Clare Chandler would take this tape to D'Arcy, along with a small notebook containing dates, times and places of other meetings between Mrs. Zachery and van Lier; this was the sword the Englishman needed to finish Richard Zachery in politics forever. That same sword would also make Aaron Paul Banner the next President of the United States. As for Dan Einstein's murder, that too had happened at just the correct moment. Gypsy was dead and Banner had no regrets; the wiretapper was greedy and boastful and in essence had killed himself.

The FBI in New York had hired Einstein to bug an East Side Manhattan restaurant owned by Mafia leader Augustino Bonnetti, in order to learn if Bonnetti had bribed a secretary to steal files from the office of a federal prosecutor. After planting listening devices and taking the

FBI's money, Einstein had turned around and told Bonnetti he was being bugged and for a price Einstein would remove the bugs. When the FBI had learned it had been double-crossed, Einstein was on his way to his grave. It had only been a question of time.

From his window Banner watched people walking toward new Senate building. On a mild May day like this Adam Danziger would walk to his meeting with Banner, rather than take a limousine. During the short walk Danziger would undoubtedly say hello to as many people as possible and in general conduct himself as a candidate for vice-president. Adam Danziger, however, was in for the greatest disappointment of his life; Banner had invited him to his office this afternoon to tell him that he was no longer being considered as a presidential running mate. Another man was to be Banner's vice-presidential candidate; another man would also make the speech that would place Banner's name in nomination at the convention. Danziger's political career was about to be destroyed because of D'Arcy, the columnist.

While D'Arcy's original columns on Adam Danziger had not been printed under threat of a lawsuit, the columnist had resorted to printing blind items on the Florida congressman. And even though Washington knew who D'Arcy was writing about, the general public hadn't and therefore Danziger had survived so far. What he couldn't survive and didn't know about was a probe of his financial affairs being conducted by Florida's largest newspaper, which had assigned its best team of investigative reporters to the story. Banner knew this because he had a continuing secret check being made on those men he was considering as his vice-president. When the Florida newspaper finished its investigation Danziger's political career would be finished as well. That's what Banner was going to tell him this afternoon, though he hadn't decided whether or not to tell Danziger that it was D'Arcy who'd tipped off the Florida newspaper and caused the investigation.

Gossip. Investigative reporting. When it came to drawing blood, thought Banner, the difference between the two was no more than the difference between a lion and a grizzly bear. Both could claw and chew a man to death. He smiled as he looked through the window and saw Danziger plant himself in the path of an oncoming black couple, introduce himself and offer his hand. Danziger was a racist who had now softened that particular stance since national officeholders had to be possessed of a more tolerant outlook. Banner smiled again. After today Danziger could go back to being himself.

When Danziger turned the corner and disappeared into the building, Banner buzzed one of the three secretaries he used. "Martha, please put in a call to Mrs. Chandler and when you get her let me know. I want to talk to her before I speak to Adam Danziger. If he gets here before I'm finished have him wait, please. Be nice to him, he's running for a place on the ticket, in case you hadn't noticed."

"I've noticed."

"Fine. Thank you, Martha."

When Adam Danziger did enter Banner's office, the Virginia senator pointed to a couch near the door and walked back to his desk, putting as much distance between himself and Danziger as possible.

The campaigning smile was still on Danziger's face when Banner began. "You and I've been friends for a long time, Adam, so this isn't easy for me to say."

Monica moved with a speed born of fear. Rolling the photographs of the dead Chindé GIs, she shoved them into her shoulder bag, along with Donald Rettig's notebook. Several of Burt's small notebooks mentioning Gil van Lier were also in the bag. At the file cabinet she yanked open a drawer and quickly looked at folders, removing any with Gil van Lier and Renata Zachery's name. There was no time to inspect each folder, so she simply took as many as she could fit in her hand. A stunned Molly stood and watched, and bit a knuckle. The telephones rang and were forgotten.

"I don't know, Miss Hollander. I really don't know."

"I do, Molly. Burt will tell you it's all right. He's on his way here now and he'll tell you all about it when he arrives. There's no time to explain. I have to take these files and notes and get out of here."

"Miss Hollander, I don't think I can let you do that. There was some trouble last week about an item in Mr. Anthony's column that he didn't put there and he said something about his notes being stolen."

Monica stopped for a second, closed her eyes, then opened them and continued pulling folders from the file cabinet. "I know about last week, Molly. But there's no way you can stop me from walking out of here with this material. Believe me, I'm only trying to help Burt. Someone else is coming here to take away this material and that's not going to help him at all. Are there any other files beside those in this cabinet?"

Molly shook her head and continued to gnaw on a knuckle. "No. Mr. Anthony hasn't been writing the column that long. I can't let you come in here and take Mr. Anthony's property and leave. I can't."

"You can, Molly. Now I've told you there's no time to explain or argue. I've got to get out of here before they take this stuff."

"They? Who's they?"

"Believe me, I'm not trying to hurt Burt. I'm only trying to help him. If it wasn't for me . . ."

Monica didn't finish the sentence. A few minutes ago she had leaped from a cab, thrown a ten-dollar bill at the driver and raced passed the doorman and into the elevator. Monmouth's security guards couldn't be more than minutes behind her. Explanations to Molly would have to wait.

"It's not your fault," she said to Molly. "Just blame everything on me. If you like you can come with me to make sure I'm only holding this material until Burt claims it. I mean that, Molly."

"I, I don't know. Did Mr. Monmouth tell you to do this?"

Monica shook her head. "No. He doesn't know about it. He soon will and when he does, I'll have problems of my own. So long, Molly. Either come with me or get out of the way, but don't try to stop me."

"Miss Hollander, please!" Molly began to weep.

Monica, tears in her eyes as well and her arms filled with folders, ran past her.

Out in the hall, Monica started toward the elevator and stopped. The indicator showed one elevator, on the sixth floor and rising. Two more floors and it would be here and if Monmouth's men, who were certain to recognize her, were on it, if they saw her with Burt's files and notes . . . Monica turned and ran toward the staircase as behind her, the elevator stopped and its doors slid open. She didn't turn to see who'd gotten off. But she heard male voices as she opened the Exit door, raced along a landing and down the stairs.

She had gone down three flights of stairs and was on the landing leading to the next when the door above her burst open and a Spanish-accented male voice shouted, "Hey! Come back here with that shit! Goddam it, come back here!"

A frightened Monica turned and saw the dark shapes of men on the landing above her. In the dim light she could make out the face of one of them, and she knew he recognized her. He was a fierce-looking giant named Lopez, a day guard in the *Examiner-World* lobby, a man who sometimes bragged about what he did to those he caught trying to break into the newspaper building.

"Lady," he yelled down at Monica, "you can get hurt doin' that!"

Monica began to run and in her haste she missed a step and then she was falling sideways, the folders flying from her hand and now she was speeding through a shower of papers, seeing it all in slow motion, seeing herself in midair and knowing that there would be pain when she landed. The expectancy that this was certain to happen was the worst horror of all.

The pain came. She crashed at the bottom of the stairs and screamed as something sharp pierced her side, but the scream ended when she passed out.

Burt was out of the elevator before the door had fully opened and racing down the hall, Action Jackson on his heels. When they arrived at Burt's apartment, the door was open and a weeping Molly stood just inside.

The apartment was a mess. File drawers had been pulled out and dumped on the floor. Desk drawers were on top of desks and a telephone had been yanked out of the wall and dumped in a wastebasket. But it should have been worse, they hadn't done as thorough a job as Burt had expected.

"What happened?" asked Burt. "Where's Monica?"

Molly held a handkerchief to her face and pointed with a trembling finger. "She's gone. She's got the files and they're after her. I saw her run toward the stairs. Mr. Anthony, those men were m-mean. They were nasty to me. They began to tear this place apart looking for your notes, but Miss Hollander has them—"

"The stairs," said Action Jackson, who turned and was out of the apartment and into the hall before Burt could catch up to him. At the Exit door, Jackson yanked it open and was halfway across the landing when Burt reached the door. Burt followed him, leaping down the stairs three at a time and in the semidarkness everything now happening to him seemed like a bad dream. Finally as they turned at a landing Burt saw three men crouched over Monica who lay at the bottom of the last flight of stairs, papers and folders scattered around her. When the three men heard the footsteps above them, they quickly looked up and one of them, papers in both hands, dropped them and shoved a hand in his back pocket for the knife he carried there. Action Jackson hesitated only a fraction of a second. Gripping the banister with both hands for balance he lifted a huge leg and kicked the guard in the face, sending him flying across the landing and crashing into a wall. The guard slumped unconscious at Monica's feet.

Then Jackson stood near the bottom of the stairs, fists on his hips. Burt stopped. The huge black man blocked the staircase and the only way Burt could see Monica was to crouch down and peer through Jackson's legs.

Jackson said, "Nobody moves, nobody gets hurt. Let's do this easy. I want to see hands. Show me some hands with nothin' in 'em. Nice, real nice. Now put 'em behind your neck."

The two guards did as ordered.

"Anybody carrying?" asked Jackson.

The guards shook their heads.

"Ain't just talkin' 'bout guns," said Jackson. "Anybody here got a knife?"

The guards shook their heads again.

"Best be that way," said Jackson, "because I'm checking you out to make sure. If I find anything you better hope it's a sandwich, 'cause you suckers are gonna eat it."

"Got nothin'," Lopez said. "We ain't here to make trouble. Just come here to get some papers, that's all."

Jackson nodded toward the unconscious guard. "Why don't you two make room for yourselves to sit down. Push him outta the way and you two sit on the top step, hands behind your neck, backs to me."

"What's gonna happen to us?" Lopez asked.

"You know the rules," said Jackson. "When you lose you don't have the right to ask shit. Why don't you sit down like I told you and don't give me no attitude. I don't like no attitude."

The two guards pulled the third out of the way and sat down as ordered, hands behind their necks, backs to Jackson.

Burt pushed his way past the black man and leaned over Monica. When he looked up at the guards, his face was tight with hatred.

"Nobody touched her," the anxious Lopez swore. "She

tripped and fell. That's the truth. I swear on my mother that's how it happened."

"You're lying," said Burt.

"Ask her."

"I will."

Lopez turned his head until he could see Burt. "We didn't beat up on no woman. We just come here to get the stuff, your notes and that's it. We chased her and she started runnin' and she fell. That's it, I swear."

Monica moaned and Burt cradled her in his arms, gently stroking her hair and face. He wanted to say so much to her, but the words eluded him. However, he had something to say to the guards. "If you laid a hand on her, I'm going to have my friend here break your back."

"You got no right," said Lopez. "Mr. Monmouth said we was just gettin' back something that belonged to him. He said it was legal."

Burt held Monica close to him and whispered, "I got the right, friend. As of now, I've got the right."

Monica made a little sound, then opened her eyes. "Burt? Burt?"

He kissed her forehead and she reached up to touch the tears rolling down his cheek.

"I'm here," he said. "I'm here. Did they hurt you?"

"No." She smiled. "Tripped. No parachute. God, my ribs. I think I broke something. And my knee."

Burt looked at the security guards, then at Jackson. "One of these clowns has a key to my apartment," said Burt. "Get it. Then see if they've got anything else of mine. After that I want you to take any identification they've got on them. Any ID. Driver's license, Social Security, anything. When I tell Monmouth his goons were here, I want proof. I've got you and Monica as witness, but I want more. Don't touch anything else but ID."

Jackson nodded.

Burt stood up with Monica in his arms and said to Jackson, "When you're finished here, turn these assholes loose and bring the notes to me. I've got to get Monica to a hospital for X rays."

Monica clung to him and said, "Don't forget my bag. Oh, God, it hurts to breathe! Do me a favor and don't make me laugh."

Burt kissed her again. "No more free falls, okay?"

She flinched, bit her lip and dug her fingers into the back of Burt's neck in a vain attempt to fight the pain. "No more job. No more. . . ."

She passed out.

Burt held her tighter and hurried out the stair exit.

# ■ ■ ■ Twenty-Nine

D'Arcy pressed the hold button, hung up the receiver then left his desk and hurried into his bedroom, slamming the door behind him. At his bed he reached for the telephone and sat down.

"Johnnie?"

"I'm here, Robin."

"Let me help you. Just tell me where you are?"

Her voice was slurred with drugs and despair. "Nobody wants to help, not even my own family."

"Johnnie, please let me help you."

"Called my family," she said. "My mother hung up on me, but she took the time to remind me about all the trouble I've caused her and how she doesn't want any more. My father's in London sucking around the Arabs. That's his speciality, sucking around people with money, which is how he got plenty of money, my father. You know what my mother's way of dealing with me is? Same as it's always been. She offered to send me an advance on next month's allowance and that's it. She didn't want to know from my problems. She fucking didn't even want to know and she never has."

D'Arcy squeezed the receiver with both hands. "Where are you?"

Johnnie's laugh was hard, brutal, brief. "Where am I? In my head. That's where I am. I'm hiding in my head and Richie's never going to find me there. He's looking all over town for me, you know. He's trying to find me and my own mother doesn't even give a shit. She's got her own life to lead, her social friends, her parties in Connecticut. My mother always hangs out with the *right* people. Know what else she said before she hung up? Said we had an *arrangement*. An *arrangement*. The family gives me money and I stay away. That's the deal, says my darling mother, and I have to keep my end of the bargain. Stay away, Johnnie, 'cause nobody wants you, except Richie and he wants to kill me."

An angry and frustrated D'Arcy shouted, "Must you always take those bloody drugs?"

Johnnie sighed into the phone. "Drugs are my friend. Drugs are definitely my friend. I fly high in the sky by and by—"

"Oh, do be sensible. Tell me where you are."

"Like hell. How can you help me against *them?* You don't know what's going on, Robin bird man. You think you do but you don't. Robin bird man. That's what Richie calls you. My family won't help me and you can't help me. Not against the mob, you can't. Nobody can."

"There are laws in this country. I'll make it my business to see that you're protected. The police—"

"Two words for the police. *Balls.* The police are the problem, man, not the solution. The police work for the mob, they work for the people who're trying to blow me away. Cops, judges, district attorneys, you'd be surprised just how many of them are owned by the mob and I know what I'm talking about. I been with a lot of these people and they are mob alllll the way. Alllll the way. That's where the money is, Robin bird man."

D'Arcy closed his eyes. "Do you need any money?"

"You sound like my mother. That's all she offered me. Money."

"I'm offering more and you know it."

"Yeah, I guess you are. I just want to get out of the city. Maybe Canada, Mexico, maybe Hawaii. But I don't have a cent. Drugs are expensive and some guy I was with last week waited until I fell asleep, then he ripped me off. Took almost fifteen hundred cash, some jewelry, my camera, some dope. That bastard did a job on me. Guess I was lucky he didn't give me the clap. Don't ever go to bed with a drummer."

She wept.

"A friend of mine got hurt yesterday," she said softly. "He's one of the people I buy dope from. Richie found him and asked him where I was and the guy gives him a smart answer. Richie broke his thumbs, both of them. Robin, they're after me and I'm scared. If I don't get out of the city soon, I'm in a lot of trouble. I can't eat, sleep. I can't. . . ."

D'Arcy was on his feet and running a hand through his hair. He looked at his watch. "It's almost eight o'clock and the banks are closed. I have a little money and I can probably get more from Fiona and Perry. I should be able to cash a small check somewhere in the neighborhood and I'll bring all the money to you. Just tell me where."

"You-you've been good to me, Robin. I wish it could have worked out for us. I don't even see how you can like me. Most of the time I don't even like myself."

"We're still alive," said D'Arcy, "and that means we've got a chance to be anything and everything to each other."

"I wish," she said, "I wish—" And then the sobbing became uncontrollable.

D'Arcy's voice was husky in his throat. "I have many wishes, my darling, and they all belong to you. Tell me where you are."

Minutes later D'Arcy was in his office counting the

money he'd just borrowed from his assistants when Perry answered a phone, placed the caller on hold and yelled, "Clare Chandler. She says it's urgent."

D'Arcy grabbed the receiver in front of him. "Yes, Clare. Make it quick, if you will. I'm on my way out."

"I'm in New York, Robin, and I have it."

"Have what?"

"The tape," she said. "I was too frightened to telephone you from Washington. I suppose I was paranoid about my own phones being tapped. Right now I'm so nervous I can hardly walk."

D'Arcy gritted his teeth. If pulling Clare's toenails out with a pair of pliers would have organized her thoughts in a straighter line, D'Arcy would have done it gladly.

"Clare, for God's sake, will you say what's on your mind? I have to get out of here."

"I'm at Kennedy Airport. Let me close the door, first. Robin, I don't want to carry this thing around with me any longer than I have to. You *have* to meet me right away and take it off my hands."

"Impossible," snapped D'Arcy looking at his watch. If he was late, Johnnie might disappear and he'd never find her. Or Richie would kill her.

"I have it, I have it!" Clare had never been this excited out of bed since D'Arcy had known her.

"Have what?" D'Arcy's impatience and irritation were no longer hidden.

"The tape of Gil van Lier and Renata Zachery making love. I've also got a notebook of facts about other meetings between them. Robin, I can't carry this around with me. It's going to explode. If you don't meet me *now*, I'm either returning to Washington this minute or I'm throwing this thing away. I'm scared."

D'Arcy took a deep breath to calm himself down. The excitement over the tape, coupled with the tension he felt over Johnnie made him dizzy. He sat down, one hand on a forehead now damp with perspiration. Everything he had ever wanted, dreamed of, worked for was within his grasp. He had just picked up the telephone and at the other end of the line was the one story that would make him the most successful gossip columnist in the world.

But there was Johnnie and she was expecting him.

He said, "Have you heard the tape?"

"Yes. It was played for me yesterday and everything you could want is on it. Names, place and some very, very hot goings on, let me tell you. I also looked at the notebook on the flight up here. Robin, all of this could make you the most important man in journalism anywhere in the world."

"I agree. Who played the tape for you? I assume it was the same man who gave it to you, the same man who commissioned the wiretapping in the first place."

She hesitated, then said, "I-I don't want to talk about that now. Can we go into it when I see you?"

D'Arcy smiled. His voice was gentle. "Of course. Why don't you come here and wait for me."

"Where are you going?"

"I must cash a check, then see a friend in need."

Clare's anger came out of panic. "I came up here to see you, not wait around while you—"

"Clare, darling, I've given my word to help this friend. It won't take long. I'll rush there and rush right back to you."

"Robin, I'm scared."

And so is Johnnie, he thought. "Clare, I'll tell you what. Come to the office. I'll try to get back as soon as I can. If I'm not here when you arrive someone in the office will know where I am. Just ask Perry or Fiona. Get the address from them and meet me there. This way you won't be alone for a minute. I'll either meet you here or at my friend's hotel."

"Where's that?"

Now it was D'Arcy's turn to hesitate. "I'd rather not bandy that information about, if you don't mind. Who knows who might be following you. Just do as I say. We'll meet in my office or at my friend's hotel and I'll take the tape off your hands. It'll be my worry then."

"Yes, Robin."

Minutes later, when D'Arcy left his apartment building, he failed to notice a man hidden in a darkened doorway across the street, a man who had been following him for the past two days. The man began to follow him once more, walking on the opposite side of the street and keeping a half block behind D'Arcy. The man, who had burn marks on the backs of both hands, was a New York City detective and extremely skillful at following people. When D'Arcy hurried into a liquor store, the detective held up one hand in a stop signal and behind him a car with darkened headlights, which had been slowly rolling down the street, eased to a quiet halt. Inside the car and hidden by the night, Richie sat alone in the back seat and tried not to remember that four hours from now at midnight his three days were up.

After fixing himself toast and tea in Monica's kitchen Burt carried it into the living room, where Monica had fallen asleep on the couch watching a televised ballet. He found a chair near the couch and bit into a piece of toast, his eyes on Monica. On-screen, a male dancer with an impressive bulge in his crotch placed both hands on the hips of a tiny ballerina and lifted her overhead. Off-screen, someone plucked violin strings in a tuneless monotone, a cue for the male dancer to begin turning slowly in a circle; above him the ballerina arched her spine, bending backward to seize both ankles with her hands. Monica stirred and Burt stopped eating. When she relaxed, sinking deeper into a drug-induced sleep, he returned to his toast, his eyes wandering back to the ballet.

Since her fall yesterday, Burt hadn't left Monica alone. He had slept on her couch, while she had spent the night in the bedroom with pain from two cracked ribs, a twisted right knee and one slight concussion. Prescribed medication had given her a little rest but . had still cried out several times during the night and each time Burt had been there. Once when it had appeared she was reliving the fall in a nightmare, he had awakened her and held her

353

in his arms. The flowers he had sent were in the bedroom; they were withered and stiff but Monica had refused to allow him to throw them away.

As Burt sipped lukewarm tea, the ballerina stood on the toes of one foot, arms pointed at the ceiling. Several feet behind her, the male dancer did a split, rested on the floor in that position and waited. Harold Monmouth had also waited. He had waited until this morning to talk about what had happened yesterday regarding the security guards and Burt's notes; the notes themselves were never mentioned and the telephone conversation, while tense, had been mercifully brief. Monica was fired effective immediately and Burt would be fired after completing five more columns; Monmouth's original ultimatum was now a final verdict.

Burt had expected the call and was ready. "Severance pay for Monica and myself," he told Monmouth. "Let's talk about it."

"My attorneys are attempting to sort that out now. You'll hear from me when a decision is reached."

"I've already reached a decision on it," said Burt. "I want all the money I'm due on my contract. Every penny of it, plus five thousand for moving expenses. I haven't decided whether or not I'm returning to California, but in case I do, it'll be nice to know I can afford it."

"I said my attorneys are working on the matter. However, I can tell you right now it's highly unlikely you'll get that sort of golden handshake from me. You disappointed me, Anthony. I don't mind telling you that. Since you failed to live up to my expectations, I see no reason why I should live up to yours."

"I think you will," said Burt. "I expect to be paid in full and what's more I want six months' severance for Monica."

"I warned you about trying to take me on," said Monmouth. "You probably have some sort of peculiar reason why I should grant what you've just asked, so let's hear it. Not that it will do you any good."

"Why don't we see what good it does me. It's amazing

354

how much of a hard-ass I can be when I know I won't be working for you much longer. Suddenly you don't look so tough. I'll begin by telling you I can identify the three men you sent over to my apartment yesterday, men who terrorized my secretary, wrecked my apartment, chased Monica down the stairs and put her into a hospital."

"Your word against mine," said Monmouth calmly. "Your word against *theirs*. You say you can identify the men who perpetrated these so-called outrages and I say you can't. Someone else could have done—"

"You haven't heard the rest of it. I can identify them by their driver's licenses, Social Security cards, their security guard ID and a few other pieces of paper. I can also produce a witness beside Monica and myself, said witness being a New York City police officer. One of your guards ought to remember this particular cop quite well. The cop loosened a few of his teeth. You still listening, Mr. Monmouth?"

"Yes," said Monmouth slowly. "Go on."

"Is that all you've got to say? You don't sound so sure of yourself now."

"Damn it, man, get to the point."

"You probably thought I'd made a mistake not having your goons arrested. I didn't. I mean what did they take? I got my property back and it's in a safe place. By that I don't mean my apartment. And technically speaking no one laid a hand on Monica, so I figured one of your lawyers would have had everybody out of court and on the street in nothing flat. That would have been too easy and I didn't want you to have it easy. Not after what happened to Monica. I'm going to tell you something about gossip: what actually happened doesn't count at all. What counts about gossip is what people *believed* happened. I didn't want a judge to dismiss yesterday's occurrence as some sort of slight misunderstanding. The guards would have gone free and you would have been off the hook. But D'Arcy won't dismiss a damn thing when it comes to you."

"D'Arcy?"

"He'd love to print this little saga and make you look like a heavy-handed retard. He'll jump at the chance to get you and we both know it. Something else: Monica's got a good case for a lawsuit against you *and* the company that does your security. It'll be the sort of publicity a security company wants to avoid. Doesn't do much for their image as public protectors."

"You could have stolen that identification," said Monmouth.

"Don't be stupid," said Burt. "It's too much of a coincidence that three men lost their identification at the same time, in the same place and in front of three witnesses. Nobody loses a nickel; they only lose their ID. Mr. Monmouth, you should have another talk with your lawyers. Between D'Arcy and a lawsuit I'd say you're being squeezed and squeezed hard. Isn't that what you told me? When you go after a thing, you said, go after it hard."

"You bloody bastard," said Monmouth. "You think you're right clever, don't you."

Burt nodded. "I'd have to say yes. You'll probably look for a way out of all this, because you just don't like to lose. But I promise you D'Arcy will get all the information he needs to drive a stake through your heart. I also think that if your lawyer knows his business, he'll tell you not to go into court to fight a female employee you fired while she was ill. D'Arcy and I can make people think this is one hell of a sad story. Monica will have so much sympathy going for her that you'll walk out of court a lot poorer than you walked in. You're probably more worried about D'Arcy making you look foolish, so I say quit fucking around and send us the money."

Monmouth took some time before answering. "You're finished as of now. As of this very second you're out of my life. Completely and utterly out of my life."

"I want the money," said Burt.

Monmouth slammed down the phone without answering.

Burt smiled at the receiver in his hand. "I think I just heard a discouraging word."

He said to Monica. "He'll pay. It's going to kill him, but he'll pay."

"And he'll never stop hating you," she said.

"He can hate me so long as he pays. You can't scare a man who's got nothing to lose and as of now, I've got nothing to lose. I used to be a good reporter; Monmouth may just find that out someday and I do mean the hard way."

More pleased at being unemployed than he had ever thought he would be, Burt telephoned Dave Tiegs and Molly to tell them the news. Both were genuinely sorry about his getting fired; Molly cried, while Tiegs, taking the news calmly, said both he and Burt would find another money tree to shake. The two men promised to have dinner soon.

The televised ballet ended and was followed by a costume drama dealing with a turbulent period in the life of England's royal family. Burt went to the kitchen for a second cup of tea and when he returned to the living room the television screen was filled with bearded men in armor glaring at each other; several of them shouted to the king that he was now dethroned. You and me, thought Burt. And I couldn't be happier.

He wasn't happy about Monica having gotten hurt; he blamed himself and nothing she had said to him could change his mind. While working for Monmouth, they had both gotten hurt and the time had come for Burt to do something about it. It was time to walk away from self-betrayal. It was time to stop being what someone else wanted him to be and start being the only thing he could be: an honest reporter. Gossip was somebody else's game, not Burt Anthony's. As for Monica, Burt was going to start being honest about her immediately. He wanted her and he would do anything to keep her.

"You're coming with me," he said to her.

"Where?"

"I don't know. It'll either be here or California and I can't promise you it'll be a life with all the bills paid on time, but you're coming with me."

"I don't understand."

"That's because you're on dope, at the moment. I'm saying I love you and I want a life with you and I'm not giving you much of a choice. Either you come with me or I'll find another woman to fall down the stairs on my behalf."

"You don't have to—"

"I do. I have to. I have to and I want to. Now take some more dope and go to sleep."

"I could be dreaming all this, you know. What if I wake up and you don't remember a word you just said. What happens then?"

He kissed her. "Then I suppose I'll have to repeat every word."

Burt, his eyes on the medieval television drama, smiled at Monica's sleepy reply. "In writing, turkey. I want it in writing."

The ringing telephone knifed into Burt's relaxed mood, annoying him, and he leaped up to answer it before the ringing bothered Monica.

"Hello?"

"Is this Burt Anthony?"

"Yes."

"Are you alone?"

Burt recognized the voice, but the shock of hearing it prevented him from speaking.

*"I said are you alone?"*

Burt switched the receiver to another ear. "No, no, I'm not."

"Leave the apartment," said Gil van Lier. "I have to talk to you and it's got to be private. Nobody, I mean nobody, must hear our conversation."

"I, I can't. What's going on? Where are you calling from?"

"I'm in Washington and I need your help. You've got to leave and get to a phone that's not being tapped. I wouldn't ask your help if I wasn't desperate."

Burt sat down. "Hey, wait a minute. Back up and run that past me again. You need *my* help? I thought I had already helped you by not printing certain information. And what's this business about Monica's phone being tapped? This is the first I've heard about it."

"Maybe it's not tapped. Maybe I'm nervous because of what I just heard. Anthony, you have got to help me. Leave the apartment and call me *now*. I'm in a public phone booth near my house—"

"I can't leave. I've got a sick friend on my hands. Monica's been hurt and somebody's got to stay with her."

"Anthony, I'm begging and that's something I never do. You're my last hope and there's not too much time left. Damn!" Burt heard van Lier strike something with his fist.

"Taking it out on the phone won't help," said van Lier. "Will you do as I ask and leave the apartment and call me here?"

Burt looked at Monica. "No."

"Why the hell not?"

"I've had it with being everybody's football. Yours, Monmouth's, whoever. Monmouth wants me to make him a big man and when it's not done the way he prefers, he fucks me over. I end up sitting on a story that can blow you out of the water; I go against everything I am as a reporter by not printing it. Well, I'm tired of people walking on my face and that includes you, Mr. Secretary."

"The vote comes up day after tomorrow, but if I don't get your help the vote won't matter. Look, if I tell you what's going on, if I tell you everything, will you please help me? Time's running out."

"Why should I help you any more than I already have?"

"Because you have integrity," said van Lier. "Because you care about doing the right thing. Because once you make up your mind to do the right thing, you do it."

"Not lately," said Burt. "In case you haven't heard, I'm out of a job. What's more, it doesn't bother me as much as I thought it would. When I leave Monmouth, I leave gossip. I'm a reporter and I don't think gossip has a goddam thing to do with reporting."

"I'm not surprised you're leaving. You'd have done it sooner or later."

"You sure about that? Dumb question. You're always sure. What about that item about Mrs. Zachery, the one with my byline?"

"About Renata being pregnant? I knew you didn't write that garbage. It was fantasy, a handful of smoke with nothing behind it. You're a hell of a lot more careful than that."

"Is that why you never called me down on it?"

Van Lier was silent. "You've got to do something for me. Clare Chandler's just left Washington with a tape. Someone's been tapping my phones and bugging my bedrooms. Jesus!" Again van Lier pounded the wall of the telephone booth.

"They, they have a tape of me and—"

He hesitated.

"Renata Zachery," said Burt.

"They have this tape and it can destroy me, her, and a few others."

"Vice-President Zachery included," said Burt.

"Christ, you ought to be down here talking instead of me. Yeah, the tape has me and Mrs. Zachery and we're involved, let us say, in a very heavy scene and Clare Chandler's taking it to Robin Ian D'Arcy. She's probably already in New York by now."

Burt sat up straight. "If D'Arcy gets that tape you've had it."

"Don't remind me. I want you to get it from him, get it before he prints one word. Clare also has a notebook with information about me and Mrs. Zachery that I'd rather not see published."

Burt licked his lips. The reporter in him could almost taste this story. "Why me? Wouldn't it be smarter to send one of your own people after something as red hot as this, someone you could really trust?"

"No way. I wouldn't trust my mother with that tape. Whoever has it can put my career in the toilet."

"Whoever has it can also put Richard Zachery's career

in the toilet. Whoever has it decides who becomes our next President. Why didn't you send Cortes after it?"

"By the time I'd learned about the tape, Clare Chandler was somewhere between here and New York. There's no way Cortes could get to New York before she does. Believe me, I tried figuring out a way to get that tape without involving anybody beside Cortes and myself, but it just didn't work. You're my only hope."

Burt said, "A tape like this could make me the biggest reporter in the business. I could write my own ticket anywhere in the country."

There was still strength in van Lier and he found it. His voice became more insistent, more persuasive. "You're a journalist, not a gossip. You never were a gossip. Everyone knew it; you were just the last one to find it out. You could have burned me more than once, but you didn't. Not just because you were holding back as a favor. You also didn't do it because you wanted to make sure of your facts. Gossips are never sure, Anthony. What's more, they don't give a damn. You do give a damn, you always have and you always will."

Behind Burt, Monica softly called his name.

He said to van Lier, "What if I use the tape for myself. What if I decide to hell with integrity and use the tape myself. What then, Mr. Secretary?"

Van Lier's laugh was short and bitter. "So I'm taking a chance. What choice do I have? I usually take only calculated risks, specific gambles and then only when forced to. That's my secret. I figure the odds, find the edge and roll the dice. So far it's worked."

"So far." Burt turned and waved at Monica, who now sat up staring at him through a tangle of hair. She waved back and cleared the hair from her face.

Burt said, "Did you know that they call you Gil van Lucky?"

"Who do you think first used that name?"

"You're taking a chance. I'll tell you up front you're taking a chance, because right now I don't know what my future's going to be. It could go in any direction."

"You're taking the chance, Burt. Whatever you decide to do about that tape is going to determine the kind of man you're going to be the rest of your life. I'm asking you to pull my chestnuts out of the fire and I'm also asking you to stop the woman I love from getting hurt."

"Love?"

"Put your tongue back in your head and stop drooling. Yes, I love Renata Zachery."

Burt exhaled. "Holy shit."

"That seems to sum it up," said van Lier. "It is one hell of a big mess, but at the moment I can't do a thing about it. The question is, will you?"

Monica limped past Burt, on her way to the bathroom. He patted her gently on the behind and said to van Lier, "A question: who clued you in about the tape and if you don't tell me, I'm hanging up. If I'm in this thing, I want the name of all the players."

"I guess you deserve to know what you're getting into. There aren't any secrets between us at this point. Do you know Senator Adam Danziger of Florida?"

"Not personally."

"He was supposed to be Aaron Banner's vice-presidential candidate. Yesterday Banner dropped him like a hot potato."

Burt was on his feet, his mind spinning. "Wait, wait. You're saying Banner's behind this whole thing, that he ordered your phones tapped? And Danziger's angry about Banner dropping him so he spilled the whole plan to you? Wow!"

"Danziger didn't do it for free. He wants his. A Florida newspaper's preparing an exposé on his financial dealings. He wants me to go to Richard Zachery and see if Zachery can either kill the story or at least tone it down. The governor of Florida and Zachery are in the same political party and they know each other quite well. I told Danziger I'd try, but I couldn't promise anything."

"You've got a lot riding on whether or not you can keep reporters quiet. You may find this a lot harder than you think. What are you going to tell Zachery?"

Van Lier sighed. "I haven't decided. I can't very well tell him the truth, can I?"

"It would be different," said Burt, "but I don't recommend it."

"Get to Clare Chandler and D'Arcy before they destroy me."

Monica smiled at Burt as she limped back to the couch. Placing his hand over the receiver's mouthpiece he said to her, "Van Lier. He needs help."

"What are you going to do?" asked Monica.

"I, I don't know. I told him I couldn't leave you."

"It's up to you," said Monica. "I'll be all right. How long would you be gone?"

"I'm not sure. Couple of hours at least."

"Burt?" It was van Lier.

"Yes? I'm still here. I was talking to Monica. She said it was up to me whether or not I go."

"Do it. I promise you I won't forget it. Do it and do it now."

Burt shook his head. "No matter what I do lately, it costs me more than I can afford. What's it going to cost me to help you this time?"

He hung up.

Burt and Monica stared at each other in silence. "He needs help," said Burt.

"Everybody does at one time or another," said Monica.

He walked across the room and sat on the edge of the couch, taking her face in both hands. "The only person who's done a damn thing for me lately is you. If you tell me to go, I'll go. If you say stay, I stay."

She shook her head. "We went through that in my office the other day. It's your life, Burt. You'll have to decide."

■ ■ ■ **Thirty**

Ignoring the gun aimed at him, D'Arcy sat down and crossed his legs, using his fingers to straighten the crease in his trousers. "In England neither our police nor our thugs carry guns," he said contemptuously, "so you should know that I am not as impressed by your revolver as I should be. You will forgive me, of course. And do try not to be alarmed when I reach inside my jacket for my cigarettes."

Without waiting for an answer, he coolly took out his cigarettes, lit one and blew smoke across the room at Richie Sweet and Sal Abruzzo. D'Arcy smiled at Johnnie, who sat rigid with fear on the edge of a sagging bed in the cheap hotel room.

"Not to worry, love," he said cheerfully, flicking ashes on the worn carpet. "We'll have this business settled straightaway."

In confrontation, D'Arcy had always found courage.

The temporary uncertainty brought about by his attachment to Johnnie had vanished in the face of their present peril. The Mafia hoodlums who now pointed guns at him and Johnnie in a shabby little room in Manhattan's Chelsea section had created a moment of tension the likes of which D'Arcy had never faced before. But he had often courted danger and above all, he had never fled from it and so he would meet this challenge, overcome it and defy the scum who now stood in front of him. They would not take Johnnie's life so long as D'Arcy had his.

The frantic rush to obtain money for Johnnie and meet Clare Chandler had pushed all else from D'Arcy's mind. It had completely slipped his thinking that he might have been watched; in truth, his arrogance wouldn't allow him to consider such a possibility. After cashing a check at a liquor store, he had rushed back to his apartment building only to find that Clare hadn't arrived. He considered waiting for her but decided that further delay might mean Johnnie would flee and he would have lost her once more. *D'Arcy had to help Johnnie.*

And so he had gambled with the biggest story of his career. He had hurried upstairs to his apartment, written Johnnie's Chelsea address on a slip of paper, then sealed it in an envelope with Scotch tape and handed it to Perry. Under no circumstances was Perry to give this envelope to anyone but Clare Chandler. If for some reason she didn't show up, Perry was to destroy the envelope and flush it down the toilet unread.

After thanking Perry, D'Arcy went downstairs where he told the doorman that if Clare Chandler came and asked for him, he was to have her go upstairs to see Perry. Then D'Arcy raced off to meet Johnnie, unknowingly leading the two Mafia hit men to her. He knocked on the door of Johnnie's sleazy room and she opened it, and neither of them heard the two men behind him until it was too late.

Richie shoved his gun in his belt and used both hands

to emphasize his words as he spoke in Italian to Sal Abruzzo.

"He's here," said Richie, "and he knows who we are and what we have come here to do."

"He's heavy," said Sal. "You don't hit somebody like him; it's trouble all the way."

"We have no choice," Richie said. "The man is in the wrong place at the wrong time. Today is the third day and if I don't settle this thing with the girl in less than three hours, I am a dead man. The Englishman is a witness. How can I leave him here to tell people I have taken the girl?"

"Talk to him," said Sal Abruzzo. "We have nothing to lose."

"His mother talks to him," said Richie. "I haven't got time to talk to the bastard."

"I don't like this," said Sal. "I don't like this man being here."

Richie's hand came to rest on his gun. "He is here," said Richie. "That is a fact."

"Talk to him," said Sal.

Richie chewed the inside of his mouth and eyed D'Arcy. He didn't tell Sal that D'Arcy definitely had to die. Sal didn't know the Englishman as Richie did. He didn't know that it was a waste of time to ask the Englishman to keep quiet about what he'd seen in this room tonight. Robin Bird Man wouldn't break, he wouldn't bend, he wouldn't give in. Richie was as sure of this as he was of the death sentence awaiting him if he didn't kill Johnnie. But he would go through the motions so that later Sal could tell the *consigliere* that Richie had tried to do what was right.

Richie said to D'Arcy, "I don't suppose if I let you walk out of here you'll keep quiet?"

"When I leave this room," said D'Arcy, "Johnnie comes with me."

Richie shook his head. "Can't be."

"Dear boy, not only will I not keep quiet, as you put it, but I shall make it my business to cause a great deal of trouble for you and your slimy associates. You, my friend, shall regret this evening to your dying day."

"I ain't your friend. Just remember: I gave you the chance to walk."

D'Arcy stood up. "Johnnie and I are leaving."

Richie looked at Sal Abruzzo as if to say I told you so.

The gun was in Richie's hand. "We're all leaving. And we're going to find a quiet place and take care of business."

"I understand that some men find it impossible to get an erection," said D'Arcy, "and therefore resort to playing with guns as a substitute. Tell me, Richie: how does it feel to be impotent? Do women laugh at you when you fail—"

Richie backhanded him in the face and the stinging blow almost spun D'Arcy around.

Turning to face Richie, D'Arcy touched the pained spot with his hand. "Our own little macho man. Do you feel more virile now?"

Richie didn't want Sal Abruzzo to see him lose control, not over something like this. Robin Bird Man was deliberately trying to make Richie come unglued. Well, it wasn't going to happen. Richie was going to do his job and look good all the way. He jerked his head toward the door. Time to get this show on the road.

D'Arcy turned to see Johnnie grip the edge of the bed with both hands, cling to it and refuse to move. Running over to her, an impatient Richie grabbed a handful of her long hair, jerked her head back and brought his thumb within a fraction of her left eye. When he spoke, his lips almost touched her forehead. "If you don't move your cute little ass, you are gonna be looking at life through only one eye. Now get the fuck off that bed and do it now!"

Johnnie ran to D'Arcy, who put an arm around her and glared at Richie. The Englishman didn't fear him and Richie knew it; D'Arcy hated him and wouldn't stop until he had destroyed him. Richie was a killer and could easily recognize his own kind and D'Arcy, in his own way,

367

was as much a killer as Richie was. That was why wasting Robin Bird Man was not only a pleasure but an absolute necessity.

When the taxi pulled away, Clare Chandler could be seen running across the sidewalk and into the rundown hotel. Burt sat in his parked cab and wondered why she would be meeting D'Arcy in such a dump. The Milton Hotel was a foul-looking dump in a tough neighborhood and the last place one would have expected to find D'Arcy or Clare Chandler.

Fifteen minutes before, when Burt's cab had been about to pull in front of D'Arcy's apartment building, an empty cab had cut in front of it in response to a doorman's whistle. Burt had been about to pay his driver and step out on the sidewalk when he saw a harried-looking Clare Chandler running toward him. To avoid being seen by her, Burt slid down in the back seat, grateful for the darkness. He could still see and hear her. Up close she looked frightened. It was understandable, considering the information she now carried. The tape and notebook in her possession would have frightened a lot of people.

Or was she still carrying it? She *was* leaving D'Arcy's building, which could mean she had already dropped off the tape and notebook. Burt watched as she hastily fumbled in her purse in search of a tip for the doorman.

The doorman said, "Thank you, Mrs. Chandler, but that won't be necessary. Mr. D'Arcy took care of things before he left. He's a precise man, as you know, and wouldn't appreciate me taking advantage of his guests."

*Before he left.*

Burt saw Clare Chandler smile weakly, then step into the empty cab and when the doorman slammed the taxi door behind her, Burt was sitting up straight in his seat.

"Follow her," he said to his driver. "There's twenty over the meter if you don't lose her."

And now Burt watched Clare Chandler disappear into the seedy-looking hotel on Eighth Avenue and 25th Street. He paid his driver, then stepped out into the street and seconds later the cab drove away, leaving him alone. The May night was mild and somewhere behind him two women spoke softly in Spanish, then laughed. A black youth on a skateboard sped in front of Burt, a transistor radio pressed against his ear. A cat screeched and a garbage can was overturned, its top rolling until it hit another can.

Burt dried his sweaty palms against his thighs and took a deep breath. When the dizziness passed, he forced his eyes open as wide as they could go. It's true, he told himself, I *might* be willing to do anything to get my hands on that tape.

And the thought that he was on the verge of throwing away all of his scruples, frightened him.

*Walk*, he said to himself. *Start walking.*

He did, keeping his eye on the faded and decrepit sign saying HOTEL MILTON.

A pale yellow bulb failed to light most of the dark hallway and also did nothing toward eliminating the odors so deeply ingrained in every inch of the floor and walls. Poor lighting and sickening smells, however, didn't concern Clare Chandler as much as did the presence of Richie Sweet and Sal Abruzzo.

"These men," she said to D'Arcy, digging her nails into his arms. "I, I don't understand, Robin. Who are they? Where are they taking you?"

D'Arcy patted her hand. "So nice of you to drop by, love. Your decorator could do wonders with this hovel. These men? Ah, yes. There's a name for them, but why go into that now. They are indeed taking us somewhere, but I'm afraid you'll have to ask them where. As yet they haven't seen fit to confide in me."

He took Clare's purse from her and flinched as Richie, his gun in his pocket, jammed it hard against D'Arcy's ribs. D'Arcy turned his head and spoke over his shoulder. "Not to worry. She isn't the gun-carrying type."

D'Arcy turned slowly and faced Richie, letting him see the tape and small notebook he'd removed from Clare's purse. "Items of some worth to me and of no consequence to you. Nothing to be alarmed about, but then you never were one for deep thought, were you, Richie?"

Richie said, "Keep talking. You just keep talking. The time's gonna come when you won't be able to talk, so you might as well get it all out while you can."

D'Arcy gave him a half smile while handing Clare's purse back to her.

Richie said, "Sal, you go first. The rest of you follow him and remember one thing: if I have to burn anybody here and now, then that's how it's gonna be. I do what I have to and I don't worry about it. Now let's all go outside."

D'Arcy looked at a terrified Clare, who was slowly becoming more aware of the danger she had walked into. The Englishman said, "He has a revolver. Both of them do and that little speech the one behind me just gave is his way of saying he'll send us all to eternal rest on this very spot if we don't do as he says."

"Kill us?" whispered Clare. "Robin, does he mean it? Is this some sort of joke?"

"It isn't a joke, Clare. Now calm yourself and do as I say. Turn around and follow—"

Richie shoved D'Arcy into Clare Chandler. "I said *move.*"


Burt was about to step from the street onto the sidewalk when he saw them pushing through the hotel's front door. D'Arcy, Clare Chandler, the blond girl Johnnie and two men. The alert D'Arcy saw Burt and reacted enough to warn Burt that something was wrong.

Burt saw the two men stop and the dark, handsome one move closer to D'Arcy, who shoved him away and yelled at him, "You silly little shit! I've had enough of your attempts at terror!" There was venom in D'Arcy's voice and his face was red with anger.

Now the three men and two women were out on the sidewalk, several feet away from Burt who still hadn't moved.

"Read my column tomorrow!" shouted D'Arcy to Richie. "Your Don Bonnetti will choke on his breakfast! You impotent little—"

The night exploded and there was nothing Burt could do to stop it from happening. He had no way of knowing that something had snapped inside of Richie, that anger now ruled the Mafia gunman, that Richie's hatred for D'Arcy demanded blood and as of this second nothing in the world was more important than killing Robin Bird Man.

Richie fired through the pocket of his suit jacket at close range, shooting D'Arcy twice in the stomach, driving him backward several feet along the sidewalk until D'Arcy collapsed, his eyes wide with disbelief. Johnnie ran.

Planting his feet, a grim-faced Richie drew his gun from his pocket and aimed carefully, a firm two-handed grip on his weapon. He pulled the trigger three times, sending Johnnie stumbling forward, arms extended to break her fall and then she fell, hitting an empty garbage can and sending it spinning in front of her.

Burt ran. He ran toward a parked car to his left, ducking down behind it, hearing Clare Chandler scream uncontrollably and feeling a hot, sour taste in his mouth that meant he was on the verge of throwing up. On the almost deserted street, cars stopped, windows opened, people shouted. Death had swiftly brought life to the street. As Burt carefully peeked over the car hood, the two gunmen raced past him and were gone. When the footsteps couldn't be heard anymore, Burt came out from behind the car.

He was at D'Arcy's side in a minute. All words seemed locked within him and the sheer helplessness he felt in the face of death made him want to scream. As he leaned over the dying D'Arcy, he saw the trace of a smile begin on the columnist's mouth. With what little strength he had left, D'Arcy moved his blood-covered hands toward Burt.

The hands held a tape and a small black notebook.

*"Guts, dear boy,"* said D'Arcy and then he died.

# ■ ■ ■ Thirty-One

**Montreal,
June 2.**

The black coffee would start Richie's day this morning. After that, he'd check out of the motel and keep running for his life.

He stood at the open window of his cabin, cup to his mouth and smelling the rain-wet pine trees around him as he stared at the lake which lay just beyond a half-filled parking lot. It had rained for the past two days, ever since he had iced D'Arcy and Johnnie, but the rain didn't seem to bother a slicker-clad fisherman in a rowboat, who was alone on the lake and patiently waiting with rod in hand, eyes on the gray, choppy water around him.

Dummy, thought Richie. You could be in a warm bed with a woman instead of sitting in some fucking boat waiting for a fucking fish to jerk your fucking line. But if he could, Richie would have traded places with the man in a second, because while killing D'Arcy had been satisfying, it had been the worst mistake of Richie's life.

When he had telephoned Carmine DiNaldi to tell him that Johnnie and D'Arcy were dead, at first the *consigliere* had been silent. Finally, his only words to Richie had been go home and stay there until you hear from me. Tell Sal to do the same thing. That was when Richie had begun to fear for his own life. The vibrations had been all bad; Richie had been around the *consigliere* long enough to know the signs. When Carmine DiNaldi said little, he was at his most dangerous. When he concealed his thoughts and actions, he was a snake coiling to attack.

Instead of going to his apartment as ordered, Richie had disobeyed the *consigliere* and gone alone to a bar. First he had lied to Sal Abruzzo, telling him the telephone conversation with the *consigliere* had been a good one, that there was nothing to worry about because the *consigliere* had a plan to smooth things over. The family had important friends, so killing D'Arcy wouldn't be a problem. Sal and Richie would have to lay low for a while, but after that there would be nothing to worry about. That was what the anxious Sal had wanted to hear. He had left for his home in the Bronx, a smile on his face, giving Richie one last thumbs-up sign. Richie never saw him alive again.

In the bar the news of D'Arcy's murder had been important enough to interrupt the programming on every television channel. Richie had nervously watched while downing drink after drink. From the bar he had checked into a hotel under an assumed name; he wasn't going near his apartment tonight, not if he wanted to stay alive. Just before falling asleep, he telephoned Sal Abruzzo. A man had answered and calmly asked who was telephoning Mr. Abruzzo. Richie, his hands shaking uncontrollably, had hung up. Sal lived with a wife and two children. The male voice did not belong there. The male voice had come to Sal's home to kill him.

Leaving the hotel immediately, Richie had used a credit card to rent a car and drove north. In Utica, he had

373

awakened a friend and borrowed a gun from him; both Richie and Sal had gotten rid of the guns used to kill D'Arcy and Johnnie. Now Richie was in a motel on the outskirts of Montreal and ready to keep moving. The story of D'Arcy's murder had even made the Canadian papers, where it was printed in both English and French; Richie was sick of looking at it. The killing was a mistake and if he could change things he would. But at the moment, all he could do was run and keep on running.

Because of him, the family was now under more pressure than it had ever been. Three mob murders in less than ten days, the New York press headlined, and nothing's being done about it. The FBI and police, in order to appear somewhat efficient, had released Richie's name and his photograph was now in newspapers all over North America. D'Arcy's friend, the well-dressed woman who had stumbled on the scene at the hotel, had probably mentioned Richie's first name. That would be more than enough, along with her description of him. If Richie were dead, the pressure would be off the family to a large degree; if he were dead, he couldn't tell who hired him to pull the trigger.

Richie turned from the window and walked back to the map spread out on his bed. From Montreal he planned to drive across Canada, through Quebec and into Ontario, Manitoba and all the way to British Columbia. After that, he would turn south and drive down into the States again. He rubbed the stubble on his face; the sooner he grew a beard and moustache the better. As for money, he could solve that problem easily enough. He had a gun and it could support him until something else came along.

Leaving his cabin, he hurried through the rain to the motel office, where he used his credit card to pay his bill. After buying a pack of cigarettes, he turned up his coat collar and ran out into the rain again, this time toward his car. He suddenly remembered he needed more gas and maybe it would also be a good idea to buy a few sandwiches to avoid eating in restaurants where he might be recognized.

On the lake the lone fisherman wiped rain from the lenses of his binoculars, then focused until the picture was clearer. He stared at Richie's car and when Richie ran into the picture, the fisherman licked his lips and reached down between his legs, pulling back a piece of oil cloth that protected a device the size of a small transistor radio.

As Richie opened the door to his car and got in, slamming it behind him, the fisherman, binoculars still to his eyes, licked his lips once more, counted slowly to five and pressed a small red button at the top of the device he held in his hand. In the car, Richie had just reached for the ignition key, when he heard and felt the heat and roar around him. He screamed as both of his legs were ripped from his body. No one heard him scream, but they did hear the explosion. The agony of Richie's horrible death lasted only a fraction of a second, for the steering wheel was driven into his chest, crushing it and pulverizing his heart.

Out on the lake the fisherman watched flames engulf the remains of the car and, when people began rushing from their cabins, the fisherman casually dropped the mechanical device overboard and picking up his rod, turned his back to the commotion on shore. He began to whistle, enjoying the drumming of the raindrops on his yellow slicker, finding it a pleasant counterpart to his tune.

After setting a pair of suitcases by the front door, Burt returned to the bedroom where Monica was packing cosmetics into a shoulder bag. He was about to pick up another suitcase when the doorbell rang. Monica dropped a compact on the table and looked nervously into a mirror at Burt's reflection.

He smiled at her. "It'll be over soon and then we can leave."

"God, I hope so." She reached for her cigarettes.

As the doorbell rang again, Burt went to her and kissed the back of her neck. "Don't quit on me now."

She reached back to touch his face. "I can't quit smoking, so how can I possibly quit you?"

"That's what I want to hear."

"He's not going to like what you've done."

"No, I don't think he will. But it's time I stopped worrying about what he's going to like. I'm in business for myself, remember?"

"Yes."

Burt kissed her neck once more, then walked into the living room. At the front door he hesitated, took a deep breath and exhaled. *Now*, he whispered and jerked open the door.

Gil van Lier said, "You're a hard man to reach these days."

Burt looked at the black diplomat whom he hadn't spoken to since the night he'd sent Burt to get the tape, the night D'Arcy was shot to death. "The FBI wanted it that way. They thought I might be in danger, but with Richie Sweet and Sal Abruzzo dead, I'm told there's nothing to worry about."

"You're a fortunate man. It seems my worries have just begun."

Burt nodded. "Yes, I would say so. Congratulations, Mr. Secretary."

"Thank you. May I come in?"

As Burt stepped aside, van Lier turned to the pair of secret agents behind him and said, "Wait here. I'm sure there's nothing to fear in Miss Hollander's apartment." He looked at Burt. "At least from guns."

"There are no people with guns here, Mr. Secretary."

Van Lier walked past Burt, who closed the door and waited as the diplomat strolled to the center of the room and stopped, his glance darting first to Burt, then to Monica in her bedroom doorway and back to Burt again. Van Lier, edgy and tense, but handsome in a tailored gray suit, nervously tapped the fingers of one hand against his thigh and said nothing.

Burt said, "Monica Hollander, I'd like you to meet

Secretary of State van Lier. Mr. Secretary, this is Monica Hollander."

Van Lier smiled at her, stepped forward and shook her offered hand.

"My pleasure, Mr. Secretary," said Monica. "Congratulations on your appointment."

"Thank you, Miss Hollander. I hope I can do justice to it."

Again the diplomat's glance went from Burt to Monica and back again.

"She stays," said Burt defiantly. "She's earned the right to be here. Besides, it's her apartment."

Van Lier looked down at the floor and said nothing.

"No," said Monica, shifting her cane from one hand to another. "I'm dying to hear what you two have to say to each other, but I don't think it's fair, Burt, to put him under this kind of pressure. He can talk a lot easier if there's no one else in the room. I'll wait in the bedroom."

Burt pushed himself away from the door. "I said that from now on you're a part of everything that concerns me and I mean it. After what you've been through—"

Monica smiled. "You can tell me later. At the moment, I think we should extend Secretary van Lier the courtesy of allowing him to work out his problems minus an audience. I'd want someone to do the same for me or you."

Burt shook his head and said softly, "Thanks."

Monica said, "It's a pleasure to meet you, Mr. Secretary, and I wish you all the luck in the world in your new job."

She dropped her cane and her hands quickly went to the doorjamb for support, but before Burt could reach her, van Lier had crossed the room and handed the cane back to Monica.

With a tenderness that Burt found moving, the diplomat said to her, "Thank you, Miss Hollander. Thank you very, very much."

When she had closed the door, leaving the two men

alone, van Lier said, "I can see why you didn't want to leave her the other day." Van Lier's smile was boyish and sly at the same time. "She's special."

"She's taken."

"I can understand that. Yes, I can very well understand that. I see you are preparing to leave. Where to?"

"California. We're driving across the country, taking our time, seeing the sights, relaxing and trying to forget the past few days. I want Monica to meet my family in Los Angeles."

Van Lier sat down on the couch. "Sounds like fun. Always wanted to drive cross country but never got around to it. When?"

"Soon. Now that there's no longer a problem. Richie Sweet was blown up in his car yesterday just outside of Montreal and witnesses saw Sal Abruzzo being forced into a car in front of his home and he hasn't been heard from since. The FBI says he'll never be seen alive again."

Van Lier placed his hands palm down on his thighs. "And Clare Chandler's in the hospital and still under sedation, which brings us to the tape and the notebook. What did you do with them?"

"I burned them."

It was the last answer van Lier had expected. "You what?"

"Burned them. I didn't trust myself with them. I don't know what I'd have done if I'd listened to the tape or read the notebook, so I burned them. I haven't the slightest idea what they contained. All I know is I'm out of the gossip wars for good and gossip is what the tape was all about."

Van Lier dropped his head back against his shoulders. "Jesus. Three days of sweating it out, of not sleeping, of worrying about the confirmation vote *and* worrying about what you might do with that tape."

Van Lier looked at Burt and continued, "I couldn't contact you no matter how much I wanted to. The FBI and the police were on you twenty-four hours a day.

And whenever I telephoned your apartment or this one, I received no answer or a busy signal."

"As of last night I've been back here with Monica," said Burt. "We kept the phone off the hook until this morning when you telephoned. Unfortunately, some of the people who want to talk to me are crazies. D'Arcy's murder has this town in a state of shock and the pressure is on to bring somebody to trial. The triggermen can't talk, but there's always the people who hired them. The FBI is out to pin something on the Bonnetti family—"

"Burned them," said a relieved van Lier, shaking his head. He smiled at Burt. "I guess I can't ask for more than that."

"There's something I'd like to ask you. When you told Richard Zachery to suppress the story on Adam Danziger, did you tell him why?"

Van Lier linked his fingers behind his head and stretched his long legs in front of him. He was Gil van Lucky once more and enjoying the role. "No. I think he's aware of a certain closeness between his wife and me, but he won't speak to me about it. It wouldn't look good for him to accuse me or her, not if he wants the presidency. He was forced to continue supporting me or say why not. Gossip can hurt, as you know by now. Presidential candidates can't afford to be hurt."

"So he closed his eyes and helped you to become secretary of state."

Van Lier shrugged. "A blunt way of putting it, but as good a way as any. I simply asked him to see what he could do for Adam Danziger because Adam had just done a favor for the party. A big favor. I let it go at that. I haven't the slightest idea how it will turn out, by the way."

Burt shook his head. The rich get richer; van Lier was off on another winning streak. "What's happening with you and Renata Zachery?" he said to the diplomat.

Van Lier looked at him for a few seconds. "I'm not a fool, Anthony. Reckless at times but not a fool. Only calculated risks, remember? It's over between us. She and her husband had a talk and then she and I had a talk and we all decided there's a lot at stake. Too much for anyone to continue walking a tightrope without a net. Her husband wants to be President and I want to stay secretary of state. Renata and I have decided not to see each other anymore. Richard Zachery is owed that much. It wasn't the easiest thing I've done lately."

"Power versus love and love loses," said Burt. "What's Aaron Banner going to do about all of this?"

Van Lier spat out the words. "Not a goddam thing. He doesn't want any part of D'Arcy's death and he doesn't want any part of an FBI investigation into the Mafia. Clare Chandler's lips are sealed. Bet on it. She just happened to be with D'Arcy when he died—"

Van Lier looked at Burt. "Like you just happened to be passing by in a taxi, saw D'Arcy and got out to say hello to your competitor."

"Which is more or less the truth. Anyway, my story held up. I had to repeat it several times, so sticking close to the truth was the only thing to do."

"Speaking of things to do," said van Lier, "what about your future? My sources tell me you've been offered a fat book contract by an English publisher, who wants you to write the story of D'Arcy's ill-fated love affair with Johnnie Gelb and how the Mafia put an end to it. You've turned down an offer from Harold Monmouth to resume writing your gossip column at twice your original salary. You've also had an offer from D'Arcy's paper to replace him. Have you decided which golden opportunity you're going to succumb to?"

"I've decided I'm a reporter," said Burt. "Which means gossip is out. The book deal sounds good. Monica and I can live off that money for a while. Did your spies tell you I'm coming back to New York in three weeks to work on another story?"

"No, they didn't. Which story?"

"A detective named Nathaniel Jackson, they call him Action Jackson, has trouble over some cocaine he's supposed to have taken from a dealer and kept for himself.

In the time I was in police custody I asked around and learned that the property clerk in Jackson's case is being investigated on suspicion of having taken quite a few items from the clerk's office—stolen property, weapons, cash and of course drugs. Nobody bothered to tell Jackson about the investigation. I'm waiting until D'Arcy and the Mafia are off the front pages, then I'm looking into Jackson's case."

Van Lier nodded, pleased. "Sounds altruistic. So you're a reporter again."

"It's what I do best. It's the way I should be living my life. Gossip is what the public wants, but good reporting is what it needs. I'm pretty well fixed for money now and I've also got a bigger name and should be able to sell a few stories without too much trouble. Especially after tomorrow."

"What's happening tomorrow?"

Burt said, "You haven't asked me about Chindé, Mr. Secretary."

"What about it?"

"I wrote the story, all of it. About you, the dead GIs, Donald Rettig, the army officers who flew over there, the secret participation of both current and ex-CIA men. I wrote it all."

Van Lier narrowed his eyes, almost knowing what was coming next.

"And?"

"It's breaking in tomorrow's paper. D'Arcy's paper. Front page."

Van Lier said slowly, *"You printed it after all."*

"I did."

"Why?"

"Because I had to. Because it should've been printed a couple of weeks ago when I first learned about it. Because I'm a reporter."

Van Lier stood up and for a second Burt thought the diplomat was going to hit him. "Do you know what you've just done?"

"Saved a few lives," said Burt.

"Like hell!" Van Lier took a step toward him and Burt backed up.

He cleared his throat. "Forget it, Mr. Secretary. You're about to tell me that people will die in Chindé because of what I've written. Maybe they will. But if I help you to cover up this thing, American soldiers will die for sure and so will a piece of this country. The longer I keep silent, the more GIs you'll send over there and the more of them will get shot up, a little fact I'd unfortunately ignored. I have a responsibility to someone other than you. To myself and to the people who expect reporters to tell the truth. I'm no flag-waver, but the people of this country deserve better than what they're getting from their politicians and press. You want me to keep quiet about anything that's going to shake your little world. Well, fuck it, man, as of now I've stopped keeping quiet. First you want to shut *me* up, then you want to shut up reporters in Florida. For Christ's sake, where's it all going to end with you? Tell me, because I'd really like to know. When are you going to stop fucking over the press because of your ambition?"

Van Lier pointed a finger at him. "We had a deal. You were to give me time. Time!"

"You're using it to send men to their death and that's a bad deal. If I give you enough time, you'll have a hundred thousand troops over there and you'll still be telling me it's all for peace and don't print anything because you only want to help. Help who? I'll tell you who. You want to help yourself, which is what we all do, which is what I did when I said I'd keep quiet. I wanted to sit next to the throne, like a lot of Washington reporters do. They all have their noses so far up the ass of the power structure that you can't see their heads anymore. It was a bad deal, Mr. Secretary. People around me have gotten hurt because of deals I've made recently. Well, the only deals I'm making now are deals I can live with. I'm a reporter and that means from here on in, watch out."

"I would advise you to do the same," said van Lier. "That attitude of yours isn't going to win you any friends."

"Reporters shouldn't have friends. Friends end up asking for favors and when a reporter does a favor he's rarely doing his job. Anyway, you're secretary of state and your private life is still your private life. You won two out of three. That's better than most people ever do."

Van Lier let his arms flop to his side. "Maybe it is. Anthony giveth and Anthony taketh away. I suppose I'll be hearing from you again, one way or another."

"Could be."

Van Lier offered his hand and Burt took it. The diplomat smiled. "You'll forgive me if I don't stay. I'm due at the UN and I also understand there's quite a story in tomorrow's paper, one I should prepare for. I can't wait to read it."

When van Lier left, Monica came into the room as fast as her injured leg would allow. "I couldn't hear most of it. Next time, will you two please speak louder? What happened? God, what did he say to you? You look—"

"I look worse than I feel," said Burt. "I feel fine. I *will* feel fine in a few minutes."

"Tell me everything."

"Spoken like a true gossip lover."

"What's that?" she asked as Burt looked at the small notebook in his hand.

"Something I just wrote down after our new secretary of state departed."

Burt showed her the page on which he'd written: *"Guts, dear boy."*

He underlined the words twice before putting the notebook away.